HEART QUEST™

HeartQuest brings you romantic fiction
with a foundation of biblical truth.
Adventure, mystery, intrigue, and suspense
mingle in our heartwarming stories of
men and women of faith striving to build
a love that will last a lifetime.

May HeartQuest books sweep you
into the arms of God, who longs for you
and pursues you always.

D0905762

A Bouquet of Love

AN ARRANGEMENT OF FOUR BEAUTIFUL NOVELLAS
ABOUT FRIENDSHIP AND LOVE

GINNY AIKEN

RANEE MCCOLLUM

JERI ODELL

DEBRA WHITE SMITH

HEART
QUEST™

Romance fiction from
Tyndale House Publishers, Inc.
WHEATON, ILLINOIS

Library of Congress Cataloging-in-Publication Data

A bouquet of love / Ginny Aiken . . . [et al.].
    p.   cm.
  ISBN 0-8423-3848-9 (softcover)
   1. Love stories, American.   2. United States—Social life and customs—20th
century—Fiction.   3. Bouquets—Fiction.   I. Aiken, Ginny.
PS648.L6B68   1999
813′.08508—dc21   98-47655

Printed in the United States of America

05 04 03 02 01 00 99
7   6   5   4   3   2   1

CONTENTS

"The Wrong Man"

1

"His Secret Heart"

87

"Come to My Love"

181

"Cherish"

289

The Wrong Man

GINNY AIKEN

*We know that God causes everything to work together
for the good of those who love God and are called
according to his purpose for them.*

ROMANS 8:28

To George,

*Because after twenty-one years
you're still the right man.*

PROLOGUE

York, Pennsylvania

If the envelope in Carrie Forster's hand contained what she suspected it did, her biological clock's ticking was going to rival Big Ben's. Half of her itched to rip the thing open and confirm her suspicion; the other half wished she hadn't received it in the first place. Or that she could just ignore it.

Glancing into Grandma Smith's mirror, which she'd hung over Great-aunt Sophie's lowboy in the tiny entrance to her condo, she saw exactly what she'd expected to see. A red-headed, thirty-something, successful career woman. And there was nothing wrong with that . . . except for the loneliness that occasionally—all right, regularly—swamped her these days.

Sure, she had friends, and Mom and Pop lived only a few miles away in Dallastown, but Carrie felt a gnawing void in her heart, right where a husband and child should be. The only problem was she hadn't found that husband with whom to have that child. At least, not yet.

And all around Carrie, her friends were sprouting bellies. Big round bellies, full of wriggling, kicking miracles conceived in joy and love.

Carrie covered her flat-as-a-pancake belly and again wondered what it would feel like to have a brand-new life growing inside her. To have a man at her side whose hand would cover hers as that life manifested itself.

A lump grew in her throat. When would her time come? Would it come at all?

Then she shook her head. "Stop it!" she ordered herself. This wasn't healthy at all.

Squaring her shoulders, she slipped a pinkie under the flap, ripped the envelope open, and extracted the invitation to Cindy's baby shower. The *third* baby shower in October. One for each of her college roommates.

As she stared at the pastel card stock, Carrie felt determination shove past her self-pity. "That does it! I know exactly what I'm going to do. And I'm not waiting one more minute to do it."

She stomped to her telephone table, yanked out the phone book, and flipped through the yellow pages. "Let's see. . . . Here we go. Just what I wanted."

The ad for Make-Me-A-Match Dating Service looked as hokey as all the others, but one of the guys at work had gone through it and found his partner for life. They'd just had their first child—exactly ten months after the wedding.

She punched in the number and heard a little voice in the back of her mind before the call went through. *What if this isn't the best way to find a life mate?*

Then a chirpy female voice chimed, "Good afternoon! May we make you a match?"

Carrie squashed the little voice, and in *her* firmest voice said, "I sure hope so."

CHAPTER ONE

Leaning back in her desk chair, Carrie stared at the fax printout on her desk. By now, the cupid-and-pierced-heart logo of Make-Me-A-Match had become disgustingly familiar and brought with it an increasing sense of failure.

She'd kissed five toads and found no prince. She had only one date left on her contract—and precious little hope. But her determination remained as strong as ever. So she'd called her contact at Make-Me-A-Match first thing after arriving at the office this morning, and her fax machine had just spit out the information on her last candidate.

She hoped he was nothing like the last one. Carrie shuddered, remembering last night's debacle.

Erwin Himmel had looked great on paper—they all did, and some looked great in person, too. But their hidden flaws overrode every manly physique, every head of artfully styled hair.

Erwin had invited her to a performance of *Cats* at the Strand-Capital Theater. Carrie loved Broadway musicals, and his choice of activity had buoyed her lagging spirits. However, he had failed to mention that dinner would be under the local golden arches, helping his ex-wife with their seven-year-old daughter's birthday party.

By the time they arrived at the Strand-Capital, Carrie's silk sheath bore the condiments from Katie Himmel's burger, and she was in no mood for adults in costume—of either clown or feline form.

She hadn't had a problem with the children. The sauce wound up on her skirt because Katie had cried when her older brother called her the birthday twerp, and those clear green eyes swimming in tears had broken Carrie's heart. The birthday girl's parents had been too busy squabbling to notice the child's pain. Carrie had comforted Katie.

Prior notice from Erwin would have been nice. She would never have worn the silk if he'd warned her. And she would then have avoided the further mess made by the very "helpful," very yellow-and-red Ronald.

But today was a new day. Bradford Kenner was a new man. And this was February, after all. Romance filled the air.

Since Bradford Kenner's name would be the last provided by Make-Me-A-Match, Carrie decided to do her best to make dating work with him. On paper they had nearly everything in common: They both had great careers; they enjoyed dinners out, pop music, and cats; and they were both ready for marriage and a family. How bad could he be?

Refusing to remember the last five candidates, who had shown her how bad they really *could* be, Carrie pushed her chair back and went to the vending machines in the middle of the hallway by the Cost-Accounting Department at the Harley-Davidson plant. A can of iced tea would hit the spot.

She heard the ticking the minute she entered her office again. To her horror, in the middle of her desk, on top of a mountain of spreadsheets and the incriminating printout from Make-Me-A-Match, sat a round, fat, red alarm clock of the old-fashioned sort. As she stared, mortification twisting her stomach, the stupid thing began to ring, its clapper hitting the two brass bells on top loud enough for everyone in the vicinity to hear.

She plunked down her iced tea and grabbed the clock, fighting to shut it up. As it continued to clang, chuckling broke out behind her. Carrie spun around and glared at her coworkers. "Who?"

As one everyone turned to the tall man at the rear of the group. "Big George thought your own biological clock would come in handy," someone said.

Of course it would be George. Married twenty-some years and with four sons—not to mention a penchant for practical jokes—the man was the logical culprit. Calling on her sense of humor to pull her past her embarrassment, Carrie shook a finger at George. "Just you wait!"

Eyes twinkling, grin plastered across his face, he answered, "Save me a dance at the wedding."

Her heart skipped a beat at the thought of a potential wedding. Her wedding. She grinned back. "Done deal."

The crowd dispersed, and before he left, George added in a serious voice, "I'll be praying for you."

Warmth filled her. She understood what he'd done. He'd gotten her to lighten up, he'd made her smile, and at the same time he'd offered support. He might drive her crazy at times, but he cared. "Thanks."

As she sat back down, she noticed the spilled tea. "Oh no!"

The sweetened amber liquid had puddled on the printout with her last date's information, blurring the black print to the point of illegibility. "Now what?"

At least she remembered his name. She could look him up in the phone book—if he didn't call her soon enough. And then it struck her. Who said she had to wait until he called?

This time she would take the initiative. After all, he'd agreed to have his information sent to her. He'd agreed to meet her. And Carrie was tired of waiting for the right man to show up. If Bradford Kenner was the right man, she wasn't going to sit around until he called. *She* was going to make the first move this time. Now is the time for all good men

She riffled through her white pages and immediately spotted the listing for Bradford Kenner—only one, so she wouldn't have to play eeny, meeny, miney, mo or guess. Then, flipping through her Rolodex, she found the number of her favorite florist. She dialed and a few minutes later hung up, satisfied with her efforts.

On impulse, she picked up the phone again, punched out her last match's number, and left a message on his machine.

Anticipation rippled through her—followed by that pesky tweak from her . . . was it conscience? Better judgment? She stifled the tweak and smiled. She'd taken action, put things into motion. All she had to do now was wait until February 14.

Valentine's Day. Now is the time for all good men

The phone rang. And rang. Now is the time for all good

Brad Kenner rolled over, ignored the ringing, and groaned.

He hated being sick. He didn't have the time to spare, especially when all that was wrong with him was a lousy cold.

Beep! "Hi! I just got your name . . . ," said a female voice to his machine—an unfamiliar female voice. Again rolling over, Brad caught snippets of the message. ". . . Make-Me-A-Match . . . looks promising . . . hope you agree . . . look forward to hearing from you . . ."

Wrong number, he decided, feeling the dopey, head-in-the-clouds effect of his heavy-duty cough syrup. Reaching over, he hit the "clear message" button on his answering machine and tried to go back to sleep.

With no success, as the percussion section in his head continued its rumba beat. His frustration grew.

He'd started his new job as principal of Christ's Academy in York last summer, and he had too much work to do to lie around blowing his nose and feeling crummy. But in Velma Myers, his secretary, he'd met his match. At the first sign of a sniffle and bleary eyes, she'd chased him and his germs right out of the office.

"Don't you know what kind of an epidemic we could have if you stayed around here sharing your wealth?" she'd asked as she shepherded him to his car. "Honestly, a grown man should know better. And a school principal at that."

Sheepishly, he'd followed orders, knowing that at least for the short term, the school would run smoothly under Velma's no-nonsense direction. She was the most efficient, hardworking, caring secretary he'd ever been blessed with. And she was crazy about kids. Having raised six of her own, she knew exactly when to comfort and coddle them and when to yank the rug out from under them.

As she often did to him. Velma reminded him of his late mother, and he'd come to care for her nearly as much.

Brad had spent months praying for a new position, one in a school that needed someone with vision to guide it toward greater service for Christ. He loved the challenge presented by a fairly new facility, one where patterns weren't set, where he could really make a difference.

God had answered his prayers with the offer from the academy. It had meant a small pay cut, but since he had few needs, the chance to help build a strong Christian school had made up for the loss in cash.

He had so many plans for reaching out to the community of believers. . . . He wanted every Christian in town to realize that this option existed for their children. And he wanted to encourage the teachers and students at Christ's Academy to excel, to become everything the Lord had created them to be.

But here he lay, flat on his back—er, side—running low on tissues and wheezing and coughing like his beat-up '57 Chevy, which, like him, needed restoring. He prayed that the Lord would restore *him* soon so he could restore his car.

When the doorbell rang later that afternoon, Brad dragged himself upright and plodded to answer the door. Only partly surprised, he found Velma on his doorstep, bearing gifts.

She bustled past him to the kitchen. "Get back in bed, young man! You'd better give me your house key before I leave today so you don't have to get up when I come check on you tomorrow."

Brad didn't know whether to laugh or cry. He wasn't sure how to handle being treated like a cross between a misbehaving six-year-old and an ailing octogenarian. But Velma, being Velma, took care of his indecision.

Shoving him gently in the direction of his room, she said, "I brought you tissues since I noticed yesterday you only had the one box left. Did you eat?"

At his halfhearted nod, she gave him that patented, disgusted-mother glare of hers that got the kids at school to do whatever they had to do and didn't want to do. "Just as I thought. Well, I made a kettle of chicken soup for you. That way you'll only have to nuke a bowl for each meal. And here's a box of crackers. Shouldn't be too difficult to get some nourishment into you this way."

They'd reached his bedside, and just as he was about to collapse again, Velma yanked him upright by the arm. "Not on that rumpled mess, you don't. Let me straighten out those sheets. One would think that was a wrestling ring instead of a bed. The sheet's come off all four corners." She turned her gimlet eyes back on him. "You didn't sleep well, did you?"

Brad shrugged, yielding to the inevitable. Velma had appointed herself his nurse and mother, and he didn't have the energy to tell her he had suffered through many a cold on his own. She was determined to ease his misery.

"You don't need to worry about that missing load of supplies anymore," she said, tugging the sheet into place. "Day before yesterday's snowstorm did delay the truck, but they delivered our order this morning. And Sandra Simmons's mother called to say she'd chaperon the fourth grade's field trip to the Baltimore Aquarium next week. So that's all settled."

Brad allowed his secretary's voice to flow over him, assuring him that everything was fine. He thanked God for Velma's efficiency, since at the moment, in spite of a mountain of guilt, he could barely dredge up any interest—much less concern—for the fourth grade's trip or the reams of paper that fueled the learning at the academy. He prayed for a quick recovery. He hated being sick.

Velma didn't stay silent for long—if she ever stopped talking in the first place. "*Now* you can lie down again," she said. "You'll feel so much better with the bed made and the pillows fluffed up. They were squashed down between the headboard and the mattress and wouldn't have given you any support. You need to keep your upper body raised so you can drain. . . ."

Brad gratefully crawled under his covers. "You were right, Velma—it *does* feel better," he croaked.

She gave him a grin and her best I-told-you-so *hmph*. "Now let's see about getting some fluids into you. Do you have any juice? Tea? Ginger ale?"

Before Brad had a chance to answer, the doorbell rang. Velma waved at him. "I'll get that and your drink. You just rest."

Her running shoes squeaked across his hardwood floor, then stopped as she opened the front door. "Oooooh!" she exclaimed in delight.

Curious as to the cause for her comment, Brad tried to rise, but his head had started to pound again, and a violent sneezing fit quickly changed his mind. Velma would let him know soon enough.

True to her nature, his secretary wasted no time in squeaking back to the room as fast as her Reeboks could carry her. "Just look at what you got!" she cried. "Isn't it adorable? I wonder who it's from . . . ?"

Stunned and bewildered, Brad stared at the generous basket of flowers and greenery in Velma's outstretched hands. A pair of heart-shaped helium balloons hovered over her head, one reading, "Be Mine," and the other, "Valentine." Even from the bed, he saw the scarlet box of chocolates tucked in among the mums, carnations, and who-knew-what-other flowers.

"So who is she?" asked Velma, ever persistent.

Brad shrugged. "Beats me."

"Oh, come on. You're telling me you have no idea who sent you this beautiful bouquet?"

"Yep."

"Then I guess we'll have to do it the old-fashioned way. There's a card, you know."

Brad again tried to rise, but Velma gave him another glare. "Don't you dare get up! I'll bring you your valentine. Then you can tell me who's courting you." She accompanied her words with a wink.

Brad warily took the envelope from its plastic trident holder and carefully lifted the flap. He pulled out the card—one of the plain kind all florists carried—and opened it. In an unfamiliar script he read,

12

*Has Make-Me-A-Match made us a match? Let's plan a
get-acquainted dinner date for Sunday, February 14, and
find out. I'll be out of town on business until late Saturday,
so you don't need to call me back. I'll pick you up at seven.*

The note was signed by Carrie Forster.

Brad didn't know Carrie Forster.

As he stared at the note, he heard the familiar tapping of a
running shoe and an impatient sniff.

"Well?" Velma asked. "Are you going to keep me in suspense?"

He shrugged again. "It's from some woman named Carrie
Forster. Never heard of her. I must have gotten it by mistake."

Velma's iron-toned curls bobbed from side to side. "No
way. The envelope has your name on it, and the deliveryman
was very clear about the recipient. That bouquet's for you."
Craning her neck, Velma tried to read the note.

Taking pity on her, Brad said, "Carrie Forster's making a
date for dinner on Sunday. But from what she says, she wants
to get acquainted then. This is weird."

Velma sighed, her expression growing dreamy. "Not at all.
It's the most romantic thing I've ever heard of."

Brad coughed his objection.

"And you know what else?" Velma asked as if he wasn't
dying right before her. "I wouldn't be surprised if God's
nudging you in the direction of romance . . . marriage. . . ."

Brad bolted upright, his head pounding like a jackhammer,
the room spinning like a Tilt-A-Whirl. "No way, Velma!
Uh-uh. God's called me to Christian education, and he led
me to Christ's Academy. I'm not looking for a woman. Besides, this Carrie Forster is *not* the one for me to romance. She

sounds too . . . wacky, too zany, and I've never even heard of her."

"That's what's so romantic about it. Come Sunday, *Valentine's Day,*" she said with a knowing look, "I bet you'll see God's hand in this."

"But—but—"

Ignoring his indignant sputters, Velma squeaked out of the room, then moments later turned on the kitchen faucet. If not for the card in his hand and the balloons bobbing over his nightstand, Brad would have sworn the cough syrup he'd taken earlier was giving him hallucinations.

Of course it was all a mistake. It had to be. He would call the florist shop and make them come pick up the arrangement. If he acted quickly, the florist could contact its client and straighten out the mix-up, since Carrie Forster's gifts had obviously reached the wrong man.

As he picked up his phone, Velma launched into an off-key rendition of "Isn't It Romantic?"

CHAPTER TWO

B ut I don't know this woman," Brad insisted for the umpteenth time. "I know she gave you my name and address and that you delivered the bouquet as ordered, but—"

The female florist's very firm voice cut off his argument—again. The flowers, balloons, and box of chocolates were his to enjoy.

He hung up, coughed, and reached for the candy. Hey, he'd tried to do the right thing. He'd tried to refuse what *he* knew wasn't meant for him. But since everyone from Velma to the florist insisted the bouquet *was* his, he might as well enjoy it.

And Brad loved chocolate.

Popping open the heart-shaped box, he studied the assortment before him, wondering if his stuffy head would allow him to enjoy the rich flavors. "Only one way to know," he murmured as he chose a pecan-topped piece.

Who would send a man gifts without verifying that she had the right address? She could at least have called—

"Uh-oh." Could Carrie Forster be the one who'd left the weird message on his machine yesterday morning?

Pushing the playback button, he heard the five short beeps

that meant he had no messages waiting. "Uh-oh," he repeated, a funny feeling settling in his middle.

Had he erased the message in his cold-and-cough-syrup-
induced misery? Brad tried to remember, but yesterday was
hazy in his mind. He remembered feeling wretched, remembered getting the weird message, remembered Velma's inva-
sion, and would never forget the arrival of the bouquet.

To his dismay, he remembered little else. Which meant he
probably *had* wiped out the message. Had it been from his
wacky Valentine?

Nah. That'd be too much of a coincidence. Wouldn't it?

His head began pounding again, and Brad took it as evidence that he'd wasted altogether too much brainpower on
the misunderstanding at a time when his brain was under viral
siege. His pillow and blanket beckoned, and before succumb-
ing to slumber again, he jotted a note to check with Velma
about the community-outreach open house he planned to
hold at the end of the month.

As he dozed off, a dozen pink-and-silver heart-shaped helium balloons chased him down the school's hallway.

With the memory of her multiple disastrous dates fresh in
Carrie's mind, she didn't try too hard to primp for this latest
one. She'd made reservations at The Gingerbread Man
downtown, a favorite of York's young singles, where casual
attire ruled. Black pants and matching blazer over a jade silk
blouse felt perfect. A final glance into Grandma Smith's
mirror told her a slick of apricot-toned lip gloss was all she
needed.

As she grabbed her handbag, excitement again bubbled in
her middle. Would Bradford Kenner be the one?

She ran to the kitchen and checked on Patches's food and

water, then left her condo, her mind still on what might lie ahead.

Carrie had thought of her final frog-prince candidate while at the conference this past week and had considered trying to reach him again by phone. But she'd been busier than she'd initially expected and didn't think he would appreciate a call at ten Pacific, one eastern standard time.

So she'd waited, anticipating their date.

The date she was about to drive to. Her stomach did a little flip as she turned the key in the ignition of her compact car.

Taking a deep breath—for the first time in about a week— Brad settled into the couch and used his remote to click on the 76ers game. Not a rabid fan, he still enjoyed watching the pros perform feats he'd never managed even in his teens.

On the cushion to his right sat a stack of sample textbooks, and to his left, a bag of sourdough pretzels. Finally human again, he could pore over the books on his teachers' wish lists for the next school year's curriculum; then when hunger struck, he could munch pretzels. Getting back to productive work, b-ball, and no more sniffles—that was Brad's idea of a perfect, lazy Sunday evening.

The doorbell rang. He groaned. Velma Myers was indisputably the most determined woman.

He yanked open the door. "Honestly, I told you a dozen times at church today that I'm fine—"

"Hi!" said the redhead on his doorstep—*definitely* not Velma. "Are you ready?" she asked.

She was beautiful. And a stranger. And he didn't know what he was supposed to be ready for. "Huh?"

After the brilliant syllable popped out, Brad could have kicked himself. How could he say something so dumb? From the look on the redhead's face, she was wondering the same thing.

"You know," she continued slowly, enunciating both words very clearly. "Dinner."

"Yeah, the last meal of the day. But . . . I'm missing something here."

"I'll say." Her wry tone did say it all. She could probably verify his suspicion that he'd lost every scrap of common sense—if not IQ—he'd ever had.

She turned and crunched down his salted steps, mumbling something about frogs.

Frogs? In winter?

At his mailbox, she wiped the snow off the number, then glanced over her shoulder. "The address is right. Are you . . . Bradford Kenner?"

That he could respond to coherently. "The one and only. And you are—"

"Carrie Forster."

This was Carrie Forster? The zany, Valentine's Day bouquet sender? Funny, she didn't look crazy. In fact, she was very pretty, with huge brown eyes and a fantastic smile—or at least, he thought she had a great smile. She'd lost it after he'd opened his mouth.

"Wait a minute," he said, turning. "Don't go yet."

He went into the house, grabbed the days-old arrangement, and ran back out. "Here. You sent it to the wrong guy. I'd never heard of you before these got here."

She'd come back to the steps and now stared at him as if he'd sprouted two additional heads.

"Oh, I'm sorry," he said, figuring he knew what the problem was. "I ate the chocolates. The woman at the florist's said I should. I mean, she insisted they were for me, and even though I was sure they weren't, well . . ."

Since Carrie hadn't moved—not even to change expressions—Brad let his words die off. He'd never been the suave kind of guy who had the perfect lines worked out. His thoughts generally tumbled out as they formed, and most women looked at him as this one was looking right now.

She blinked. "You *are* Bradford Kenner, right?"

He decided to stick with monosyllabic responses. "Right."

"And you said you were the one and only, didn't you?"

"Yes." So far, so good.

"Well, then I can't figure out what the problem is. You're the only one listed in the phone book," she added, as if that explained everything.

Brad propped the sad-looking bouquet on the porch railing and rubbed his chin. "You make a habit of sending flowers, chocolates, and balloons to guys who are the only ones listed by that name in the phone book?"

When she gaped, he winced. Oh, brother. He'd gone and done it again. Monosyllabic responses—he had to remember that in the future. "I'm sorry—"

She laughed, cutting off his apology. "I guess when you put it that way, it does sound silly, doesn't it?"

He'd been right. She had a great smile. He smiled back. "I'm sure there's been a misunderstanding—"

"I'll say!"

They both chuckled again, and Brad remembered that it was well below freezing. "Would you like to come inside while we sort all this out?"

"To be honest, I'm ravenous, and I have reservations for seven-thirty at The Gingerbread Man." She paused and nibbled on her bottom lip. Then, as if she'd come to a decision, she added, "There's no point in wasting them. Would you like to come along? We can sort out the misunderstanding then. Besides, I'll bet you haven't had dinner yet."

"Guilty as charged. And if you're serious, I'll take you up on it. The Gingerbread Man sounds better than my frozen meat loaf. But only if it's my treat."

"No way. *I* sent the bouquet, *I* made the date, and *I* just offered again. My treat."

Brad shook his head. "I have a better idea. Since I'm the wrong guy, how about if we forget the whole date thing and just go to dinner—as new acquaintances. No pressure."

Carrie took another nibble at her bottom lip, and Brad thought again how pretty she was. Then she smiled and nodded. "Sounds great. Put that thing—" she gestured to the droopy, brown-edged flowers and wilting balloons—"out of its misery, and let's go eat."

After a few minutes' discussion of transportation—Carrie's or Brad's car—they decided to each drive, since it *wasn't* a date. Carrie shrugged, wondering why he continued to deny he'd heard of her before the arrival of the bouquet. Was she that great a disappointment?

He sure wasn't. With his clear blue eyes, brown hair, and resonant voice, Bradford Kenner was enormously appealing. As was his awkwardness when he'd opened the door—especially after the super-lady-killers with flawless lines she'd met. Hopping into her car, she heard him call out, "By the way, call me Brad."

Brad. Brad Kenner. Carrie said the name out loud, test-driving it, then decided she liked it. It seemed to suit him better than the formal Bradford.

The trip downtown was short, and she soon arrived at the restaurant on the Codorus Creek. Moments later Brad joined her, and they were shown to a table with a view of the waterway. The moon sparkled in the clear winter sky, its reflection shimmering on the icy surface.

As soon as the waiter left with their orders for iced tea,

Brad pinned her with his crystal blue eyes. "OK. I've been trying to figure this thing out on the way here, and I'm getting nowhere. How about if you tell me your side of the story from the beginning; then I'll tell you mine."

Carrie grimaced. "You want to hear the whole thing?"

Curiosity dawned on his face. "Now that you put it that way, I *really* want to know."

Buying time, she shook out her napkin and spread it on her lap. Then she picked up her fork and walked its tines up and down the edge of the table. Finally, after glancing at his open and interested expression, she went with her impulse.

"What can I say? I signed up with a dating service, and they sent me names. Yours was the most recent."

"Whoa! Don't you have to be a member for them to have your information to give out?"

Carrie nodded.

"I've *never* joined a dating service."

"Come on—if I can admit to joining, so can you."

"I would if I had, but I really haven't. I haven't done much dating in a while. I've been too busy."

"I guess work keeps you pretty tied up."

"I don't mind. It's my choice, of course, and I really care, so I give it my all."

Carrie smiled at his sincerity. "I'm impressed. I always heard it was the power that drove those in your position. You must be an exception in corporate law."

Brad frowned. "Corporate law? I'm not a lawyer."

It was Carrie's turn to frown. "You're not?"

"No. I'm the new principal at Christ's Academy."

Tapping her short fingernails on the tabletop, Carrie turned that piece of information over in her mind. "You're Bradford Kenner, but you're not a lawyer."

He nodded. "I'm a school principal. I have a master of education degree in administration."

"And you've never joined Make-Me-A-Match?"

The waiter arrived with their iced teas and menus. As they perused the lists, the young man offered suggestions, preventing Brad's response. Once Carrie had ordered her crab cakes and Brad his steak, the waiter retrieved the menus and departed with a smile.

"Well?" she asked.

"As I told you earlier, I've never contacted a dating service. I'm suddenly embarrassed to admit I can't even remember when I last went out on a date. Running a school is a challenge—especially a Christian school, since they usually encompass all twelve grades. It's not a nine-to-five job, so I have very little free time."

Carrie chewed on her bottom lip. "OK, let me get this straight. I got your name from a dating service, but you're the wrong guy—wrong job and not even a member. But you are the Bradford Kenner in the phone book, right?"

He nodded, grinning crookedly.

"It's not that common a name. . . . How could the mix-up have occurred?"

"Beats me. Why don't you go back over the sequence of events? You joined the dating service, and they sent you a name—Bradford Kenner."

"Not exactly. They sent me five names, then yours."

Brad's eyebrows rose. "Five?"

Carrie chuckled. "Not a one was right for me."

He whistled softly. "And I'm not even the right guy—I mean, the guy who wanted to be matched up. Maybe you can get your money back . . . or another name . . . or something."

"No. My contract specified six names. Yours is the last

one, and that's one membership I'm not renewing. If I'm meant to remain single, then it's up to me to reach the point where I can accept it. Not necessarily like it, just accept it."

As his gaze lifted to hers, a hint of confusion entered his expression. "What's wrong with being single? I'm pretty happy with my life."

"It's different for a guy."

"Oh, don't give me that. It's a matter of . . ."

Carrie waited, but Brad suddenly seemed reluctant to continue. "Of what?"

He stared at her for a minute . . . two. Then he rapped his knuckles sharply on the table. "OK, we're getting to know each other, even if this isn't a date. Since I've already told you I'm the principal at a Christian school, you know I'm a Christian. I believe life is a matter of seeking God's will. Acceptance is much easier once you know you're walking in his will."

"I'm a Christian, too. I mean, I go to church with my parents every Sunday, and I believe in the Trinity. But I'm not so sure my marital status is that big a deal for God. I mean, there are so many more important things to concern him. I'm just a little speck down here."

Brad's blue eyes grew intense. "God cares about *every* aspect of your life, and he will guide you if you seek him. That's one of the most important things I try to teach my kids. It's the second most basic fact of the Christian faith."

"The first being . . . ?"

"That Jesus is the Son of God and that he died for our salvation."

She nodded. "That I know, but I'm not sure about the other. I'll have to think about it."

The waiter arrived with a basket of bread, and Carrie took a sip of her tea. Brad felt the urge to say more, but he realized this wasn't the right time. Still, he wondered about a woman who felt so distant from God that she had sought help from a dating service rather than her heavenly Father.

"You know what?" Carrie said suddenly. "I think I've figured out how the mix-up happened."

"The mix-up?" he asked, his mind on deeper matters.

"You know. The Bradford Kenner lawyer/principal thing."

"Oh, that."

"Mm-hmm, that. Make-Me-A-Match faxed me the information at the office. Shortly afterward, I went to get a can of iced tea. A group of fellow employees . . . followed me into my office, and as we were speaking, I accidentally spilled the tea over the printout. Because your name is so unique, I remembered it and found it in the phone book."

He nodded. "I'm the only Bradford Kenner listed. I can see how that could happen. You know what that means, don't you?"

"What?"

"That I'm definitely *not* the one and only as I told you earlier. Somewhere in York there's another guy with the same name and an unlisted number. A lawyer who joined Make-Me-A-Match. I bet you'll hear from him soon."

"Hmm . . . you could be right." Her gaze turned speculative. "Tell me, Brad, even though you've never joined a dating service and you say you're perfectly happy as a single guy, you wouldn't be interested in . . . dating, would you?"

Her directness caught him by surprise. "Hey, it's not that I don't find you pretty or anything, because I do, or that I wouldn't like to go out with you, because I probably would, but it's just that I came to York as principal of Christ's Academy, and I really feel God led me to this position and not to marriage, and I'm really committed to—"

"It's OK," she cut in, laughing. "I'm not offended. But I would like to get to know you better. As friends. You're easy to talk to, and that's no mean feat."

"Ouch!" he said, mashing his eyes closed and shaking his head. "Next thing I know you'll tell me I have a great personality. Does wonders for the old male ego, you know."

"After my last few dates, friendship and conversation have become very important to me. I mean, once you've gone out with a throwback to *Saturday Night Fever* who spent the evening slicking back his do and discussing the latest dance tunes, you come to appreciate simple things."

Again, Brad felt the urge to witness to Carrie, but he tamped it down. "Who knows? Maybe the other Bradford Kenner will still turn out to be the right man."

"Maybe," she said as the waiter slid her plate of crab cakes before her.

"I'll pray for you," he said and was rewarded with a beautiful smile.

"Thanks. I need all the help I can get."

CHAPTER THREE

Too bad Brad Kenner had turned out to be the wrong man, Carrie thought as she opened the door to her condo an hour and a half later. She'd had a great time at dinner—the best time she'd spent with any of the men she'd met recently.

"Mrrreeooow," Patches reproached.

Carrie reached down and scrubbed her pet's head. "Excepting you, of course. Then again, I've known you a while now. Besides, Brad's human, and that's a big plus."

As she took off her coat and gloves, Carrie heard her answering machine's chirp. Hanging up her outerwear, she realized she was missing her scarf. "Hmm . . . probably left it in the car again. Have to remember it tomorrow," she murmured to Patches, who had begun his usual between-the-ankles dance.

Carefully dodging his paws, she went to the kitchen and pressed the "play message" button on the machine.

"Hi. This is Bradford Kenner. I received your printout from Make-Me-A-Match, and you look great—on paper, of course." His chuckle matched his voice, brisk and direct, but definitely not Brad's.

"Since I missed you tonight, I'll try again tomorrow. I'd like to talk and set up an initial date. Take care."

As the tape whirred back to its starting spot, Carrie smiled. Brad had been right. He'd bet she would hear from the other Bradford Kenner, and she had. This one sounded very different from the man she'd met tonight.

Tired as she still was from the long conference she had attended during the week, she decided to call it an early night. In her room, she turned on the twenty-four-hour news channel and went to the bathroom, removed what little makeup she wore, brushed her teeth, and ignored the news.

Her mind replayed the topics she and Brad had covered during dinner. Especially the one about seeking God's will for your life. She'd never thought of making choices that way but rather let impulse lead her as often as not.

And wound up in trouble just as often.

Carrie chuckled. She'd been fortunate this time. Showing up at a strange man's house with all intentions of going on a date with him was one of her most misguided ideas. Especially since the man on whose doorstep she'd landed was not the one who'd been prescreened by her expensive, highly selective dating service.

That was one impulse she would never follow again. She planned to talk with Bradford Kenner number two, then maybe—hopefully—go out with him. But Carrie had a feeling she was done with the dating-service industry—even though she still wanted love, a husband, kids.

As she fell asleep, she decided to give Brad's suggestion of seeking God's will careful thought.

The conversation with Bradford Kenner number two—"Ford," as he liked to be called—went well, if quickly. He was headed for an appointment, and they only had time to choose a place and time to meet and to have just enough additional chatter for Carrie to decide she was still interested in meeting the man.

So after a week of catching up on work that had piled up in her absence, Carrie was looking forward to dinner at a French restaurant in Harrisburg on Friday night. Ford had chosen it since he was handling the acquisition of a York company by a large Harrisburg enterprise and he'd be spending most of the day in the capital city. She'd agreed that his plan made sense.

As she locked the door on her way out, Carrie heard the phone ring. With a glance at her watch, and ever mindful of the eternal construction delays on I-83, she decided to let the machine get the message.

She was on her way to meet frog-prince number six.

"So," Brad said to Carrie as she slid in next to him on the gym bleacher the next evening. "Tell me that long story about your date with my namesake."

She held out her hand. "Give me back the missing scarf you called about in the first place. Mom crocheted it, and I'd be a dead duck if I lost it."

Brad grinned. "Here—"

The exuberant cheers of the crowd watching the high school basketball game drowned out the rest of his words.

"Thanks," she said when the noise died down to a muted roar. "I'm glad you found it and called."

"Well, are you going to tell me about that date?"

She rolled her eyes. "If you're *that* curious. It was . . . a date. A first date. Nothing special—if a little . . . different."

"How different?"

"Well, Ford is a corporate attorney, as the dating service had said, and he's handling a tricky merger right now. He asked me to meet him in Harrisburg, and I agreed—"

Again the crowd rose to its feet and yelled for the team in red. When the racket mellowed some, Carrie said, "From the pain in your expression, it's safe to say that's not your team."

Brad smiled crookedly and shook his head. "We're in the blue. And to be honest, we stink. But we have heart."

Carrie chuckled. "That's what counts."

Just then, a short kid in a blue-and-gold uniform stole the ball from a lanky six-footer in red, dashed between two more, and dribbled furiously to the basket at the far end of the court. When the ball went in, the spectators stared in awe. The room fell silent for a moment. Then surprised shouts of "Way to go!" rang out.

Carrie glanced at the man at her side. Perched on the edge of the wooden bench, Brad beamed, looking every bit the proud papa. "Did you see that?" he asked.

"Everyone did," she answered.

"That's Doug's first basket. Ever. He has spent hours practicing, determined to prove himself a part of the team despite his height. He approaches every aspect of his life that way—even his studies. I think I'll treat the team to sundaes after the game to celebrate his achievement."

Admiration rippled through Carrie. "You're a nice guy, Brad Kenner," she said.

He groaned. "I told you the other night you'd wind up telling me I had a nice personality. Next you'll compare me to your favorite slippers."

Carrie laughed. "Not . . . quite," she answered, studying her companion. From his shiny dark hair—mussed from raking his fingers through it—to his blue eyes, his crooked grin, and his solid build, Brad Kenner was a great-looking man. No matter what, she would never see him as just a comfortable companion.

Just then, she realized how very attracted she was to

him—to that great personality he kept groaning about. If only he weren't quite so focused on his career.

A loud buzzer rang, distracting her from her discovery.

"Game's over," Brad said, rising as the two teams lined up to shake hands. "Are you meeting my namesake?"

"No. He said he'd call to set up another date. His schedule's crazy, from what he was telling me."

"And speaking of telling, you never finished your story. Tell you what, let me congratulate Doug, give the coach the cash and the go-ahead to take the guys to DQ, and we can go grab a bite to eat. If you're hungry, that is."

"I haven't eaten yet, so that sounds great. I'll wait for you here."

Brad clambered down the bleachers onto the glossy wooden court, then crossed over to where the blue-and-gold team was again gathering at the bench. His easy stride ate up the distance, and a moment later, he caught up the slight player in a gruff bear hug.

The boy blushed to the roots of his buzz-cut blond hair, basking in Brad's attention. The rest of the team surrounded the man, who exchanged high fives with the other players.

He spoke to the coaches briefly; then, dropping his arms onto the shoulders of two boys, he lowered his head and joined the team in prayer.

Carrie's admiration grew, and she debated saying something as he returned to her side. "Ready?"

She laughed. "I was the last to ask that, and I left you speechless, as I recall."

Brad blushed. "Don't remind me. That wasn't one of my finer moments."

"But this was," Carrie answered, nodding toward the court. "You were great with those kids. I understand why you feel the way you do about your work. You obviously like them, and they like you right back."

"It's my calling," he said with a self-deprecating shrug. "It's where God planted me."

Carrie nodded slowly. "I can see where you would think that."

"Hey, enough about me. Where do you want to eat?"

"I'm not picky. I'll eat about anything."

"Well, I'm a sucker for beef, so how about it? There's a great steak house on the west side."

"Sounds good."

"This time, though, I'm driving. It makes no sense to take two cars. I'll bring you back to get yours after we eat."

Carrie smiled. Tonight was different. Her instincts told her she could trust Brad with her life. "Let's go."

As they drove across town, they discussed Christ's Academy's fledgling sports program, the upcoming outreach events Brad had planned, and the pleasantly surprising increase in early applications for the next school year.

He then asked Carrie about working for a company with a folk-legend image like Harley-Davidson. She spoke of their emphasis on the uniqueness of the bikes and the fascinating characters she met at company events and offered to take him on the plant tour.

The steaks were great, as was the continuing conversation. Finally, when a stuffed Carrie turned down the offer of dessert, Brad turned his laser-bright eyes on her. "How about the rest of that . . . different-date story?"

She wrinkled her nose and chuckled. "It was different, all right. Ford got there late. We had reservations for eight-thirty, since he'd said he was sure the meeting would be wrapped up by then, but he wound up rushing in at nine-thirty as I was about to leave. The restaurant, a very intimate, froofy-type place, closed at ten, so we had to order fast, eat, and run."

She laughed, remembering. "The waiter stood at my elbow the whole time. In his black cutaway, he was this . . . this dark *presence* that hovered . . . and checked his watch every five minutes. Just about each time Ford's cell phone rang again."

Brad smiled. "Not what you were hoping for, was it?"

"Oh, and that's not the worst of it. When I had nearly finished, I set my knife down, then placed the fork on the plate to take a sip of water. By the time I put the goblet back on the table, the guy had whisked my place setting away!"

"Talk about fast food!"

"A drive-through would have been more leisurely. And you know, it wasn't even the rushed meal and the waiter on the run that bothered me, it was . . . the feeling I got from Ford."

Carrie paused to gather her thoughts, wondering if she should even bring them up. After another glance at Brad, she decided a male perspective had plenty of merit, so she went on. "He had an agenda, and a get-acquainted date was part of it. Between the hours of eight-thirty and ten, you understand. Then he was off to sleep so he could be fresh and ready for today's appointments."

Brad rubbed his chin, keeping silent for a moment. "Maybe he behaved like that because he's so busy with this deal he's handling."

She thought back on the evening. "Maybe. But you know what? My career's very important to me, and it's still not everything. I have to wonder if his is."

"There are people like that," Brad said noncommittally.

Carrie shrugged off her negative feelings. "Maybe I'm just being judgmental, and I shouldn't be. After all, he's just the kind of candidate I've been looking for—he's a successful career man, ready to settle down with a wife, and he wants the traditional 2.3 kids, too. I'll give him the benefit of the doubt, even though he said he'd be working all weekend long."

"You won't?"

Carrie laughed. "Nope! I like my weekends. Today I did the stuff I never have a chance to do during the week—you know, cleaning and shopping and all that. Tomorrow's church with Mom and Pop; then I'm free to relax."

"Sounds healthy."

"What do you do on weekends?"

Brad gave her his lopsided grin. "Catch up on school stuff."

She laughed.

"But seriously, I do relax," he said. "Tomorrow's a good example. I figured I'd take advantage of last week's storm and go skiing. I hear the local slopes are in good shape."

Carrie studied Brad. "Funny. I wouldn't have pegged you for a skier."

"Oh? You know so many skiers you can sniff one out?"

She laughed again. "That was a dumb thing to say, wasn't it? Actually, I don't know any."

"Never been skiing, then?"

Carrie shook her head, still smiling. Brad really liked that smile of hers. And he thought it would look great against the snow. Before he thought it through, he asked, "Want to try it?"

"What? Me ski?"

"Yeah. I'll help you. We'll have a blast."

Catching her lower lip between her teeth, she thought it over for a minute. "It's dangerous, isn't it? I always see people in casts and hear about the accidents."

"True, there's an element of danger in skiing, just as there is in any sport, but we'll be careful. And I promise I'll only take you to the bunny slope."

She groaned, then laughed some more. "Half of me is ringing alarm bells, but the other half tells me I can trust you. What time and where do you want to meet?"

They made arrangements and drove back to the academy's parking lot. As Brad leaned against her open car door waiting for Carrie to turn the ignition, he said, "Uh . . . about tomorrow? Well . . . ah . . . I don't want you to get the wrong idea—"

"I know," she cut in with a grin. "It's *not* a date. You're too busy with your new position to get involved in a dating relationship. We're friends."

Brad sighed in relief and grinned back. "I'm glad you understand. That's one of the best things about you."

She arched an eyebrow. "Oh? So *you're* the one bringing up the great personality bit!"

Cheeks blazing, he shrugged. "Hey, if you got one, flaunt it! I had a good time again tonight. And I think you're going to be a natural on the slopes tomorrow."

"Don't say another word until you get York's greatest klutz on skis! See you at two-thirty."

As she drove away, Brad couldn't help but remember how much they'd laughed each time they'd met. If he *did* have time to think about marriage, Carrie would fit the bill quite well.

But he wasn't looking for a romantic partner, even if he was attracted to her. At this time in his life, Brad's goal was doing his best at the school, and that was all he could handle.

He went home, mulling over what Carrie had told him about her date last night. It didn't sound as if Bradford Kenner number two—Ford—was quite what Carrie was looking for, and more than ever, he knew she needed to trust her life to Christ. She needed to seek the Father's will for her future.

Besides, she appeared to be looking for a guy kind of like him. Well, one who was ready for marriage, of course, but someone who liked kids and wasn't in such a rush through life as the high-octane lawyer.

Once home, Brad went straight for his Bible, hoping to regain perspective since the image of Carrie's smile and sparkling brown eyes seemed etched in his memory. He'd sought the Lord's will many times, and he knew he was meant to be at the academy. He didn't want an attraction to a pretty woman to distract him from serving Christ.

Then why'd you go and invite her skiing tomorrow? a mischievous part of his conscience asked.

Kneeling, Brad turned to Psalm 119. "Your word is a lamp for my feet and a light for my path," he read, the familiar words reminding him of God's promise to guide him. *Father, lead me to the right path,* he prayed.

Carrie wasn't really York's *greatest* klutz—but pretty close. The moment she stepped into her bindings, her feet flew out from under her and she crashed at the end of the chairlift line. They laughed it off.

And they continued to laugh their way down the bunny hill and back up the lift. Brad couldn't remember when he'd had more fun, even though he usually enjoyed the rush of the air, the glide of the skis over the snow, the turns, and the speed. Today the sport consisted of hauling Carrie out of snowdrifts and retrieving her lost skis.

It had to be the company.

He glanced sideways and smiled. Carrie had closed her eyes and leaned her head against the backrest of the chairlift, her lips curving up gently. She sighed. "Isn't it a beautiful day?" she asked.

"How would you know with your eyes closed?" he teased.

"Just smell it! The cold, the freshness, the sun . . ."

"You can't smell the sun."

"Ah, but a cloudy, snowy day doesn't smell like today, so it has to be the sun we smell."

"Hmm . . . interesting theory, but if you don't want to fall and make the operator stop the lift again, I suggest you open your eyes. We're almost there."

Poising on the edge of the seat, she clutched her poles in one hand and focused on the top of the lift. "I'm not falling off this thing again! I've learned at least that much today." Then she lurched off the seat and, with arms windmilling, skied off the landing.

"See?" she asked as she awkwardly snowplowed to a stop inches away from a massive pine. "I told you I wasn't going to—oh, oh, oh—ow!"

Yet another close encounter with a snowdrift.

"OK, OK," Brad said, precisely braking about five feet away from her and bracing himself against his poles. "So you've mastered getting on and off the lift. Now all you have to do is learn to stay on your feet."

Her brown eyes narrowed. "Think I can't do it, huh?"

"Mm . . . mm . . . mm . . . ," Brad hummed noncommittally, studying the cloudless sky.

"Just you watch."

He faced her again and never saw it coming. The snowball caught him smack in the middle of his forehead, bursting and showering his face with powdery crystals.

"Oh-ho! So *that's* the way you want it." He bent and scooped a handful of snow, dodging her next missile. A second later, he cried, "Gotcha!"

"Take that!" she countered, spitting out the flakes that had landed on her lips.

He responded with another shot.

In less than five minutes both looked like snowmen and sounded like defective radiators, out of breath from the skirmish. As Carrie ran a hand over her eyes to wipe off the remains of his last hit, he skied to her side, grabbed another load of snow, and waited until she could see him again. "Truce?" he asked.

She narrowed her gaze. "Are you admitting defeat?"

Brad widened his eyes. "Who's standing ready to rub whose face with more snow?"

"Hey, I started out on the ground so I could reach the snow more easily."

"What kind of line is that? You fell. We did battle. I won."

"No, I won."

He stared at her, noting how beautifully the dark red hair that escaped her forest green hat contrasted against the snow. Her cheeks and lips glowed rosy from the cold, and her large brown eyes sparkled with pleasure.

Magnanimous, he said, "OK, OK, we both won. Want to call it quits and grab a cup of hot chocolate at the lodge?"

"Don't even have to think about it." She held out her hand. "Help me up?"

Clapping the snow from his gloves, Brad took both of his poles in his left hand and grasped her hand. Next thing he knew, he was flying through the air, the sound of Carrie's laughter ringing out through the clear winter air.

When he landed at her side, he turned to glare at her but lost the desire as he found himself only inches from her face. He caught his breath.

"*Who* won?" she asked, an impish grin on her lips.

Brad couldn't look away and saw surprise change the texture of her smile. It warmed, sweetened, grew more personal.

For a moment they both stared at each other, the silence of the snow deep and cushioning. He liked this woman, he thought yet again—really, really liked her. And he was very glad she'd sent that crazy bouquet to him by mistake.

"We both did," he murmured.

CHAPTER FOUR

On Wednesday evenings, Carrie volunteered at her church's nursery to give parents the opportunity to participate in various activities sponsored by the congregation. She, in turn, relished the opportunity to cuddle the babies and study the antics of the toddlers.

She could have done without the diaper changing, but she chalked it up to advance practice. She *really* wanted a family of her own, especially after hearing all the details about Cindy's, Willa's, and Beth's wonderful new bundles of joy. She wasn't really jealous of her three college roommates—she just wanted what they had found.

As she snuggled with the Doerrs' new daughter in the roomy rocker, she heard the congregation enter the sanctuary over the intercom on the nursery wall. Mom had said they were having a speaker tonight instead of the usual activities.

Carrie nuzzled the baby in her arms, savoring the scent of talcum powder and infant. She began to hum and let herself dream.

As if from a distance, she heard the opening hymn and prayer followed by Pastor Williams's mellow voice introducing the guest. She was idly wondering about the presentation when trouble erupted right at her feet.

"'S mine!" bellowed Tyler Moore, a two-year-old tyrant.

"Mine," disputed dainty but determined Missy Hayes.

"Mine!" repeated Tyler.

"Mine," countered Missy.

Carrie hurriedly placed her sleeping angel in a crib and dropped to toddler level. "Hey, I've got lots of stuff in here. Neat stuff, but I'm not sharing."

Missy's teary brown eyes and Tyler's gray ones beamed on her.

"Gimme it!" demanded the male autocrat wanna-be.

"Me, pweeze," wheedled the future female diplomat.

Grinning, Carrie led her two charges to the toy boxes in the corner of the room. As the three of them rummaged through the treasures within, she heard a familiar voice say, "Good evening."

Brad! What was Brad Kenner doing at her church?

She found out soon enough. He was, of course, presenting information about his school, inviting parents to enroll their children. In his clear, resonant baritone, he described the school's programs, its mission, its goals. Then he opened the session for questions.

Carrie grinned. He was good. If she had a child, she'd be the first in line after the meeting to request a registration form.

To her relief, her charges were picked up promptly, and she cleaned up the room in no time. Hoping to catch Brad before he left, she ran out into the narthex.

She found him thanking Pastor Williams for the chance to address the church. When Brad spotted her, he flashed her his infectious, crooked grin. "Hey! I know you."

"That's right, Mr. Big-Shot Principal," she answered, grinning back.

The reverend smiled, murmured something polite, and approached a cluster of parishioners a few feet away.

To Carrie, Brad said, "Were you here tonight? I didn't see you."

"I was in the nursery, but we have a loudspeaker there."

He gave her a penetrating look. "Practicing, were you?"

Instead of squirming as she wanted to do, she shrugged. "Mm-hmm."

"More to your liking than skiing, I'll bet."

Carrie laughed. "I had fun exploring snowdrifts!"

"So did I," he answered, and suddenly the memory of a brief, intense moment hung between them. Then he gave a sharp shake of his head and asked, "Any more dates with Ford?"

"We're going out on Friday night. A traveling company is performing *Oklahoma!* in Baltimore. I love Broadway musicals." His expression altered marginally, but Carrie couldn't decipher the change. "How about you? You going skiing again?"

Brad shook his head. "Not this weekend. I'll have catch-up reading to do on Sunday because the senior class has a missions activity on Saturday. They're volunteering at the soup kitchen downtown. I'm in charge of the project."

"Sounds challenging—and very worthwhile."

"I hope my kids learn how little it takes to make a difference in someone else's life."

She thought those kids would more than likely learn that lesson simply by being around this man, but she doubted he'd want to hear her say that. "Let me know how it turns out," she said instead.

"All right. I'll call you next weekend."

"Great." She turned, looking for her parents but realized that the church had emptied. Only Pastor Williams remained, obviously waiting for the two of them to leave. "It was good to see you again."

"Enjoy *Oklahoma!*" he called as they headed for their separate cars.

Carrie drove home, unable to stop wishing that Brad were the one taking her to the show.

The phone rang before the crack of dawn on Saturday morning. Carrie grumpily reached for it, wondering who on earth would call at such a time. "Hullo?"

"Carrie? This is Brad. I know it's really early, and you're probably tired from the show last night, but we have a flu epidemic going through the school that everyone's blaming me for, and even teachers and parents have come down with the bug."

This did *not* make sense. She crawled upright on her pillows and blinked to wipe away the morning cobwebs. "Uh . . . Brad? I'm not very swift in the morning, but . . . why are you calling *me?* I'm not a doctor."

He laughed sheepishly. "I know, and I know I'm not making much sense. I'll be blunt. I need help. Right now, I'm the only adult supervising fifteen seventeen-year-olds at that soup kitchen. I thought—hoped—maybe you'd bail me out . . . ?"

"You can't get *anybody* else to help you?"

A long silence followed. "Well . . . not anyone I'd like to share a tough day with."

Pleasure flooded her then, and despite his insistence that he wasn't interested in romance, Carrie couldn't help wondering if maybe romance was interested in him.

Impossible hope burrowed into her heart. Especially when she thought about last night. She shook her head. What a strange evening. She had to remember to tell Brad about her latest dating-service experience.

"At what time and where do you need me?"

"You're a lifesaver!" he exclaimed. "If you give me your address, I'll swing by and pick you up by seven-thirty. We're cooking the meals, you understand."

Suddenly feeling much more alert, Carrie gave Brad directions, then hung up and ran to the shower. As she lathered, she remembered bits and pieces of conversations they'd had, odds and ends she'd picked up from his talk at church on Wednesday. Seeking God's will had featured prominently in his speech.

How did one come to know God's will for one's life? she wondered, sudsing her hair. And did God *really* care about the little things? Smaller-than-Ten-Commandments stuff? Like who to date and what to do on a Saturday morning?

Was helping at the soup kitchen God's will for her day?

She'd have to discuss it with Brad. Since meeting him, she'd found herself considering deeper issues more frequently than ever before. She had a strong feeling he would love to talk about this as much as he'd enjoyed their skiing escapade.

Just one more thing she'd come to like about him.

Hours later Brad stood at the doorway to the dining hall at the soup kitchen, surveying the action. His kids were doing great, and he knew their hearts were in their efforts.

Then he saw her. Carrie sat at a far table next to frail, old Mrs. McFarlane. Having volunteered here a number of times already, he had come to know the regulars. The tiny lady was his favorite, her delicacy and gentle nature appealing to his protective side.

Carrie, with her red curls and emerald sweater, presented a

radiant contrast to the older woman in dove gray and rose. With animated gestures, she chattered away, winning polite laughs from her companion, all the while cutting turkey, baked potato, and steamed broccoli into manageable pieces. Mrs. McFarlane, who never asked for help, appeared so absorbed in the conversation that she seemed to forget the severe palsy that normally mortified her. The morsels that fell from her fork were either caught unobtrusively by her companion's napkin-covered hand and returned to her plate or toed into a neat pile at Carrie's feet.

Brad's heart took a dip, and admiration filled him.

Oh, Lord, he prayed silently, *a woman with a heart so great shouldn't have to rely on a dating service to find love.*

He grinned sappily. He'd known it was the right thing to call her that morning. Not only was she fun to be with, but Carrie Forster was one terrific lady. Every day that went by, he liked her more and more.

As he walked to the industrial-sized sink in the kitchen, Brad nearly tripped over his feet when he realized where his thoughts had been headed. He groaned. Why on earth was he thinking of Carrie that way? She was husband hunting, while he was committed to his calling.

And he *knew* God had called him to Christ's Academy. And right now that didn't leave time for courting a potential wife.

Praying for guidance, self-control, and wisdom, he attacked the few items that didn't go into the industrial dishwasher with a vengeance.

"You're gonna scrub that steel right off that pan," Carrie sang to the tune of the *South Pacific* song moments later. "You have a problem with it?"

"No," he answered shortly, determined to keep his interest from wandering where it wasn't meant to go.

46

Parking herself at his side before the mammoth sink, she said, "Then let me help. The poor pan will appreciate it."

Distance, he needed distance—and then he remembered *he* had been the one to call *her* that morning. It no longer seemed such a wise move. With a sudsy finger, he pointed toward a counter ten feet away. "Towels are over there. You can dry."

As she grabbed a clean cloth, he mentally scrabbled for a risk-free topic of conversation. He nearly laughed in relief when he pounced on the perfect one. "How'd your date go last night?"

Carrie did the laughing. "You really want to know?"

"Hmm . . . I think we did this the last time. Yeah, I'm curious about this dating-service experience you're having."

Obviously thinking, she rubbed a kettle's bottom to a gleam. "I'm not sure it's the dating service that's responsible for my . . . wacky dates."

"Oh, so this one was wacky while the other one was different. Tell me about it."

She set down the kettle and grabbed the baking pan he'd just abused. "Ford had just picked up his new car at the dealership, and he was really excited about it. Get this, it's a brand-new, fire-engine red Corvette—with more bells and whistles than a steam locomotive."

Brad frowned. Did a showy car mean something to Carrie? "A 'Vette, huh? Ford must be doing well."

He stole a peek to gauge her response to his statement and caught the droll look she sent his way as she swabbed the baking pan. "And he's not shy about it," she said. "To give you an idea how pleased he was with his new toy, he kept buffing the thing with this chamois cloth each time he got out. You know—in my driveway he did the right fender. At the theater parking lot he did the hood. You know what I mean. Oh, and he kept pointing out its features to me."

"Loaded?"

Carrie shrugged. "I guess." Then the mischievous gleam he had come to know appeared in her brown eyes again. "Yeah, that's right. He said the upgraded friggledorp button on the dash would make the dooglemaow shranattub faster. Oh, and the custom muckobrog meant the yackupoosh—"

She stopped when he collapsed against the sink, whooping with laughter.

"Get the picture?" she asked with a wink.

Gasping, he nodded. "I take it . . . you're not . . . a . . . car buff."

"A car's a car. It gets me where I want to go."

"Remind me not to show you *my* toy."

"Uh-oh. A car?"

"The car."

"Elaborate, please."

"He's a gem. Well, in the rough, you know. Abner's a '57 Chevy. Someday he's going to look brand-new again."

"Abner? I thought guys named their cars after women."

"Yeah, others do, but I figured that was too . . . common for my pal. He's Abner, and it's the two of us guys—and my sidekick, Elbow Grease—against the forces of corrosion and time."

Carrie chuckled. "Somehow I can't picture you all grunged up under a pile of rust and bolts."

"Hush, woman! Don't you offend my buddy that way."

She laughed. "To each his own."

"Yeah, I'll keep Abner, and Ford can keep his 'Vette. Anyway, how was the show?"

"Great. *Oklahoma!*'s one of my favorites."

"And how do you feel about Ford? Now that you've gotten to know him better."

Carrie grinned wryly. "I'm not so sure I've gotten to know him at all."

"What do you mean?"

"Well, we got to the theater, he buffed his hood, studied his profile in the paint job—to check the gloss, he said. Then, when he finally tore himself away, we went inside. But before we got past the ticket taker, he said he'd forgotten something and dashed outside again. He ran back in, and we sat and talked about his big merger until the lights went down. I settled in, loving every note of the overture, and then . . . I noticed the light."

"The light?"

"Mm-hmm. One of those carry-with-you reading-lamp thingies."

"Let me guess. Ford had brought it with him to read the program since he's a Broadway-musical fan?"

"Wrong. To read the 'Vette's owner's manual 'cause he hates show tunes."

He tried. Brad really tried to stifle his laugh. But that not-so-perfect-but-wholly-human part of him triumphed. He chortled at the image in his mind. "I'll bet . . . everyone around you . . . loved it."

"Right. I've never heard an audience with so many scratchy throats."

He whooped again. "Still think dating-service introductions are the way to find the right man?"

Carrie considered the question for a moment. "I'm not sure. I don't really know Ford yet."

"But do you still *want* to know him?"

Brad's question caught her off guard. She thought back over her dates and conversations with Ford Kenner. She thought of the things they had in common—and those they didn't. Then her reason for joining the dating service popped back into her mind.

"On paper, he looks great," Carrie said slowly. "Oh, you know what? Ford said the same thing about me in the first message he left on my machine. Interesting, don't you think? Anyway, I would hate to make a hasty judgment. He *is* my last frog-prince, after all."

"Frog-prince?" Brad choked out.

Carrie blushed. "That's what I began calling the guys whose names I got from the service. I've figuratively kissed a bunch of frogs and come up with no prince yet."

Brad squashed the irritation he felt at the thought of Carrie's kissing those guys. Then he remembered that she'd said *figuratively*. He felt better—marginally. "So, do you think Ford's the prince?"

"I don't know. And I wish I could know."

They fell silent as Brad wiped the stainless-steel counter. "We're done here," he said. "Let's round up the kids and head back to school."

As they traveled to the east-side campus, Carrie mulled over their conversation. And once again the matter of God's will returned to her mind, even though Brad hadn't brought it up. She suspected it had been foremost in his mind. That's how well she was coming to know him.

Was Ford Kenner God's will for her life? Like Christ's Academy was for Brad's?

Carrie decided the time had come to figure it out. And Brad was the man to help her do it. She would not forget to ask him on their way home.

She bided her time, watching him make sure each kid had a ride home, waving good-bye, pausing to glance heavenward and smile. As he came back toward the car, emotions swelled inside her, and she found herself wishing again that Brad weren't so determined to avoid romance.

This man was special, and the woman who won his heart would be very fortunate and well loved. If only she could be the one. . . .

But she wasn't, so she had to stop thinking like that. She had to focus on finding the right man *for her*. And if Brad was right and a dating service wasn't the best way to do so, then maybe he was also right in insisting that God would provide the answers she wanted.

"All set?" he asked, sliding behind the wheel.

"Oh yeah," she said, her mind on higher things. She waited until he pulled out of the parking lot. "OK, Brad. You've mentioned a few times—and a whole lot more times kept yourself from mentioning, I'm sure—that you feel I need to seek God's will for my life. I've grown up a Christian in a Christian home as a member of a Christian church. But . . . I'm not sure how to go about seeking God's will. And I don't even know that my dating situation really matters to God. I mean it's not that important, and I'm only one of zillions of people on earth—"

"Stop right there," he said. "In his Gospel, Luke quotes what Jesus told his disciples about God's interest in his children. Our Lord said, 'What is the price of five sparrows? A couple of pennies? Yet God does not forget a single one of them. And the very hairs on your head are all numbered. So don't be afraid; you are more valuable to him than a whole flock of sparrows.'"

"But—"

"No *buts*. You matter; he cares."

Carrie softly said, "Enough to send his Son to die for me."

"Exactly!"

"OK, so God *does* care about me, even about the hairs on

my head. How does that translate into my finding his will for my life?"

Brad thought for a moment. "Well, when you care about someone, don't you let them know what you think is best for them?"

"Hm . . . yes, but—"

"Hey! No *but*s, remember? Scripture speaks to this very thing. Psalm 37 is the one I go to when I'm seeking God's will."

"I'm embarrassed to admit I don't know it offhand."

"You can read it later, but I'll tell you the four steps I find most useful. First, you need to trust in God and do good. If you do that, the psalm says that you will live safely and prosper."

Carrie considered his words. "That makes sense, and it's pretty practical, too. Doing good leads to a good life."

"Our God is very practical. But he wants to do more than care for our basic needs. Which leads me to the second step. That one tells us to delight in the Lord so that he can give us our heart's desires."

"You really think he wants to give us our deepest desires?"

"Yes, when we delight in him. When we put him first in everything and rejoice in his power, his majesty, his glory. All I can say is that when I do immerse myself in his Word and turn to him first, my wants fall in line with his—or at least, that's how it feels."

"I'll have to look this up when I get home. Go on, tell me step three."

"Gladly. That one says we must commit everything we do to the Lord, and he will help us."

Carrie nodded slowly. "And the fourth?"

Brad gave her his crooked smile. "This one's the hardest

for me. We're to be still in the presence of the Lord, waiting patiently for him to act."

"And God wants me to bother him with even my desire to marry? Oh, why even ask? You just told me what the Bible says, and it says just that."

Brad chuckled. "Think about it, Carrie. And I'll pray for you."

She again felt the pleasant warmth that her heart had begun to associate with him. If only . . .

But, no. She had thinking and reading to do. And praying. "I'll pray for me, too."

As he let the engine idle in front of her condo, Carrie gave in to impulse and threw her arms around Brad's neck. She hadn't meant it to last more than a second, but suddenly his arms went around her, and it felt so good . . . so right to have him hold her. Emotion rose to her throat.

"Thank God we met," she whispered, giving him a peck on the cheek and flying out of the car before melting into an embarrassed mush.

She fumbled her key three times, knowing he was still in the driveway waiting for her to go inside. But how could she stick the puny piece of brass into the slim slice of a hole when her every sensor beeped a furious *danger, danger, danger* at her?

Finally, after what seemed like an eternity, she succeeded, opened the door, and slammed it shut behind her. Dropping her purse on Great-aunt Sophie's lowboy, she made a beeline for her bookshelf and pulled out the Bible Mom and Pop had given her as a graduation present all those years ago.

CHAPTER FIVE

The slam of Carrie's condo door shattered the ice that had formed on Brad's brain when her arms wrapped around his neck. Oh, man, was he in trouble.

He'd liked that hug.

Too much.

Just like he liked *her* too much, too.

And he shouldn't since he wasn't looking for romance and marriage. Besides, she was hoping to establish a relationship with Ford. And, oh, how that name was beginning to grate on Brad's nerves. What'd the guy think he was? Some sleek sports car of the *mucho* money kind?

As he turned onto his street, Brad realized what he'd just done—felt. "Uh-oh. The green-eyed monster's put in an appearance," he muttered, trying to ease the sting of self-knowledge with the worn-out cliché.

As the automatic garage door whirred shut, he sighed. He'd urged Carrie to seek God's will. His feelings for her had him so confused that he felt the need to cry to God for guidance himself.

After spending some time with his Bible and in prayer, Brad went about his usual evening routine, still feeling restless, unsure of his direction. He'd never been one to waffle, to let good and appealing things distract him from a higher calling. Why did this have to happen now? Why with Carrie?

Although he turned on that evening's television shows, he couldn't have told anyone what he'd watched. He saw only Carrie's smile, her eyes, heard her laughter, her voice, felt her arms around his neck.

He turned in early, after spending yet more time in prayer. But as he fell asleep, the snowball fight ended very differently from the one they'd already lived out.

This time it ended with a kiss.

"God? I'm new at this, you know." Carrie swallowed hard, her hand covering the Bible page on which she had found Psalm 37. "I'm going to try it Brad's way—well, your way, really. From now on, I'm going to commit everything I do to you. I'm going to trust you and use the talents and abilities you've given me to do good for you. I'm going to delight in you, spend time getting to know you, and I'm going to do my best to be still in your presence—even though you know I'm not good at keeping still."

Carrie winced. Was she doing this right? Then she wondered . . . was there a right or wrong way to speak to God? If she understood her Bible correctly, he knew everything about her even before she knew it, so what was the point of changing in order to approach him? Sincerity and simplicity probably worked best.

"Oh yes," she added, "I'm praying that you'll give me my heart's desire—you know, that family I want—if it's your will. And I'm going to wait patiently for you to act. But, God? You know patience is not my strongest suit, so you're going to have to help me with that one, too."

When she realized the magnitude of the privilege she had

just used, the enormous gift she had in being able to call on God, tears welled in her eyes. "Thank you, Father, for caring enough about me to count the hairs on my head. Thank you for sending your Son to that cross for me. Thank you for listening, and thank you for . . . Brad."

Even though he didn't want romance, Brad wanted friendship. And that friendship had come to mean a great deal to her.

As Carrie putzed around the rest of the evening, she kept coming back to the conversations she and Brad had shared, the fun they'd had together, the good they'd done at the soup kitchen earlier that day.

And she again found herself wishing . . . wanting . . . then reminding herself to stop. Brad was *not* interested, and unless she wanted to ruin a great friendship, she had to focus on seeking God's will for her life.

Would it be Ford? Would she come to respect, admire, and plain old like him as much as she already did Brad?

Would she come to love him?

When she went to bed, she found herself more tired than she had thought. In moments she drifted off, the snowball fight she dreamed of more hilarious than before. This time, however, it came to a very different end.

This time, it ended with a kiss.

Tuesday after work, Carrie received two phone calls. The first was from Ford. He expected to close the big merger on Friday, and his law firm planned a celebration in his honor. He wanted her to attend as his date.

Of course she agreed to go. She wanted a fair chance to get to know him, and celebrating something that obviously meant so much to him would offer insight into the man.

She hoped.

Brad called a short while later. He wanted to know if she'd found the psalm as meaningful and helpful as he did. Carrie shared with him how his encouragement had led her to commit to a deeper walk with God, which then brought them, inevitably, to talk of his work at school. Before they realized it, two and a half hours had sped by. Patches had begun eyeing Carrie malevolently, *mrrreeooowing* his objection to being ignored for so long.

At the last moment, as he was saying good-bye, Brad paused. "Are you still there?" she asked.

"Mm-hmm . . ."

"What's up?"

"I was thinking . . . we have this fun event for the whole school on Saturday, and I was wondering if you'd like to come. It'll be an all-day thing, and I won't be able to leave until it's over, but from what I've heard about the last three years' Doldrums Days and with everything I've planned, I figure we should have a good time. I mean, it's nothing fancy—on the contrary, come in jeans and a sweatshirt, since it could get messy."

She'd come to know him well enough to suspect he might actually be asking her on a date, a *real* date. Carrie's heart kicked up its beat, and butterflies did a jig in her middle. "How messy?" she asked, trying to keep her cool.

"Messy as in me being dunked in a vat of slime. It's a baseball throw, with the proceeds going to our missions' collection. Whenever anyone hits the target, the bench I sit on falls out from under me. I understand sliming the principal is every student's goal."

Carrie giggled at the thought. "How about the adults?"

"Hey! You're supposed to be on my side!"

"Oh, sure. I will be. The front side, with my throwing arm

warmed and primed." She paused for effect. "Did I ever mention that back in high school I was the star pitcher on the girl's softball team?"

Dead silence. "No-o-oo . . . ," he said ever so slowly, "you forgot to mention *that* when you called yourself York's greatest klutz. Anyway, if you'll come, I'll forgive you for dunking me."

"It sounds like too much fun to miss."

"I'll pick you up at eight-thirty Saturday morning."

Carrie groaned. "Ever heard of sleeping in on Saturday mornings?"

"Why waste the time?"

She sighed with patently fake long-suffering. "OK, only because you asked so nicely, I'll be ready."

"It's a date, then."

She caught her breath as she heard the disconnecting click from his end. Did Brad realize what he'd said?

And what did it *really* mean? In the greater scheme of things. For the two of them.

Breathing a prayer, she tried to settle the now dive-bombing butterflies and replaced the receiver. In her heart of hearts, she wondered if God was already revealing his will for her.

"Love that sweatshirt!" a compact, iron-haired, fifty-something woman in Levi's and Reeboks exclaimed as Carrie removed her coat.

"'Hu-huh, hu-huh, I'm Goofy,'" quipped Carrie, imitating the Disney character. "I'm a longtime fan."

The woman came closer and gave her a sharp once-over. "I don't know you, and around here there's *no* one I don't know." She stuck out her hand. "I'm Velma Myers, the school secretary. Who're you?"

"I'm Carrie Forster, Brad's—"

"Valentine!" Velma burst out with glee. "I knew it! I just knew it!"

"Knew what?" asked Brad as he backed through the door, his arms full of boxes.

"I knew God's hand was on that bouquet you got when you were so sick. And you thought it was nothing more than a big mix-up. See? Here you are, and here she is, and, boy, is she pretty! Just right for you, I'd say."

Carrie's cheeks blazed at Velma's exuberance. She peeked at Brad, wondering what he thought of such bluntness, and caught his matching blush—all the way to his earlobes!

"Velma," he said, a warning note in his voice. "There's no need to embarrass Carrie."

Carrie had a feeling Brad was even more acutely aware of his own embarrassment than hers.

Velma waved dismissively. "I'm not one to dither, and you know it. I'm glad to meet you, Carrie, and I hope you have fun with us today. I gotta run." Matching action to words, she squeaked away, singing—off-key—what sounded to Carrie suspiciously like "Isn't it romantic?"

Brad cleared his throat, obviously uncomfortable. "Ignore her," he said. "She's the best school secretary there's ever been, but she's incorrigible. And she's decided that since my own mother's long deceased, it's up to her to take over the job. Never mind that I'm a full-grown man. So she never minces words around me, and she bullies me mercilessly. She even poured gallons of homemade chicken soup down my throat when I was sick, thinking I couldn't take care of myself, which is why she was there when your bouquet arrived—"

"Brad," Carrie cut in to put him out of his misery. "Yeah, she was a little embarrassing, but I liked her. And it's pretty obvious she likes you. Don't worry about me. A blush here and there won't kill me. Besides, the woman sings show tunes!"

"Just as long as you don't hold her against me."

"Nope. I'll just get even when you're perched over a vat of slime."

He groaned, then headed for a set of closed double doors. "Here," Carrie said as she ran to open them for him, then found herself in the gymnasium where they'd watched the basketball game. "How's Doug?"

"You remember?" Brad asked, delight in his voice.

"How could I forget? He was great, and you were so proud of him. That was a fun evening."

"Great steak dinner, too."

"And the company matched if I do say so."

"Thank you kindly, ma'am." Dropping the boxes next to the steps to the stage, Brad leaned back to stretch his spine. "And speaking of company, how'd last night's date go?"

Carrie's laughter exploded. "I have now officially flunked out of the dating-service experience."

"That good?"

"If it weren't so funny, it'd be terribly sad," she said, remembering the episode. "I'd told you Ford was closing that big deal he'd been working on. As expected, it went through, and he was elated. His colleagues congratulated him over and over again. Then we went to dinner. Since Ford was the guest of honor, we sat at the head of the table."

She paused to take a breath, and Brad said, "So far, it sounds pretty nice."

The mischievous part of her made another appearance, and she waggled her eyebrows at him. "We're only now getting to the good part. Ford began to expound on the value of a brilliant, well-honed brain. 'It's all about mind over matter,' he said about a dozen times."

"Oh, brother."

"Exactly. He later told me, 'I believe a very intelligent person can develop his brain to such a level that he can move spoons with only the power of his mind.'"

Brad howled. "Tell me you're making this up. Please."

"Can't do that. I'm serious. Worse, *he* was serious."

"So did he?"

Carrie chuckled. "In a way."

"What way?"

"Naturally, he felt driven to demonstrate. So he scrunched up his eyes, wrinkled his nose, pleated his forehead—basically, he pruned up his face. Seconds trickled by, and he just concentrated harder."

"What did you do?"

"Hey, by that time, visions of ambulatory utensils danced in my head. And I distinctly remember the music from *The Twilight Zone* playing once or twice through my thoughts."

As Brad chortled again, Carrie grew serious. "You know, in the middle of this goofy scene, I realized Ford had nothing more than self-esteem and ego to count on."

"Smart woman."

She smiled smugly. "I'm even smarter than that. And compassionate, too. Why, seeing how hard he was trying to prove his point, and seeing how much he was relying on his brainpower, I began to suspect his ego was about to get zapped in the middle of his celebration. I felt sorry for him, so . . ."

Brad's eyes widened. "You didn't?"

"I sure did. As he turned red from focusing, I reached across the table and nudged the spoon a couple of inches to the right."

Whoops of Brad's laughter caught the attention of those preparing the booths for the upcoming attractions. He dropped onto a step, hugging his middle as inquiring glances came their way. "You rat!"

"Not at all," Carrie maintained. "I was being kind. I really did feel pity for him." She thought back over her intent last night. "All right. Maybe I was a rat—a little. And that was wrong. I probably owe him an apology. But you should have seen how pleased he was when I exclaimed that I'd seen the spoon move. Which I had."

"You just . . . never mentioned . . . you'd . . . helped it . . . along," Brad said between more laughs.

"Would *you* have?"

"Probably not."

"Anyway, I decided right then, I was out of there. No more dates with strangers for me."

"Good decision. But you know," he said, growing serious, "we shouldn't laugh—it *is* as sad as you said. We should pray for Ford, that he comes to know Christ. The entire episode just goes to show, once again, how right Scripture is. Look at what can happen when a man relies on his own understanding instead of leaning on the Lord."

Carrie caught her breath. Yes, she saw exactly what could happen. A woman could come to see the difference between two men more clearly than she ever had before. Whereas Ford depended on himself for his success—not to mention his monumental embarrassment—Brad depended on God for everything. There was no contest between the two men.

Not anymore.

Carrie realized right then that if Brad never decided he wanted romance, marriage, or her, she might well remain single for the rest of her life. As clearly as if he had spoken out loud, God had shown her that. Ford, dating services, and all the rest were not right for her.

The question now remained—was marriage God's will for Brad and her?

Carrie enjoyed every minute of Doldrums Day at Christ's Academy. It was part fund-raiser, part carnival, and all fun, and she pitched in to help wherever anyone needed a hand.

She learned a lot by keeping eyes and ears open. The staff held Brad in high esteem, even though he was considerably younger than a number of them. The parents were well pleased with their new principal, many pausing to speak with him while he dripped green goo from his bench.

The next time he took a reprieve from slime duty, he caught her eye and gestured her over. "Come join me for a cup of punch in the teachers' lounge," he suggested.

"Need to get away from the noise?"

"No, I want to dry out a little, and I'd love some company. Are we working you too hard?"

"How could you think that?" she asked, sincerely surprised.

"Well, I invited you, and all I've done is wriggle in glop. I see Velma's put you to work, and I began to wonder why you'd agreed to be tortured like this."

"No torture. In fact, Mr. Big-Shot Principal," she said mischievously, "I'm learning all kinds of fascinating things."

"Uh-oh."

"Mm-hmm," she responded, giving him a pointed stare. "All kinds of things about the wonderful, talented, fair, intelligent, kind, wise, assertive new princi—"

"Stop!" he cried, his cheeks red. "No punch for you. Not after *that*."

"OK, OK. Seriously, Brad, they really like you, and I enjoy hearing their comments. It's nice to know others share my good opinion of you."

He didn't respond but stared at her, his expression unreadable. Then he reached over and took her hand between both of his. "The feeling's mutual, you know."

And as the moment stretched, minute by charged minute, the hall in a noisy school building suddenly reminded Carrie of a hushed, snow-covered ski run.

"Carrie—"

"Hey, Mr. Kenner!" called a dark-haired male missile that stopped mere inches from Brad's knees. "Mrs. Myers says you're taking too many breaks to do the missions collection any good. She says you better get back on the job."

Brad gave her his crooked grin. "Gotta go."

"Your clamoring public awaits you," Carrie offered, disappointed that the boy had arrived just when he had. "I'll get back to the baked-goods booth. We're doing quite a business there."

Brad started toward the gym. "Don't eat too many of your wares. The sixth-grade teacher and her husband have invited everyone who worked today to wind down at their home after we close up here. She promised bowls of her killer chili to all who come—and *no noise, no stress.*"

Warmth careened through Carrie. *Two dates in one day.* "Excellent. See you later."

She gave him a wave and only then noticed the slime dripping from her hand. Veering toward the ladies' room, she thought she'd better get used to school-age interrupters and gloppy messes. If God were to give her the desire of her heart, she would be blessed with many more years of the like.

Because, against all odds, she was falling in love with the wrong man.

CHAPTER SIX

Hey, lady! We need us a cookie here," said a cleaned-up, slimeless Brad as Carrie swabbed the counter in her booth. "Do you have any left?"

Turning, she saw the most heart-mushing sight she'd ever seen. Tall, solid Brad Kenner stood before the baked-goods stand holding a weepy toddler in the crook of his arm. With his large thumb, he wiped a tear from the little girl's cheek, then rubbed his nose against her temple.

"It's OK, Susie-Q," he murmured. "I know there's no more ice cream, but my special friend Carrie is going to find you the most splendiferous, stupendous cookie ever. Then you and I are going to help your mommy and daddy pack up the beanbags so they can get you home in time for supper."

If Carrie hadn't already realized she loved this man, all doubt would have vanished right then. *Dear God, thank you for bringing Brad into my life, and if it is your will, let him want me as much as I want him.*

Clearing her throat of the emotion there, she held out a snickerdoodle. "This is the last of my absolute favorite cookies in the whole wide world. Just for . . . Susie, you said?"

"Susie's my girl," he said with a wink. "And if my lady is done here in about a half hour, we'll head on out to the Allens'."

67

The "my lady" sent ripples of pleasure up and down Carrie's spine. "I'll be done in five minutes. Maybe Velma will have something else to keep me busy until you're ready. Don't worry about me. Finish what you need to do."

"Wise and generous as well as lovely," he answered, dipping his head in a bow before sauntering away, a smiling Susie raining crumbs all over his clean shirt.

Of course, Velma had plenty to keep Carrie occupied, not to mention questions and comments aplenty. Blunt and direct, the secretary revealed her heart of gold and unshakable faith in Christ. When Brad returned for Carrie, she felt she knew the older woman as if they'd been friends all their lives.

With a farewell hug, Carrie said, "I hope to see you again soon."

"Hah!" Velma retorted. "We've got you now. Before you know it, you'll be a fixture around here. After all, God didn't land that bouquet in Brad's lap for nothing!"

"OK, Velma, good night now," Brad said, hustling Carrie away from his outspoken secretary before the woman thought up another outrageous thing to say.

"She's not coming to the Allens'?" Carrie asked as they left the school building.

"No. She has to go home and check on her husband. He's a serious diabetic and recently underwent an amputation."

"And she came today anyway?"

Brad unlocked the passenger door and held it open. "Neither she nor Roger would have it any other way," he said. "Even though I insisted she spend the day with him. Last I heard, Roger was still muttering at his new wheelchair for his lack of proficiency with it. That's what kept him from coming and helping today."

Closing her door, he ran around the car. When he slid in,

Carrie said, "I'd already decided I could come to love that lady. Now I'm pretty sure I'll love her husband, too."

Brad smiled. "Smart woman."

She gave him a penetrating look, her expression serious and gentle. Brad gulped and nearly missed her murmuring, "Let's just say not as blind as some."

They fell silent, and the drive to the Allen home was made to Schubert's Unfinished Symphony. At the gathering, bowls of steamy, spicy chili were pressed into their hands, and they were shown to a comfortable couch. Conversation was of the "Did you see how well the fishing booth did?" variety.

As Brad finally began to relax, his pager went off. He groaned and checked the phone number—not one he recognized. "Excuse me," he murmured to Carrie, showing her the small, black receiver. "It'll only take a minute to see who's calling."

It took him even less time than he'd thought. He returned to her side immediately. "I'm sorry, but I have to leave," he said, his voice low, not wishing to alarm the others. "It's the police. There's been a break-in at the school. Vandals. I need to view the damage, decide whether to press charges—that kind of thing. I'll be back for you as soon as I'm done."

Carrie stood. "Forget it. I'm coming with you."

Brad's protective instincts kicked in. "No way. I don't know how dangerous the situation is, and I will *not* expose you to any risk."

"*You* will expose me to no risk. *I* will choose what risk I can reasonably take. And since it was the police who called you, I'd say things are under control."

"But—"

"No *buts*. You're just wasting time. Let's get to the school."

They executed this ride as silently as their earlier one, but with much less ease between them—and no Schubert. Brad worried about Carrie, and she remained glaringly stubborn. He only wanted to make sure she stayed safe, that nothing happened to her. He . . . *cared* for her, and he couldn't stand to think she might get hurt.

He pulled up in front of the main entrance and, as he opened the car door, faced her again. "Carrie—"

"Don't. Let's go."

Clenching his jaw and praying for help with this obstinate woman, he ran inside. Carrie's equally rapid footsteps followed him to the office, where a sliver of light shone beneath the closed door.

"Hey, Tom," he said to the policeman who patrolled the school property. "What did you find?"

"You missed it?" asked the large African-American man. "How could you? It's all in bright red."

Feeling stupid—especially since he'd stormed in stewing over Carrie's bullheaded attitude—Brad asked, "What's all in red?"

"Er," Carrie offered from behind. "You might want to go back to the lobby, Brad. Then again . . . you might not."

He gave her a glare and noted her efforts to stifle a grin. Without a word, he strode from the office to the vestibule.

And he saw it—all of it.

In red—ketchup red.

"Great! That's just great." When she snickered, he spun and shook a finger in her face. "Stop it. It's *not* funny. Besides, we have to catch whoever did this."

"You don't find 'Principal Kenner's a green-slime kissy-face' funny?"

"Not in gaudy lipstick across floor-to-ceiling windows at the front of the school," he answered, his cheeks scalding hot.

"Hey, it's not permanent, and it's obviously a prank. The police are here, and I'm sure they'll catch whoever—"

"I've caught whoever—red-handed." The policeman chuckled at his play on words. "Come back to the office, Brad. I'd like to see you handle this one."

"That's what you said when Keith Bennett stole the new math books and refused to return them because they didn't make sense," Brad said, shaking his head. "You wanted me to do something about it? Other than tutor the kid so the books would make sense?"

Tom raised both hands, grinning. "Hey, in my book, theft is theft."

"In my book, it's a call for help. And tonight's the same," Brad added as he passed Velma's immaculate desk on his way to his office. He jolted to a stop when he spotted the small body in his chair. "Mindy? Mindy Slater? What are you doing here so late?"

Hazel eyes spit rage. Pointed chin jutted forward. Thin arms crossed a narrow chest. Tight lips offered nothing.

"I found her in the boys' john copying her message on the mirrors there," Tom said as he followed Brad. "She informed me that you are a hypocrite and a liar and that she hates you. Her efforts tonight are meant to tell the whole school what a rotten slime you are—her words, not mine." Slapping a printed form onto a leaning tower of folders on Brad's well-papered desk, he added, "Sign here so we can press charges."

Brad waved Tom away. "Did you notify her parents?"

Tom didn't budge. "Right before I called you. They live in Dover, so they won't be here for at least another ten or fifteen minutes. Sign, would you?"

"Mindy," he said, ignoring Tom's paper and approaching the child, "why did you tell Officer Marks those things? It's pretty clear you're angry at me, and I'd like to know what I did to upset you."

If anything, the little chin protruded farther, and the white-rimmed lips got thinner. Mindy offered not a sound.

"I would like to talk about . . . whatever," he said, crouching next to the girl. "But I can't if I don't know what's wrong."

"Oh, *you* know what's wrong," Mindy suddenly said, her words drenched with contempt. *"You* were in that hall, dripping slime all over *her* hands and staring all googly at her."

Her words struck him so hard that he lost his balance and landed on his tail end. His face went hot again, as did his ears. He hadn't thought anyone had noticed them in the hallway—not that holding Carrie's hand was such a terrible thing to do. "I . . . er . . . was thanking Miss Forster for her help with the baked-goods booth. She's not a parent or a teacher—"

"Yeah, we noticed," Mindy muttered.

"Who noticed?"

"Everyone with eyes," she spit out.

"Like?" Brad persisted.

"Oh, Sarah Mitchell, Wendy Harris, Trina Collum."

"But—"

A squeeze on his shoulder made him stop. He turned and met Carrie's gaze. "Mr. Kenner, Officer . . . Marks, did you say?" she asked. When Brad nodded, she went on. "This strikes me as something to be discussed between women. You two are superfluous here. Please leave the room for a moment."

"But—"

"But—"

"No way," she said, cutting off both Brad and Tom. "I'll call you when we need you—*if* we need you. Go!"

Carrie's expression told Brad she wouldn't yield. Since he knew no harm would come to either female by leaving them alone, he conceded defeat. Tom followed him to Velma's throne room. Curious, Brad parked himself where he could not only hear but also see what transpired between Mindy and Carrie. Tom pressed up behind him.

"First of all," Carrie said as she sat on the edge of Brad's desk, across from Mindy, "forget the Miss Forster stuff. I'm Carrie."

Mindy glowered in response.

Carrie seemed unaffected by the venom. "Besides, I think I know what the problem is."

"Yeah, right."

"Mm-hmm. I don't know how old you are, since you look pretty mature to me, but when I was, I think about twelve, I fell head over heels for . . . Mr. Potter . . . my science teacher. . . ."

Carrie donned a dreamy expression. "I hated science, but I sure did like that man. And he was soooo nice to me. I was sure he was *the* one for me."

Mindy's arms relaxed. "So?"

"So I followed him *everywhere*—in school, of course. I even hid in his classroom closet one day."

Brad groaned.

Tom snickered. "Start checking your closet come Monday, Teach."

Mindy leaned forward. "What happened?"

Brad read triumph in Carrie's grin. "His *wife* came to pick him up that day!" she exclaimed, grimacing. "I didn't know he had a wife, and I had to watch him *kiss* her. Was that ever awful!"

Brad chuckled, and Tom shook his head. "Women," muttered the very married father-of-two-with-another-in-transit.

Mindy sat back, her bottom lip quivering. "But you didn't wind up . . . *arrested*."

"Noooo, but Mr. Potter needed his coat, you see—this happened in February—and guess what he found when he opened that door?"

"Oo—o—oh . . ."

"Exactly. I wound up suspended. And grounded. And I swore I hated Mr. Potter to everyone who would listen."

"Did you *really* hate him?" asked Mindy.

Carrie shook her head. "I thought I still loved him. For a long time after that."

"So what happened? You're not married to him or anything."

"No, and I'm very glad I'm not."

Brad nodded in silent agreement.

Tom whispered, "Looks like she's not the only one."

Brad gave the officer a quelling glare, which merely made Tom laugh again.

"Why?" asked Mindy, leaning forward.

Carrie placed her hand on the girl's thigh. "Let me tell you something. I *thought* Mr. Potter was the right man for me back then. And I *thought* I was in love with him. But you know? He wasn't, and I wasn't. I learned that later."

"How did you learn that?"

"Oh, learning he wasn't the right man was easy. He was nearly twenty years older than me back then. That's a huge age difference."

"No, Miss Fors—"

"Carrie."

"OK, Carrie. I meant, how did you learn you weren't really in love with him?"

"I forgot about him. Until tonight."

"Oh," Mindy said in a little voice. "And did you learn how to know if someone's right for you? If you're *really* in love?"

As Brad waited for Carrie's answer with even more interest than Mindy, Rod and Audrey Slater ran in. Brad and Tom turned sharply, motioning for silence.

"Funny you should ask," Carrie said. "I only learned that very recently. I was again making a hash of things—"

"But you're a *grown-up!*" Mindy exclaimed in shock.

"And still goofing up—on occasion," Carrie answered. "But a very wise man told me exactly what I needed to do to find the right match. This smart man told me to seek God's will for my life, and if there was to be a man in my future, our heavenly Father would lead me to him."

Brad felt his cheeks warm as he dodged Tom's inquiring look.

"So did God answer?"

"He sure did! He showed me the wrong man pretty clearly, and how silly it was for me to stubbornly try to do everything on my own."

"Wow," Mindy breathed. "D'you . . . do you think God will show me if I ask him?"

"I know he will, Mindy. And I'll tell you something else this very special man showed me. When you go home, look up Psalm 37. It'll give you simple steps to follow to help you find God's good and perfect will. If you do what it calls you to do, then God will protect you, help you, guide you, and bless you with everything you need."

"It's that easy?"

A rueful note underscored Carrie's chuckle. "I didn't say it was easy, I just said the steps were simple, and the psalm is clear. I learned that I needed to remain open to God's leading instead of focusing on what I thought was the best and most logical way to do things."

"How about the best way for getting out of trouble? Do you think God will show me *really* quickly? Like right now?" Mindy asked, twisting her fingers.

"I bet you know what to do, what God wants you to do. First you have to confess, then ask God's and Mr. Kenner's forgiveness, and finally make restitution."

"Restitution?" the girl asked, suspicion in her voice. "Is that what I think it is?"

"If you think it's cleaning up the mess you made," Carrie answered, "then, yes. It's what you think it is."

Mindy groaned. "I was afraid you'd say that."

"Because you figure it's what Mr. Kenner will say."

"And Mom and Dad."

"Guess there's no getting around it. You'll have to come back tomorrow after church with window-cleaning spray and lots of paper towels."

Mindy nodded reluctantly.

"Tell you what," Carrie added, standing up. "I'll meet you here. Since we've had this woman-to-woman talk, I think you and I can become friends. How about if I help you clean up the mess?"

Mindy's jaw dropped. Then she scrambled to her feet. "You would do that? After what I thought . . . what I said . . . what I wrote . . . ?"

"Sure. You did all that before we got to know each other. Now we're friends, and friends help friends when there is trouble."

"Oh, Miss Fors—I mean, Carrie, I'm so sorry I did what I did." Tears flowed down freckled cheeks, and Carrie wrapped her arms around the girl.

Brad entered the room, eyelids tingling. "Time to go

home, ladies. Mindy, your parents are here, and, Miss Forster, you've been out and about since nearly the crack of dawn. Your chariot awaits to whisk you away."

Mindy swiped her wet cheeks, nodded, and murmured a sincere, "I'm sorry, Mr. Kenner. You're not a green-slime—well, you know. And Carrie's really neat."

"Yeah, Carrie's really neat," echoed Tom, waving his form. "But I need a signature on this report."

"What report?" asked Brad, snatching the page and tearing it up. "You're only verifying that everyone's gone after the Doldrums Day event. As you can see, Mr. and Mrs. Slater and their daughter are leaving, as are Miss Forster and myself."

Tom shook his head, grinning. "Sounds good to me."

The Slaters thanked everyone profusely; then, with her mother's arm around her slim shoulders, Mindy left, saying to Carrie, "See ya," as she went.

"Yeah, Teach," Tom said, touching a finger to his hat. "See ya."

"Hopefully not too soon," Brad responded.

"Tomorrow at church."

"So long as it's not here again. Say hi to Marcie."

"Say hi to her yourself in the morning." Then Tom turned to Carrie. "We could use you at the station. Thinking of a career change?"

"Not in the near future," she answered. "I knew exactly how Mindy felt since I lived through the same thing."

"You mean you didn't make that up?" Brad asked.

"Of course not," she said, her voice indignant. "I wouldn't do that to her. Don't you know me by now? Haven't you figured out yet that . . . *things* . . . happen to me all the time?" She huffed an irritated breath out of the corner of her mouth. "And here I thought you were so wise."

"That's my cue to leave," Tom said with a laugh. "Congrats, Brad. The lady's a keeper."

Carrie turned away and stalked to the darkened window. Brad stared at her rigid spine. He thought he read pain in her posture and regretted causing it. Because he cared. And especially after what God had revealed to him as she spoke with Mindy Slater.

"Carrie?"

"What?" she spit back.

"I'm sorry I hurt you. More than that, I'm sorry I've been so resistant."

She drew in a sharp breath.

Brad went on. "I heard what you said earlier tonight. And while I think—I hope—I understood what you meant, I must confess I've been blinder'n a proverbial bat."

"You won't get an argument from me," she murmured, still facing the window.

He came closer. "You were right when you told Mindy that a person must always remain open to God's leading instead of stubbornly focusing on what they think is the right thing to do."

"What are you trying to say?"

"That when God tried to bring a new blessing to my life, I continued to focus on what he had already given me, where he had already led me. I turned a blind eye to God's efforts to transform me into that new person he wants me to be. I was so set in my thinking that I nearly missed learning what God wanted for me, how really good and pleasing and perfect his will is. I almost missed an unbelievably wonderful gift."

She took a shuddering breath. "And what is that wonderful gift God's brought into your life?"

Brad placed his hands on Carrie's shoulders, admiring the

courage it took to ask that question. "You. Tom is right. The lady is a keeper, and I intend to keep her. If she'll let me."

"Oh, Brad," she murmured, turning to face him.

The tears on her cheeks dealt him a direct hit to the heart. "I'm so sorry," he murmured. "I never meant to make you cry. Please forgive me for being such a . . . a . . . ."

"Speechless again?" she asked, a hitch in her voice.

"I'm not surprised. You see, it's the first time I've ever told a woman that . . . that I love her." He cupped her chin in his palm and rubbed a finger over the soft skin of her jaw.

"Just as it's the first time that woman's told a man she loves him."

As he stared into her brown eyes, he cupped her other cheek as well. "You'll make a great principal's wife, you know. With the way you handled Mindy tonight, you'll only enhance my efforts. . . ." He let his words trail off when he felt her laughter through his hands. "What's so funny?"

"You."

"Me? What'd I do now?"

"You left out a few details."

"What'd I forget?"

"Well, a proposal might be nice, and I wouldn't object to a kiss . . . or two. . . ."

Brad let his head drop back, squinching his features into a tight grimace. "I guess since I'm no Romeo, I'd better stick with the great personality, huh?"

Carrie reached up and tugged on his hair until he met her gaze again. "I'll have you know I fell in love with that personality, and it's not too late to catch up on the Romeo part."

"Well, will you?"

She huffed in clear frustration. "What, Bradford Kenner? Will I *what?*"

"Will you marry me?"

Closing her eyes, Carrie turned her face heavenward. "Thank you, Lord, for making things work together for the good of us who love you and who you've called according to your purpose. Thank you for even making the wrong man right." She met Brad's anxious gaze. "I was afraid you'd never ask. Yes—"

Brad cut off the rest of her response with a heartfelt kiss.

EPILOGUE

The chapel at Christ's Academy couldn't accommodate another soul. White roses, lilies, ferns, and baby's breath adorned every pew down the center aisle, and on the simple altar, a larger mass of the same waited patiently.

Brad followed Pastor Williams out of the vestry and came to stand slightly to the right of the arrangement. As he faced the guests, he caught Velma's knowing wink, Tom Marks's thumbs-up, and Mindy Slater's grin.

He couldn't believe this was actually happening. To him. The man who'd thought his life was perfect as a bachelor.

In the months since meeting Carrie, he'd come to appreciate what she brought to his life more each minute that went by. He was a happy man today. And planned to grow happier with every day to come.

As the first notes flowed from the organ's pipes, a terrible thought occurred to him. He looked at his older brother, Craig, and mouthed, "The rings? Do you have the rings?"

Craig nodded and smiled indulgently. He patted his breast pocket. "Got it covered," he whispered.

And then everyone stood. Brad faced the entrance. The vision in satin and lace on her father's arm stole his breath away.

Carrie.

Dear God, he loved her. So very much.

And she looked more beautiful than she ever had before. The white veiling barely shielded her pretty features, and below the flowered crown that held it in place, her red hair glowed with the vibrancy he'd come to associate with her.

She smiled at him and drew steadily closer.

He noted the simple elegance of her gown—a lace-dusted, fitted sheath of satin to her waist, then a smooth cascade of fabric to the floor.

And in her hand, she carried his bouquet—a very special, unique bridal bouquet he'd had made to order. Among the orchids and roses nestled a miniature pair of heart-shaped balloons, one reading, "Be Mine," and the other, "Valentine."

A Note from the Author

Agift of flowers is always special, and some bouquets are more special than others. Over the years my husband, George, has given me flowers for various reasons. The occasion that stands out in my memory as the most romantic might surprise some.

Thirteen years ago we decided to build a new house—at the same time that I was expecting our third child. By the time my due date approached, warm weather came, too. Pregnant, with a preschooler and a toddler and a house to maintain in "show" condition, I was exhausted. One hot Friday afternoon, two weeks after my official due date, I reached the end of my rope. By the time George got home from work, I was in tears at the kitchen table while the boys reveled in the mess of toys they'd spread everywhere. To my amazement, George sat me on his lap and handed me a bouquet of Tropicana roses, just like the ones I'd carried in my wedding bouquet.

"Because you're so beautiful, and I'm so glad you're my wife," he said, in answer to my drippy "Why?"

That afternoon, as he held me and loved me in spite of my mood, I felt the human version of unconditional love. No matter how cranky, how weepy, how gargantuan I grew,

George loved me. And regardless of our temperamental and personality differences—imagine a writer married to an engineer—he was, and still is, the right man for me.

Ginny Aiken

ABOUT THE AUTHOR

A former newspaper reporter, Ginny Aiken lives in south-central Pennsylvania with her husband and four sons. She discovered books early on and wrote her first novel at age fifteen. (She burned it when she turned a "mature" sixteen!) That first effort was followed, several years later, by the winning entry in the Mid-America Romance Authors' Fiction from the Heartland contest for unpublished authors.

Ginny has certificates in French literature and culture from the University of Nancy, France, and a B.A. in Spanish and French literature from Allegheny College in Pennsylvania. Her first novel was published in 1993, and since then she has published numerous additional novels and novellas. One of those novels is a finalist for *Affaire de Coeur*'s Readers' Choice Award for Best American Historical of 1997. Ginny's novellas appear in the anthologies *With This Ring, A Victorian Christmas Quilt,* and *A Bouquet of Love.*

When she isn't busy with the duties of a soccer mom, she can be found reading, writing, enjoying classical music, and preparing for her next Bible study.

Ginny welcomes letters written to her in care of Tyndale House Author Relations, P.O. Box 80, Wheaton, IL 60189-0080, or by E-mail at GinnyAiken@aol.com.

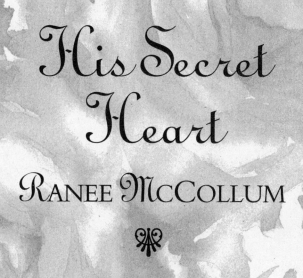

His Secret
Heart

RANEE MCCOLLUM

To Mom and Dad,

Thanks for all your

love and proofreading.

CHAPTER ONE

The Beast has done it again!" Gwen Dalton dropped into her office chair with a cross thump, glared at her computer, and thought wistfully of the days when ancient CPAs used pebbles and charcoal to figure out their clients' taxes. A computer was a necessary tool now, but the inexpensive machine Gwen had been able to afford gave her no end of trouble. She had dubbed it The Beast within three days of purchasing it, and it deserved several other names, on which she tried not to dwell. Gwen was more than ready to hasten the now two-year-old computer's demise, but the thought of buying another one brought no joy either. She didn't like computers. She didn't understand them. In college, her computer-course instructors had referred to her as The Problem Child.

"Computer locked up again?" Susan Gambert asked from her desk across the room. Gwen nodded and rolled her eyes at the older CPA with whom she split the rent of this small office space.

"I guess so," she grumbled. "It keeps giving me this error message." Gwen leaned forward and tapped her index finger against the mouse's buttons harder, as though that would make a difference. "It says . . . I don't know what it says. It says the program is not responding . . . but I punch End Task and it just sits and smirks at me."

Susan came to hover over Gwen's shoulder, and the smell of magnolia perfume invaded Gwen's nostrils. Susan was obviously longing for springtime on the Emerald Coast, even though it was barely January and the magnolias wouldn't bloom here in the panhandle of Florida until late April. Or maybe she was looking forward to the end of tax season, which coincided.

"Give it the old three-finger salute," Susan suggested after reading the error message and also reaching out to tap the mouse buttons.

Gwen shook her head. "I never know what to do after control/alt/delete," she said. "I always end up losing everything I just entered." Gwen could feel Susan's eyes swerve questioningly from the computer screen to the top of her head. Susan had twenty more years' experience than Gwen did, and it was wonderful to have her wisdom at hand, but she didn't understand Gwen's difficulty with computers. Susan had learned everything at a three-day seminar several years ago and had easily kept up with the many changes since. Gwen knew Susan considered her a sharp, conscientious CPA, someone she could recommend without a qualm. For Susan, Gwen's perplexing computer illiteracy was more of an oddity than an encumbrance.

Gwen sighed and confessed.

"Yes, I forgot to save it. How was I to know it was going to lock up like this?"

Susan, fortunately, was also very kind.

"Maybe if you call tech support, they'll have some ideas," she said.

"But it's got my phone line tied up, too. I was trying to fax this to Loper and Simms."

"Use my phone," Susan offered.

"I don't want to tie up your phone line." Although she and Susan shared office space, their clients—and their business problems—were their own. They had always meant to install more than one phone line apiece, but they hadn't done it yet. "I'll go use a phone next door. Adam has plenty." Gwen grabbed the number for tech support on her way out.

In this strip of storefronts, the office space next door to Gwen and Susan belonged to Software, Inc., a computer store Gwen had no reason to frequent. Why should she abuse herself like that? No, Software, Inc., was better left to people who actually *liked* computers.

The bell on the door sounded a melodic, computerized chime as Gwen passed through. Adam's self-designed door-warbles were always the first bar or two of familiar hymns, and today she recognized "How Great Thou Art." Cute, granted, but if this was what the man did for fun, he obviously lacked a social life. He had a new warble every week.

Gwen threaded her way through neat shelves full of software boxes and other computer paraphernalia and reached the back counter.

"Hey, Adam," she said to the man standing behind it with his eyes glued to a computer screen. "Can I borrow a phone? My computer has gone haywire."

Adam Langford looked up, smiled hesitantly, and shoved his thick-rimmed glasses up the bridge of his nose. "Should have bought it from me. I mean from us. From this store," he said, leaking confidence as he spoke. He grimaced and looked away.

"Should have moved your store in two years earlier, and you would have had a sale," Gwen said, trying to tease him back from whatever precipice from which he wanted to throw himself. His words never seemed to come out right.

Gwen had long ago formed her opinions about the sole owner and manager of one-year-old Software, Inc. Sort of sweet, incredibly shy, mostly socially inept, Adam Langford was of average height, with blond hair that was always neatly cut. He looked like every computer geek she had ever known—dark blue tie; short-sleeve, white dress shirt; and probably the same glasses he'd owned in high school. Occasionally he told Gwen strange computer jokes that zoomed right over her head, and she would laugh politely while he snorted merrily. Then he would realize she hadn't gotten the joke and would stumble through an explanation and then an apology. Sometimes Gwen thought he was from another planet entirely. His preoccupation with his computers didn't help her opinion. Every once in a while Gwen and Susan would find a bouquet of supermarket flowers on their office doorstep—with Software, Inc.'s latest sale bill attached. Adam's store was wildly successful in the Pensacola area, but Gwen had never really pursued the friendship.

Gwen didn't see how they could *have* a friendship when all their conversations ended, at some point, with the two of them smiling inanely and uncomfortably back and forth at each other.

Like now. Gwen waited expectantly while her usually bright smile went stale. Finally she bit her lip and asked again. "May I borrow one of your many phone lines? I don't want to tie up Susan's."

"Oh! Sure!" Adam jumped as though he'd been stung, then bent and fumbled loudly beneath the counter before coming up with nothing. He stared at Gwen, consternation written across his face. Finally, he reached down the counter for his regular corded phone—which he used at the sales desk, he'd told her once, because sometimes the computer interfered with a cordless phone's reception—and pulled that one over.

"Use th-this one," he said, shoving the phone at her.

"But that's your main line." She didn't want to tie up Susan's line; she certainly didn't want to cause Adam to lose business because she was on his phone.

Adam shook his head violently. "That's OK. I don't mind."

Gwen took the receiver he offered, reluctant to press the point. She didn't know if it was her presence that always made Adam nervous or if it was just Adam, but she suspected the latter.

"What . . . what is it you're having problems with?" he asked as she dialed.

"The Beast's all locked up," Gwen said. "I tried to fax some stuff, and now the phone is off the hook, so to speak, and although I can move the cursor, nothing happens when I click."

A recorded voice on the phone welcomed her and asked her to punch 1 if she would rather fax her question, 2 if she wanted the E-mail address, or 3 if she wanted to talk to a technician. She jabbed at the 3 button. What she wanted was to toss her whole computer out on its ear and sue the company, but—

"Uh, Gwen?" Adam ducked his head up and down, trying to capture her attention but reminding her of a blue heron in the process. She blinked at him while another canned message informed her that she could expedite her call by knowing what the problem was and asked her to listen to the options. Gwen snorted. She hated this. She wanted to talk to a human.

"Uh, Gwen?" Adam asked again.

"What?" she asked as she tried to make sense of tech support's choices. Software problem? Press 1. Hardware? Press 2. How did she know? Which number did she push for total ignorance?

"I own a computer store?" Fluorescent light bounced off Adam's glasses as he peered at her uncertainly. "I could maybe help you out?"

"I know," she said, "but as you've pointed out, I didn't buy the system from you. And I couldn't ask you to leave your store." She gave her attention back to the phone, punched a random button, and tapped her fingers on the counter as yet another message informed her that they were terribly sorry but everyone was too busy to take her call.

"How Great Thou Art" warbled again as a customer entered the store. Adam slapped his hands against his thighs, nodded in Gwen's direction, and went off to offer his assistance.

Absently, Gwen turned to watch. Adam was certainly knowledgeable about computers. His professionalism in dealing with this elderly lady who didn't know a mouse from a rabbit was diverting to witness. Gwen's lips turned up in a smile as Adam tilted his head to one side, listened to the lady's request, then made a suggestion. Adam was no high-pressure salesman, and he had never once treated Gwen like a technologically inept female. He had always been a perfect—if rather uncoordinated—gentleman.

Gwen had known that Adam was a Christian the first time she met him. Just hours after Software, Inc., moved in next door, Adam had visited the office to introduce himself to her and Susan. He wore a little gold fish on his tie.

"I like your tie tack," Gwen said after they had run through the normal pleasantries.

"Thank you," he said. "Did you know this is a very ancient symbol? The early Christians used it to subtly identify themselves to others."

"I did know that," Gwen replied. "I guess I should wear my fish earrings more often."

They smiled at each other in acknowledgment of their shared faith. She had thought then that he was a very nice guy, but she hadn't realized how little they had in common until a few days later. After waving to Adam in the parking lot a few times, Gwen had made a point of going next door to see his store. The computerized door chime played the first line of "Jesus Loves Me."

"Wow," she said to Adam as she looked around his spotless store. "This looks . . . nice. Very neat." Because she knew so little about computers, she didn't know what other comment to make. In fact, she was a little disappointed. But Adam smiled and began to point out different features in his store.

She tried to be attentive during his little tour, but the experience was unnerving. Adam ricocheted from inspiring to comical to alarming. For a few wild seconds, Gwen thought of asking where the other two Stooges were hiding, but Adam didn't need any help from them! She felt a little sorry for him, though, and tried to find a balance between concern and unawareness. When Adam tripped over an electric cord while hurrying to answer a suddenly ringing phone, Gwen turned away and became politely engrossed in a rack of instruction manuals. When he brushed against a rack of boxed programs on his way back, sending them tumbling to the floor, Gwen brushed off his embarrassed apologies and helped him restock the shelf. She tried to act like everything was normal—like she wasn't caught in a farce called "Computer Nut Goes Berserk"—perusing the title on each software box as she picked it up. After a moment or two she began looking closer, her attention caught by a definite trend. Noticeably absent from Adam's inventory were any games with parental warning stickers.

"I advertise as a family-friendly store," Adam explained when she commented. "Parents know they can come in here and let their kids pick something out without worrying about the content." He seemed to realize she was genuinely interested.

"Look over here." He went around the end of the aisle to the other side, narrowly avoiding stepping on two boxes still on the floor. She followed him with care, and he showed her a small selection of specifically Christian software.

"My dream," he said, his voice surprisingly firm and sincere, "is for there to be a lot more of this well-programmed, entertaining yet educational software with a God-view, not a world-view." Gwen thought that a very worthy aspiration and told him so, and Adam stared at her, swallowed, and stuttered a thank-you.

She hadn't developed the friendship as much as she could have over the last year, she supposed, because the only things Adam seemed capable of talking about with any confidence were computers, computer programs, computer accessories, computer capabilities. . . . Anything else, with the possible exception of his faith in Christ, seemed to stump him. And since Gwen was not fond of talking about computer *anything* . . .

The "terribly sorry" message from tech support ran again, interrupting her recollections. Gwen watched Adam escort his still-undecided customer to the door and return to the counter. He started whistling. The sound was soft and unobtrusive, but Gwen recognized the tune: the theme music from *Jeopardy!*

A grin tugged at Gwen's lips. She wanted to talk to a human? She had one. Even if she would never understand his world, even if they had nothing else in common. Adam would know what was the matter with her rotten computer. Abruptly she put down the phone.

"Oh, all right," she said, smiling. "If you could take a look at The Beast, I'd appreciate it."

Adam broke off in midwhistle. "Really? Oh." An awkward pause ensued. "Uh, I mean, sure—"

Flustered, Gwen backpedaled furiously, thinking she must have misunderstood his offer. Maybe by "helping her out" he meant he could sell her something. That was it. Of course he didn't mean he was personally going to fix her machine.

"I mean, if that's OK," she said quickly. "I don't mean to take up your time. If you've got a manual I could look at or something . . ." Hadn't she seen a book somewhere called *What to Do When You Jump to Conclusions?*

"No!" Adam said, his voice too loud. "I can fix it. I can't leave the store right now—"

"Whenever!" Gwen cut in. "I'll just . . . work on something else." She backed away from the counter, forcing a smile. If he couldn't leave the store, her computer and phone were probably dead for the day unless she reset The Beast and lost what work she hadn't saved, but that was her own fault.

"Wait, Gwen." He attempted to follow her and got tangled in the phone cord, which, because of her, was not in its normal, neat, coiled position. She stopped.

"What?"

Adam located a cellular phone and handed it to her before he answered. "You go sit at your desk and call me on that, and I'll talk you through what you need to do to fix the problem."

"Oh! Right!" He could fix her computer over the phone? Well, wasn't that what tech support was going to do? That was just it, she *hadn't* known what tech support would do.

She didn't understand computers! Embarrassed that she hadn't understood, Gwen turned abruptly. "I'll call you."

She flew through her own office doorway and sat down at her desk, waving the cell phone at Susan, who was on her own phone. She wished she didn't feel like she was somehow using Adam. She had never paid much attention to the guy, and here he was helping her out—but that was his option, wasn't it? Brushing off the feeling, she studied the phone in her hand and realized she didn't know how to work it. Helpless, she glanced back at Susan, who nodded and held up one finger, indicating that she would be off the phone in a minute. Gwen scowled at the cell phone, wondering why things couldn't be simple anymore. She didn't even own a cordless phone. She had an old-fashioned alarm clock with the bell on top. She had finally bought an automatic-drip coffeemaker last month, after her old percolator had finally stopped perking. She didn't like all this high-tech stuff. She and Adam were worlds apart.

Susan hung up her phone and came to Gwen's rescue.

"Power, then the number, then Send," she demonstrated, then handed the phone to Gwen, who managed to dial one of Software, Inc.'s secondary numbers.

"Adam, it's Gwen," she said when he answered. "I'm ready. What do I do first? I really don't want to lose this information."

"You didn't save it as you were going along?" His voice was concerned but not incredulous.

"No . . . I composed the fax, and I guess I thought I would save it when I got through faxing. Sorry." Gwen gritted her teeth. Pen and ink didn't require fourteen steps. It was simple. Simple! At least Adam wasn't rolling his eyes at her. Or at least she couldn't see him if he was.

"That's OK," he said. "Tell me what you were doing and what happened exactly."

She told him, figuring she sounded so dumb he wasn't going to be able to understand what she was talking about, and finished by reading the error message on the screen.

"OK, that's not that bad. A customer just walked in, so I might have to put you on hold in a minute, but we can get started."

"Great! What do I do?"

He talked her through the entire process, and in blind trust she followed his instructions, not understanding half of what appeared on her screen. Twice Adam had to leave her hanging to help a customer, but when he got back on the line, he always knew precisely where he had left off.

"OK, now start your program again, and let's see what happens."

"OK, here goes." Gwen clicked the appropriate icon. She waited, anxiety warring with hope in her stomach.

"By the way," Adam said, "have you ever had the unit cleaned?"

"Cleaned?"

There was a beat of silence, and then a soft chuckle sounded in her ear. "Computers do get dusty."

"Really?" Dust? Who cared about dust? *Where* did Adam get that chuckle? She hadn't ever heard Adam laugh like that. It was almost . . . kind of— Before she could think of what it was like, her file flared to life on the screen.

"Oh, here it is!"

"All your data is there?"

"Yes, every bit . . . well, wait. A few lines here and there have been converted to asterisks. What does that mean?"

Adam grunted. "That means it's lost, I'm afraid. Is it a whole lot?"

"No, not really." She scrolled down the page, relieved that most of her morning's work was still there. She laughed. "This is great. You're like my own personal tech-support person. Thanks so much."

For the first time in their whole conversation she heard him stutter.

"It—it's not problem. Not *a* problem."

Gwen felt a pang. Where was the guy who had chuckled? Why did she care? "I'd better let you go. I've taken enough of your time."

"Let—let me know if you need anything else."

"I will. Thanks."

After she hung up, Gwen went to work repairing the slight damage to her documents.

"Lord, thank you for Adam's help," she mumbled as she typed. "He's a smart guy. He can't talk about anything but computers, and we can't have an intelligent conversation be-cause I detest computers—" she glared malevolently at The Beast—"but he's a nice guy. Not my type, but nice." She held her finger down on the delete key, eating up another row of asterisks.

That laugh. That wonderful, deep, movie-star chuckle. . . . In contrast to Adam's normal nervous stumbling, she found it intriguing. *Intriguing?* Yikes, what a word to use in describing Adam Langford, computer geek! But there was something about that laugh. . . .

Too late, she pulled her attention back to the computer screen. Jerking her finger off the delete key, she groaned. She'd just deleted five rows of good type while lost in thought about Adam. Breathing deeply, she went to work re-placing them.

CHAPTER TWO

The sky over Pensacola, Florida, hung dark with clouds when Gwen pulled into one of Calvary Community Church's four parking lots. The soggy Sunday morning was between showers at that moment, and she parked her four-year-old Ford Escort as far away from the old brick church building as she could. Gwen knew Calvary Community's elderly members appreciated the closer spots, many of which were already filled with cars owned by early—and crazy, Gwen thought—risers. She felt a grudging respect for people who got up in time for the eight o'clock Sunday school classes, but the thought of voluntarily leaving the comfort of her cozy flannel sheets at six o'clock in the morning on any day of the week was laughable. Arriving twenty minutes early for the nine-fifteen Sunday school class was just like going in to work: she didn't have to get up until seven-thirty.

She glanced at her watch, nodding in satisfaction. Being early, not just on time, to church had been a New Year's resolution, and so far she was keeping it. Gwen grinned and rolled her eyes heavenward to share the witticism with God. Today was the first Sunday of the year.

Gwen gathered her purse, umbrella, Bible, and notebook

and stepped out of her Escort. Cool, cloying mist—actually visible in the air as small, drifting droplets—instantly engulfed her, and she grimaced. Another perfectly decent hairdo almost instantly reduced to dripping strands! After living all of her twenty-seven years in Pensacola, Gwen was used to the Gulf Coast's interminable humidity, but it still annoyed her when the stuff turned physical. Her baby-fine brown hair didn't have a chance of holding up under the assault.

Picking her way carefully through the wet parking lot, Gwen noticed a car with its headlights on. An unwritten law encouraged Florida motorists to use their headlights when it was raining, and this mist was close enough to rain to make lights worth it. She looked again, frowning. Last week was the first time she had noticed the red 1969 Oldsmobile 442 convertible, which had had its lights on then, too. That particular muscle car would have been hard to miss anyway, since it was similar to the one her brother, Matt, had owned back when he was in high school and Gwen was in junior high.

Last Sunday, out of curiosity, she had walked over to get a closer look at the 442 and its neglected lights and decided that the driver must be one of those dedicated eight o'clock church kinds of people since the car's hood was cool. She thought about trying to find the owner in the enormous church building but rejected that notion. Finding anyone in that old maze was a pain, let alone when you didn't know whom you were looking for. Remembering the list of dos and don'ts Matt had drilled into her before letting her drive his car, Gwen proceeded to the driver's-side door.

"'Never, never, never lock a convertible, Gwen,'" she had repeated her brother's words. "'Thieves just slit open the top to get to the radio.'"

Gwen had tried the door, smiling in satisfaction as the latch gave way. This Oldsmobile's owner apparently lived by the rule, too, although possibly because of real-life experience. A ten-inch gash in the white top, just behind the driver's seat, was stitched together with heavy-duty thread, evidence of just the sort of villainous activity her brother had warned her about. Sympathizing with the owner, Gwen reached inside to push the lights off. She took a quick look around the spotless car, thinking fondly of her teen years. Matt's Olds had been a fixer-upper; this car was beautifully restored, except for that stitching. Sometime she'd have to call Matt, who was living somewhat unwillingly in snow-covered Minnesota, to tell him about it. Gwen had been the typical bratty little sister, always fussing over the car, asking for rides, and generally making a pest of herself. As a testimony of Matt's generosity, on the day Gwen got her license, he let her drive herself and two friends to the movies. Driving Matt's Olds with the top down on Santa Rosa Island on a summer's day was a treasured memory, unbearable humidity or not. She had loved that car. Gwen smiled again and started to shut the door, then paused. She opened her notebook and scribbled a note. "Your lights were on," she wrote to the forgetful owner. "I turned them off for you. Hope your battery is OK. Great car!" She decided to be anonymous with her good deed, drawing a smiley face in place of her signature. She put the note on the driver's seat and went in to Sunday school, late as usual.

But today Gwen checked her watch and shook her head.

"Slow learner," she muttered. She was *not* going to bail the Oldsmobile's owner out this time. A dead battery would make a better point, and she was *not* going to make herself late for Sunday school again. Gwen managed to ignore her twinges of conscience right up to the point where she opened the church door to go inside. The "do unto others" refrain just kept getting louder. She sighed, turned around, and marched back to the convertible. Muttering under her breath, she yanked open the driver's-side door and reached inside for the lights. As her hand came in contact with the knob, a piece of paper that had been carefully propped there fluttered to the floorboard. Surprised, she picked it up and turned it over.

> *Thanks for turning the lights off! Counting on your sense of responsibility to turn them off again so you'll find this. The battery was fine—it's new, and so is the car. I mean the car is new to me! I don't normally forget to turn the lights off, but since I don't drive it except for Sundays and special occasions, it must have just slipped my mind. Where's that pesky warning bell when you need it??? Thanks again. Oldie.*

Gwen was surprised at such a verbose reply to her simple note. Oldie, whoever he was, was obviously a friendly sort. Oldie. Probably an older man, she thought. *Oldie* could be a reference to the make of the car, but why would anyone call himself old if he wasn't? She read the note again. The tone was a little scattered. Maybe Oldie was a retired naval officer. Maybe he was recently widowed and had bought the car to keep himself busy. He sounded a little lonely. Whatever the reason he owned the car, such a sociable note deserved a decent reply. Gwen turned the piece of paper over, dug a pen from her purse, and wrote:

> *Hi, Oldie. You're lucky I checked! I might not have noticed it at all, but my brother had a car like this. I see you're less fanatical about the convertible top than he was. He wouldn't ever put the top up, even in the winter. He paid our parents rent for full-time use of one side of the garage! If it looked like rain, he stayed home. The one time we tried to put the top*

*up, we discovered it had been down for so long it had corroded
and was stuck. We used up every can of WD-40 in the garage getting it free.*

Gwen hesitated for a second. She hadn't meant to go on and
on about one of her favorite memories. Oldie wouldn't care
less. Well, it was already written. She put pen to paper again.

*Anyway, congratulations on your purchase. It's a really nice
car. (But watch for rust!)*

She signed her smiley face again and put the note on the
seat. Glaring first at the miserable weather, then at her watch,
Gwen groaned. Late again!

The rotten weather persisted until Wednesday, when the
clouds finally dispersed. Gwen hopped out of her car and into
the office, full of energy and beaming at the newly revealed
sun. She smiled brightly at Susan.

"You're in early," Susan observed.

"What? It's eight-forty-five."

"And you don't have to be here until nine."

Gwen shrugged in good-natured acceptance of Susan's
teasing. She was a night person, not a morning person. It was
nice to be early for a change. And she could tease right back.

"The sun woke me," she said, her voice deliberately too
light and bubbly, "and I was so *stupendously* happy to be rid of
the rain—what in the world is Adam doing?" Gwen's tone
changed abruptly as she peered out the window beside Susan's desk. Adam was walking around the parking lot with
what looked like a piece of two-by-four in his hands. He kept
staring at the ground and moving something on the board.

"He's testing some sort of prototype robot thing he invented," Susan said. "He's been out there off and on since seven."

"Seven!" Gwen shuddered. She hadn't even been awake at seven. Seven was on the verge of being uncivilized. She moved closer to the window, wondering what was so all-fired interesting that Adam was out at the crack of dawn to play with it. She could barely see the small buglike object on the ground in front of Adam. It couldn't have been much bigger than the palm of her hand. It had legs. It looked like a large spider. She watched Adam maneuver it around a Dumpster and a shrub, then shook her head.

"I'm going to Joe's for orange juice," she informed Susan. "You want anything?"

She waited while Susan dug in her purse for money, then went next door to their other neighbor, Joe's Bag o' Donuts. Joe's didn't make them like Krispy Kreme did, but he was closer and better for Gwen's waistline. If she stopped at three Krispy Kremes, she was happy with her willpower. Joe's didn't take that much control. Gwen ordered, then took the two bags, one with her orange juice and Susan's coffee, the other with two cake donuts, and walked out the door. Suddenly she stepped on something.

Something that moved.

She yelped and jumped frantically backward, instinctively trying to take the weight off the guilty foot. Running into something behind her, she lost her balance. She flailed both arms, dropping both bags and creating an explosion of coffee and orange juice. Her brain screamed through the options of what she could have stepped on. Kitten? Frog? Giant bug?

Two strong hands grasped her shoulders, steadying her and holding her up. At the same time, a clatter on the ground caught her attention. The two-by-four that Adam had been using to control his robot had joined the drinks and donuts on the ground.

Gwen looked down at the hands on her biceps, then swiveled her head around to look up into Adam's face.

For a second she was frozen. She was quite certain she had never been this close to him before. It wasn't at all like she had expected. His hands, with their long, capable fingers, were warm and secure. His blue eyes behind his glasses were sharply concerned. He had a lovely, firm jaw and chin.

Abruptly deciding that her near fall had warped her sense of perception, Gwen struggled to put all her weight back on her own two feet, instead of leaning back against Adam like some Victorian lady in a swoon. He let her go when she was upright again, then crouched down to pick up his control board. He set it against the side of the building and reached for the donut bag.

"They're squashed," he said after peering inside. He bent to pick up the drinks.

Gwen took a deep breath and turned to collect the pieces of Adam's little bug robot, which she had smashed with her foot. Three of its eight legs were broken completely off, and its antenna was bent.

"At least they aren't Krispy Kremes," she heard Adam mutter as he tossed both soggy bags into the trash can by the curb.

"The donuts are no big deal," she said, going to stand next to him with the remains of the bug in her hands. "But I think I ruined this. Sorry."

Adam took the robot from her, examining it with care.

"I don't think it's as bad as it looks," he said after a moment. "The casing probably protected the chip inside, which is the important part." He flipped the robot over and pried open its abdomen. Two more legs fell off, but he ignored them. Gwen realized for the first time that the robot's body was the casing for a computer mouse. She leaned closer.

"The casing cracked here—" Adam pointed—"and here. But see, the chip itself is fine."

"What is it supposed to do?" Gwen asked, interested in spite of herself. "Some military application or something?" She had just read—or rather, skimmed over—something in the paper about the military using tiny robots for reconnaissance. She hadn't really been interested.

"Nothing so top secret," Adam said. "It's a toy. I want to make a couple of these remote-control pets for my nephew. He got a remote-control car for Christmas, and that got me thinking." He flipped the robot back over and held it up. "It's my 'pet' project."

Gwen laughed. "It's cute. Or it used to be, anyway. Was it working before I smashed it?" She reached over and prodded at the cracked case in Adam's hand. She felt Adam freeze. She pulled her hand away and glanced into his face.

Adam backed up quickly, nearly falling off the sidewalk in his haste. Gwen backed away from him, concerned and mentally off balance. What had just happened?

"If I can help with anything, just let me know. I mean, I can't really help, I guess. I don't know anything about robots. I could give it a decent burial, I suppose," she tried to joke.

Adam made an attempt at a smile. "R-really, it's no problem. I'll just take it in and fix it," he said. He was backing down the sidewalk as he spoke. "No problem. I'll show you. I mean—" He had reached Software, Inc.'s door, and he glanced inside. "Phone." At Gwen's blank look, he opened the door and pointed. "The phone's ringing."

"OK," Gwen said. "You'd better get that." She heard the door-warble sound as he went inside. *Amazing Grace.* Gwen shook her head and bent down to pick up another severed leg. She returned to Joe's and explained what had happened. He generously gave her new drinks and donuts, and Gwen went back to her office.

"You OK?" Susan asked as Gwen handed her the food. "You look a little dazed."

"Small problem involving a small robot," Gwen answered. "I'm afraid I almost killed Adam's latest project."

She sat down at her desk and stared for a minute at the small metal robot leg in her hand, wondering what it had been before being pressed into service as an appendage. She shrugged, set it on the top of her monitor, and forgot about it.

She had barely thought about the Oldsmobile, but that Sunday Gwen was not really surprised to see its lights on again, even though the day was sunny. She didn't hesitate. Inside, on the driver's seat, was another note. Gwen smiled and opened the door to retrieve it.

"Hi, Smiley," it began. Gwen paused, considering. Smiley had been her nickname in high school, but she hadn't been called by that name since then. She had always had a smile to which people responded. Except Adam, she reflected. He always seemed to back off when she smiled at him. Shaking her head, she wondered briefly if Oldie might be someone she knew—someone that had seen her smile. Then she remembered that she was signing her notes with the smiley face. "That's where he's getting it," she mumbled and read the rest of the note.

That's pretty funny about your brother. I'll bet he got a lot of strange looks. Truth is, I'd have the top down, too, in this weather (that's part of why I moved to Florida!), but the mechanism is broken. Just waiting for a new part so I can fix it. But you probably aren't interested in that! I've wanted a car like this for a long time, and I'm looking forward to playing around with it. Glad you like it, too. By the way, I have two brothers (possibly not quite as eccentric as yours), and they both wonder what I was thinking to buy a car like this. Something about being out of character! But I told them sometimes you just have to take a chance.

I'm sort of assuming you've lived your whole life here. I think that's kind of cool, having roots, knowing the town inside and out. My family was military. We moved everywhere. My dad was stationed here for a while, and the place grew on me, so I came back. I love the beaches. I love the seafood. (Except oysters. I don't like oysters.) I'm not so fond of the humidity, especially in August, but the rest of the year is great! I think I'll stay here forever, God willing. He's certainly blessed my endeavors this year. What about you? What has God said to you about the rest of your life? Have a good week! Oldie.

What had God said to her about the rest of her life? Gwen laughed, sat down in the seat, and wrote on the back of the same piece of paper:

Oldie, God still has to deal with me on a day-to-day basis, I'm afraid. I've never taken for granted that I will stay in Pensacola, but for now it's where I want to be. Like you, I like the beaches, and the food is wonderful. Have you driven east on Hwy 399? Have you been out on Perdido Key? I can't imagine how anyone can believe that it's all just a cosmic accident. Have you ever been on the beach at night—especially one of the beaches away from the city—and looked out at the stars over the ocean? I feel so tiny. I was out this last week, when it was halfway warm, listening to the waves.

The waves farther down the beach sound like one big continuous roar, but you can hear each individual crash from the ones right in front of you. I always sort of thought that's how God wants us to look at life. If you try to listen to the waves down the beach, sometimes you miss the ones that are right in front of you, the ones that are so much clearer and more personal. Anyway . . . sometimes my personal philosophies get out of hand. I'd probably better get inside and listen to someone smarter than I am!

I hope the part for your top comes in soon! January does have some really nice days as far as weather goes. Have your brothers ridden in this car? I'll bet that would convince them you aren't crazy. Have a good week. Smiley.

Gwen left her note on the seat and thought about Oldie most of the day. "Have a good week," he'd said. To her, that sounded like he was planning to write again. And his questions were not rhetorical; Oldie sounded like he truly wanted to know. She was less convinced now that he was an older man, although that possibility remained. Mostly, Gwen thought wryly, because tall, dark, handsome, and available would be too good to be true! She considered coming right out and asking Oldie about his age, but that might be considered rude. And not knowing was sort of fun. A small mystery to keep her diverted. And if Oldie did turn out to be someone she could be interested in, she would find that out eventually. And if he was older, it didn't matter. This unexpected friendship was enjoyable. Gwen was content with the notes. For now.

CHAPTER THREE

Monday the weather turned seasonably cold. Gwen wrote an E-mail to Matt in Minnesota, telling him the temperature had finally dipped into the forties. She grinned, imagining his response. Minnesota was below zero. She finally remembered to tell him about the Olds in the church parking lot and how she had known that the car would be unlocked. She didn't mention the notes to Oldie. She didn't want Matt to tell her she was crazy to exchange notes with a man she didn't know. Later in the morning, Matt sent a response, expressing appreciation for the 442 but threatening to send her some snow. She was still smiling over that when Adam walked into the office. She transferred her smile to him. He smiled in Susan's direction before crossing to Gwen's desk.

"I wondered if you had it," he said, gesturing toward her computer.

"I'm sorry?" Gwen asked, bewildered. True, she'd just about had it up to there with The Beast, but she didn't think Adam was asking about her emotional trauma.

"The leg. I thought you might have the leg."

Gwen just stared at him. Was "leg" some new computer term she was supposed to know? Would she know it if she had it? Adam had once asked how much memory she had, and Gwen had told him it depended on the day and how much sleep she had gotten the night before. After several terribly confused minutes, she had finally realized he was asking about her computer's capabilities, not hers.

"Leg?" she asked, her mind still blank. Adam reached over her desk and plucked something off the top of her monitor. She stared at it a second before she realized it was the broken leg off his robot.

"Oh, Adam, I'm sorry!" she exclaimed. "I put it there last week, and it must have slipped back far enough that I couldn't see it. I forgot about it. I'm sorry."

Adam nodded. "It was stuck in the air vent back there," he said. He waved the leg at her and turned to go.

Before she knew what she was doing, Gwen stood up. "I was wondering what it used to be?" she asked.

Adam looked down at the leg in his hand. "Just an old piece of metal," he said.

"Oh." Gwen felt ridiculously disappointed. "I thought it might be something more interesting."

Adam shrugged and looked at the leg like it might tell him something. "I—I don't think so."

She was making him nervous now, she could tell. "OK. Well, I hope you get it fixed. I'm sorry I forgot about it."

He left, nearly running into the doorjamb in his haste. Gwen stared after him for a minute, then rubbed her forehead and decided it was time for a break. She dug a granola bar out of her desk and ate it while she thumbed through the latest copy of *Florida CPA Today*. An article entitled "How to Set Up Your Own Web Page" held her interest for all of three seconds. She could set up a decent letterhead, and her spreadsheet program gave her minimal trouble, but she would probably shut down the entire Internet if she tried for a Web page.

After a bit of aimless page turning, it occurred to Gwen that she didn't know where Adam lived. She suspected he didn't live far, which made her wonder if he might live in an apartment complex she passed every day on the way to work. She didn't remember seeing his car there, however, so he probably didn't. He drove an old beat-up Vega, which he parked behind the row of offices.

"Where the color and such won't prevent people from patronizing our businesses," he had told her once. The Vega was an indescribable shade of faded green, and it made horrible noises, especially on cold mornings. She had laughed and concurred that patrons of Joe's Bag o' Donuts probably appreciated that.

Gwen sighed and tossed the magazine aside. Crumpling the granola bar's wrapper, she eyed Susan's trash can, took aim, and tossed the wrapper in. Then she flipped open a file on her desk, preparing to organize a client's tax return.

W-2 form, good. Form 1099, good. Receipts neatly organized, wonderful. . . .

Adam was an early riser, she thought as she worked. That was a negative. He liked Krispy Kreme donuts. Positive. He had at least five computers that she knew of. Negative. He was a Christian. Positive. They really had nothing in common but that. Negative. Shaking her head, she redirected her attention to the tax return.

"Concentrate on your work," she scolded herself. "Don't go off thinking about a guy who is a first-class nerd."

A first-class nerd? Where had that come from? She was shocked that she would think such a thing.

"I'm not that shallow," she murmured, then paused.

Aren't you?

"Of course not!"

"Talking to yourself again, Gwen?" Susan asked from across the room.

"Sorry. It's nothing." Gwen slapped both hands to her cheeks. Her brain was tired, obviously, and low blood sugar probably accounted for her lousy mental meanderings. The granola bar hadn't been very big. And it hadn't had chocolate chips. Gwen glanced at the clock.

"I think I need some lunch," she said to Susan. "I'm going to run home for a minute."

Driving to her house took fifteen minutes, during which time Gwen tried to gain control of her thoughts.

She had always believed that when God brought people to her mind at unexpected times, she ought to pray for them. Judging by the way his name kept popping up, she was to do an *awful lot* of praying about Adam. But why? She had to be missing something.

She parked at the curb in front of her small Victorian-style cottage. The garage was behind the house, and it was actually closer to walk up the sidewalk from the curb. The house was a rental unit, and Gwen longed for something of her own, but it would be a good while yet before she could afford that. In the meantime, this elderly house was home. After climbing the wooden steps to her small, swing-equipped front porch, Gwen paused with her key in the lock and finally gave in.

"OK, God," she said, "what?" She waited. Except for her stomach's growling in anticipation of some food, she heard nothing. *Sometimes, Lord, a loud, booming voice from heaven would be nice. Or maybe a telegram. Oops, you would send E-mail now, wouldn't you? And I'd probably accidentally delete it. Let's stick with the loud, booming voice!*

Entering the familiarity of her small house was soothing. The old wooden floors creaked just where she knew they would. The wood-framed windows let in just the right amount of light. In the living room, a woolen area rug covered burn marks where sparks from a long-ago fire had been left to smolder. Gwen figured that must have been when the landlord decided to fill in the fireplace. He'd left the mantel, though, and Gwen had situated her cream-colored love seat in front of it and flanked it by two potted ferns. An oak bookshelf stood at attention beside her armoire on the adjacent wall. She could sit on the love seat, look through the window onto her front porch, see the street, and have her books close at hand too.

"Hello, Brutus!" Gwen waved to the bright blue Beta fish swimming in his bowl on one of the shelves. A fish was the only pet the landlord allowed. Matt had given her the fish when she moved out of her parents' house. He'd told her that its name was Brutus, the Attack Fish. Brutus wasn't much company, but he was better than nothing.

At some point in the house's history, someone had knocked out the wall between the kitchen and the living room and put in a counter instead, so Gwen had put her small TV on a swivel stand and was able to watch from either room. Gwen kicked off her shoes and pulled plastic containers from the refrigerator, wondering with vague detachment if Adam was in some kind of trouble. What was the matter with the man that she needed to pray for him? Nothing startling occurred to her while she wandered around her small kitchen, waiting for leftovers to heat up on the stove. She had a microwave but rarely used it, except to heat water. She thought microwaved coffee was the worst, and that inhibition carried over to food as well.

Pulling out a plain white china plate that had been her grandmother's, Gwen spooned her own version of chicken piquant onto it. Rolling the capers back to the middle of the dish with an antique silver fork, she remembered she had used up the last of the anchovy paste and needed to put it on her list for the next time she went to her favorite specialty food store. She took a seat at her oak dining table and sighed. Thinking about gourmet cooking wasn't helping.

Why all this angst about Adam all of a sudden? What was different about today?

Adam. What was different about Adam?

She remembered his chuckle when he was helping her fix The Beast. She remembered the last, stuttered sentences of that conversation. Until that point, she hadn't been aware of his usual gracelessness. On the phone, talking computers, she would have never known that he oftentimes stumbled over his words and, more often than not, over his own feet. She could easily have pictured him as a successful businessman, confident in his abilities and kind enough to help her out.

She put down her fork with an astonished clank. Adam *was* a successful businessman—and anyone who could fix her computer without even looking at it was obviously confident . . . and generous and understanding and patient.

And strong. She could still remember the feel of his hands on her shoulders as he kept her from falling. Her mind could picture, without much trouble, the handsome face behind the glasses.

Could she possibly have been judging Adam—erasing him from the book of her true friends—on the basis of his chess-club tie and his geeky glasses? His unfunny jokes that she didn't get maybe simply because she didn't understand computers? His clumsiness? His stumbling speech?

Stricken, rigid in her chair, Gwen realized she thought she was better than he was. Even worse, she had the feeling that he knew it. He probably figured she'd seen the computer geek and hadn't bothered to look further because she was too disdainful of his profession and his interests. Maybe *that* would explain his nervousness around her, his bumbling and stumbling. That would explain why he was more at ease with other people. He could sense her coolness! She remembered the ease with which he had talked about his "pet" project—until she had gotten too close. He must have wondered what sort of game she was playing.

Dear God, she prayed, *I'm so sorry. Please help me see him as a man, not a stereotype. Please forgive me for my arrogance. Please help me show Christian love.*

Her heart rate slowed. Taking a deep breath, Gwen sank back against her seat. She shook her head in dismay. Why had she never thought of this before?

His chuckle. Unexpectedly, Gwen felt herself blush. That's what had broken through. That laugh had felt personal. Like it was meant just for her. A sort of verbal hug.

Gwen grabbed her fork. All God expected her to do was look at Adam as a beloved child of God. And she could do that. No hugs necessary.

"Not again!" Gwen sat back in her chair with a resigned sigh and looked over at the light on the phone. Sure enough, The Beast had locked everything up again.

She hated to go running to Adam, especially since she had pretty much forgotten what he had told her to do last time. He'd probably think she hadn't been paying attention. She had been! But not enough to duplicate what he had done. And besides, she'd had taxes on her mind, not rotten computers that didn't work.

Susan walked by with raised eyebrows. "Just use my phone and call Adam," she said. "He's got a crush on you anyway. He'll do whatever you want."

Gwen stared at Susan's back. Computer problems weren't enough. Oh no. Now her coworker had to start acting like a lunatic.

"I'm going to pretend I never heard that," Gwen said, rising. "But I *will* borrow your phone." Susan just laughed. Gwen's lips formed a serene smile as she dialed Software, Inc.'s number. This was her first chance to show Adam that she saw him as a real person—that she valued his advice and his expertise. Susan was so far off in her interpretation of Adam that Gwen didn't give it a second thought.

Adam was in their office two minutes after Gwen explained the problem. Susan slanted a glance at Gwen, who tried to ignore her. Adam sat down in Gwen's chair and peered intently at her computer screen. He tapped keys confidently while Gwen perched beside him on the edge of her desk. Susan was humming something.

Gwen recognized it as "Goin' to the Chapel."

"I've been thinking of taking a class," she blurted, jumping up. Adam looked up at her in surprise, his hands pausing over her keyboard. Susan guffawed.

"Maybe," Gwen added, flinging her hands into the air and glaring a warning at Susan. "It's just that I know so little about computers, and I realize I didn't really pay much attention to the classes I had in college. . . ." She finished with a shrug, mentally berating herself for not being able to come up with a better subject. She hadn't done well in college because she and computers were like oil and water. And why would she take a class? She had Adam right here.

And Susan knew it. "Why don't you just ask Adam to help you?" she asked, her tone too sweet. "He knows everything." Adam turned away from the screen, ready to say something.

"Sure," Gwen said, although she didn't want to. She wanted to take this sincere friendship thing slowly. To give

Adam a chance to see that her change was heartfelt. But now she was caught. Susan was still wagging her eyebrows around. Gwen turned to where Adam sat, his eyes locked on hers.

"That is, if Adam's willing." Gwen's smile was brilliant. Apparently it took a few seconds for Adam to realize that was his cue.

"Water," he croaked instead. "Might I have a glass of water?"

"Oh, sure!" Caught off guard by his apparent refusal, Gwen fled to the back room. She filled a glass with ice and water and returned to the front room, handing the glass to Adam.

"Thank you." He drank, then searched for a place to set the glass down.

"Here, I'll take it." He handed it to her, and she hesitated. Maybe he didn't want to put himself through tutoring her, but was that so terrible? She couldn't really say she would be a good student. Or maybe he had missed the whole exchange. Maybe he was trying to figure out how to tell her that The Beast was completely dead.

"Is something really wrong?" she asked.

"Huh?"

"With the computer? I saved everything this time, I think. Did the hard drive crash or something?"

Adam seemed to wake up. "No. No, nothing major. You've just got a small hitch. Actually, several small hitches. I think it would be best to uninstall the program, though, and start over."

"OK." Gwen was relieved, not only because her computer was OK but also because Adam was speaking in coherent sentences again. "I'm sure you can take care of it."

"Yes, I can. But do you mind waiting until after I close the store tonight?"

"No, that's fine," Gwen hastened to assure him. "You need to get back to work."

"I think this will do what you want for a few hours." Adam rose. "I'll be back after six."

"Thanks. I may swing home and come back." The stores in the strip mall set their own hours, and Gwen and Susan normally closed up shop at five.

"See you then," Adam said.

"I'll bring supper," Gwen offered spontaneously.

Adam misjudged the distance around her desk and banged his thigh on the corner. Gwen winced for him.

"Are you OK?"

"Fine. And supper fine. I mean, *supper will be* fine, too. Thanks." Gwen watched as he escaped out the door.

Susan swiveled her chair to smirk at Gwen.

"What?" Gwen asked. The wariness in her voice grew with Susan's grin.

"That boy has it bad for you." Susan held up a hand at Gwen's sputtered protests. "Running over here at the drop of a hat, working after hours, forgetting how to talk."

"Susan, you're dreaming."

"He's had a crush on you from the beginning."

Gwen couldn't believe how this conversation was spiraling out of control. "What? No way." She turned to her desk and tried to look like she was getting back to work, but Susan wouldn't quit.

"And you've never paid the slightest attention. Ignoring him, breaking the poor guy's heart . . ."

Unfortunately, that point was hard to argue with. But Susan's explanation of Adam's foibles was all wrong.

"It's true that I've been ignoring Adam," Gwen said. "I recently realized I haven't had a very nice attitude, and I'm going to try to change it. But I'm not interested in Adam that way, and he certainly isn't interested in me."

"Uh-huh. That's why you offered to bring him supper."

"He's fixing my computer. I'm being nice."

"Uh-huh."

"I'm actually kind of interested in someone else," Gwen said in desperation, then berated herself for speaking before she thought. Susan leaned forward to give Gwen her full attention.

"Do tell."

Gwen grimaced. "I shouldn't have brought it up. It's nothing really."

Susan just kept looking at her.

"Oh, all right. It's just that there's been this '69 Oldsmobile 442 convertible in my church parking lot for a few weeks now, and I turned the lights off once, and now the owner and I have sort of got this pen-pal thing going."

"Really?" Susan was intrigued. "And it's a young guy? Dating material?"

"Well . . . I don't really know. Maybe. It might be an older man. He calls himself Oldie."

"You've never seen him?"

"No."

"But you've seen the interior of the car, right?"

"Yes. So?"

"What sort of stuff was lying around on the floorboard?"

The question made Gwen pause. "Now that you mention it, nothing. Clean as a whistle. But that makes sense. Oldie said he'd waited a long time for this car. He's going to keep it as nice as he can."

"Yeah, and it also means you can give up any hope you had about the guy being young and single."

"I never had any hope of that!"

123

Susan rolled her eyes. "Never had any hope, my eye," she muttered. "You tell me you aren't interested in Adam because there's someone else, and now you tell me he's an older man. You are one confused girl, but you can give up on this Oldie person. If this guy was young and single, that car would have something in it. Young, available men don't have time for housecleaning." Susan turned back to her computer, disinterested. "What you've got there is some elderly gentleman whose wife taught him to pick up after himself."

Gwen didn't quite follow Susan's reasoning—Oldie had said the car was new. Maybe he hadn't had time to junk it up yet. Or maybe he was just neat. Or maybe it really was an older man. Gwen felt a little twinge of disappointment. But Susan was off her back about it, and Gwen made a mental note not to bring it up again. It didn't matter how old Oldie was, right? He was her friend. Now if Susan would only forget about Adam!

CHAPTER FOUR

Gwen returned to the office that evening carrying a homemade but previously frozen vegetable lasagna, a green salad with raspberry vinaigrette made from her own recipe, and a loaf of seven-grain bread she had made two days ago. Her parents had bought her the bread machine for Christmas, and even though its small keypad looked alarmingly similar to a computer, she had figured it out and was actually enjoying it. Maybe there was hope for her yet.

Gwen unloaded a plaid tablecloth, two blue stoneware plates, and flatware rolled in linen napkins from her picnic basket and arranged them on the small table in the office's back room. She had decided against candles or flowers. This was a working supper. Hearing a knock at the front door, she went to let Adam in.

"Hi," she said. "I just got back. Are you hungry?"

Adam drew in a deep breath. "Lasagna?" he asked.

Gwen smiled at his wondrous look. *OK,* she thought. *He's obsessed with computers, but he's also interested in food. Good.* "Yes. I'm afraid it has been in the freezer for a few weeks, but it should still be edible."

Gwen led him into the back room, where she scooped a healthy portion of lasagna onto a plate. She set it before him, then opened the small refrigerator.

"Looks like we have diet Coke, diet Coke, or diet Coke," she said, looking back at him. He was gazing rapturously at the steam rising from the lasagna.

"Hmmm. Diet Coke sounds good."

Was that humor? With no stutters? From Adam?

Still thinking about that, she tossed him the can.

"Here."

He looked up in time to see the can flying toward him, but he fumbled it. The can rolled behind him to the filing cabinet. He picked it up and set it gingerly on the table.

"Just tap it on the side a couple of times," Gwen said, scooping lasagna onto her own plate. "It makes the bubbles go down."

He looked at her, doubt evident in his expression. "You probably eat at the computer, too, don't you?"

Gwen winced. From anyone else, she would have put that comment in the humor column. But from Adam, it was deadly serious. "Just, um, carrot sticks, gummy bears—the stuff that doesn't have crumbs."

"Uh-huh." Adam's gaze was wistful as it drifted to the salad bowl. "So, er, should I ask the blessing?"

Gwen bit back a smile. "Go ahead."

He prayed nicely, Gwen thought. Respectful, humble, confident. But then, he wasn't looking at her either. Gwen felt a pang. As long as he wasn't paying attention to her, he didn't have this shy, nervous, bumbling problem. Adam's voice, talking to God, was beautifully calm. She appeared to be the only thing that made him lose his composure.

Great. Perfect. She was a nincompoop.

He said amen and looked up at her. She looked back, and something in her face made his go bleak.

"I forgot to bless the food, didn't I?"

Gwen didn't want to say she hadn't noticed. That would

only make him think she hadn't cared enough to listen, when in reality she had been tuned in to the sincerity in his voice, not the content of his prayer.

"I'm sure God understands," she said, her words soft. "Go ahead and eat." Adam paused a moment, then unrolled his napkin. She followed suit. She was going to do everything possible to help him see that she had reformed.

He took a bite of lasagna, chewed, then sighed deeply.

"That good, huh?"

"Sometimes I get busy and forget to eat."

"That never happens to me," Gwen said. She hoped she didn't sound like she was dismissing his habits. "I love to cook, and eating is high on my priority list."

His gaze swept her. "You don't look it."

"Um, thanks," she mumbled. *Yikes, maybe Susan is right.* Gwen forked some salad onto Adam's plate, then her own. He was so involved in the lasagna, he didn't seem to notice.

"I like to jog," she added.

"Really? I hate it. I mean—" Adam looked away from his lasagna in consternation. "I didn't mean to disparage your exercise program. I jog, too, when I can force myself, but I don't like it much. I'd rather go to the gym." He discovered the salad on his plate.

"Whatever works." Then she blushed. Going to the gym was working pretty well, it seemed, for Adam, and she suddenly wondered why she had never noticed his broad shoulders, his muscled forearms, his—Gwen realized she was staring and looked away. Adam was still inhaling the food, so perhaps the tension she felt was all her own.

Adam reached for the bread.

"Did you make this?"

"Yes. It's seven grain."

"You do a lot of cooking. I knew that."

Gwen thought he sounded like he was talking to himself. She knew he could lose himself in a computer screen; she hadn't realized food would do the same thing.

"You know," Adam said, "I don't even own a dining-room table. Most of the time I just eat over the sink."

Gwen had always pictured herself and her future husband in the kitchen with matching aprons, feeding each other bites of whatever culinary delight they were preparing. They would sit down at their antique oak table and light the candles and listen to Mozart. The kitchen sink would be used strictly for washing, not eating over. Food would be enjoyed, not scarfed down. Although whatever it was Adam ate over the sink probably wasn't terribly enjoyable anyway.

Gwen jumped when Adam rose. He rinsed his empty plate in the bathroom sink, swallowed the last of his diet Coke, and threw away the can, then peered at Gwen.

"So . . . are you ready?"

Gwen looked down at the food she had barely touched. Why was she thinking about the qualities of her future mate while having supper with Adam?

"G-Gwen?"

She gave herself a stern mental shake and rose from the table.

"Weren't you hungry?" Adam asked. "Or is there something I should learn?"

She quirked an eyebrow at him, and Adam sighed.

"I meant *know*. Is there something I should know?"

Gwen was still too far off the subject to catch his meaning.

Adam laughed awkwardly—not the laugh that she liked—and shook his head.

"I should *not* attempt to tell jokes," he murmured.

The light finally dawned for Gwen. "You mean about the food? Is there something you should know about the food?

Why I didn't eat it?" Her laugh was a little hysterical. "No, the food's fine. It's just me. I'm sorry."

"You want me to wait till you finish?"

"No, that's OK. I'll eat later. Let's go ahead and get to work. I'll try to pay better attention this time."

"I'll write some stuff down for you."

"That will help."

She followed him out to the office, where he pulled Susan's chair over to Gwen's desk but left enough room for Gwen to sit in her own chair beside him. He booted up The Beast and cleaned his glasses while he waited. Gwen took the opportunity to study the lines of his face. She swallowed. The computer beeped.

"Now," Adam said, "the first thing we do is—"

He lost any vestige of awkward shyness while he worked. He turned to Gwen frequently, making certain that she understood what he was doing. After a few minutes, Gwen was able to focus on what he was saying. She owed him her complete attention. She was going to hang on his every word.

He turned her computer inside out. When he was finished, the screen didn't look at all like it had before, but she finally knew the functions of all the icons. Adam had taken off all the programs she never used and had even run next door to his store to grab a disk or two that he thought she couldn't live without. He traded places with her and made her run programs and showed her what to do after control/alt/delete.

When they finally looked at the clock, it was after eleven.

"I didn't mean to keep you so long," Gwen apologized.

"I should be the one saying that. I know I get carried away with this stuff."

"I know how that goes. And I really appreciate it." Gwen hesitated. "I know what you're going to say, but I don't feel right about not paying you for your time. . . ."

Adam held up a hand. "Consider it a favor from a friend."

"I know, but that software must have cost you something—"

"Tell you what. You can do my taxes this year. I mean, if that's OK. You really don't owe me anything—"

"Personal *and* business taxes. Deal," Gwen interrupted and extended her hand. Adam reached to shake it—with his left hand. Gwen flipped her hand to accommodate his, but he yanked it back and offered his right. After a few flustered seconds, their hands finally meshed. Adam's grip was strong. The sudden warmth that infused Gwen's body startled her. Perhaps it startled him, too, because he didn't let go.

"Can I walk you to your car?" he asked. "It's late."

He didn't want to leave her alone, she thought warmly.

"Sure. Let me get the picnic basket," she said. He realized he was still holding her hand and let go suddenly. In the back room, she gathered her things with quick motions and returned. Adam took the basket from her, and she locked the door behind them. At her car, he placed the basket on the seat and nodded at her.

"Thanks for supper," he said.

"Thanks for fixing The Beast. I might have to find another name for it now."

"I hope so. I mean—" he shook his head—"I hope it works for you. Let me know if you have other problems." He might have been talking to a customer in his store. Gwen said good night and drove away. She looked in the rearview mirror as she exited the parking lot and saw Adam still standing where she had left him.

At home, her lack of supper caught up with her, and she decided to heat up some lasagna in the microwave. She sat at the table and ate, wondering at her dissatisfaction with the evening.

She made him nervous. He was a shy, intelligent man who deserved more than her passing glance, and she had apparently trampled on his ego so thoroughly that he could barely look her in the eye. She felt guilty. She felt sympathetic. She felt *frustrated,* and she didn't know why. They had nothing in common. He ate over the sink, and she was a gourmet cook. He rinsed his plate, and she never dusted. He loved computers, and she tolerated hers. It wasn't like they were ever going to be more than friends anyway. So why did she feel like she was missing something? Perhaps it was due to the fact that she hadn't come right out and apologized for her attitude. Gwen snorted.

"Oh, sure, make the guy more uncomfortable than he already is by telling him you used to think he was a nerd. That'll do wonders for your friendship." She remembered Adam in the parking lot, standing in the dark. He'd looked a little lost. Gwen shook her head. She was going to have to do better.

On Sunday Gwen was not surprised to see the Oldsmobile's lights on again. Even though the sky was overcast and many drivers were using their lights, Gwen knew Oldie had left her a note. She began to get a funny feeling in the pit of her stomach. Maybe he really was interested in her. She had thought about last Sunday's notes, wondering how they were getting so personal so fast and debating if that was wise. But he didn't know much about her, she reasoned, at least not the kind of things that could be dangerous, like her address or where she worked. Even while she was acting friendly, she was being prudent. She knew there were some strange people out there, but she didn't think Oldie was one of them.

Nevertheless, while she read the note, she made a conscious effort to listen to God's leading.

Hi, Smiley. How was your week? Can you believe it—the part for my convertible top came in, and it was the wrong one. But since the weather isn't great, I guess it doesn't matter so much. I'm afraid I'm becoming acclimated to Florida; although I wanted to go out to the beach yesterday, I wimped out and stayed home, listening to tunes in front of the fire instead. (When I moved here I thought having a fireplace in Florida was a crazy idea. I still think that. After I lit a fire in mine, I had to open a window to cool the place off. But the ambience was nice.)

Oops, late for church. Gotta go, Smiley! Later, Oldie.

"Wimped out." "Tunes." "Later." The nickname "Oldie" had to refer to the car, Gwen thought. No doubt about it, this guy was young. She pursed her lips, trying to think of how best to deal with this revelation. The notes were not flirtatious. Confident, yes. Intelligent, humorous, thoughtful, yes. But solitary. No mention of someone with him in front of that fire. Trying to stem the rising tide of excitement, Gwen penned her words with care.

Oldie, my brother, Matt, has been in Minnesota for several years. Whenever I go to see him—and it doesn't matter if it's midsummer—I freeze. But he's become used to it, although he still misses Florida.

What kind of tunes do you listen to? I've always listened to a little bit of everything, but lately I'm partial to Mozart and other classical stuff. It makes me feel intelligent! But if I'm cleaning house, I like something with a decent beat. For some reason it helps speed the drudgery along.

I hope the part comes in soon.
I'm almost late for church, too! See ya! Smiley.

She dashed into her Sunday school class with thirty seconds to spare. And everyone kept asking her what she was smiling about.

"Aren't you leaving?" Susan asked on her way out the door at four-thirty on Wednesday. Susan's day had started at six that morning. Gwen felt a little guilty about not coming in until nine o'clock, even though Susan had no reason to care.

"I've got several things to catch up on," Gwen told her. "There's no time like the present."

"I'll see you tomorrow, then." Susan waved.

After Susan left, Gwen glanced out the window at the fading light. The day had been mild and sunny, and the evening looked too nice to waste. Gwen decided to grab an apple and a bottle of water and go across the street to the small park that formed a green belt between the stores and a residential area. She stepped out the door, then turned back for her sweater, noting the almost total absence of cars in the parking lot. She knew it was slow for the few retail shops, including Adam's, that did business here, or anywhere. Too soon after Christmas and too far from a tax refund for most people to think of going shopping.

Gwen crossed the street and pulled her sweater tighter. Maybe this wasn't such a good idea after all, she thought. The air was colder than she had anticipated. She noticed a pickup basketball game going on not far away and wandered over, hoping that having something to watch would take her mind off the chill in the air. Several teenage boys and a couple of men were heavily involved on the small asphalt court. They certainly didn't look cold, Gwen thought as she sat down on a bench to observe. Most of them were wearing T-shirts. Gwen wondered about Oldie's car and whether he had managed to get the part he needed to fix the convertible top. Not that he would want the top down in this weather. She grinned to herself. This was just the kind of weather that had made people turn to look in astonishment at Matt.

She chewed her apple and watched the game. Basketball wasn't really her sport. She wasn't a bad shot, but she could never anticipate her opponent's next move—the other player would feint left, and she would go left, while the opponent dribbled past on the right. As she watched, one of the men threw a three-pointer and then high-fived one of the teens. The group was playing under a single basket, so the teams regrouped and started again. One of the kids flubbed a shot, and the man who had shot the earlier basket caught the ball on the rebound. He dribbled expertly for a second while an opponent moved in to guard him. Gwen couldn't see his face, but she had the funny feeling she knew him. Just as she was thinking about that, the man passed the ball to the teen who had made the mistake, who then made a neat basket.

"Good job!" the man called out. Startled, Gwen looked closer. Blond hair, right height, no glasses for some reason—but there was no mistaking Adam's voice. As Gwen watched, mesmerized, Adam got possession of the ball again and worked his way gracefully through his opponents to slam-dunk the ball into the hoop.

Gwen couldn't take her eyes off him. Was this *Adam?* The guy who stumbled over inventory in his own store? Who couldn't catch a soda can? Being ashamed of the way she treated him was one thing, realizing just how far off her misconceptions were was quite another. Obviously, either she was completely blind or "computer geek" didn't mean what it used to.

Gwen watched Adam effortlessly guard his opponent, following the man's feints and turns. One of the teens came too close, trying to help his teammate, and Adam backed into him, knocking the boy to the ground. In an instant, Adam had dropped his guard stance and offered a hand to help him up. Meanwhile, the other man rushed up to the hoop and shot but missed.

The lights around the court came on, and Gwen realized how dark and cold the night had become. She could see her breath, and she had to squint at her watch. She needed to get back. Eyeing the game, which was back on in full force, she wished she could stay. Idly, she wondered why Adam had left his store before closing time, but then she remembered the lack of customers and cars in the parking lot. She turned to look. Sure enough, from here she could see the parking lot and realized that Adam must be keeping an eye on his shop from the court.

"So you do get your nose off the keyboard occasionally," she murmured. She wondered spontaneously if he would like to go to a movie sometime. Well, maybe not a movie. That was too much like a date. Maybe the naval museum. Lots of high-tech stuff there but also vintage aircraft that she liked to look at. And it was free, so they wouldn't have that awkward "who's going to pay" scenario. Just a friendly outing.

She wondered if Oldie had been to the naval museum yet. He liked old cars; she'd bet he liked old airplanes, too. And afterward they could go to Semolina's and have pasta.

She glanced at her watch again and sighed. No use fantasizing about a date with a man she hadn't even met. She needed to get her mind in gear and get back to work.

Just as she took a step, the game ended. Gwen hesitated.

Maybe Adam would walk back with her. She walked forward to the court, noticing a gray sweatshirt on the ground beside a light pole. She could just make out the letters *S-o-f-t-w-a-* before the fold made it impossible to see. But the shirt was Adam's; she knew that much. She picked it up and straightened in time to see him walking toward her across the court. He was too far away to have noticed her yet.

"Hey, Adam!" she called. "Great game!"

He looked up and stumbled. On the same flat surface where he had been playing a challenging game just moments before, he stubbed the toe of his sneaker and almost fell.

"Sorry!" she said. "Didn't mean to startle you." She dismissed the whole museum idea. If just the sound of her voice threatened to cause him severe bodily harm, she wasn't going to torture him with a whole afternoon in her presence.

"Are you working late?" Adam asked after he had recovered his balance and joined her under the light pole.

"I was," she answered, handing him his sweatshirt. "I decided to come out and eat an apple since the day looked so nice." Unconsciously she shivered. "It's colder than I thought it would be."

Adam paused in the middle of pulling on his shirt. "Are you cold?" Without waiting for an answer, he yanked the shirt off and handed it back.

"Really, Adam, I don't need it," Gwen protested. "It's not that far." She tried to give it back to him, but he stepped away, shaking his head, and narrowly missed backing into the light pole. Gwen thought quickly. She had to save Adam from himself. She dragged the shirt over her head, and he stopped retreating.

"Nice shirt," she said. It was bigger than she thought it would be. She caught a trace of a pleasing cologne. And she was much warmer. The shirt probably even looked halfway decent with the denim skirt she was wearing. "Thanks. Are you headed back to the store?"

Adam didn't seem to hear her.

"Adam?"

He dragged his eyes to hers.

"Are you going back to the store?" she asked again.

"Yes."

Gwen waited, but he didn't add anything. "Well . . . so am I." She took the initiative and started walking. Adam fell into step beside her.

Neither of them said anything until they were standing in front of Gwen's door. She looked down at the shirt she was wearing.

"Keep it," Adam said, his tone abrupt. "I don't need it tonight." He made a sort of patting motion on her arm, then drew his hand away.

Gwen decided that the best thing would be to agree with him. "Thanks. I'll get it back to you when it's warmer."

"Sure."

There was an awkward silence.

"I guess I'll see you tomorrow, then," Gwen said. Adam nodded.

"Good night."

"Good night." Gwen unlocked her office door and went inside. For a long time she sat staring into space. She wished she didn't make Adam so nervous. From the glimpses she got of him interacting with other people, and from the rare instances when he forgot who she was and how she had treated him, she knew he was a man she wanted to get to know better. She shook her head. It shouldn't matter so much. She wasn't "after" Adam. But she wished she knew how she could make him feel more comfortable around her!

CHAPTER FIVE

Gwen accomplished a lot that week: organizing files she hadn't touched in months, catching up on publications, cleaning out her desk. She brought something for supper and worked until nearly eleven every night. On Saturday she was so set in her routine that she felt pent up staying at home. At about six o'clock in the evening, she finally gave up trying to relax and went to the office, where she updated her Rolodex. After that, she decided to go to work on her business-card files.

"But first, coffee," she said aloud. She had stocked the office with several different flavors of gourmet coffee beans after Susan bought her a fancy bean grinder for Christmas. Gwen had one at home, but this one had three different settings for grind. Gwen measured and ground and glanced out the back room's small window. She noticed Adam's Vega still in the parking lot. While she waited for the coffee to brew, she debated. Taking Adam coffee would be friendly. Making him so nervous he spilled coffee on a computer would be disastrous. Biting her lip, Gwen reasoned that Adam would never let liquid come within three feet of his computers. Her thoughts ping-ponged back and forth. Perhaps he had forgotten to eat and she ought to take him something besides coffee.

She checked the fridge. Dismally empty. She had cleaned it out this week.

The coffee finished dripping.

A friendly cup of java was better than nothing. Decision made, Gwen grabbed two mugs and the carafe and headed out the door.

She expected the door to Software, Inc., to be locked for the night, but it gave at her experimental push, and the chime sounded. "Holy, Holy, Holy." She heard chair springs creaking in the back room.

"Adam?" she called.

"I'm sorry, we're—Gwen?"

"Are you busy?" She waved the mugs at him when he appeared in the doorway. "I just made some coffee and thought you might like some if you're working late."

"That—that would be great." He paused. "Would you like to come back here?" He gestured behind him. "I'm working on your—I mean, my robot."

Gwen followed him into the room, where various computer parts were spread out on a tall, white Formica table. Adam's back room was as neat as the rest of the shop, she noticed. And it was carpeted, giving it a very homey feeling despite the various containers of mechanical parts and the boxes of inventory on shelves against the back wall. Gwen set the mugs down on top of a smaller table, then looked around for something on which to set the hot coffeepot.

"Have you got something—"

"Here," Adam said. Gwen took the mouse pad he offered and laughed.

"That will work." She poured coffee into the mugs and handed him one, which he took with utmost care.

"Hazelnut," he said after one cautious sip.

"Yes, it is," Gwen said. Her surprise must have sounded in her voice.

"I like to go down to the, um, bookstore sometimes," Adam explained, sitting down on a wheeled stool, which squeaked alarmingly, whether from the wheels or the tilting seat, Gwen couldn't tell. "Just to sit and read and have coffee."

"Really? What do you read?" Gwen rested a hip on the Formica table and eyed Adam's precarious perch. The stool seemed awfully tall and wobbly—probably not a problem for Adam under normal circumstances—but now she was here. She could just imagine what would happen if he suddenly turned nervous. She needed to keep the conversation going.

"Some fiction," Adam answered. "But mostly computer manuals and magazines."

"Now why did I know that?" Gwen teased gently and was pleased to see a small, wry smile on Adam's lips.

He had nice lips.

Gwen cleared her throat and took another sip of coffee. "What are you working on here?" she asked.

Adam swiveled on his stool to face the parts on the table. He seemed unaware of Gwen's growing concern.

"This is the next generation in my pet project," Adam said, his voice segueing into professionalism. "I used the untimely demise of the first unit as a catalyst for making improvements." He went on to explain several new commands he was going to load onto the robot's chip and held up several unidentifiable parts for her inspection. Gwen tried hard to follow him but in the main just nodded at random intervals.

"But the problem I'm having now is finding something big enough to carry all that but small enough to look cute. The mouse casing won't work anymore."

"Hubcaps," Gwen said. Adam stared at her.

"That's perfect," he said. "Why didn't I think of that?"

Gwen shrugged and smiled, pleased that she had been able to come up with an idea that Adam approved of. Hey, she didn't know a byte from a gigawatt, but she knew hubcaps. Oldie's 442 had very nice ones.

Adam pulled out a notepad and a pen and started sketching a hubcap bug. Gwen surveyed his back room. In the corner, past the Formica table, sat an overstuffed chair. An open bag of Chips Ahoy! shared space with a Bible on a table nearby. Gwen walked over and sat down in the chair. A rocker, she discovered, and leaned back. The Bible was open to 1 Corinthians 9, and several verses were underlined with the precise lines that only a straightedge could have produced. Gwen glanced at the cookies. Nearly gone. She resisted the temptation and sipped her coffee instead.

"Where do you go to church, Adam?" she asked after a few moments.

He barely looked up. "I recently started attending Calvary Community."

Gwen's jaw dropped. "That's where I go!"

"I know."

"You must go to the early service," she said. "Otherwise I'd have seen you."

"I do." Adam stretched across the table to pick up a metal bug leg.

"Do you know anyone named Oldie?"

The words were barely out of her mouth when Adam's wheeled stool suddenly whooshed out from under him, sending him sprawling. Gwen set her coffee mug down on the table with a bang and jumped up, hovering uncertainly. After a quick mental review of what she had said, she could remember nothing that would have made Adam nervous. She had to assume it was just the stool's time to go.

"Are you OK?" she asked. Adam sat up without answering, reached over to where the offending stool lay on its side, and yanked the casters out of its legs.

Gwen couldn't help it. She laughed.

Adam's face was determined, then thoughtful. He held up one caster.

"This would make a perfect robot leg," he said. He scrambled to his feet and shook one finger thoughtfully in the air while his eyes flickered back and forth. Gwen grinned as she watched the wheels turning in his head.

"Perfect as long as it doesn't have to climb stairs," she said. Adam's eyes zoomed in on her and narrowed as he considered that minor difficulty. Gwen smothered laughter as she watched him right the unwheeled stool and pick up the notepad again. She went back to her easy chair.

There was no tension in the air at all. She felt very comfortable. Rocking, watching Adam think, drinking coffee—she liked this. She gazed around Adam's office again. A small, neat stack of books was next to her chair, and she picked up the top one. *The Light Princess* by George Macdonald. *Perelandra* by C. S. Lewis was under that. Then *Piercing the Darkness* by Frank Peretti. Gwen glanced up at Adam. She had all three of these on her bookshelf at home. She stacked them back in order. Mostly computer manuals, indeed. Adam had been holding out on her. She grimaced. Not that she had ever given him much of a chance to discuss reading material before this.

She finished her coffee and let her mind drift. Tomorrow was Sunday. It was supposed to rain again, so even if Oldie had his top fixed, he wouldn't have it lowered. She'd probably find another note. She hoped so. She glanced at Adam but decided not to bring up Oldie again. For one thing, Adam was concentrating awfully hard, and for another, it didn't seem fair to Oldie to be asking questions about him behind his back. Oldie deserved to tell her things about himself in his own good time. She wanted to keep the integrity of their little friendship. She liked the notes. The concept was so old-fashioned. Handwritten notes took time. In this age of E-mail and answering machines, a person really had to care to take the time to write something on paper. Gwen sank down a little farther into Adam's rocking chair. A person had to care. Did Oldie care? She thought he did. She hoped he did.

She noticed a wooden mantel clock on the shelf above Adam's head. She pondered its incongruity in this store of high-tech gadgets and then realized the hands read eleven-thirty. Gwen jumped up.

"Adam, I have to go."

He looked around and seemed to realize for the first time that she was still there.

"Gwen, I'm so sorry for ignoring—" He tried to push his stool back, but without the wheels, the legs caught on the carpet. The stool tipped and threw him over backward.

Gwen's first instinct was to spring forward and catch him, but she was too late. She dropped to her knees beside his inert body instead.

"Are you OK? Does anything hurt?" She waved her hands over him with ineffective gestures.

"My ego," he muttered. "My dignity."

Gwen laughed in relief and sat back on her heels. "You look kind of cute down there," she said and wished she had bitten her tongue instead. Good night! Was she flirting? With *Adam?*

He turned his head, and they blinked at each other. Hopping to her feet, Gwen offered him a hand up, hoping he would just let the moment pass. She thought back to what she was saying before the stool tipped.

"Oh, ah . . . at any rate, I didn't feel ignored tonight," she said. Adam let her hand go as soon as he was on his feet. Gwen reached for the coffeepot and mugs. "I think I was in need of some company."

Adam found his voice. "Well . . . I'm glad. Thanks for the coffee."

Whew, back to normal.

"No problem." Gwen moved back through the darkened store, Adam trailing her. "Maybe we can do this again some-time." Behind her, Adam ran into a display case. Gwen cringed but chose to ignore it. "What's your favorite kind of coffee?"

"Er, chocolate macadamia nut."

"Mmmmm, that sounds good." She reached the door. "I'll see you Monday."

Adam had stopped very close behind her. She figured he was having trouble with his distances again. When she turned her head, she had to look up to see his face. Unexpectedly, she felt his hand on her cheek, gently pushing a strand of her hair back. *Uh-oh.*

"Monday," he repeated her word, but Gwen almost didn't hear it. His hand remained, softly touching the top of her shoulder. She started to turn her cheek into his palm and stopped herself. What was she doing? What was *he* doing? Gwen forced one foot to take one step back; then her eyes met his, and she was caught.

If he laughs now, she thought, *it will be that chuckle I heard on the phone.* A verbal hug. From a man who liked her.

Before she could think further, Adam drew his hand away and reached past her to the door.

"Good night, Gwen," he said.

"Good night." She went home, kicking herself for flirting and wondering what she was going to do now.

Sunday morning was overcast and as gray as Gwen's thoughts. She retrieved another note from the Olds, and it only confused her more.

> *Hi, Smiley. I went out on the beach this last week and listened to the waves and thought about what you'd said. And I heard them, and I felt a little ridiculous because I hadn't heard them that way before. Sorry for the short note, Smiley. I was up too late last night and am running late. Have a good week, and I'll write more next Sunday! Later, Oldie. PS, there's a sand dune out there with smiley faces drawn all over it.*

He was drawing her name—or at least her signature—in the sand? What did that mean? What did she want it to mean? After last night, after Adam's touch?

Gwen had to think for a moment before she wrote. She had brought her own paper this morning so that she could take Oldie's note with her, and so she would have more room to write, but her note was short.

> *Hi, Oldie. I was up late last night, too, talking with a friend I should have gotten to know a long time ago. Would you pray for me this week? I'm in need of some divine guidance. I think I may have been ignoring the waves in front of me. Thanks. Smiley.*

Gwen put the note on the seat and went into Sunday school. She sat alone, vaguely aware that she was, for once, early. While she was waiting for the class to begin, she read Oldie's note again.

Drawing her name in the sand. Was that a good thing? Was she pleased?

She was. Her relationship with Oldie was fascinating and pleasantly puzzling. Unlike her relationship with Adam, which was baffling.

She didn't feel very good. She glanced at the clock. People were filtering in. The Sunday school teacher looked like he was on his way over to say hello. She would not wimp out now. She knew the feeling in the pit of her belly wasn't physical but mental. *Lord, I am really confused,* she prayed, *but I know you will help me figure out where to go from here.*

Gwen made a determined effort to put it out of her mind. The Olds was gone, as always, when she came out of church. She spent the whole afternoon at home with a fit of the dismals, which she thought about blaming on the gloomy weather but decided probably had more to do with her own dilemma. She'd had more than enough dilemmas lately. When five-thirty rolled around, Gwen decided to quit using tax season as an excuse to get out of going to Calvary Community's evening service, like she had been doing since January, and hopped into her car.

Several friends greeted her as she walked in, and she spent a few diverting minutes talking to them. Then she saw Adam come into the sanctuary. Excusing herself, she walked toward him.

"Hi, Adam!" she called out, forcing cheerfulness into her voice. She couldn't possibly walk up to him and ask him what he meant by his actions last night—she couldn't even explain her own. And she couldn't ignore him. She would be friendly and go from there.

Adam looked startled when he saw her.

"Gwen," he said. She thought he looked almost disappointed. "You don't usually come to this service."

"No, I don't," Gwen said. "Do you?"

Adam nodded. He seemed to be on the verge of saying something else, but though Gwen waited with an expectant look on her face, he didn't continue. She didn't blame him for being uncomfortable, but he could at least be consistent! How could he strike sparks in her one minute and turn around and be so tongue-tied the next? The moment was decidedly awkward. Gwen decided to put them both out of their misery.

"Well," she said brightly, "I'll see you around."

Gwen sat by herself in the balcony, knowing she wouldn't be good company for anyone. One look at her and her friends would declare an emergency. The hymns almost made her cry. She stared at the pastor but barely heard the sermon and was disgusted with herself afterward for not paying better attention. Rising after the benediction, she noticed Adam talking with another man and two women. He laughed easily at something one of the women said, and Gwen glared. Why couldn't he be like that with her? Why did she care? She watched despondently as the foursome left through one of the back doors. Adam never stumbled.

Gwen made her way out of the church to her own car. Sliding down in the seat, she closed her eyes for a few seconds, wishing she had never gotten up that morning. Better yet, she should have stayed in bed all week. She shook her head. Straightening, she was about to turn the key in the ignition when she noticed the Oldsmobile. She hesitated, then let her hand fall.

If she really wanted to know who Oldie was, she told herself, the smart thing to do would be to go back into the church, stand up at the podium, and ask in a loud voice who owned the '69 Oldsmobile 442 convertible in the parking lot. She choked back a laugh. There was no way she was doing that. For one thing, what if no one answered? For another, what if someone wanted to know why she wanted to know? She'd probably burst into tears trying to explain, and they'd haul her off to the loony bin.

The honest thing, of course, would be to write Oldie a note and ask: Are you dating material? Are you interested in me? Can you explain to me how the male mind works?

Gwen slunk down in her seat. She *could* sit right here until Oldie came out of the church. At least then she'd have one straight answer tonight, as devious as this was. She felt like a spy.

People drifted to their cars. She thought several were headed to the Oldsmobile, but they all went right past. Her heart rate jumped every time she saw a man she thought might be Oldie and plunged again when they all went to other cars. After about fifteen minutes, she realized that there were only two other cars besides her Escort and the Olds. She pondered her options. He'll be out soon, she told herself. Perhaps Oldie was on the cleanup committee—but the church had a janitorial service. Another fifteen minutes went by. Gwen tried not to think about how cold she was getting. Her mind began to invent scenarios. Maybe Oldie had seen her waiting and was hiding behind the church's sign because he didn't want to be recognized. Maybe he was an escaped felon using church attendance as a cover for his nefarious activities. Maybe he had gotten a ride home with someone else.

Gwen looked at her watch. She'd waited sixty-four minutes. She could see her breath.

Suddenly the absurdity of what she was doing hit her, and she grabbed for the keys. All the way home she chastised herself. Yes, she admitted, she had been hoping for tall, dark, and handsome. Yes, she was acting like a lovesick fool. Yes, if she wanted to know so desperately who Oldie was, she should just ask him.

But that was it. She didn't really want to lose the uncomplicated pen-pal thing they had going. She didn't want to mess it up with questions that got too personal too soon. She sighed. Even without her interference, the whole situation was convoluted. Oldie was writing her name in the sand. Adam was touching her hair. She was thinking strange thoughts about both of them. What in the world was going on here?

She tossed and turned in bed until midnight. At last she reached over to her bedside table to turn on the light, then pulled her Bible from the shelf beneath it. Every other time in her life that she had experienced this out-of-control feeling—from the time in fifth grade when a boy had asked her to "go" with him, to the weeks before her CPA exams—only one thing had comforted her. She had gone through Psalms once, chapter by chapter, marking with a blue crayon at least one verse that spoke to her in each. Now those marked verses were as familiar to her as her own home, soothing by the very fact that they had sustained her before.

I will lie down in peace and sleep, for you alone, O Lord, will keep me safe. . . . But I trust in your unfailing love. I will rejoice because you have rescued me. . . . The Lord is my strength, my shield from every danger. I trust in him with all my heart. He helps me, and my heart is filled with joy. . . . Commit everything you do to the Lord. Trust him, and he will help you. . . . Send out your light and your truth; let them guide me. Let them lead me to your holy mountain, to the place where you live.

Gwen let the words flow over her, allowing the peace to penetrate her confused mind.

"Thank you, Lord," she whispered and fell asleep.

CHAPTER SIX

By Tuesday she could face Adam calmly. She knew she could, which was good because he stopped by about lunchtime. Gwen looked up in surprise.

"You said you would take these whenever I had them ready," he said, handing her a manila folder. He did not look the least bit uncomfortable or nervous.

"These are your tax records?" she asked to cover her surprise. "Business and personal?"

"Yes, ma'am." He attempted to rest one hip against the edge of her desk and knocked over the jar holding her ink pens. Pens went everywhere.

So much for his poise. Gwen jumped up and went around her desk to help him pick up the scattered pens.

"I'm going to lunch," Adam said after setting the jar back on her desk with great care. "I was wondering if, er, if . . ."

Gwen regarded him, thoughts buzzing like bees. Adam was going to lunch? Since when did he go to lunch? He got so busy he forgot to eat! Belatedly, Gwen realized he was asking her to go.

"I can't. I'm sorry," she said. "I have a client coming at twelve-thirty."

Adam nodded his head in understanding, but Gwen hated disappointing him.

"Catch me some other time, OK?" she said. *OK, Lord. Why, when I've decided to relax about Adam, does he ask me to lunch? Why does the timing have to be terrible? Would you please tell me if I actually* want *to go to lunch with this man?*

"OK. Are you all right?" he asked.

Gwen realized that she was usually the one asking that question. She attempted a smile. "I'm fine, Adam. I just . . . just wish I could go to lunch." *I think.*

Adam nodded and reached for the office door just as her twelve-thirty client was opening it from the outside, and the two men came within inches of colliding. Gwen waved at Adam after he made it out the door, but she didn't think he saw her. She put him out of her mind and was able to speak with her client about tax shelters and IRAs with some semblance of intelligence. After he left, however, Gwen turned to Susan with the question that had been plaguing her for the last forty-five minutes.

"How is it that Adam can go to lunch?"

"Hired an assistant," Susan said. "I think he's finally realizing he can't run that store all by himself and still have a life." Susan's smile was wry. "Although by the looks of his assistant, he's not going to have to go very far for that."

Gwen's stomach dropped.

"What do you mean?"

"I met her this morning. Yesterday was her first day."

"Her?" Gwen asked.

"Oh, very definitely her." Susan grinned.

Gwen was perplexed. She went home that evening and re-read her last note from Oldie.

"Oldie, whoever you are," she said, "I may need your friendship more than ever."

"What's this?" Gwen walked into the office Wednesday morning, and her gaze swung from the bouquet of flowers on her desk to Susan's face.

"They were leaning against the door this morning. Adam must be going to a new florist, though. That's a much nicer bouquet than usual."

The arrangement certainly didn't look like it came from the local Winn-Dixie grocery store.

"So . . . why are they on my desk?" Usually she or Susan put Adam's offering in a vase and set it on the table by the chair in the waiting area. Gwen picked up the flowers. Poking prettily out of green tissue paper were daisies, mums, a stalk of snapdragons, and some baby's breath. And one rose. A fluke, of course.

"And where is Software, Inc.'s sale bill?"

"Aha!" Susan said. "Now the light begins to dawn."

Gwen forced a laugh.

"You've got to be kidding. You think Adam left these for me?"

Susan swung around. "Did I say that? I don't believe I said that. Maybe you're *wishing* they were for you, hmmm?"

Gwen gave her a warning look. "Susan, you're incorrigible. I think I'll just go thank Adam for these and ask him for his new flyer, since he *obviously* forgot."

"You just go ahead and do that," Susan said, smiling.

Gwen placed the flowers back on her desk and bounced out the door.

Adam's door chime warbled the first line of the doxology. Adam's new assistant stood at the sales counter—pretty, blonde, and about Gwen's age. Gwen refused to be worried. The girl looked up with a smile.

"Good morning," she called. "How are you today?"

"I'm fine," Gwen said with an answering smile. She held out a hand. "I'm Gwen Dalton from next door."

"Paige Olsen," the girl said as they shook hands. "So nice to meet you."

"Is Adam around?"

"No, he had to step out for a minute. Is there something I can help you with?"

Gwen considered. "I was looking for a copy of your new sale bill," she said.

Paige looked around the countertop. "I don't believe we have a new one," she said. "Just this one from last week. It's good until next Sunday—well, Monday, actually."

Gwen took the flyer and confirmed that it was the same one she had seen in Adam's store last week. She had been so certain Adam had simply forgotten. What in the world would Susan make of this?

"This is fine," Gwen said to Paige. "Would you tell Adam I stopped by?"

"Here he is now," Paige said. The doxology rang through the store.

Gwen turned. "Thanks," she said over her shoulder to Paige. She intercepted Adam in the middle of the store.

"Thank you for the flowers," she said. She noticed that his eyes were tinged with red and he wasn't wearing his glasses. Come to think of it, she hadn't seen him with his glasses since before the basketball game.

"You're welcome." He noticed the sale bill she held. "Did you think I forgot?"

Gwen glanced away before she answered. "I thought you might have."

"I didn't."

Gwen nodded. "I met Paige," she said, unsure why she

didn't want to pursue the subject of the flowers. "She seems very nice."

"She is," Adam said. "She knows computers, too."

Gwen's smile was faint. "I wouldn't expect you to hire someone who didn't."

"Having an assistant does give me more time. Which reminds me—I forgot to give you a few receipts for the business. I cleaned out a file, and I had some stuck in the wrong place. Is it too late to give them to you?"

"Not at all. Do you have them handy?"

"Hang on a second."

Gwen waited while he went to the back room. As he passed Paige, she said something to him, and he smiled broadly and nodded. Gwen turned away to look out the window. The sun was shining. She wondered if Oldie had gotten the convertible's top fixed, if perhaps he was out driving around somewhere. Gwen glanced toward Adam's back room, then back at the sunshine.

Would she rather be out driving with Oldie or drinking coffee with Adam?

"Here you go," Adam said as he walked up behind her. "I really appreciate your doing this."

Gwen took the receipts back to her office and quietly put them aside.

"So did he forget to attach the sale bill?" Susan asked without looking up from her computer.

Gwen sighed. "No."

Susan nodded, and Gwen thought that was the end of it. She should have known better. Susan started whistling again. "The Wedding March."

Gwen wadded up a piece of scrap paper and threw it at her coworker. She missed by a mile. Nevertheless, Susan stopped whistling. But only because she was laughing so hard.

Gwen could hardly wait for Sunday. She arrived at church more than half an hour early, parked closer than she normally did, and hurried to the 442. Oldie would calm her down. He knew nothing of her inner quandary. His notes were simple and sincere. She needed that.

> *Dear Smiley, I hope your week went well. You sounded like you needed a shoulder to cry on last week. I'm glad you chose me. I prayed for you. I prayed for me, too. We all fall off the path occasionally, but hey, it sounded like you were crawling back on! I know God is watching over both of us. I don't think this relationship was a random chance any more than I believe God didn't create anything. (That didn't quite come out right, but I think you know what I'm trying to say!) At any rate, I hope you are feeling more at peace this week. Let me know. I care about you. Oldie.*

Gwen read the note three times before she let herself believe Oldie was for real. For him to realize, from her brief note, how rotten she had felt last week—well, Gwen was impressed. And disarmed.

"Oldie," she wrote back, "thank you for your prayers and your understanding. I look forward to these notes! I needed someone to talk to last week, and you were there! I had made a big mistake—I didn't look at the heart. I think he's forgiven me, but I don't know if I'll ever be able to express how sorry I am for the way I treated him."

Gwen stopped writing. Oldie would have no idea who "he" was, and she realized that talking about Adam to Oldie was a strange thing for her to do anyway. But it was honest.

And she had to be honest. She didn't want to lead Oldie on, even if she was still confused about how she felt about Adam.

I guess I should explain that Adam is a friend I'm getting to know, sort of like I'm getting to know you. I can't really say any more than that right now. Your friendship is precious to me. I'm trusting that God will lead me in the right direction. 'Til next week, Smiley.

Tuesday evening Gwen said good-bye to Susan and walked next door to ask Adam a question about his taxes. The door chime warbled the doxology again, and she was surprised that he hadn't changed it since last week.

Paige wasn't in—Gwen had discovered that she only worked mornings—but Adam was not in sight. Gwen paused beside the sales counter before taking the initiative and walking to the door of the back room.

She poked her head in and saw Adam sitting in his overstuffed rocker, his elbows on his knees, his head in his hands. As she watched, he pulled his glasses off and rubbed his eyes.

His glasses. She hadn't seen him wear those in weeks.

"Adam?" she said softly. Startled, he shoved his glasses back on and straightened.

"Hi, Gwen," he said. He sounded so despondent that Gwen went to perch on the arm of the rocker.

"Rough week?" she questioned. To her surprise, he smiled.

"It's only Tuesday," he said.

"Some weeks are like that."

He nodded. "Well, it's nothing, really. . . ."

"*What* is nothing?"

He indicated his glasses. "I got new contacts a few weeks ago. . . ."

"I noticed."

"Well, I can't wear them. For one thing, they can't seem to find a prescription that's crystal clear—and for another, my eyes just don't seem to like them."

Gwen remembered his red eyes of a few days ago. "So you have to go back to glasses?"

"Yeah. That or surgery." Adam took off his glasses and inspected them at close range. "Can you believe I've had these things—this particular pair of frames—since high school?"

Gwen looked at the thick black rims. She bit her lip.

At a range of eighteen inches, Adam didn't need a prescription to see her face. "You can, can't you?" he asked. But he was smiling.

Gwen grinned. "They still work, though."

Adam's smile faded. "I upgraded to a new pair anyway." He snatched a pair of stylish wire-rimmed glasses off the table, put them on, and looked at Gwen. "I don't know if I like them. What do you think?"

Gwen, sensing that her answer was important to him, studied his face for a moment before answering. She looked too long and had to fight to keep her voice steady. The glasses were fine, but she couldn't say that she noticed. Her heart was beginning to pound. "I think those are very nice," she managed. Adam nodded and looked down at his short-sleeve shirt.

"I've been thinking I need to go shopping, too," he continued. "Nobody wears a tie with this type of shirt, do they?" His fingers fumbled at the knot, loosening it, finally drawing the thing from around his neck. He unbuttoned the top button and drew a deep breath. "Ah! That feels better." He looked up at Gwen. "What else would you change?"

Gwen stared at him. She had watched this startling display in astonished disbelief, but the physical changes were barely registering. "Nothing," she said and swallowed hard. "Absolutely nothing."

Adam chuckled. That beautiful, personal chuckle she had heard only once before.

She jumped up. "I have to go, Adam."

He rose with her. "Of—of course."

Gwen heard the stutter and almost could not believe it. She wanted to fling her arms around him and beg him to believe that she—

Gwen clamped a lid on that thought. She didn't. Did she?

She made it out the door, to her car, and into her house before she admitted it.

She did. Maybe.

She looked around her living space. Yes, she could see Adam sitting at her antique oak dining table, eating a meal she had prepared for him. She could see him in the kitchen, where he would measure ingredients with absolute precision. She could picture the two of them building robots together out on the porch or maybe in the garage. She could see him sitting at his dusted computer, which they would place in her antique armoire. She remembered now that she had taken a picture of that piece of furniture into work nearly a year ago to show Susan, and Adam had also admired it. She wondered what his house looked like. Her gaze drifted to the bookshelf. They would read C. S. Lewis together while drinking chocolate-macadamia-nut coffee. He would get a kick out of Brutus, the Attack Fish.

Gwen flopped onto her love seat and groaned. Adam was still prone to stuttering when he talked to her. What was she doing falling in love with him? And where did that leave Oldie?

CHAPTER SEVEN

All week, Gwen wondered what she was going to say to Oldie. If he did happen to be young and available, he would not be interested in hearing that she might be in love with another guy. On the other hand, it wasn't fair to him to lead him on, no matter how much she enjoyed the easy camaraderie they shared. Gwen sighed as she walked toward the Oldsmobile on Sunday morning.

She looked through the window, then opened the door to pick up her note.

Hi, Smiley. I got the part for my convertible top, but now the weather has turned cold! You know, I was thinking—it really sounded like you liked that guy you told me about. Does he know that?

Gwen noticed that the dot below the question mark was large and smudged, like the writer had let his pen sit on the same spot for a long time.

It's probably none of my business, Smiley. I'm enjoying our friendship as it is, and nothing will endanger that if you want to continue writing. But I don't want to get in your way. I'd better get in to church. Oldie.

Gwen stood for a long time before walking back to her car and getting in to write a reply.

Oldie, thanks for your honesty. You make me think.

After agonizing over it, she could think of nothing more to say, though she sat until she was nearly late for Sunday school. Finally realizing that maybe her mind's silence was God's way of telling her to keep her mouth shut, Gwen left her short note on the seat of the Olds and went inside. She prayed for wisdom.

On Tuesday Gwen walked out to her car after dark and had to jump out of the driver's seat again to take something off the windshield. She thought at first it was a piece of junk mail left by a solicitor but then realized it was a large envelope. With *Smiley* written in Oldie's handwriting on the outside.

Gwen was startled. She had had no idea Oldie knew where she worked or even what kind of car she drove. For the first time, a note from him made her wary. She looked toward Software, Inc.'s door, wondering if Adam had an X-ray machine or some other device that would let her see the contents of the envelope before she opened it, then shook her head. Adam had left that morning on an overnight business trip. She shook her head. This was Oldie she was dealing with. She opened the envelope. Inside was a sheet of the same paper on which Oldie always wrote his notes.

Smiley, I know this is unusual, but I couldn't wait. I'd like to meet you face-to-face. Would you give me the honor of escorting you to the church's Valentine's banquet next Sunday

evening? You can put your answer in the Olds next Sunday
morning. Have a good week! Oldie.

Gwen was intrigued. Oldie was laying all his cards on the
table—and quite romantically, too. She glanced at Adam's
door again.

The pang of longing that hit her surprised her. She had his
friendship. He had her . . . deepest affection. Gwen closed her
eyes. He probably had more than that.

But here was Oldie. Her friend. Her confidant. Her pal.
The guy who practically read her mind. The guy who had invited her out on a date first. How had she gotten herself into
this mess?

Gwen wavered for three days. She prayed. She read her Bible. In spite of her conundrum, she felt peace. She would follow God's leading.

On Friday night she called Software, Inc.'s secondary
number, the one Adam gave out only to friends.

"Adam," she said, "I need to ask you a question."

"The Beast acting up again?"

"No," she said. "Nothing like that. It's kind of personal." She
could feel the change that came over him, even over the phone.

"OK."

"I've been asked to the Valentine's banquet by someone
I've never met but maybe you have. Do you know anyone
who goes to our church and calls himself Oldie and drives an
Oldsmobile convertible?"

Adam paused for so long she was almost afraid he wouldn't
answer.

"Adam?"

"I know him."

Gwen's relief came out in a rush. "Do you? Is he nice? Can
I trust him?"

"You're going to go to the banquet with him, then?" Adam's voice sounded strangled.

For the first time, Gwen hesitated. "A lot depends on what you think of him, Adam," she said. "And . . . no one else has asked me." There. She had given Adam a chance. She had practically screamed that she would entertain another offer—his. But she had given him a way out, in case he didn't want to make that offer.

"I am quite sure that Oldie's intentions are honorable," Adam said. Gwen couldn't hear doubt in his voice anymore. She closed her eyes. She didn't know whether to be relieved or upset.

"Thanks, Adam," she said. "I really do value your opinion."

Saturday Gwen spent much of the day thinking about what she would wear to the banquet on Sunday. Eventually she decided on a cream-colored lace dress that she had worn only once before, as a bridesmaid in a friend's wedding last year. It had been a fun wedding, she remembered, but standing behind her radiant friend, Gwen had wondered if she would ever find someone to whom she could say those sacred vows.

She still wondered that.

Adam. She had known Adam then. Or rather, she had known *of* Adam. She hadn't truly seen the man behind the name.

But why was she thinking about Adam now? Oldie would pick her up tomorrow. Gwen sighed, wondering if this date was a foolish venture. She meant simply to explore all her options—pass through all the doors that God held open for her—and then see where he wanted her to go next.

She sighed and turned her thoughts to easier subjects. She

would wear her hair in a twist, she thought. Tomorrow's weather was supposed to be sunny and unseasonably warm. Her brother, Matt, wouldn't have let something so mundane as a hairdo prevent him from putting the top down; and Oldie had waited too long for nice weather to want to leave the top up now that he had it fixed. She would have to use more hair spray than usual. Gwen smiled wryly to herself. Even if the evening went awry, her hair wouldn't, and she would have something to tell Matt about.

She didn't accomplish as much as she wanted to at the office that day, so she stayed late to make up for it. And she might as well get used to it, she thought. Tax season was not for slackers. She worked until hunger made productive work impossible. Adam may have been able to forget about his appetite, but the thought of leftover London broil in the refrigerator at home wouldn't allow her to concentrate.

Walking out to her car in the dark, Gwen noticed Adam's green Vega, apparently stalled, in the parking lot. The hood was up. Walking over for a closer look, she saw Adam staring at the engine.

"Need help?" she called out.

He banged his head on the raised hood as he straightened. Rubbing the sore spot, he shrugged. "I know what's wrong with it. If I had some tools, I could fix it, but I don't have any with me."

"Can I give you a ride to your house to get some?" Gwen asked.

Adam appeared to think about it. "If you wouldn't mind, that would be great."

Gwen inclined her head to her Escort. "Hop in."

She followed his instructions to his house. As she suspected, he didn't live far, and the red-brick house he pointed out to her was much nicer than she would have expected for a bachelor who spent most of his time at work.

"This is nice," Gwen commented. She put the Escort in park and turned it off.

"Thanks. . . . Would you like to come in while I get the tools?"

"Sure."

As Adam put the key in the lock, he hesitated and half turned. Gwen supposed he was going to tell her not to mind the mess or that he wasn't much on decorating or something. He didn't; he didn't say anything after all, just held the door for her to precede him into the house.

Once again Gwen had to remind herself that jumping to conclusions was a bad idea. Adam's house was very neat and clean, but what charmed Gwen—and made her stomach flop—was his taste in decor. The furniture was not new, but it looked inviting. At one end of Adam's sofa was an old flat-topped trunk with a lamp and neatly stacked books on top. On the other side of that was a comfortable-looking leather recliner, with a small stereo close by. Those pieces faced a brick fireplace with pictures on the mantel. To her left was the kitchen—she could see through it to the table-less dining room.

But for that, this could have been her house. The potted plants, the artwork on the walls, even the way the furniture was placed—she felt right at home. She had suspected that she would.

"Would you like something to drink?" Adam asked. His voice seemed a note deeper. There was something about him tonight, Gwen thought, and tried to come up with the word.

"No, thanks. I imagine you're anxious to get your car running." She smiled so that it wouldn't seem she was trying to hurry him.

She wasn't. But the longer she stayed in this house, the more she would think going out with Oldie was a bad idea.

Adam nodded and turned down the hall to the door to the garage. Gwen peered after him, noting that he closed the door securely behind him after he went out. Left alone, she circled the sofa, peering out the French doors into the shadowy backyard. What did he have out there? she wondered. Maybe she could finagle an invitation to come again sometime.

After her date with Oldie, of course.

The framed photographs on the fireplace mantel beckoned. What must have been a photo of Adam's family caught her eye first. His parents, his brothers, one woman she assumed was a sister-in-law, and one boy, maybe ten years old. The family resemblance was clear. That was who he was making his robot for, Gwen remembered. *That's what Adam's kids would look like,* her brain added. To take her mind off that she forced her gaze to the next picture, which was of the same boy, probably taken at school.

The next picture in line was of Adam standing next to a car.

Gwen froze, and then her heart broke from a comfortable pace to an alarmed gallop.

Adam was standing in front of Oldie's car. Oldie's 1969 Oldsmobile 442 convertible. The one with the repaired rip in the top behind the driver's-side door.

Gwen stared at the photo, her hands going up of their own accord to pluck it off the mantel and bring it closer. Maybe it was her brother's car, she thought. Maybe Adam had owned it before Oldie.

Yeah, right! Gwen, you've been a fool!

Gwen heard the door to the garage open. In slow motion

she turned to see Adam. The stricken, guilty expression he wore told her all she needed to know.

She glanced down once more at the picture and then set it carefully back on the mantel.

"Gwen—"

"Adam," she said. "Oldie." She turned to look at him, her face carefully blank. "I should have known."

"Gwen—" He looked miserable. "I was going to explain everything tomorrow."

Yes, that's right. He had been. She was going to meet Oldie tomorrow. To go to the banquet. Perhaps tomorrow the experience would have been romantic and hilarious and touching. Right now, it was embarrassing and humiliating and awful.

She let none of that show on her face.

"Fine," she said. "You can explain everything tomorrow. Right now I'm going to take what's left of my composure and go home."

She turned and walked out. He didn't come after her, but suddenly she knew how to describe how Adam had been acting tonight.

Sheltering. Protective. She had thought he was protecting her. But he hadn't been.

He'd been guarding his secret.

She drove around to the other side of Adam's block and parked until her hands stopped shaking. While she waited, she mentally reviewed the last few weeks. She remembered the night in Adam's office when she had asked him if he knew Oldie and he had fallen off his stool. She remembered all the notes from Oldie since then and her phone call to Adam last night.

Tears stinging her eyes, she remembered the look on his face after she found the picture.

He'd been disappointed that she had found it.

Gwen shoved her car into gear and drove home, trying not to think until she got there. She parked her car and ran up the stairs to her room, hoping the exertion would relieve some of the explosiveness she felt. Jogging would help clear her mind, but she didn't like to go out this late on a Friday. She slipped off her low-heeled pumps and trotted down the stairs again. Up. Down. Up. Four more sets, and then she was winded. In the middle of her bedroom, she stood still, clenching her fists, knowing that running might help short term, but it wouldn't get rid of the real problem.

Adam and Oldie had *lied* to her. OK, maybe that was too strong a word. But they—he—had certainly been keeping a secret for much longer than she felt was appropriate. Gwen fell facedown on her bed and tried to think logically. What would make them—him—do such a thing?

Why couldn't Adam just be honest?

She rolled over onto her back and let her tears fall. They fell into her ears, but that wasn't as irritating or humiliating as what Adam and Oldie—Adam—

Her mind ran in circles, trying to remember every detail of her conversations with Adam, her correspondence with Oldie, and how the two fit together. She had thought she was getting to know two men. Now there was only one, and she wasn't sure, after this revelation, that she knew him at all. On that thought, Gwen drifted into sleep.

When she awoke, the house was pitch-dark. She had been so distracted, she hadn't bothered to turn on any lights when she came in. She got up, undressed, and washed smeared makeup from her face. She drew a chenille robe around her and went to her window. If she had hoped to see any-thing—the Oldsmobile, the Vega—it wasn't out there.

"Good," she muttered. And sniffed.

She went downstairs and into the kitchen. She pulled cof-fee beans from the refrigerator, then put them back. She wasn't having coffee. She might never drink coffee again. Maybe vodka.

Gwen snorted out a laugh. No, she wasn't doing that ei-ther.

She had a glass of water instead and went to sit on her love seat. Brutus waved his fins at her.

"Get him, Brutus," she said, but the humor helped only for a minute. She put her head down on her knees.

She hurt, and she was ashamed of it. She was embarrassed and annoyed. She felt like a schoolgirl whose diary had been passed around among all the boys. Adam's actions toward her had been influenced by his knowledge of her notes to Oldie. His seemingly incredible perception of her moods was noth-ing more than a cheap trick.

Gwen shook her head. In her mind, she was still seeing Adam and Oldie as separate people. And she still didn't know why Adam had perpetuated such a myth. How did he think she was going to react when she found out? Fall into his arms and thank him for playing a neat joke on her?

Look at his heart.

Gwen grunted at that thought. How did you get to know someone when that someone was pretending to be someone else?

"I'm disappointed," she whispered. "I thought both Adam and Oldie were nice, respectable men, and this just seems like a childish prank." She laughed miserably. "A silly, childish prank that I fell for."

Sunday morning she felt better, but the whole situation still nagged at her. Yes, Adam/Oldie was wrong to lie to her or keep secrets from her or play tricks on her—no matter why he had done it, he owed her an apology.

Of that much she was certain.

Gwen measured out coffee and then realized what she was doing. Last night she had been going to throw all her coffee away, and here she was making a pot like nothing had ever happened. She sighed. The truth was, while she was peeved at Adam, she still remembered their friendship—and it was a friendship, even though he had let her down. She still knew how comfortable she was in his company. She still knew how well she and Oldie had communicated through the notes, even though Adam had taken unfair advantage. She still remembered Adam's laugh, his touch—

Gwen abandoned trying to make coffee and sat at her dining table, looking out at her small backyard and the birds flitting about. After a while, it occurred to her that while Adam's deception hurt her, his actions were those of a man trying to get close to something without scaring it away. He was using a disguise. Camouflage.

Would she have given him a chance if he had tried courting her as Adam?

Yes. In fact, she had, finally. But before that, she had a long history of ignoring Adam as a man, and she knew he was having trouble overcoming that. He had probably thought he had a better chance camouflaged as Oldie.

Gwen rose and dressed for church. If she had been nicer, less blind, to begin with, Adam wouldn't have felt it necessary to engage in his double life. He would have felt free to pursue a romantic relationship with her without the secrecy.

Though that took some of the blame from his shoulders and put it squarely on her own, Gwen thought, it certainly didn't excuse him.

She was late for church, and the Olds was not in the parking lot when she pulled in. She wondered if Adam had come to church today. Attendance was certainly a struggle for her. But as she sat in church, her mind felt clearer. And then the sun hit one of the stained-glass windows and lit up the sanctuary with reds and golds. Gwen turned, watching thoughtfully. She would apologize. She would listen to what Adam had to say. They would go from there.

Twice that afternoon she nearly picked up the phone to call Adam, but something stopped her. Whether it was the belief that it was more his duty than hers to initiate a conversation or just the fact that she didn't know what to say, she wasn't sure. She dinked around the house, putting things in order, plopping down at the table every now and then to read a passage in her Bible, and mostly wondering if Adam was ever going to call.

At about four o'clock she was upstairs considering rearranging her bedroom when the doorbell rang. Adam. It had to be.

Standing in front of her closed door, she took a deep breath, composing herself for the confrontation.

She opened the door. No one was there. At least not at eye level. The Olds was parked next to her curb, obviously newly washed and waxed, with its convertible top down for the first time—and its lights on. And traveling toward her down the sidewalk was a small metal contraption made out of two hubcaps and four casters. Gwen gaped as it stopped at the bottom of the steps. The robot had a white flag strapped to its back.

Gwen looked at both sides of the porch, but Adam was no-where in sight. She stepped down to the robot's level and plucked the flag off its back. On the other side of the cloth, in Oldie's familiar handwriting, were the words *I'm sorry* followed by a tiny heart. Gwen felt her mouth turn up in a small smile.

"You can come out now," she called. "I won't bite."

Adam poked his head out from around the left side of her house, where the driveway led to the garage. Gwen registered the wire-rimmed glasses, the stylish sports coat, the cautious, hopeful look on his face. He walked around and stepped up onto her porch without stumbling once.

"We need to talk," he said.

"Yes," Gwen said. "We do." She moved to her porch swing and sat on one side, leaving the other side open in plain invitation, but Adam stood, hands shoved in his pockets, in front of her. Finally he started to speak, staring down at the wooden porch floor.

"I know I'm not who you expected," he said. "I know that you deserve more. I can't blame you for being disappointed in what you see—" He started pacing in front of the swing. "I know you were hoping Oldie was some really handsome guy, someone who didn't stumble around and knock things over. I've never been great to look at, and I realize that—"

She was beginning to hear what he was saying, and she was appalled. This was the stuff *she* was supposed to be apologizing for.

"Adam—"

He ignored her. He just kept pacing and lamenting and apologizing for his looks, his speech, his Vega—

She jumped up, setting the swing in motion, and planted herself in front of him.

"Adam, that's not it." She had to back up a step because he

almost didn't stop in time, but she stopped his pacing. "You never had to change for me. At least, I never should have made you think you needed to change for me. I know, and I know you know, that at first I couldn't see past the computer-geek label I put on you. I'm sorry for that, but I changed. You know I did." She had his full attention, and her voice softened. "I don't want you to be anyone but who you are. *You* didn't need to change; my perceptions did. Don't you understand? It's your deception I'm upset about, nothing else! I feel so foolish—" She broke off, biting back all but the most important point. "You could have told me much sooner that you were Oldie," she continued. "You should have."

He blinked at her, and a small smile played on his lips. "I was going to get around to apologizing for that next," he said.

"Well, get on with it!" Gwen was appalled to feel tears start in her eyes. She had thought she was done with that. She'd put on mascara because she was so certain.

Adam sobered. "Gwen," he said, "I'm sorry. I didn't know it was you writing the notes until you asked me if I knew Oldie. And then I was so incredulous I couldn't think straight." He reached out suddenly to draw a strand of her hair into his fingers. "You've always been the girl of my dreams, Gwen. And I had a chance to get to know you without fear of falling over my own feet or saying the wrong thing. Which I only do because I'm so afraid—" He stopped, her hair still wound around his fingers. Gwen lifted her gaze to his.

"Afraid of what?" she asked. Adam's fingers traveled down her jaw, and he stepped closer.

"Afraid this moment will end, and you'll never forgive me for what I did," he said. "Afraid you'll never be able to see past my secrets to the truth. Afraid you'll never see what's in my heart."

Look at his heart.

Looking at Adam now, she couldn't believe she had ever been so blind. How could she have missed so much? Gwen swallowed hard and placed her palm flat on his chest. She could feel his heart beating strongly under her hand.

"And what is in there, Adam Langford?" she asked, already knowing.

"Love," he whispered. "Love for you." He bent his head and kissed her. Nothing Gwen had ever experienced had felt so absolutely right. Nowhere she had ever been had felt more like home. She felt bereft when he pulled away, even though he kept his arms around her.

"I have dreamed of that," he said. Gwen laughed, and the sound was shaky.

"I have a feeling I will dream of that," she answered. He laughed and pulled her closer.

"I love your laugh," she told him. "Do you know that was the first thing I ever loved about you?"

"Really? What else do you love about me?" His voice was teasing.

"Everything. But mostly—your car!" she teased in return, grinning. Adam pretended to pout, then looked at his watch.

"Speaking of the car, we still have time to go to the banquet," he said. "Will you go with me, Gwen? As my valentine?"

"Yes, I will," she said, her eyes sparkling, "but only if you'll kiss me again." He did, and then she left the circle of his arms reluctantly. "Give me fifteen minutes."

"I'll wait," Adam said.

Gwen hurried. Thanks to Saturday's daydreaming, she already had everything planned. The cream-colored dress slipped neatly over her head, and as Gwen checked herself over in the mirror, she realized just how much she looked like a bride. She paused, her heart skipping beats at the thought.

"Give the guy some time, girl," she murmured to herself. Smiling at the thought of the man waiting downstairs, she hurried with her hair and makeup.

Swirling out onto the porch, she found Adam swaying comfortably on her swing. He looked the way she knew he would: confident, capable, and very happy to see her. He rose from his seat, and his smile made her want to sing.

Thank you, God.

"Shall we?" he asked, offering her his arm. They walked down the sidewalk to the Oldsmobile, and Adam held the door for her. He went around to his side and got in, and for a moment he just looked at her.

Gwen stopped staring in appreciation at the sky in clear view above her and glanced at him.

"What?" she asked, smiling.

Adam smiled back, laughed the way she loved, and started the car.

A Note from the Author

My husband, Gary, and I were married on the twenty-eighth of November, 1987. On the twenty-eighth of every month for the past eleven years, Gary has brought me a flower. Most times it's a red rose surrounded by baby's breath. Often, it's a blossom off a tree or something from the flower bed. Occasionally, it's just a pretty weed!

Since he's in the air force, we're often apart on the twenty-eighth, and he has to be creative. He's sent me pictures of flowers and earrings resembling flowers and has even enlisted the help of friends or family. Sometimes he has to wait and make it up to me when he gets home.

Whatever the flower looks like, Gary's offerings are a wonderful reminder of his faithfulness and dedication. I truly appreciate this regular "bouquet of love."

Ranee McCollum

ABOUT THE AUTHOR

Growing up, Ranee McCollum wanted to be a veterinarian. After receiving a D in chemistry in her second year of college, however, she realized she was on the wrong track and became an English major. She promptly received a D in modern poetry. Her Prince Charming rescued her from the clutches of this wicked grading system and carried her off to become an air force wife, a nomadic life for which she's much better suited.

At present, she lives with her husband and five-year-old son in eastern Kansas. When she isn't packing or unpacking, Ranee enjoys reading, visiting antique shops, and exploring the local area. Also, this year she plans to take up golf and English horseback riding.

In addition to "His Secret Heart," Ranee has written two inspirational novels, *Watercolor Castles* and *A Thousand Hills* (both published by Heartsong Presents).

Ranee welcomes letters written to her in care of Tyndale House Author Relations, P.O. Box 80, Wheaton, IL 60189-0080.

Come to My Love

JERI ODELL

❦

*Then Jesus said, "Come to me, all of you who are
weary and carry heavy burdens, and I will give you rest.
Take my yoke upon you. Let me teach you, because
I am humble and gentle, and you will find rest for
your souls."*

MATTHEW 11:28-29

THIS BOOK IS DEDICATED TO MATTHEW, KELSY, AND ADAM,

my precious children.

Being your mother is such a privilege,

and one of life's greatest blessings.

And to Audrey, Dell, Kelsy, Nancy, and Pat,

who gave me encouragement, prayer

support, and editorial advice.

And always to Dean . . .

CHAPTER ONE

Harrison Jorgenson watched in numb disbelief as the police officers trampled over the wet lawn on the way back to their patrol car. Harrison's gut feeling, good news never knocks on the door at 5 A.M., proved correct. Clarissa lay in the hospital morgue, waiting for him to identify her body and arrange for a mortuary to pick it up.

"Clarissa's dead," he whispered to the silent house. He closed the front door, leaning heavily against it. "Clarissa's dead . . . and I'm free." His voice sounded hoarse and raspy in the early morning stillness. Guilt overwhelmed him at his response. His wife had died in a car accident only hours before, yet he felt only relief; the nightmare had finally ended.

His eyes shut, and he sighed—a long, loud, deep sound that echoed through the large entry hall. Opening his eyes, he stared at the staircase curving up to where Benjy and Abby snuggled in sound sleep. How do you tell a five- and three-year-old that their mother died on her birthday, while celebrating with another man?

He didn't know the answer, but he knew someone who would—Karl McCoy. Oh, why hadn't he taken his father's advice and married one of the McCoy girls?

Korby McCoy adjusted her graduation cap. Almond-shaped ebony eyes stared back at her from the mirror, a sadness reflecting from their depths. She ran a smoothing hand over the back of her caramel brown hair, which hung to her shoulder blades. The silky strands glimmered in the California sunlight that shone through her bedroom window. A knock took her attention from the mirror.

"Come in." Korby turned to face her dad as he entered. He stopped in the doorway, and she noticed tears pooling in his eyes as he regarded her attire.

"Korby Bear, you're all grown up and looking gorgeous. My fourth college graduate, and I couldn't be prouder." His voice sounded slightly choked up. "Why the sad face on your big day?"

His tenderness reached Korby's sorrow, which had been hovering just below the surface. A lone tear trickled down her cheek. "Oh, Daddy," she sobbed, "why can't I be more like my sisters? All six of them know exactly what they want to do with their lives." She sniffed and pulled a Kleenex from the box sitting on the nightstand beside her bed. She dabbed her eyes, trying not to smear her mascara. "They all want to do something great. I only want to get married and have a family."

"Korby, caring for a husband and children is a worthy calling. If that's the desire God has given you, then when the time comes, be the best wife and mother you can." His blue eyes smiled at her as he spoke. Exactly the kind of husband she hoped for, her dad exuded gentleness and strength.

"How can I when there is no one in my life? I don't even have a boyfriend." The tears flowed anew. "Dad, why hasn't

God granted the desire of my heart? I thought for sure I'd find someone in college, but I barely dated."

Karl McCoy wrapped his arms around his middle child, bumping her cap off in the process. They both laughed, breaking the tension. "I hate to sound trite, but God's timing is much different than ours. When he's ready, he'll bring a wonderful man into your life. Until then, quit worrying about your sisters, and be the best Korby you can be." He kissed the top of her head, where her cap had perched moments before.

"What do I do with my life while I'm waiting? I don't even have a job."

"Let's pray and see what door God opens."

They knelt beside her bed, beseeching God to guide Korby's future according to his will. "And give her the patience to wait on you, Lord. Amen." They rose, and her dad hugged her once again. "You fix your cap, and I'll meet you at the front door in five minutes."

She nodded and smiled. "Thanks, Dad. I love you."

"And I love you, Bear." Her dad had a pet name for each of his seven daughters.

While Korby fixed her makeup, she tried to muster some joy and anticipation over tonight's event, but none came; instead, she felt dread and confusion about her future. Since she was a tiny girl, she'd dreamed of one day having a husband and lots of children. She'd anticipated a tender man declaring his love and showering her with roses. What if God never answered her prayer and she ended up an old maid?

Harrison trudged toward his downstairs office, making a mental list of the things he needed to take care of this morning. *Call my parents, her parents, a mortuary, the McCoys.*

Tell Benjy and Abby. . . . The thought brought an ache to his heart as he pictured his honey-haired cherubs trying to understand death.

He sat down in the leather chair behind his massive desk. Everything in their home exuded elegance and expense; Clarissa would have it no other way. He flipped through his Rolodex until he found his parents' number.

Harry and Rose Jorgenson would be wide awake because their day in South Africa was almost half over. His stomach knotted as he picked up the phone and dialed the international code, followed by the rest of the number.

"Hi, Mom."

"Hi, honey! How are you this wonderful May day? You know May is still my favorite month." He shook his head, realizing that some things never change, one being his mom's enthusiasm for life.

"I'm fine. Is Dad around?"

"Normally he's not at this time of day, but this must be your lucky day. One moment, sweetheart." His lucky day? He sighed at her choice of words, knowing she'd soon regret them.

"Hello, Son, how are you?" His dad's voice boomed over the line.

"Dad, can you get Mom on the phone, too? I need to tell you both something."

"We only have one, but we'll share. Rosie, Harrison wants to speak to both of us." After a brief pause, his dad instructed him to go ahead.

"Clarissa died last night in an alcohol-related accident. The driver of the car she was in hit a tree, and they both died instantly." He couldn't bring himself to admit that another man had been escorting his wife.

"The kids?" his mother asked.

"They're fine. They were home with me." He heard his mother release her breath upon hearing his answer.

"Son, we're so sorry. We'll get back to the States as soon as we can."

"I knew you would. I'm planning the funeral for next week to give you time to get here."

"Are you OK?" Concern rang in his mother's words.

"I'm numb."

"The grieving will come later, Son."

How could he tell his parents he'd already been mourning the loss of his wife for almost four years? The only feeling he anticipated coming later would be guilt over the relief he felt now.

"We'll be praying, sweetheart. We'll call you as soon as we know details."

"Harrison, we love you."

"I know, Dad. Thanks. I love you, too. I'll talk to you soon." Harrison laid the phone receiver back in its cradle and rested his head in his hands. He'd disappointed his parents by marrying Clarissa, yet they had never stopped loving him. Thank God they hadn't asked for details of the accident. He knew that during this visit he would no longer be able to hide the true Clarissa from them. At least they would have the grace not to say, "I told you so."

Harrison walked to the kitchen to start the coffee. He'd wake the kids soon and take care of them before he drove to the Coppersmiths' home to inform them of their daughter's death. Somehow his parents' prayers would get him through the day.

The graduation ceremony blurred as Korby battled the tears that insisted on making an appearance. Two of her sisters had flown home to celebrate the event, so the whole family surrounded her on the football field afterward.

When they arrived home, the ringing phone called out to them. "I'll get it in my study," her dad volunteered. "Then we'll have cake and presents." He winked at Korby as he left the room.

Her mood lightened considerably as she and her sisters caught up on each other's lives. She loved all of them dearly, for they'd always been a close-knit family. Karly, the oldest, had them all laughing with her sidesplitting tales about other med-school students.

Finally Karl returned. His sober expression quieted them quickly.

"Dad, what's wrong?" Korby asked.

"Harrison Jorgenson's wife died early this morning in an accident. He asked if I'd do the funeral."

"Oh, Dad, how awful!" Korby felt deep sorrow for their old friend.

"Doesn't he live in Nashville?" Karly questioned.

"Yes, but he doesn't know any clergy there. I think having a stranger officiate at a funeral would be hard."

"How can he not know a pastor in his own town? Hasn't he lived there six or eight years?" As usual, Karly wanted everything spelled out.

"I don't think he attends church. When he married Clarissa, he pushed God to the back of his life."

"His parents were heartbroken over his marriage," Kettie McCoy informed her daughters. She returned her attention to her husband. "Can you free up your schedule to fly back there?"

"I think I'll have to. His father is my oldest and dearest friend. I'll preach tomorrow, get things organized at the office Monday, and fly out midweek. Korby, why don't you come with your mom and me? You could help with his children."

"Sure." Why not? After all, they all knew she had no plans, no future. She might as well be of use to someone.

"How many kids does he have?" Karly's curiosity drove the conversation onward.

"Two," Kettie replied. "A boy and a girl."

"Remember when he had a crush on you?" Korby asked Karly.

"Yes, and I think all six of you had a crush on him," she teased her sisters. "He was cute."

"Yes, and such a nice boy," Kettie said. "He loved coming to the States on sabbatical with his parents and spending time with our family, since he had no siblings of his own."

"Dad, remember the missions fair when I decided to be a medical missionary? Didn't he commit to becoming a missionary pilot at the same time?" Karly questioned.

Karl nodded, a sad expression on his face. "Yes, but his involvement with Clarissa waylaid those plans. Now, how about cake and presents?"

Korby smiled, noticing how her dad had tactfully changed the subject before their discussion turned to gossip.

The following Wednesday, Korby and her parents gaped at the large southern home from the windows of their rental car. "Wow," was all anyone said. The impressive two-story colonial home stood before them, stately and regal.

A weary and much-older-looking Harrison answered their knock. Korby noticed the gold flecks in his honey brown hair. His tawny eyes studied her. "And which of the seven Ks are you?"

"This is Korby," her dad answered for her.

"Ah, K number four. I didn't recognize you all grown up." He shook her father's hand and hugged her mother as they crossed the threshold. He seemed uncertain how to greet her, so he just nodded. "Come meet my kids."

They followed him to a downstairs playroom. "Benjy, Abby, come meet Daddy's friends." Two light brown heads popped up from the floor, where the children were lying on their tummies watching a Barney video. They jumped up and ran to their father. Benjy looked like a miniature replica of his dad. Abby's shy gray eyes must have been her mother's contribution. Her chubby cherub cheeks begged Korby to kiss them. She resisted the urge since Abby didn't know her and the behavior seemed too forward for a stranger. Her heart ached for these motherless children, and she vowed to shower them with love and attention while she was there.

Harrison led them to the guest room. "Korby, do you mind sharing with Abby? I only have two extra rooms in the main house and thought if you didn't mind, I'd give the downstairs one to my parents. I do have a separate guesthouse if you'd prefer."

"I'd love to share a room with Abby. But what do you think, Miss Moppet?" She couldn't resist touching Abby's curls. Abby shyly nodded her head and smiled up at Korby. "Will you show me where your room is?" Korby asked. After another nod, she took Korby's hand and led her up the stairs to their destination.

Abby's room embodied femininity, decorated in pink frills and lace with a canopy bed in the center. Clarissa's taste appeared impeccable from what Korby had seen of the house so far. The Jorgensons were obviously financially well off. After hanging up her navy dress and stowing her luggage out of the way, Korby decided to take a self-guided tour of the house.

In the formal living room, she stopped to admire a portrait that she assumed must be Clarissa. The woman's eyes resembled Abby's.

"That's Clarissa." From the doorway behind her, Harrison confirmed her unspoken thought.

Korby nodded. "Abby has her eyes. She was very beautiful. You must miss her terribly." Her voice took on a wistful sound as she thought dreamily of the fairy tale Harrison and Clarissa's life together must have been. It seemed so romantic to lay aside all your plans and dreams because you love someone so much that nothing in life is worth more than having her. Harrison had done that for Clarissa; he must have loved her with a deep and passionate love.

"Beauty is only skin-deep. Don't fool yourself into thinking too highly of my dead wife. She was nothing but a tramp."

Korby gasped. She turned around to see eyes filled with hurt and pain. The look on his face verified the bitterness she'd heard in his voice. And something in Korby McCoy's heart wanted to reach out and help this broken, hurting man.

CHAPTER TWO

I'm sorry. I didn't know." Uncomfortable, Korby looked down at her tightly clasped hands. "It's just . . ." She paused, glancing back at the portrait. "Well, she's very pretty, and you're—" Suddenly embarrassed by what she had almost said, Korby felt heat rush to her face. She glanced up at Harrison, whose eyes reflected amusement at her faux pas. "Anyway, you were an attractive couple—" she lifted her chin a fraction—"with beautiful children and a nice home, so everything appears fairy tale–like."

Harrison smiled at her, and his tawny eyes warmed. "No fairy tale here." She noticed that he swallowed hard. "Our lives were about as far from 'happily ever after' as one could get." He sighed and rubbed the back of his neck. "Things are seldom as they appear. I'm sorry. I hope I didn't sound rude earlier, but you were bound to hear the truth sooner or later. It's in all the local papers."

"What do you mean?"

Harrison walked into the room and sat on the edge of a straight-back chair. He rested his arms on his legs in a stooped position. He looked like a man burdened by the weight of bad choices. Korby's heart ached for him, and she longed to bring him comfort. She took a seat in an identical chair and waited for him to continue.

"The Coppersmiths, Clarissa's parents, are an old Nashville family from way back. They are newsworthy. The fact that their married daughter died in an alcohol-related crash, with a married man who wasn't her husband—also from a society family—is fodder for the inquisitive people who thrive on that sort of thing."

Korby's watery eyes wouldn't quite focus on the man sitting with his head hanging down, his gaze on the floor. She tried to swallow away the lump lodged in her throat. What could she say to bring him solace? Jesus' words from Matthew kept replaying in her head: "Come to me, all of you who are weary and carry heavy burdens, and I will give you rest." *Lord,* Korby prayed silently, *help Harrison to find his way back to you.*

"I'm sorry," she said quietly. She sensed the deep hurt and betrayal he felt. Somehow his pain became her own.

Harrison looked up into her eyes and smiled the saddest smile she'd ever seen. "My parents warned me, begged me, to stay away from her. My mother said sometimes the devil has gray eyes. I remember my dad telling me that temptation comes packaged as exactly what we think we need and want." He glanced up at Clarissa's image in the painting. "He said anything that distracted me from God and his plan, I needed to resist. Now I wish I'd listened. . . ." He looked back at Korby and continued. "Enough of that. I'm glad you came. You and the other Ks are like sisters to me. Do you remember my last visit to California?"

Korby nodded. "Right after you graduated from college."

"And you from eighth grade."

"And Kinsy from high school."

"Your mom had a party for all three of us."

"You stayed with us almost a month."

"Then I had to leave to start school at Moody Aviation. I missed you all so much, and besides your mom, only Kelsy wrote to me. She wrote me weekly until I got married; then I never heard from her again."

"As a second grader, she planned to be your wife someday. She cried when she learned you'd chosen another." They laughed together.

"Do you remember our nightly basketball games?"

Again Korby nodded.

"Your dad, you, and I took on the other six girls. We always won."

"Yeah, but you guys rarely let me touch the ball. How did I get stuck on your team, anyway?"

"It seemed fair to give them the three biggest and the three smallest, so we took the middle one."

"That's the story of my life. Never the biggest, smallest, prettiest, or smartest, just plain old Korby." She said the words jokingly, but she knew from the way his eyes bored into her soul that he had picked up on something more.

"There never was anything plain or ordinary about you, Korby, and there doesn't appear to be now, either."

Their gazes locked briefly. Then her dad spoke from the doorway. "When do you expect your parents, Harrison?"

Harrison's eyes left Korby. "Tomorrow evening. It's been over three years since they've been Stateside. Abby was a tiny baby. It'll be good to see them."

"For me, too," Karl agreed.

"If you'll excuse me, I think I'll go make friends with Abby and Benjy." Korby smiled at both men.

"Korby, good visiting with you. Thanks for listening." She nodded to Harrison and went in search of his children.

She marveled at how easily the conversation with him had

flowed. She'd always loved that about him. Rarely could she talk to a man, other than her dad, without feeling nervous and shy. Time fell away whenever Harrison came back into their lives. It felt like he belonged, like he was one of them, even now.

Harrison was amazed at how easily Korby had won Abby and Benjy's love in only three days. The adoration on their little faces when they looked at her made him smile. Other than the impending funeral hanging before him this afternoon, he was enjoying being with his parents and the McCoys again. He dreaded today, but maybe it would at least be the last time his heart would break over Clarissa.

In his pride he didn't want to face all the people who'd look at him with pity because his wife had been unfaithful or those who'd whisper behind his back. Some would think he hadn't been man enough to keep her. He'd made a huge mistake involving himself with Clarissa, one that couldn't be erased, rectified, or forgotten. A mistake that had forever changed the direction of his life. He wondered for the thousandth time how he could have been so blind when he met Clarissa. He had ignored his parents' warnings, and his heart had paid many times over for his choice.

He watched from the window as Karl and Korby shot hoops with the kids, using Benjy's miniature basket. He smiled, remembering their first day, when Korby had implied that she thought he was handsome and her cheeks had turned bright red. There was something refreshing and real about her.

"Have you thought about child care for the kids after Korby leaves?" his mom asked, joining him at the window and wrapping an arm around his waist. "Since your flights often take you away for several days, a live-in nanny might work best."

"Yeah, I've thought about it but haven't done anything yet. How does a person go about hiring someone to raise his children? We've all heard the horror stories."

"What about Mrs. Coppersmith?"

"She doesn't have the time with her charity fund-raising, her bridge club, and all her social events. Besides, we don't see eye to eye on much."

"What about Korby? She could live in your guesthouse."

Harrison looked at his mother with a puzzled expression on his face. "Korby's a college graduate. I'm sure she's looking for something a little higher up than a nanny position. Besides, she lives in California, not Nashville."

"Kettie mentioned that Korby is struggling with her own future. Maybe this would give her a few months' reprieve until she figures out where God is directing her. The kids obviously love her, and she's great with them." Both watched out the window as Korby scooped Benjy up into her arms and kissed an "owie."

"OK, Mom, I'll ask her." He hoped she'd say yes, for his life would be much easier if she agreed.

Korby brought the kids inside and sent them down to the playroom to watch a video so she and her mom could prepare lunch. They'd done all the cooking since their arrival.

"Korby, wait—" Harrison stopped her. "My mom said she'd help with lunch so I can speak to you in my office."

Korby nodded her assent, but he saw a look of hesitation cross her face. They hadn't been alone together since the picture incident, and he wondered if she had been trying to avoid another heavy conversation.

"Have a seat." He motioned to a chair facing his desk as he sat in the leather chair behind the desk. "I can't thank you enough for all you've done: cooking, cleaning, child care. I'm glad you came," he told her for the second time.

"Me too. It's been good being with you and your folks again." Korby appeared to relax as she leaned back in her chair.

"What does the future hold for you now that college lies behind you?"

A frown creased her brow. "I have no idea."

"What would you like it to hold?"

"Mr. Right racing up in his white sports car with a dozen red roses, whisking me away to the land of marriage and children," Korby answered, tongue in cheek.

"Ah, the land of happily ever after." Harrison nodded. "So what's the lucky fellow's name?"

"I don't know. I haven't met him yet. I don't even have a prospect on the horizon."

"No beaus pounding your front door down, dueling in the streets for your love and affection?"

"Not even one."

"Korby McCoy, I find that hard to believe. The men in California must be either blind or stupid—or both." Korby blushed at his compliment. "So you'd like to get married and have kids, but what about career goals?"

"Those *are* my career goals. I'm not driven like my sisters. All I've ever wanted to do is have a family." Harrison saw sadness in her eyes when she spoke of her dreams.

"How would you like to be my nanny?"

"What?" Surprised eyes looked into his.

"Not forever or anything. Just for a few months while I work on a more permanent solution. I have a housekeeper, and I can hire a cook, so you'll only have to worry about Benjy and Abby."

"Are you serious?"

Her reaction made him feel stupid for even asking. "Dumb idea, right? My mom mentioned that you were struggling with the future, and I thought it would give you time to figure your life out. I'm sorry. Desperate men take desperate measures." He was starting to rise when she finally spoke.

"Yes."

"Pardon?"

"Yes, I'll do it. Only I'll cook, too. You can keep the housekeeper, but I can do everything else."

He felt his smile reach his eyes. "Are you sure? I don't want a pity nanny."

"It's a great idea. I do need some time, and I love kids and cooking, so why not?"

"I'll pay you the going rate, whatever that is, and you can fix up the guesthouse out back to accommodate you. When I'm home, you're free to live your own life." He scrutinized her expression to evaluate her motives. She looked happy and relieved. "Thank you, Korby. I know my children already adore you."

"No thanks needed. This relieves the pressure for me, too, for a while anyway. Who knows, maybe my future is racing around Nashville in that little car instead of Southern California. Do you have any friends looking for a wife?"

"Not that I know of, but I'll keep you in mind in case I run into someone. Let's go have lunch." They both rose and headed for the kitchen. Harrison realized that though Korby joked about finding a man, it was the true desire of her heart.

Straightening his tie before the funeral, Harrison found himself pondering the strangeness of the human species. They attend funerals, weeping, mourning, and wailing, then leave, meet at a prearranged destination, and stuff their faces almost like a party. He dreaded the reception at his in-laws' more than the funeral itself. He was counting on his parents' prayers to get him through it.

He paused in the doorway of the playroom, listening to Korby's quiet voice reading a story. Both kids snuggled on the couch against her. He hated to break the tranquil scene, but glancing at his watch, he realized the time to leave had arrived.

"Give Daddy a hug," he whispered upon entering. Both kids jumped up and ran to him. "I'll be back to pick you all up in about an hour." He had decided that the kids were too young to attend the actual service, but he planned to take them along to the Coppersmiths' afterward.

Korby nodded, and her somber eyes reached out and touched his soul with compassion. Without her ever saying a word, he knew that she, too, would pray him through this day.

The funeral proved more difficult than Harrison had anticipated. He found himself weeping that his life with Clarissa had ended so tragically. They had failed each other. After a rocky beginning, their life together had spiraled ever downward. They had come from two different worlds and collided in a passionate attraction of lust, but they had never quite learned to love each other. They'd even fallen short of mutual respect and admiration.

As he looked upon her lifeless face for the last time, he whispered, "I'm sorry, Clarissa. I failed as your husband." *And I failed you, Lord, and my parents. . . .*

Korby's intake of breath at the mansion towering in front of them said more to him than words. The maid opened the front door and invited them to enter. Harrison placed his hand on the small of Korby's back to propel her into the foyer. She held each of the children's hands.

Suddenly Mrs. Coppersmith appeared, resembling a pit bull with teeth showing and ready to attack. "How dare you bring her here!" she hissed. Korby and Harrison froze in their tracks, his hand remaining against her back.

"Mrs. Coppersmith—"

"Don't try to explain to me," she interrupted with a fierce whisper. Her eyes shot hatred at them both. "Clarissa told us she got no love at home. You showered it on all your other women friends, leaving none for her. Now you disgrace her memory by bringing one of your lovers to her parents' home on the day of her funeral."

"Mrs. Coppersmith?" Karl McCoy spoke from behind her. "This is my daughter Korby. She came with my wife and me from California to watch the children."

"Oh . . . I'm sorry, Reverend." Harrison heard his mother-in-law apologize for the first time ever. "But what was I to think?" she asked in her sweetest southern drawl. "He broke my daughter's heart with a countless string of women. Forgive me, please." She raised her chin and walked away without looking back.

CHAPTER THREE

Korby looked down at Abby, who had begun to cry in response to Mrs. Coppersmith's outburst. Picking her up, she saw that Benjy had grabbed hold of his dad's leg, terror in his eyes. Korby was upset by the scene, but a glance at Harrison verified that he was hurt even more deeply. His face had lost all color, and his body trembled. His pulsating jaw was tightly clenched.

"Let's grab a breath of fresh air." Her dad's calm voice was a welcome relief as he ushered them all out the front door.

Abby held on to Korby for dear life, and Harrison carried Benjy out. Korby sat on the step, taking Benjy from Harrison. Her dad began to walk with Harrison, speaking soft words of comfort and encouragement. Her heart ached watching him face yet another difficult battle today. She knew instinctively that Harrison had never done the things his mother-in-law had accused him of. *Dear Father, please touch this man with your comfort, your peace, your hope,* she prayed silently.

"Auntie Korby, why was Grandmother so mad? Why did she yell at Daddy?"

Korby hugged Benjy closer to her side. "She's just upset, sweetheart. Sometimes when people are hurting or sad, they're mean to others when they shouldn't be. She said she was sorry, remember?" He seemed content with her explanation.

When the men returned a few moments later, she could tell from Harrison's swollen and bloodshot eyes that he had wept out some of his pain. She ached to say something to make him feel better, but no words came. He joined her on the step, lifting Benjy onto his lap and holding him in a tight hug.

Finally her dad spoke. "Let's go find your Grandma Rose. I bet she'll find something good for you to eat." He lifted Abby into his arms and took Benjy's hand. It seemed strange to Korby that her dad was leaving her and Harrison alone after the scene that had just transpired.

Harrison cleared his throat. "I'm sorry you had to witness that. You must be wondering what you're getting yourself into." He sighed, then continued. "I never cheated on Clarissa. She just tried to justify her own behavior by lying about mine. There's never been another woman—ever. But if you want to change your mind about the nanny position, I'll understand. Mrs. Coppersmith may try to sully your reputation."

"No, she can't scare me away. I know you, and I didn't think it was true. The sad thing is she doesn't realize that."

"And probably never will." His flat voice held no hope. "In her mind I've been branded a womanizer, and Clarissa took the truth to her grave."

Korby reached over and squeezed his hand. Her parents had taught her that touch brings healing to the hurting. He looked into her eyes, and she said, "Those who love you know the truth."

Nodding, he patted her hand. "Thanks, Korby. You'd better get inside before more rumors fly. I just didn't want you to think—"

"I don't," she interrupted. Korby rose and walked into the house, leaving him alone.

Harrison's mind reeled back to the battle he and Clarissa had launched into before she left the house for the last time. He'd returned home from a flight to find her in a strapless gown, leaving to meet her lover.

"Where are the kids?" His voice had sounded flat and weary.

"They're spending the night with my parents."

"I want them home with me."

"Then go get them. I have plans. It is my thirtieth birthday, you know." Nose in the air, she picked up her silver beaded bag and marched past him toward the front door.

He grabbed her arm. "I'm sick of you flaunting your string of lovers in my face."

"Too bad." Fire shot from her gray eyes; her voice dared him to take action. "Now take your hands off me." He could still hear the clipped, icy tone she'd used.

He tightened his grip on her arm. An urge to slap the smug, haughty look from her face welled up inside him, but he would not stoop to wife abuse, no matter what she did. "Look, Clarissa, why don't we just agree this marriage is a farce and call it quits?"

"This arrangement works fine as far as I'm concerned."

"What about Benjy and Abby? Soon they'll be old enough to realize their mother's a harlot."

"I'm hoping they'll figure out what a hypocrite their father is first. You spout off your religious philosophies, but who's happier—you or me? I have a great time every night, while you mope around wishing you'd never met me. Men can't resist me. You couldn't, and neither can any other man I decide I want. I have power, and you have nothing. Who do you think I want the kids to learn from? Now let go of me."

Harrison released her arm, and her heels echoed through the hall toward the front door. She paused before exiting. "Don't wait up." Her smirk only served to increase his anger.

Clarissa had learned to cast her spell on men at age thirteen, using her beauty and body to her own advantage. Although at one time he hadn't been able keep his eyes or hands off of her, her physical attraction had lost its power over him long before she died. In the end, she hung around his neck like an albatross, choking the life from him.

Now, having just come from her funeral and having to face her mother once again, he took a deep breath, trying to find the courage to go back into the house. At that moment, his dad stepped out onto the porch. "Son, I heard what happened. I'm sorry. Come inside with me, and I'll make certain no one else says anything cruel." True to his word, Harry Jorgenson never left his son's side.

Harrison attempted to make polite conversation with the few who approached him with sympathy. Most avoided him completely, apparently not knowing what to say.

The following day the McCoys flew home, without Korby. She gave them a list of personal belongings to pack and ship to her. Harrison's parents had to leave the day after that due to a prescheduled missions conference his dad was leading.

As his mother gave Korby a good-bye hug, she said, "Korby, thank you so much for helping Harrison out. It's much easier to leave, knowing you're here to care for him and the children."

Harrison noticed Korby discreetly slip away, giving his family a few minutes alone together. She had moved from

Abby's room to the guesthouse earlier in the day. His mom had helped her clean it and get situated. Korby was out of sight when he and the kids came out a while later. "Knock, knock," he called from the porch.

"Be right out. I'm just making up my bed."

"So what do you think of the place? I know it's small."

"It's perfect! I love it. My favorite part is the rocker on the front porch." She opened the screen door, and Harrison, Abby, and Benjy entered her small abode.

"Have you ever visited Nashville before?" he asked.

"Never."

"Why don't we all go out for pizza and some sight-seeing? I thought we could all use a break from the heaviness of life these last few days."

"Sounds great. Give me five minutes."

Korby stood at Harrison's front door five minutes later, wearing jeans, sneakers, a pink T-shirt, and a sweatshirt tied around her waist. She'd pulled her hair back into a ponytail. Her ebony eyes sparkled when Harrison and the kids sauntered out.

"Well, you have a choice: really good pizza and sad children, or really bad pizza but very happy kids."

Korby looked into Benjy's upturned face, his eyes pleading with her to make the right choice. "Bad pizza it is." She bent down and hugged him. "Happy kids are much more important than happy tummies."

Harrison smiled at her and winked. "Thanks."

They suffered through the pizza but enjoyed watching the kids play games, ride the merry-go-round, and win prizes. Afterward Harrison drove past all the hot spots in Nashville, showing Korby the pediatrician's office and the nearest grocery store.

After the kids had their baths and bedtime stories, Harrison took Korby on a tour of the cupboards and closets so she would be able to find everything she might need. "I talked to Bruce, my partner, this evening, and he insisted I take another week off. I thought it might be fun to play tour guide and actually visit some attractions instead of just doing a drive by. Does that interest you at all?"

"Yes, I'd love that. I've never been in the South before."

"We'll start tomorrow. Be ready at nine."

"See you then. Good night, Harrison."

"G'night, Korby." He watched her walk to the guesthouse, then locked the back door and flipped off the downstairs lights. He then climbed the stairs to his room, checking each child one last time. In his room, he began to search for his long-lost Bible. He needed to find his way back to his heavenly Father.

Harrison packed each day full of activity, so each night exhaustion made it impossible to think. Keeping the kids busy helped them not to miss their mom, though she'd never been a big part of their lives anyway. They had spent more time with the housekeeper than with their own mother. He and Korby slipped into a comfortable friendship, and he appreciated her sensitivity to the three of them. They laughed easily and often. He'd almost forgotten how good it felt to laugh. He sure hadn't had much to laugh about during the nightmare of the past few years.

"I saved the best for last," he announced the following Saturday. "Today we're going to Opryland."

The kids cheered.

"Is that an amusement park?" Korby's face lit up when she asked.

"Yes. You like the idea?"

She nodded. "That's the part of me that never grew up."

Abby and Benjy enjoyed the rides. They waved to Harrison and Korby each time they passed.

Throughout the morning, Harrison kept noticing an older lady staring at them. Everywhere they went, her eyes seemed to be upon them. When they sat down for lunch, she approached them with a young child in tow.

"Excuse me," she said. "May I say what a beautiful and happy family you have? It's so refreshing to see." Then she grinned at Harrison. "Your wife radiates joy and is quite lovely."

Harrison glanced over at Korby, whose red face reflected her embarrassment. "Thank you for saying so, and yes, Korby—" he looked away from the woman and directly into Korby's eyes—"is beautiful inside and out."

For the first time he really saw her. No longer the awkward adolescent who hated playing basketball on his team, she had blossomed into a lovely flower. He swallowed hard at the realization. She squirmed under his frank gaze, but he couldn't take his eyes off of her. Korby McCoy was a woman, an intriguing, intelligent, invigorating woman. How had he spent the last two weeks with her and just figured it out?

"Why didn't you tell her I wasn't your wife?" Korby whispered as the woman walked away.

"I didn't want to spoil her illusion. Besides, I avoided a complicated explanation."

Korby nodded. "Do I have ketchup on my nose?"

Harrison laughed. "No."

"Then why are you staring at me like I have three eyes?"

"Sorry, I just noticed that you've grown up." Again he saw her blush. She'd never liked attention shined upon her. Korby held the title of "shyest McCoy."

Suddenly his senses were alive to her. Her voice sounded

melodic, her laughter like music. Her smile flooded him with joy, and an accidental touch sent his heart into flip-flop mode. This seemed crazy. He was a grown man, a widower with children, but inside he felt like a schoolboy with his first crush.

After the kids were in bed, Korby made hot chocolate and carried it to the living room. "I know it's spring, but your nights are chilly to this California girl," she explained, offering him a cup.

He'd drink anything to spend a few more minutes in her company. Soon reality would bring him back to earth, but for now, he'd enjoy orbiting through space with these new feelings sending him upward.

"Tomorrow's Sunday. Do you mind if the kids go with me to church?"

"No, not if you don't mind taking them."

"Not at all. Do you . . . know a good place to go?" she asked, fidgeting with her spoon.

Sadly, he didn't. "No." He wondered why she seemed anxious.

"Uh . . . would you want to go with us?" Her voice reflected her hesitancy to even ask. She stared at the spoon in her hand rather than his face.

He swallowed hard, and a knot of dread rose in his stomach. He'd read his Bible each night for the past week, but was he ready to darken the doors of a church? Finally she looked up, probably wondering if he had even heard her. "Maybe. I'll let you know in the morning."

"I'm not trying to pressure you. I just wanted you to know you're welcome. So . . . what do you do for fun when you're not touring this fair city?" He appreciated the way Korby sensed when to back off. She often steered conversations in different directions at just the right moment.

"I'm a workaholic. There's not much time for fun."

"Why do you work so much?" she asked with a frown.

"To avoid thinking."

"So the rumors are true?" Her voice teased lightly.

"What rumors?"

"That you are ambitious, successful, and driven." Her eyes unknowingly beckoned him to fall in love with her.

Reality brought him crashing back to earth. He was too old and had made too many mistakes to ever be part of Korby's life. He had to let her see who he really was so that she'd never return his affection. Yes, he'd make certain Korby McCoy saw the true Harrison Jorgenson.

"The truth is I'm a failure, Korby. I failed at my Christianity. I failed at my marriage. I failed to obey God's call on my life. I failed as a son and broke my parents' hearts. I've failed every important task in my life." Rising quickly, he hustled up the stairs, leaving a stunned Korby sitting on his couch with her mouth open. She'd have to let herself out tonight.

CHAPTER FOUR

Korby hadn't slept well. Harrison's declarations had left her emotions reeling. He'd made his share of mistakes, that was for sure, but he wasn't a failure, at least not in her eyes. She'd never forget the look of self-loathing on his face last night. *I want to see this man restored to you, God, for the kids' sake as well as his own.*

She glanced at the clock and jumped out of bed. It was after eight, and she hadn't intended to sleep so late. Slipping into a pair of gray sweats and a white T-shirt, she ran a brush quickly through her hair. She hurriedly brushed her teeth and rushed over to the main house.

Upon entering the kitchen, she found Abby and Benjy already dressed for church, sitting at the table in the breakfast nook, enjoying pancakes. "Good morning, sleepyhead." Harrison's voice greeted her; he wore a warm, teasing smile. The cozy scene touched her heart and drew her even closer to this family.

"Good morning." Korby returned his friendly greeting. She realized she'd been holding her breath, uncertain what to expect this morning. Relief flooded her—Harrison seemed like his old self.

"If madam will take a seat, a scrumptious breakfast shall be placed before her." Korby smiled at his butler imitation and obediently sat down next to Abby. He placed a huge stack of pancakes before her, grinning his lopsided grin. That endearing smile—what a welcome sight.

"I thought I was the cook," Korby commented, taking her first bite of his melt-in-your-mouth pancakes. "But mind you, I'm not complaining."

Harrison took the seat across from her. "You are, but we could have starved to death before you made it over here. I had the children's welfare to consider."

Even though his tone was teasing, Korby felt her face grow hot. "I'm sorry—"

He held up his hand to stop her. "Don't be. I'm only teasing." They ate for a few moments in silence. "By the way, I decided to go with you and the kids to church this morning. According to the phone book, there is one about a mile from here that starts at nine-forty-five. That should give us plenty of time."

"I'm glad." *Thank you, God! And thanks for hearing my prayers last night. Harrison is back to himself again.*

When had he decided that? What he'd decided was to offer them a ride, but looking at the dark circles under Korby's eyes, he realized he'd cost her a decent night's sleep, and he felt guilty. He'd planned to treat her with a cool indifference, but somehow seeing her this morning looking tired and vulnerable made those plans fly out the window.

"I'll do the dishes." Korby said as she rose and started gathering dirty plates. "Come here, you two, and we'll wash your sticky hands." He loved watching her with his kids. She was much more maternal than their own mother had been. He kept reminding himself how young she actually was. She acted mature beyond her years.

"I'll get ready and meet you at the door at nine-fifteen." He had to get away from her and stop thinking about how incredible she was. Just as he had learned in flight school, you don't depend on how things feel or look as you're soaring overhead; you depend only on your gauges. No matter what he felt, his gauges declared Korby McCoy off-limits—today, tomorrow, and always.

Harrison and Korby settled into a crowded pew almost at the back of the church. He sat pressed against the edge but couldn't escape her nearness. He breathed in the scent of her, and their shoulders touched. *Korby, how can I quit thinking about you when you smell so good?*

"What are you wearing?" he whispered in her left ear as they waited for the service to begin.

"What?" He had no idea what she thought he asked, but her face had turned a deep shade of red.

"Your perfume. It smells nice." She immediately appeared relieved.

"Oh. Happy."

"It suits you." And it did. It smelled light and breezy and uncomplicated, just like Korby.

"Were you surprised the kids responded so well to strangers?" she asked.

"Not really. They love preschool and probably equate Sunday school to that."

"I thought Abby might cry, but she was a trooper." He heard the pride in Korby's voice.

"Thank you for loving my kids." He felt so touched by her devotion to them.

"How could I not? After all, I love their dad." For a brief moment his heart soared on wings of hope. "You're the only almost-brother I've ever had." She smiled up at him.

Thanks, Korby, for being my gauge.

They were interrupted by a cheerful voice from the front of the sanctuary. "Welcome! What a beautiful May day to come together and worship the Lord."

Harrison tried to remember the last time he had sat in a Sunday morning church service. Sometime shortly after he met Clarissa. The old ache returned—not an ache for her, but an ache of regret for the mistakes he'd made with her.

After the welcome and a few announcements, they all began to sing choruses, most foreign to Harrison. Luckily, they appeared on a screen for all to see. Finally, the pastor prayed and invited everyone to take a seat. He began his sermon by asking everyone to turn to Matthew 18:12-14.

The pastor read the passage aloud: "If a shepherd has one hundred sheep, and one wanders away and is lost, what will he do? Won't he leave the ninety-nine others and go out into the hills to search for the lost one? And if he finds it, he will surely rejoice over it more than over the ninety-nine that didn't wander away! In the same way, it is not my heavenly Father's will that even one of these little ones should perish."

Harrison knew he was that one sheep that had wandered away. He let out a sigh, not sure if he was ready to hear this sermon. Part of him wanted to find his way back to God, but the other part knew it was a long, hard road. Was he strong enough to make the trek? Could he do it, or would it just be another disappointment to his parents when he failed again?

Somehow with all his introspection, he missed most of the sermon, but the ending he would never forget. "It's not about you getting back on track. It's not about you making right choices from here on out. It's not about *you* at all. Did you hear me? It's not about you!

"It's about Christ. It's about repentance and surrender. Do you see what he is saying a few chapters back in Matthew? He's inviting you to come, and he promises to relieve your burden and give you rest. All you need to do is come. Are you willing to come today?"

Was he? His heart pounded in fear. His palms felt sweaty; his mouth went dry. His breathing was rapid and shallow. Did he have the courage to walk down that aisle and recommit his heart and life to Jesus? It might be now or never. He had to do it.

He glanced at Korby; she seemed to sense his inner fight. Tears streamed down her face when he asked, "Will you get the kids and wait for me?" She nodded, squeezing his hand. A smile lit her face, and he realized those tears were for him. He gave her hand a quick squeeze and walked down the aisle before he lost his courage.

Korby wept with joy over Harrison's trip up the aisle. She visited the rest room to compose herself before picking up the kids. Then the three of them waited for him under a magnolia tree. The kids chattered about their morning, but Korby couldn't seem to concentrate on their words. She thought of how drastically their lives would change because their dad had chosen to return to the God of his youth. Her heart overflowed with thankfulness.

Korby watched Harrison's approach, noticing a new lightness to his step. His smile looked bigger and brighter than before. Without thinking about what she was doing, she ran into his arms, happiness overflowing in her heart for him. He briefly held her tight, then backed out of her hug.

"Oh, I'm sorry," she said, blushing. "I didn't mean to embarrass you. We McCoys forget that not everyone comes from huggy families."

He smiled at her. "Forget it. I just haven't been around any demonstrative people in years."

On the ride home Benjy and Abby sang the new songs they had learned in Sunday school. As they rounded the corner onto their street, Korby spotted a Mercedes sitting in front of the house. "Who could that be?"

Harrison sighed. "My in-laws."

Korby remembered their last encounter with Mrs. Coppersmith, and her stomach knotted. "We'll get through this," she whispered to him, squeezing his hand where it rested on the gearshift knob.

Harrison pulled into the driveway, turned off the car, and handed Korby his keys. "Will you take the kids into the house? I don't want you to have to deal with this woman, and I don't want to traumatize them any more than they already have been."

Korby nodded. "Are you sure you don't want me to stay with you?"

"I'm sure. God is with me now." Harrison opened his door.

"He always has been."

He glanced back at Korby. "I know."

Korby took the kids inside and steered them toward the playroom. As they settled in with a video, Korby heard the doorbell. She closed the playroom door and went to the front entrance to answer.

"Sorry to bother you." Harrison grinned sheepishly. "I gave you my keys. You remember Mrs. Coppersmith?"

"Yes. Nice to see you again." Korby felt a twinge of guilt

for lying through her teeth. *Horrible to see you again* would have been a more honest greeting.

"Mrs. Coppersmith, you remember Korby McCoy, don't you?"

"Why, yes." Her voice carried frost with it. She raised a brow in a look of disapproval. "I understood you traveled from California for the funeral. How is it you are still here?"

Harrison took charge of the situation. "Mrs. Coppersmith, why don't you join me in my office, and we'll discuss whatever it is you wanted to talk over. In the meantime, Korby, will you get Mrs. Coppersmith a glass of iced tea?"

Korby collected the iced tea, and by the time she entered the office, voices were raised. Mrs. Coppersmith hissed at Harrison, "What is she doing here? It's completely improper for her to be living alone in this house with you. It's obvious she is a complete innocent. How long will it be before you ruin her life, too?"

Korby froze just inside the doorway, and neither noticed her presence. "Korby lives in the guesthouse, and I would never do anything improper with her—"

"Why not? You did with my daughter. Does this Korby deserve more respect than my Clarissa did? You stole her purity and tainted our family's reputation." Now Mrs. Coppersmith stood, emphasizing each word with her hands.

Harrison rubbed the back of his neck and answered in a controlled voice. "I've explained that Korby is like my sister. We grew up together. She lives in the guesthouse and never comes upstairs if I'm up there. She loves the kids and cares for them." *Better than their own mother did.* "Isn't that the bottom line?"

"Let me have them. Give me custody. I can provide for them much better than you can. I'll see to it that they have everything they'll ever need. You'll be free to live immorally if you so choose, without their having to witness it."

Harrison slammed his fist on his desk and stood to face his accuser. "Mrs. Coppersmith, I would not give you custody of my children if you were the last person on earth. Now get out."

"I will get those children. You watch yourself, because you make one wrong move, and I'll have Child Protective Services over here so fast your head will spin. You'll regret the day you challenged me to this fight."

Mrs. Coppersmith stormed out of the office, running into Korby and knocking the tea glass to the floor. The shattering of the glass was still echoing when the slamming of the front door resonated through the house.

"I'm sorry you had to witness another scene at the hands of my mother-in-law." Harrison took her hand and led her toward the playroom. "You check the kids, and I'll clean up the mess."

Korby only nodded. That woman had left her feeling stunned both times they'd met. The kids were engrossed in the video, so Korby sat down on the couch, absorbed in her own thoughts. Her heart ached for Harrison.

Lord, give me the strength to love and encourage this family with everything in me. Harrison needs you now more than ever. And, Lord, I'll stay here forever if I have to, just so that woman doesn't get these precious kids. I love them, Lord, and want them to know you. Please don't let her take them from Harrison. She already ruined Clarissa. Please don't let her get her hands on Benjy and Abby.

As Harrison cleaned up the shards of glass, he wondered exactly when Korby had walked in on the conversation. Once again Mrs. Coppersmith had painted an untrue picture of him, accusing him of stealing her daughter's innocence. If she only knew. . . .

With Mrs. Coppersmith's help, it shouldn't be hard to convince Korby that he was not worthy of her time or attention. Clarissa's mother had a way of shining the worst possible light on him. He decided to tell Korby the whole sordid story tonight after the kids went to bed. In the meantime, he'd call Bruce and catch up on everything going on at work. Tomorrow was his day to return.

Harrison spent the afternoon in his office. Korby fixed dinner and spent the day with the kids. After dinner, he heard her strumming a guitar. From his office, he enjoyed several songs. Closing his eyes, he let the music soothe his soul. Instinctively, Harrison knew she was playing praise songs, even though he didn't recognize them. She played well. He smiled, acknowledging another asset in her favor.

She'd make some lucky man a fine wife. That thought brought a pang to his heart. No use wishing—it could never be. He smiled, thinking back to her spontaneous hug that morning. As she had run toward him, he had longed to scoop her up and plant a kiss on those very kissable lips. Instead, he had stood stiff and awkward.

The scent of her had filled him, and his fingers had longed to curl into the silky strands of her hair. He wished he could have whispered the feelings building up in his heart. Instead, he caused her to feel embarrassed for being Korby. He sighed. *Quit thinking about her. She's off-limits.* If only it were that easy.

Shortly after eight, she rapped on his office door.

"Come in."

"The kids are ready for bed. Would you like to tuck them in, or shall I?"

"I will, but then can we talk?"

"Sure." She looked puzzled.

"Why don't you wait here? Propriety and all, you know." He sounded sarcastic and hadn't meant to. She nodded and kissed each child before he departed with them.

"How did your day go?" he asked upon his return, trying to make some small talk before he dropped his bombshell.

"Good." Korby still looked puzzled, and he wanted to put her at ease before getting into the subject at hand.

"Did you feel deserted?"

"Not at all. I just thought you were giving me a trial run since tomorrow is my first real day alone with the kids."

"Are you ready?"

"Absolutely. I'm looking forward to getting into a routine."

"Tomorrow I'll set up a household account for you to use on groceries and the kids. That way if they need anything or you want to enroll them in a basket-weaving class, you can."

"Basket weaving?" Korby looked perplexed.

"Sorry, my not-so-funny sense of humor."

Korby smiled. "Got it."

"About Mrs. Coppersmith—"

"Harrison, there's no need to explain anything. She's the most evil woman I've ever encountered, and I don't believe anything she says."

"Do you believe I should give her my kids?"

"Of course not! Surely you're not considering that, are you?" Korby's voice sounded shrill.

"No. I just wondered what you thought."

"I think you are a terrific dad with two wonderful kids. I know you'll make a great Mr. Mom, and I'm so proud of you for getting things straightened out with God today. I know

that wasn't easy." Her eyes sparked with her passionate proc-
lamations.

"Korby, I'm far from wonderful."

"You keep telling me that, but it's not what I see with my
eyes or with my heart."

"Hearts can't see."

"But they can know."

*Does yours know what you do to me and how badly I want to fall
in love with you?* Harrison cleared his throat. "Did you know
Clarissa was the woman Proverbs speaks about? Her lips were
sweet as honey, but the result as bitter as poison."

CHAPTER FIVE

Korby shook her head, and he continued. "My mind screamed *run,* but she was the only girl who'd ever been interested in me. What if I ran, and she was my only chance for a wife? I'd had a crush on your sister Karly most of my life, but she wasn't interested. In college, girls barely knew I was alive. I didn't want to go to the mission field alone.

"I was at Moody Aviation in Elizabethton, Tennessee, feeling lonesome and bored. Most of the guys were married and went home to a pretty wife every night. Then Clarissa entered the picture, also feeling bored and lonesome. She was spending the summer with her ailing grandparents and decided seducing the poor, innocent missionary boy sounded like a challenge."

Harrison sighed. "No doubt about it, she was beautiful, and her body should have been illegal." He rubbed the back of his neck and noticed a blush on Korby's cheeks. "Sorry. Anyway, I was a game to her. I held out for part of the summer, enjoying the flirtation. But in the end she captured my heart, and I gave in to the physical desire as well.

"Summer ended, and Clarissa returned to Nashville with no plans of ever seeing me again. I was devastated, realizing the entire summer had been nothing more than a diversion for her. Then two months later her father showed up looking for a husband for his pregnant daughter."

"I had no idea. I'm sorry." Korby swallowed hard.

"Her parents dragged her kicking and screaming into a loveless marriage with me. She wanted to be a single mom, but her mother opposed that idea. Mrs. Coppersmith always gets what she wants, so within the week Clarissa and I vowed to love and honor one another until death do us part. The only part of our vows we managed to uphold was the 'until death' part."

Korby's heart ached as Harrison let out a long sigh and continued his story. The raw pain in his voice confirmed the high price he'd paid for his sin.

"The Coppersmiths told everyone we'd secretly married during the summer, so no shame would tarnish Clarissa's reputation. I think everyone, except her mother and I, already knew what kind of girl she was.

"So there I was—a Moody dropout with no job; a pregnant, unbelieving wife who resented me; and my future in ministry lying crumpled at my feet. My parents felt heartsick about the sin in my life, but you know they never condemned me.

"My father-in-law got us an apartment, paid for my flight time so I could get my commercial license, and financed my charter service." His tone became sarcastic. "He wanted to ensure that Clarissa would be supported in the manner to which she was accustomed.

"I thought if I just loved her enough, everything would be OK." His voice cracked. "But it never was." He ran his hands through his hair. "She hated me and blamed me for the pregnancy. She resented the kids. Right after Abby was born, she started seeing other men, and I never touched her again.

"God is a just and angry God. I know I deserved everything she put me through. I can't count the times during my childhood that my dad told me every choice has a consequence, and I'm certainly living proof of that."

A heavy sigh indicated that he'd reached the end of his unhappy tale. Korby waited a moment, then said gently, "But God is also a loving, forgiving God, Harrison. Yes, we live with the results of our choices, but we can go on to bear fruit for our Father. Look at the apostle Paul. God can still use your life if you'll let him."

"Always the optimist." Harrison smiled a tired, defeated smile. He rose from his desk chair. "I think I'll call it a night. I'll walk you out. Can you be here about six in the morning? And don't expect me for dinner. I'll have a lot to catch up on."

Korby nodded and led the way to the guesthouse. His chivalry touched her.

She couldn't understand why women, including Karly, hadn't been interested in Harrison. Korby herself had had a crush on him once upon a time. He'd always been too serious—maybe that had scared them off. He had a way of looking at a person with those light brown eyes of his that made one feel like a bug under a microscope, but truthfully she found him endearing. She'd always thought Harrison quite handsome. He was tall and lean. His strong, square jaw spoke of determination, and she loved the creases in his cheeks when he smiled. How could any woman in her right mind not find him incredible? And the tender man inside made him that much more so.

He stopped at the edge of her porch. "Good night, Korby. Don't forget to lock up."

"I won't. Thanks." He waited until she was inside before he walked the short distance to his own back door.

Korby sighed, looking out the window at the main house. Harrison was carrying so many burdens. She would ask God to send a wonderful woman to love him, someone who deserved him.

Coming downstairs after changing out of his church clothes, Harrison smelled rolls warming in the oven. Korby had started making most of their bread during the weeks she'd been with them. He could hardly believe it had been more than two months already.

The summer was flying by in a comfortable routine, and already August was upon them. Korby was fitting into the family perfectly. She ran the house in an orderly fashion, cooked delicious healthy meals, and made his heart trip over itself every time she smiled at him. Harrison found himself more in love with her each day.

The kids rarely mentioned Clarissa anymore. She hadn't been a hands-on mom like Korby. Clarissa had sent them to day care and play groups to get them out of her hair. But Korby—Korby spent almost all her time with the children, and their little faces showed how much they adored her.

Mrs. Coppersmith seemed content with her Saturday visitation schedule, which gave Korby an afternoon off each week. His mother-in-law made no more mention of custody, though he often wondered if she was waiting to drop another bomb. He tried not to worry but prayed instead.

As he entered the kitchen, the scene before him was so domestic, so tranquil. Korby was adding her poppy-seed dressing to a pasta salad. Her hair was swooped up off her neck in casual fashion. He longed to wrap his arms around her waist and kiss the back of her neck, the way he'd seen his dad do to his mom at least a thousand times while she stood working at the kitchen counter.

He'd been working hard at being aloof and withdrawn, even though sometimes he just wanted to enjoy Korby's company. He knew his hot and cold moods baffled her, but he couldn't help himself. Some days it was so wonderful just to be with her, he couldn't bring himself to withdraw. Today was one of those days. Still, realizing the direction his thoughts were going, he had second thoughts. But before he could turn to leave, he heard Abby beckon him.

"Daddy, look! Me and Benjy set the table."

"I see that, sweetheart." He didn't see at all. His eyes never left Korby. She'd turned to greet him, and her smile mesmerized him. He'd never forget how beautiful she looked, not in the sophisticated way of Clarissa, but in a pure, natural way.

"You hungry?"

He nodded, wondering how Korby would feel if she knew his heart beat only for her. Probably repulsed. He must seem ancient to her.

"Have a seat. It's almost ready."

After Benjy took his turn to say grace, Korby started the conversation flowing as she served each plate. "Do you realize that in a few weeks our Mr. Benjamin will be starting kindergarten?"

Our Mr. Benjamin? "So he will." Harrison smiled at his firstborn. "I still remember my first day of school. I had to tell the class my name, my favorite color, and what I did for summer vacation." Poor Benjy had had no vacation—what would he share? Harrison didn't take time to weigh his next suggestion—which he normally did.

"Korby, let's take the kids and go somewhere this afternoon." Her stunned gaze caused him to smile. "We could all use a minivacation. I know of a perfect spot for a picnic and a day away. The kids and I went up there for the Fourth of July last year. You'll love it. What do you say?"

"I say *bon voyage.* How soon do I pack the picnic basket?"

"Do you want to go right after lunch and have a picnic dinner on the Cumberland River?"

Korby shot a perplexed look in his direction. "This isn't like you. You're never spontaneous. Are the cops after you or something?"

"No, just my conscience for neglecting my kids much of the summer."

"OK. I'll throw something together as soon as we're done eating. Can you give me an hour?"

"You've got it. I'll get the kids ready."

As they were walking out the door an hour later, Korby was surprised when Harrison asked, "Would you bring your guitar?"

"My guitar?" Surely she had misunderstood his request.

"I thought you could serenade us later this afternoon." He smiled sheepishly at her.

"OK, sure." She hadn't even known he liked her guitar playing.

The kids took their afternoon nap during the drive to Clarksville. Korby pulled out her book and started reading. After about half an hour, she closed it to rest her eyes.

"What are you reading?"

"*Reunited.* It's an anthology about couples who meet again after years apart."

"Love stories?" He sounded cynical.

Korby nodded, feeling embarrassed.

"Surely you don't believe in that happily-ever-after stuff?"

She raised her chin a degree. "Surely I do." Her voice held a defensive edge. Riding the roller coaster of his moods sometimes exhausted her. She kept reminding herself that he was grieving and that this too would pass.

"Let me assure you, there are no men like those men. There is no love like that love, and *nobody* finds endless, eternal happiness."

"I will in heaven, if not before." *As for men like that, living with you is sufficient evidence to prove you're right.* "Harrison, I'm sorry you got a raw deal, and I'm sorry your heart's been broken, but most of all I'm sorry that you may never find love again because you don't believe it exists. You'll never give God or yourself a chance to find her, wherever she is.

"But I know that kind of love is real. I see it in my dad's eyes every time he looks at my mom, and do you know what else? I'm really tired of playing emotional volleyball with you. One minute I'm your best friend. Then without warning, I'm suddenly the enemy. You're either warm and tender or distant and rude. I'm tired of paying for Clarissa's mistakes. I should have stayed home today and let you and your kids picnic alone."

After a moment of stifling silence, he asked, "Are you through?"

She nodded, expecting him to rip into her regarding respect for your boss.

"Is that all you need to say?" He'd pulled over to the side of the highway and stopped. Was he mad enough to drop her off?

"Yes. I'm sorry—"

"Shh." His quiet voice continued, "Korby, I'm the one who's sorry." She heard deep emotion in his voice, and her eyes were drawn to him. "None of my struggles are your fault. Please forgive me for taking them out on you." The regret on his face brought a lump to her throat. She reached out and wrapped his hand in hers.

"Harrison, I love you." Her heart lurched at her own words. A deep sadness etched itself on his face. His penetrating eyes held hers. Many emotions played across his face before a tenderness settled there.

"And I love you." For one brief moment, Korby thought Harrison might kiss her. Even more surprising, she found herself wishing he would. The spell was broken when he smiled and said, "My almost little sis."

"Yes—your little sis." She released his hand, and he pulled back onto the freeway. She must have imagined the whole kiss thing. What did she know about kissing anyway? No one had ever kissed her. Maybe no one ever would.

Harrison closed his eyes briefly before pulling out onto the freeway. His feelings for Korby had absolutely nothing to do with brotherly love. Maybe it was time to find other child-care arrangements. How much longer could he share his life with her, love her, and remain immune to her? *Immune to her—what a joke!*

That's it. They'd spend a wonderful day together, and then he'd run an ad for a new nanny. Preferably someone over sixty. Making the decision helped him relax. He could do this. A few more weeks with the most perfect woman he'd ever known. She was right that happily-ever-after love probably did exist, but he had given up the right to it himself when he married Clarissa.

When they arrived at the Cumberland River Walk, Korby proclaimed, "This is wonderful!" She sent him a smile that was even more wonderful.

"You ain't seen nothing yet. Wait until we take the *Queen*

of Clarksville for a sunset river excursion. I think you'll love it."

The day passed in perfection. They walked along the River Walk. By dinner they had found the perfect picnic spot. After dinner, Korby strummed her guitar, and they sang the kids' favorite Sunday school songs. Then they wandered back to the car and stowed everything away before boarding the *Queen of Clarksville.*

They found a spot on the upper deck, and Korby leaned against the rail with her back to the sun, watching Benjy and Abby. They stood a few feet away, looking over the rail, singing "Row, Row, Row Your Boat."

"Turn around," Harrison instructed.

"Oh, Harrison!" She gazed at the view he'd wanted her to see. The sun was setting low in the sky, and the river resembled liquid fire.

He went to stand close behind her, and when she turned back, the sun glimmered off her hair. Of its own accord, his hand reached out, touching the strands of silk. His fingers intertwined themselves in her caramel locks. Her eyes met his in a half-afraid, half-inviting look.

"Korby." Her name came out sounding hoarse and raspy.

As he lowered his head to taste the sweetness of her lips, he fought an inner battle. One voice taunted, *Are you crazy?* Another said, *Once, just this once, know how it feels to hold her in your arms. Then you can send her back to California.*

CHAPTER SIX

The view from the boat was incredible, but Harrison's kiss drove every other thought from Korby's mind. The kiss was gentle and tender and everything she had dreamed a kiss would be. When it ended, he loosened his hold on her. His eyes were warm and soft; a slight smile touched his lips. "You're so beautiful," he whispered, and once again his hand found its way back to her hair. Somehow Korby knew there was a *but* coming. She sensed him withdrawing from her. *Was the kiss that bad?* From her point of view, it had seemed perfect.

"Korby, kissing you was a mistake."

How could he label the most incredible moment of her life a mistake? She stepped away from him and swallowed hard. Tears of disappointment welled up in her eyes. She had to get away before they fell. She bolted for the bathroom on the lower deck. He called her name, but she kept going until she was safely locked inside.

The storm began, and the tears flowed like rain from heaven. What had gone wrong? How could she ever face him again? Finally, the raging sobs calmed to a deep ache.

Korby realized that somewhere along the path of mothering Harrison's children, praying for him, and encouraging him, she'd begun to love him—not as a friend, nor as a sister, but as a woman loves a man. She loved him with a deep love that had grown from friendship, respect, and admiration. She loved his children fiercely, too.

"Korby?" Harrison knocked on the bathroom door. "Can we talk?" Her face heated up as she thought about how this must look to him, her pining away in there because he had rejected her.

"Later." She hoped her voice sounded normal.

"OK. The kids and I will be on the upper deck when you want to join us."

"Thanks."

"Well . . . see you later." She heard the uncertainty in his voice.

Korby waited a few minutes, then found a seat on the lower deck in a dusky corner. The sun was gone now, but the remnants of its light remained—just as his kiss was over, but the memory of his lips lingered. Everything between them would be different now. Her heart ached with that reality.

Harrison stood at the edge of the deck, listening to Abby and Benjy giggle about something. What was it about kids and life? He smiled, wishing he felt as carefree as those two. Boy, had he made a mess of things with Korby.

His smile lingered, remembering the kiss they'd shared only an hour ago. He could have gone on kissing her forever; instead, he cautiously kept it short. He closed his eyes, cherishing the memory of it—very sweet, just like Korby. A tenderness flooded his heart for this precious woman. Guilt followed on its heels as he pictured her stricken look when he had callously declared that kissing her was a mistake.

Shame filled him at the recognition of his own selfishness.

He had wanted to hold her and kiss her, just this once, with no regard for what it might do to her. Why didn't he stop to think about how she might feel after he carelessly tossed her aside?

He hadn't thought it through at all. When she had looked at him with such hope as the kiss ended, he knew he'd made a grave mistake. He had a habit of making grave errors when it came to women. Now Korby sat locked in the bathroom, crying her eyes out because of his self-indulgence. Would he never learn?

Only the light of the moon now lit the night. How could he ever make things right with Korby? The irony in all this was that holding her once had only increased his desire to hold her again. Now it would be that much harder to resist her.

Somewhere along the way, Korby had become the sole bright spot in his life besides his kids. Somewhere along the way, he'd fallen head over heels in love with her. He found himself wanting her with all his heart, yet knowing he must deny himself, even if she wanted him, too. He could never have Korby McCoy as his own. His mistakes with Clarissa made it impossible.

Korby and Clarissa were complete opposites in almost every way. He saw in Korby everything he wanted in a wife and in the mother of his children. Everything he wished he'd waited for. He wondered what kind of woman God might have brought him if he'd waited for just the right one. Maybe it would have been Korby.

Korby finally rejoined Harrison and the kids just as the boat was docking. She avoided his eyes. She felt so embarrassed by her behavior. The ride home was a silent, uncomfortable affair. At last she was locked away in the guesthouse, away from his probing eyes. She headed straight for the shower, hoping to wash away the pain of the day.

After her shower, wearing a bathrobe, her hair in a towel, Korby stood facing the mirror. How could she have ever thought someone like Harrison—a man attracted to beautiful women like Clarissa—could fall in love with someone as plain as she was? She'd long ago come to terms with the fact that she was the least of the McCoys, least in looks and least in ambition.

Korby examined herself in the mirror, comparing what she saw to the memory of Clarissa's portrait. Clarissa appeared sexy and sassy; Korby looked wholesome, like the girl next door. They both had long hair, but Clarissa's was blonde and styled with sophistication. Korby's hung straight, brown, and boring. Both women were thin, but Clarissa had curves that Korby could only dream of. Clarissa's full pouty lips invited a man's kiss.

Korby sighed, realizing this comparison was only making her feel worse. Nothing about her could compete with Clarissa—not her looks, not her figure, and certainly not her knowledge regarding men.

She didn't want to be like Clarissa per se, but she wished she possessed some of her assets. Then maybe Harrison would fall in love with her. She sighed again. *Oh well. If I die an old maid, at least I can say I've been kissed. And it was an enjoyable kiss—a tender, chaste kiss.* She fell asleep dreaming of her one kiss.

When Korby awoke, the sky still held the hues of early morning. The day lay still and quiet before her. She threw on jeans and a sweatshirt, then grabbed her Bible. The front-porch rocker invited her to come and meet with God there. After brushing her hair and teeth, she did just that.

Korby turned to the Psalms, a place in the Bible she often went when life dealt her hard blows. The rejection of the man she loved felt devastating. Finding Psalm 91, she began to read, "Those who live in the shelter of the Most High will find rest in the shadow of the Almighty. This I declare of the Lord: He alone is my refuge, my place of safety; he is my God, and I am trusting him."

"Lord," she whispered into the stillness of the day, "help me to trust you. I feel angry that you won't give me the desire of my heart. All my life I've wanted a husband and a family, and here is one that needs me. I love him, Lord. Why can't he feel the same way about me?"

Korby shut her Bible and pulled her knees up to her chest, resting her chin on them. She looked over at the main house, wishing the deep ache in her heart would stop. "Korby?" She jumped as Harrison's voice broke the quiet surrounding her.

He must have been out walking because he was coming from the opposite direction of the house. She watched him take a seat on the top porch step. She noticed that he was carrying the baby monitor so he could hear the kids if they awoke. "About that kiss—"

"That silly, meaningless mistake. Don't think about it again. It meant nothing to either of us." Her shrill voice belied her words.

"Is that how you really feel?"

With his eyes boring into her soul, how could she lie? "No." She looked away from him and back toward the house.

"That's not how I feel, either."

"It's not?" The tenderness in his voice caused hope to soar, and she looked at him, puzzled. He reached out and took her hand, gently stroking her thumb with his.

"Korby, I think you're the most terrific woman who walks

on the face of the earth." She could hear the unspoken *but* hanging between them again. His eyes roamed over her face, and she knew he was just letting her down easy.

He sighed and continued, "The kiss was a mistake because I'm way too old for you."

"It's not like I'm still in first grade and you're in ninth. We're both adults now." *Why am I arguing?* She knew by the set of his jaw that his mind was made up. Besides, she wasn't going to beg him.

"Not in age but in living. I've made too many mistakes, and you haven't made enough—not that I want you to. It's just that . . . you deserve someone who's led a pure life like you have. Somebody's out there waiting for you. Find him, and never let him go." His voice cracked with emotion.

At that same moment the monitor came to life with the sounds of movement and voices of waking children. "I've got to go." He brought her hand to his lips, kissing it. His gaze begged her to understand. "I once settled for the wrong person. I don't want you to make that same mistake." She watched him trudge toward the house through tear-blurred vision.

Was he the wrong person? He felt so right. . . .

Their week went from bad to worse. By the following week, the strain was wearing on them both. Korby didn't believe Harrison's declarations about how wonderful she was and that she deserved more. Convinced that he was only trying to let her down easy, she felt distance growing between them. The easy camaraderie disappeared, and being together proved difficult.

As the next week progressed, they spoke less and less until not at all. What a disaster one kiss could bring. Soon Korby would be returning home—Harrison had informed her that he was searching for a new nanny. The thought of leaving Abby and Benjy was so painful that she wondered if she could really leave.

When supper duty ended each evening, Korby shut herself away in her little house. One evening she lifted the phone to call home, aching to talk to people who loved her.

"Mrs. Coppersmith, my lawyer will be in touch!" Harrison slammed the phone down in her ear. Then Mrs. Coppersmith called him a name and banged her phone down. Korby felt guilty for innocently intruding into this private conversation.

She quietly laid her receiver back in its cradle. Moments later a banging brought her to her front door.

"Korby?" Harrison's impatient voice sounded from the other side of her door. "May I see you in my office?" *Is he going to yell at me for eavesdropping?* When she opened her door, he was already gone. She found him sitting at his desk, tapping a pencil against his light.

"I'm sorry. I didn't realize you were on the phone." She decided to take the initiative and clear the air.

"What?" His puzzled expression showed that he had no idea what she was talking about.

"Nothing. What did you want?" Her voice sounded abrupt, even though she hadn't intended it to.

He drew his lips together in a tight line. She saw the struggle on his face and wished she'd been kinder. "I need you." He let out a long sigh, rubbing the back of his neck. The weariness in his expression grabbed hold of her heart.

"What do you mean?" she asked softly, refusing to even consider where this conversation might go.

"Mrs. Coppersmith has filed a private petition to adopt Benjy and Abby."

"What? Is that legal?" At his nod she continued, "How can she do that? I don't understand."

"Apparently anyone can file. It doesn't mean she will get them, but I'm in for the fight of my life. I'll be investigated. Our lives will be disrupted. In the end, a long court battle will ensue, and a judge will decide who raises my children."

Terror struck Korby's heart. She swallowed the raw fear threatening to choke her. *What if Mrs. Coppersmith wins? What if she takes his children?* Korby couldn't stand that thought or the thought of Harrison without them. Her gaze found his; his expression echoed her concerns. His eyes mirrored her own fright.

"I need you to stand beside me through this ordeal. I know I'm asking a lot, considering how awkward things are between us. I'm sure you want nothing more than to get out of here ASAP and back to California, but will you think about making peace with me? I need you."

His eyes begged her to stay, to forgive the kiss and the rejection that had followed it. She knew she'd do anything for him. She loved him. She loved his kids. Nodding her agreement, she said, "I'll stay as long as you want me to, but can we somehow go back to the way things used to be?"

"We'll try. We'll both work hard toward that goal." His gaze made her heart beat a little faster and ache a little stronger. "Korby, thanks. I don't deserve you or how good you are to me. I do appreciate it, though."

She longed to hug him but didn't. She sat glued to her seat, hoping they could attain their new goal of being cordial to one another. *God, please get us through this, and please don't let Mrs. Coppersmith take the kids from Harrison.*

The phone rang, jarring her out of her prayer. "Hello. . . . Hello, sir. . . . Yes, she's well and right here as a matter of fact. . . . Sure, one moment please." To Korby, he said, "It's

242

your dad." Harrison handed her the receiver and left the room, closing the door behind himself.

Korby felt relieved to have an excuse to escape him. "Daddy!" she spoke into the phone as the door closed. After she updated him on her life, her dad asked if everything was all right.

Korby paused, uncertain how to answer. "No." Her voice cracked, and tears began a slow descent down her cheeks. Then the truth poured out like a river over a dam. "Daddy, I've fallen in love with Harrison."

"How does he feel about you?"

Korby told her dad the whole story, knowing he'd have wise advice for her. He always did. "I don't understand this whole 'God will give you the desires of your heart' concept."

"Korby, recite Psalm 37:4," her dad patiently instructed.

" 'Take delight in the Lord, and he will give you your heart's desire.' "

"You're so focused on your heart's desire that you are completely forgetting the most important part. Are you delighting in the Lord, Bear? Is he your reason to smile? Or are you too busy wanting your own way to delight in him?"

As always, her dad had nailed it. He was her spiritual coach. When Korby faced problems, her dad gently provided guidance to steer her back to the right path. "I can't remember the last time I've truly delighted in just being a child of God. Thanks, Dad. I'll focus on him and how wonderful he is instead of how lousy I think my life is."

"I'll be praying for you, and so will Mom. We'll pray for Harrison, too. Now you go spend some time delighting and sleep tight, Bear."

"'Night, Daddy. I love you."

She felt better already. She walked back to the little house she was beginning to think of as hers, got out her Bible, and read Psalm 37. Verse 5 reminded Korby: "Commit every-thing you do to the Lord. Trust him, and he will help you." She got out her journal and wrote, "Delight in him. Trust him." She read on. In verse 7 she found another challenge: "Be still in the presence of the Lord, and wait patiently for him to act." She confessed that she'd been anything but pa-tient in her desire for a husband.

Lord, teach me to delight in you and to stop fretting over my fu-ture. I know in my heart that your plans are best, and, Lord, I want a man like my dad—a man who will lead me closer to you.

CHAPTER SEVEN

Harrison needed Korby now more than ever. That thought scared the life out of him. Needing her was neither safe nor sane. Avoiding her, sending her back to California made more sense, but he found himself in a predicament where that proved impossible.

He had barely slept last night. He called his lawyer at home and scheduled an appointment first thing this morning, but that was still hours away. He spent much of the night searching Scripture for hope and truth. Korby had once told him she loved to read the Psalms when she needed hope and assurance. He found a great deal of comfort in Psalm 18.

Grabbing his Bible off the nightstand, he turned there once again. Verse 1 he now knew by heart: "I love you, Lord; you are my strength." He did love the Lord, always had. That's why his guilt weighed more heavily than he could bear.

He remembered back to a time when, as a young boy, he'd made a childhood commitment to Jesus Christ. Karl McCoy had spoken of how sin separated people from God, but Jesus was the bridge that overcame the gap of sin. In his little-boy heart, he knew he'd done wrong things and needed to ask Jesus to forgive him and come into his life to help him make better choices. He had done so that very day.

Now he cried out to God again. *Lord, be my strength as I meet with my lawyer. Give me strength to treat Korby with kindness and gentleness yet not give in to my feelings for her. Give me strength to get through the months ahead as I fight for my children.*

As he read the rest of the psalm, he found peace and hope in the words penned by David. Verse 19 nearly jumped off the page at him: "He led me to a place of safety; he rescued me because he delights in me." Harrison's vision blurred as he read it again. *"He rescued me because he delights in me"!*

In that moment truth became clear. God delighted in Harrison Jorgenson. Not only had God forgiven him and removed his sins as far as the east is from the west, but God delighted in him! Harrison found himself weeping before the almighty and most holy God. The weight of the past fell away as he realized that God loved him just as much as he had before Harrison sinned with Clarissa.

Harrison rose from his knees, not only feeling loved by God for the first time in years, but also knowing, as he knew his own name, that this whole mess with Mrs. Coppersmith and with Korby would work out. He had the assurance that God would walk through this battle with him and rescue him—just as he had done for David a few thousand years before.

Harrison was late getting home that evening. He called to let Korby know that he'd miss dinner but that he'd like to see her in his office at nine o'clock to fill her in on his meeting with the lawyer. He found her waiting there for him.

"Did you eat?" Korby asked.

He smiled, noting how well she cared for him. "More or less." He settled behind his desk and loosened his tie. He felt exhausted. Korby looked weary, too.

"Can I get you something?"

"Maybe after we talk." He sighed, rubbing the back of his

neck. "The lawyer assured me that they don't have a case, but we still have to go through the motions."

"Meaning?"

"We'll have to face interviews, investigations, and a judge. They may assign a CASA, a court-appointed special advocate, for the children. That person will spend time with the kids and evaluate their home life. It's very important that the court see a stable environment, which is why I need you to stay. It may not look good if they are on their second nanny since their mother died three and a half months ago."

Korby nodded her agreement. "I understand."

"I hope you and I can be adult enough to put our problems and hurts aside. I take full responsibility for all of it, and—" *regret kissing you more than you'll ever know*— "wish we didn't have to deal with all this awkwardness along with Mrs. Coppersmith."

"We'll just force ourselves to get back to normal. If we act like everything is OK, hopefully it soon will be. Come in the kitchen, and let me fix you a sandwich or something." Korby rose and led the way. "So, tell me when and how you knew you wanted to be a pilot." He knew she was searching for a safe and easy topic to keep the conversation comfortable.

He followed her into the kitchen, grabbing a stool at the counter while she fished through the refrigerator. "I was seven years old. I'd always been fascinated with birds, kites, and planes. It was a lazy, hot African day. I was lying on my back looking up into the sky, watching the birds overhead, and I knew. I knew I wanted to be up there with them, not a spectator from the ground."

Korby set a ham sandwich in front of him. "Why can't *I* know? I think and think, and there's nothing I want to be except—" Her cheeks grew red. "Sorry, not a good subject.

Enjoy your sandwich; I think I'll hit the sack." She made a beeline for the back door.

Except a wife and mother. It must seem cruel to Korby that he could offer her those dreams but didn't. "Lord," he whispered, "please help her to understand that I'm not the answer to her quest. She may have a little crush on me, but I'll pale in comparison when she meets the man of her dreams." When she did meet that man, he knew his heart would break into a million pieces.

Coming from Southern California, Korby found autumn to be a wonder. She and the kids were in the front yard raking leaves one afternoon when Harrison unexpectedly came home early from work. The kids ran to greet him, and Korby longed for the freedom to run to him as well.

While life had returned to a semblance of normalcy, Korby knew she had been placing walls between herself and Harrison. She guarded her thoughts, words, and actions, no longer feeling free to be open with him. She noticed that Harrison also treaded carefully, avoiding any sort of intimacy. He kept conversations light and made sure he didn't touch her, even accidentally. His eyes looked into hers less and less.

His face looked more relaxed than she'd seen it since before their kiss. He smiled at her, something he rarely did anymore. That was all it took for her heart to respond; of its own volition, it gave a little jolt. She smiled back, watching him and the kids walk toward her.

"Great news!" he said, waving an envelope in the air. "I couldn't wait to tell you." He looked so handsome that her heart melted into a puddle at her feet. She waited in anticipation.

Suddenly he picked up Benjy and gently tossed him into

the pile of leaves. He grabbed Abby and followed suit. They both screamed in delight.

"Everything on our case has come back with glowing reports! The lawyer feels confident all this nonsense might end by Christmas."

"That's great," she replied—but her voice sounded flat. She watched as he tossed the kids back into the leaves. Her heart had soared with his words *"I couldn't wait to tell you."* Then it had plummeted when she heard *Christmas*. Only a couple of months from now, and she might be leaving them forever.

Suddenly Harrison lifted her off the ground. Laughing, he spun around and dropped her into the leaf pile next to the children. The kids squealed, jumping on top of her. Whenever they tried to escape, Harrison threw them back down. Finally, Korby and the kids ganged up on him, pulling him into the pile with them.

As Harrison pushed Korby over, she somehow managed to pull him down into the leaves with her. Time lapsed into freeze-frame as she lay on her back with Harrison's face close enough to feel his breath on her cheek. He lay on his stomach right next to her.

Korby watched as a kaleidoscope of emotions flickered across his face. Her heart beat faster, and she swallowed hard, anticipating what might follow. He looked at her the same way he had on the riverboat, and just like before, she longed to be in his arms with his lips touching hers. She felt certain he wanted the same thing, though he made no move in that direction.

Why was she doing this? A moment of pleasure wasn't worth the days of pain and rejection that would follow. "I need to go make dinner." Her voice sounded husky. He jumped up, pulling her to her feet. He began to pick leaves from her hair and the back of her sweatshirt.

"I got most of the bigger pieces," he told her a moment later.

"Thanks." Their gazes seemed locked together. Korby felt that they both had things on their mind, words they longed to say, but neither said them. "I'll call you when it's ready."

"What?"

"Dinner. I'll let you know when it's ready."

It was his turn to swallow hard. She walked toward the house. Once inside, Korby leaned against the counter, closing her eyes. Maybe leaving by Christmas was a good thing. Her emotions couldn't take the ups and downs of sharing life with him.

Lord, help me to remember that whatever my future holds, it's the delighting in you that counts, not my own desires.

"We reraked your piles of leaves," Harrison told Korby when he came in later. "You know, I don't expect you to clean the yard. I'll do it on the weekends."

"I did it for fun." At his astonished look, she explained. "We don't have a fall to speak of in L.A., so it's all new and wonderful. You'll see what I mean when we're there for Thanksgiving, and you'll have a new appreciation for raking leaves."

He laughed. "You seem to find pleasure in the smallest things. That's really nice. I hope the kids learn that from you. Speaking of the kids—Abby's birthday is coming up. What do you think we should do?"

She loved this *we* stuff. "I think we should ask her. After all, it is *her* birthday. What did you do for Benjy's birthday last spring?"

"Nothing. Clarissa wasn't big on giving parties for the kids."

"Why don't we do a joint party? Abby will be four, and Benjy will be five and a half."

After a family meeting, Korby took charge of the party. She needed something to think about besides Harrison. Since neither child had ever had a birthday party before, having a joint party seemed most logical. She jumped right in and enjoyed the planning more than the kids did.

The day of the party arrived, cool but sunny. Korby had hired a clown, and he brought a pony. Friends from preschool and kindergarten came with presents and smiles. Everything seemed perfect until Mrs. Coppersmith arrived. She cornered Korby in the kitchen.

"Well, well, well, aren't you the perfect little hostess?" It sounded like a compliment, but Korby knew by her tone of voice that it was anything but. Mrs. Coppersmith raised a disapproving eyebrow as she spoke, and the smile on her lips came nowhere near her hate-filled eyes. Korby sensed a tongue-lashing awaiting her. *Lord, please send Harrison or someone to rescue me.*

"Hello, Mrs. Coppersmith. I'm glad you could come," she said to the woman in front of her.

"You may fool others, but I see right through your little charade."

"I beg your pardon?" Fear rose in Korby's heart. Unused to dealing with people like this, she wanted to run.

"You heard me. The good-little-preacher's-daughter act doesn't work with me. I know what you're about. You think you can come in here and make my grandchildren forget their mother. They come to my house, and it's *Korby this* and *Korby that*. Why, they never even mention their own mother! But I won't let them forget her."

"I'm sorry. That was never my inten—"

"You say that, but I'm not buying it. You're trying to worm your way into their hearts to win their father's affection. That will never happen! You don't have the sophistication, figure, or beauty to captivate a man like Harrison. Oh, he may toy with you briefly, but he'll never settle for someone like you. And I don't think you should throw yourself at him in front of the children."

"What?!" Korby was trying not to let the woman affect her, but she felt her chest getting tight. "I most certainly have never—"

"They told me about the riverboat ride." Korby felt her face grow hot. "How you kissed him, and he told you it was a mistake, and you ran to the bathroom—"

"Mrs. Coppersmith!" Harrison's angry voice broke into her rendition of their disaster. "Please leave immediately. You are no longer an invited guest."

Korby saw his jaw pulsating. She hung her head in shame, mortified that the kids had witnessed and described that scene.

"You don't think that will shine an interesting light on Miss McCoy's character when she stands before the judge?" Mrs. Coppersmith had turned around and now addressed Harrison.

"I asked you to leave."

As she sauntered toward the exit, Mrs. Coppersmith added one last taunt. "She is only using your children to become bedfellows with you. Don't be fooled, Harrison! She wants your money and your home, not your children."

If Korby could have disappeared at that moment, she gladly would have. She leaned against the counter, not having the strength to hold herself up. Suddenly Harrison's arms were around her. His gentleness broke the dam holding her tears at bay.

"Korby, I'm so sorry," he whispered near her ear. "Oh, baby, I'm so sorry." She felt him place a tender kiss near her temple.

"Why? Why does she hate me?"

"She hates *me*. Hurting you gets to me." He held her a moment longer. "We have a yard full of kids. I'll take over the party, and you take as long as you need." He lifted her chin. His tender eyes bored into hers. They spoke of love. He kissed her cheek before walking away.

CHAPTER EIGHT

Thanksgiving with Korby's family arrived. Harrison found himself both anticipating and dreading it. Every day the roots of his love for Korby burrowed deeper into his heart. How he'd ever find the strength to let her go, he wasn't sure, but he had to. She deserved a man who had no past to overcome.

Since the kids' birthday party, he'd treated her with a special tenderness. Seeing the hurt Mrs. Coppersmith had caused Korby, he found himself unable to continue in aloof indifference. He refused to inflict more pain upon her; she'd already experienced plenty because of her association with him.

Their flight went well. Sunny weather greeted them upon their arrival, and her dad was there to pick them up. Korby ran into waiting arms. He hugged Harrison and the kids as well.

"Karl, it's good to see you. Thank you for inviting the kids and me to share your family holiday."

"We're delighted you could join us, and we've missed this one." He smiled at Korby. "When she was at Biola, we saw her nearly every weekend. This has been a long stretch without our Bear. Her mom and I are more than ready to have you kids here for a visit, even if it's only for four days."

Entering the McCoys' home, Harrison could smell all the wonderful kitchen scents associated with Thanksgiving. He remembered at least two such holidays he'd spent in this house when he was a kid. The warmth of this family filled him to overflowing.

Soon the whole family was sitting around a huge table. After Karl prayed, he asked them all to share one thing they were very grateful to God for. Harrison sat between Karly and Abby, with Korby and Benjy across the table. His eyes constantly returned to her, and he knew there was only one answer he could give.

When his turn came, he cleared his throat. "I'm thankful for Korby and what she means to the kids and me." He watched her face darken to a reddish hue. His eyes never left hers as each person shared their heart.

"I'm thankful that Harrison found his way back to God." Korby smiled ever so sweetly. "And for each one of you." Her glance included all of them. "I've missed you. It's great to be here." He noticed that her eyes got misty.

"Yeah, I like the way you arrive after the work is done!" Karly teased.

"I say we give her dish duty," another of her sisters suggested.

"I say we give it to Harrison," Korby piped back. "He's the one who arranged the flight times."

"Yes!" All the girls agreed at once.

"Harrison and I will take dish duty, but only because your beautiful mother deserves a break." Karl smiled tenderly at his wife.

The women decided to walk to the park with the kids. "Probably afraid we'll renege," Karl joked.

Once the table was cleared and the dishwasher loaded, Karl filled the sink with soapy water to finish what wouldn't fit in the machine. As he washed and Harrison dried, the conversation turned personal.

"Harrison, I'm concerned about something, and I'll get straight to the point. What are your future plans regarding Korby?"

Harrison felt taken aback. "I'm not sure what you mean."

"My understanding was that this nanny position was temporary. Korby has worked for your family for almost seven months. I'm concerned about your children. It won't be easy for them to lose her after already having lost Clarissa."

Harrison nodded, uncertain how to answer.

Karl continued, "I'm concerned for you and Korby as well. A person would have to be blind not to see that feelings have developed."

"What do you suggest, sir?"

"I think you need to seek God's will in this, but if you and Korby don't have a future together, the sooner you make other arrangements, the better for your kids. I hope you'll forgive me for being so direct, but this can't go on indefinitely. There are too many hearts at stake." Karl's words only reinforced what Harrison already knew, and he and Korby definitely did not have a future together.

Korby slipped into her dad's study late Saturday evening. She smiled, knowing she'd find him prayerfully studying his sermon notes one last time. "I look forward to hearing you preach tomorrow. Our pastor isn't quite as good as you."

"I think you may be a tad prejudiced." Her dad graced her with his smile.

"No, just truthful." She sat in the straight-back chair across the desk from him.

"How are things between you and Harrison?"

She was glad he asked because she needed to talk things over with him and hear his advice.

"In so many ways things are perfect. I'm content. I almost think I could go on like this forever. Sometimes I feel like his wife, and Benjy and Abby feel like my kids. If this is the closest I get to having my own family, I think I can live with that."

Her dad looked concerned. "What if he meets someone else? How will you feel then? Will you be content to be the nanny if there is another woman in his life?"

She hung her head. "I see your point, but, Daddy, I know he cares about me. I can see it in his eyes."

"And he's a man. One day he'll long for a woman to share everything with, not just his kids."

His words hurt. "I wish you could see us together. He's tender and thoughtful. We have a comfortable routine. We feel and act like a family. It's all cozy and homey when we're together." With each justification, she felt her case grow weaker.

"And you're in love with him. You told me that yourself. Korby, you're playing with fire. The potential is high for at least one of you and both of the children to be badly hurt. Don't you see that?"

Yes, she did. Her gaze was teary. "I guess I hoped he'd eventually realize he loved me back and didn't want to live without me."

"Oh, honey." Her dad rose and came to sit in the chair next to hers. He took her hands in his. "My little dreamer." He smiled gently at her. "While your sisters planned and schemed, you waited and dreamed. I love that about you."

"I don't like that about me!"

"Prayerfully give those dreams to God."

"I have been delighting instead of desiring. I think that's why I'm suddenly so content with the way everything is."

"That's my girl! I just don't want you to wait too long. I'm especially concerned for the children. Abby considers you her mommy, and how does a four-year-old cope with losing two moms?" He paused, then asked gently, "Can we pray about this?" He settled on his knees in front of the chair, and Korby joined him.

"Father," he prayed, "I ask you to direct Harrison and Korby. You know each of their hearts and the plans you have for them. Give them wisdom as they seek your will for the future, and may they be mindful of Abby and Benjy and what is best for them. In Jesus' name I pray. Amen."

As they stood, Korby hugged her dad. "Thank you, Daddy." She gave him a peck on the cheek. "I love you."

"And I love you. Sleep well."

Her last night in her old room caused her to feel a little nostalgic. Abby was sharing Korby's childhood bed with her. She scooted Abby over and climbed under the sheets, cuddling the little girl against her. She stroked her finger against Abby's chubby cheek. "Tomorrow we go home," she whispered. *Home.* Somewhere along the way Nashville had become home to Korby's heart.

A lump formed in her throat as she thought of the conversation with her dad a few moments ago. He was right. She and Harrison needed either to do something permanent or to move on. The risk to the kids was too great. *Father God, please show us your plan. I love him, but he doesn't feel the same about me. I wish he did. . . .*

As Christmas drew near, Harrison and Korby shopped together, decorated together, and laughed together. She'd become his best friend. He loved being with her and couldn't imagine his life without her, but her father's words haunted him day and night.

"Don't forget we have to pick up my parents tonight. We'll need to have an early dinner," Harrison called from the foyer on his way out the door.

"I didn't forget." Korby rushed out from the kitchen, handing him his lunch sack. She reached up and straightened the collar on his coat.

He grinned down at her. "See you tonight." Once again, as he had done every morning for weeks, he squelched the desire to kiss her good-bye.

Abby and Benjy pressed their pug noses against the window, watching planes taxi down the runway. Finally Grandpa Harry and Grandma Rose arrived. After hugs were shared and luggage collected, they headed home.

"Mom, we have a surprise for you." Harrison informed his mom while unlocking the house.

"We saved the tree for you," Benjy announced proudly.

"I remembered how much you love decorating the tree, so we saved that job for you."

"Thank you. That is still my favorite part of Christmas, other than buying presents for you two," she said to Benjy and Abby. They both giggled.

Harry, Rose, and the kids started trimming the tree after the luggage was carried to the upstairs guest room. Korby went into the kitchen to fix hot chocolate, and Harrison strode toward his office to check his messages.

A few moments later he joined Korby. He knew his grin was ear to ear. "What are you so happy about?" she questioned from where she stood, leaning against the counter.

He grabbed her around the waist, lifting her off the ground and spinning her around the kitchen. When he stood her back on her feet, she swayed into him. He didn't loosen his hold.

Her face glowed with happiness. "I'm sorry. I'm suddenly feeling a little dizzy," she joked. She held on to his upper arms to steady herself.

"So am I," he whispered. *Forget her lips.* He stepped away from her, and she leaned back against the counter. "The Coppersmiths are dropping their petition. Their lawyer convinced them they are spending big bucks on a no-win situation."

"That's . . . wonderful!" Relief and worry seemed to cross her features simultaneously. "You must be thrilled."

"I am. I was hoping you would be, too." He wondered what she was thinking.

"I am."

"But . . . ?"

She turned away from him, looking out the kitchen window. *What can she possibly see? It's pitch black out there.* He heard a small sniff and turned her toward him. "Korby, why are you crying?"

"Relief."

He didn't believe her. "Please tell me what is going on."

She looked directly into his eyes for only a moment and then down at her clenched hands. "Right before this case, we both decided it was time for me to return to California. Now the case is over. . . ."

He lifted her chin. His hand remained there, resting against her neck. "I don't want you to go." His quiet voice sounded anguished. Her eyes begged him to give her a reason to stay. He raised her chin a fraction higher as his mouth found hers. He hoped this would be reason enough, for now.

There was a constant war going on within him, the war between selfishly asking her to stay versus the voice of right and reason. At this moment his selfish side won out, and he allowed himself to fall prey to her lips.

"Please don't say that was a mistake." Her eyes held a touch of fear.

He smiled at her whispered plea. "I won't." Even as he spoke, guilt welled up within him, nearly choking him. *Dear Lord, what am I doing?* He could almost hear her dad say, *"The sooner you make other arrangements, the better for your kids. . . ."*

Marrying Korby sounded like a wonderful idea. It would be the answer to his child-care problems, since the kids already loved her. Losing her would be harder than losing their own mother had been. More important, *he* loved her. He didn't want to imagine life without her. That thought brought a pang of guilt because he knew he must do the right thing for her sake.

Korby felt more confused than ever. Harrison had cooled considerably after the kiss in the kitchen. "I don't want you to go," he'd said, but he had avoided any contact with her since then. Both times he had kissed her, she had ended up feeling cheap and used because it obviously meant nothing to him. She no longer even felt like a friend.

She wanted him to love her and let the world know. She wanted him to be the first and only man to buy her roses and open his heart to her. Her dad had cautioned her that Harrison was a man and would one day need more than a babysitter for his children. He would need a woman. Had that day arrived? Why couldn't she be that woman?

After the Christmas Eve service, Korby went to pick up the kids, leaving Harrison to introduce his parents to the pastor. When she returned, she found that it wasn't the pastor they

262

were meeting but Stephanie. Korby froze in her tracks and watched from afar as jealousy raced through her veins.

Korby had watched Stephanie flirt outrageously with Harrison for months, but he'd never seemed to notice. She always sat next to him in their Sunday school class, but he basically ignored her other than giving polite answers to her questions. Now Stephanie had placed her hand on Harrison's arm, a rather forward and possessive move in Korby's mind. All four of them laughed, and Stephanie coyly shined her bright smile on Harrison.

Tonight he no longer seemed unaffected by her charm and beauty. She'd always reminded Korby a little of Clarissa. Her bleached blonde hair was styled to perfection. It hung to her shoulders, and she had a way of flipping it back with her hand, a flirtatious, attention-getting move in Korby's opinion.

Her blue eyes spoke volumes as she smiled up at Harrison. Her full lips had a sulky, seductive look to them. Harrison returned her smile. Suddenly Korby's stomach churned and her heart ached. He was on the prowl, and Korby wasn't the woman on his mind.

Finally Korby gathered her courage and approached them. She held Abby's and Benjy's hands. Harrison smiled at their approach, but it was all she could do not to glare back at him. "You remember Korby?" he asked Stephanie.

Ice blue eyes chilled Korby to the bone. "Oh yes. She's your nanny." Never before had anyone said the word *nanny* so distastefully. Stephanie turned back to Harrison and said something softly. They both laughed, leaving Korby feeling like she may have been the joke.

Rose seemed to sense Korby's discomfort. "We need to get home now, Harrison. The kids are ready to open those presents."

"Can I speak to you for just one minute in private?" Stephanie batted her eyelashes in Harrison's direction. "I'll only keep him a moment," she assured his mother. Stephanie placed her hand in the crook of his arm, dragging him away.

Korby noticed Harry give his wife a worried glance. Obviously she wasn't the only one who saw this woman as a threat. They made their way to the car, and by the time everyone was settled and buckled, Harrison had joined them. He seemed distracted.

The Jorgenson tradition was to open presents on Christmas Eve after the church service, and tonight would be no different. Korby struggled to kill the green-eyed monster roaming around in her mind. She hated these thoughts and feelings of jealousy. She couldn't quite capture the festive mood that this occasion deserved.

Abby and Benjy ripped open package after package, delighting in each new thing. Harrison opened the new Bible Korby had purchased for him. She'd gotten the New Living Translation with his name embossed on the leather cover. He appeared genuinely pleased.

The kids got her a new Christian romance novel. She glanced at Harrison, remembering their argument. "I hope you haven't read that one." Rose's voice surprised her, and she realized that Rose had purchased the gift, not Harrison. Disappointment now ebbed its way into her heart and joined the jealousy already seated there.

The last gift under the tree was to her from Harrison. Nervous anticipation filled her as she tore away the wrapping paper. She'd hoped for something personal and felt her disappointment increase when she found a couple of Christian CDs and two music books for her guitar. She wondered if his mother had picked these out as well.

"Thanks so much to all of you." She tried to fake enthusiasm but thought she sounded insincere. She couldn't even look at Harrison. "If you'll excuse me, I think I'll go call home." Suddenly very homesick for her own family, Korby gathered her things and headed to her little house. Home is where the heart is, and her heart wanted to be anywhere but in Nashville, Tennessee, with Harrison Jorgenson.

CHAPTER NINE

Harrison sensed rather than saw a change in Korby. She'd seemed disappointed in her gifts and near tears as she left the room. *What happened?* Guilt surfaced and reminded him how aloof he'd been with her since the kiss in the kitchen.

While his mom got the kids ready for bed, he cleaned up the living room, throwing away boxes, bows, and wrapping paper. He placed all the toys back under the tree. He was actually killing time until Korby got off the phone. He needed to see her tonight. When he figured he'd given her plenty of time for her conversation with her family, he went out the back door, walked over to the guesthouse, and knocked lightly on Korby's door.

"Just a minute," she called. Harrison waited several minutes before she answered. "Sorry, I was on the phone with my dad."

His heart wrenched at the sight of her. She'd been crying. Her red nose and bloodshot eyes gave her away. He reached for her to give her a hug, but she backed away. Her eyes accused him of things he didn't understand.

"What do you want?" Her crisp words left no doubt he'd made her angry.

"Korby, what's going on? What did I do?"

She glared at him. He'd never seen this side of her before. "Nothing."

He rubbed his neck. "Please don't play these childish games. Why are you angry?"

"You think I'm a child. I might as well act like one."

"I never said that. Did you not like the gift I got you?" He truly felt dumbfounded by her behavior. He was also starting to feel annoyed.

"The gift was fine. I just don't want to play your little games anymore. What did you want tonight? Another kiss? Three's a charm, you know." Sarcasm dripped from her words.

"What are you implying? I've never treated you with anything but respect." Now he was angry.

"I don't feel very respected when you sneak out here after everyone goes to bed or when you corner me in the kitchen when no one is looking. Why are you here?"

Her accusations stung. He hadn't meant to make her feel cheap. "I came here tonight—" he kept his voice quiet and calm—"because I wanted to make sure you're OK. I care about you."

"That was certainly hard to guess tonight at church or this past week."

Suddenly the light dawned for Harrison. Korby was jealous. "Stephanie means no harm. That's just her way."

"She was throwing herself at you. You didn't seem to mind much, either."

Harrison had to admit that he felt flattered by Stephanie's attention. She was a very beautiful woman and a possible diversion to get his mind off Korby. "It was harmless flirtation. Besides, I have no commitment to anyone." He knew the minute the words left his lips that they were a huge mistake.

"No, you certainly don't. Now please leave. I'm feeling

rather tired." She closed the door on his next words, and he heard her lock it. He laid his head against her door, hoping that tomorrow they could clear the air.

Korby cried herself to sleep. Morning light only made her feel worse. Between seeing Stephanie hanging from his arm and his impersonal gifts, reality hit her square in the heart. He wasn't in love with her, nor would he ever be. She was wasting her time dreaming her silly dreams.

Her heart ached. The pain was so severe that Korby wondered if she'd live through it. Part of her wasn't sure she wanted to. If not for Benjy and Abby, Korby would catch the next flight home, but they needed and loved her.

It was early in the morning, and Korby hoped everyone was still sleeping. She planned to quietly sneak into the kitchen, make coffee, and hide away in her house until mid-morning. She froze in her tracks just outside the kitchen door when voices carried to her. Unprepared to face anyone yet, she spun around to return to her private haven.

"Korby is in love with you. You can't just ignore that." Rose Jorgenson's voice spoke with empathy.

"What do you plan to do about it, Son?" Harry asked.

"I'm not right for her. No matter how much I wish things were different." His same old excuses drained any remaining hope she had left.

"Are you right for that Stephanie person?" his mom asked. Korby heard the concern in Rose's voice.

"I have no idea. Why does everyone keep bringing her up?"

"Son, she draped herself around you like a cheap suit. Any man would be flattered by such attention from a fine-looking woman, but I see too much of Clarissa in her to feel good about it. Please guard your step."

"Why did she need to speak to you alone?" Rose's voice sounded suspicious.

"She asked me to escort her to a New Year's Eve party." Korby's heart hurt more now than before.

"You told her no, didn't you?" Now she heard fear in Rose's words.

"Actually—" Harrison sounded slightly defensive—"I told her I'd call her later this week." A deep sorrow clutched Korby's heart. *Why hadn't he told her no?* "I'm trying to find a way to get my mind off Korby. Maybe dating someone else would help."

His confession didn't lessen her pain in the least. It increased it. He wanted to get over her. She quietly left the main house, silently shutting the door behind her. She whispered, "Merry Christmas, Korby," but felt anything but merry.

Harrison had to admit that life with Korby declined rapidly after his parents left. Her disposition moved from cool to frostbitten. She avoided all contact with him and was barely civil when she spoke. Her looks froze his heart. Resigned, he gave up any hope of their returning to neutral ground. He missed her and longed for the old Korby, but deep in his heart he knew their days together were numbered. Neither of them could live in this hostile environment much longer.

He decided to accept the date with Stephanie. He could barely stand to be at home anyway. He purposefully chose not to fill Korby in on his personal life. After all, it wasn't any of her business whom he spent time with; she'd just glare at him with those frosty eyes of hers anyway.

Up in his room tying his bow tie, he faced the fact that he didn't want to go out with Stephanie, never really had. Part of him wanted to hurt Korby since she so frequently elected to hurt him. He had never thought he and Korby would stoop to this level, but they both had. Now it was a competition to see who could be the meanest.

When Harrison came down the stairs wearing his tux, Korby did a double take but said nothing. Her eyes said it all for her. His date was hurting her, and he hated himself for it. He left the house feeling every bit the heel.

Stephanie greeted him in a slinky dress, a little too slinky for a Christian if you asked him. She was fun, but she wasn't Korby. As the evening wore on, he saw more and more of Clarissa in Stephanie. At the end of the night she invited him in for coffee, but he declined.

He drove down to the river and sat on the bank. As the river raged by, it matched the force of his emotions. He loved Korby, and finding a diversion wasn't working. *What now, God? What now? I love her, and I know I can't have her. Give me the courage to send her home before we end up hating each other.*

He swallowed hard, but the lump wouldn't dislodge from his throat. His eyes burned. His heart ached. When he finally forced himself to return to his car and drive home, dawn had touched the eastern sky. The first day of the new year awoke before his eyes, but he felt no joy or anticipation, only an empty, lonely ache. The silence that greeted him upon entering the house served only to increase his pain.

He longed to wake Korby from her slumber on the couch in the playroom and share his misery. He ached to see her smile, to hear her voice, to touch her hair. He paused at the entrance to the playroom on his way to the staircase, but he knew she would no longer welcome him. His legs carried his weary body up to his room.

Korby heard his key unlock the door. She'd barely slept at all, listening for him to return. Sometime during the night all her stored-up anger had drained, and all that remained was unbelievable pain. She heard his footsteps pause outside the playroom, and she wondered why.

In her mind's eye she saw him and Stephanie laughing until dawn. She pictured Stephanie, looking beautiful and sexy in a formal gown, toying with his emotions and his heart. He didn't stand a chance. Gorgeous blondes were his weakness.

Oh, Lord, if she's the right one for him, give me the grace to accept that, and if she's not, please give him the strength to walk away. I love him, Lord. I love him. Please bring healing and forgiveness between us. A lone tear rolled down her cheek, dropping onto her pillowcase, followed by another and then another.

Korby watched the clock tick away the time until it was seven o'clock in California. She'd let Benjy and Abby stay up until midnight last night to watch the ball on TV drop, so they were still sleeping. She dialed her home phone number.

"Happy New Year!" her dad's voice greeted her.

"Hi, Daddy." She couldn't match his enthusiasm.

"You OK?" Concern filled his words.

"I made a decision and wanted you to know. I'll be here six more weeks, and then I'm coming home."

"I wish you sounded happier about it. Tell me how this came about."

"You were right. I can't be just the nanny while Harrison dates other women. I can't stand to see him with anyone else. My heart is unwilling to share him. His parents are on sabbatical for this coming year. Right now they're traveling for six weeks to several missions conferences, but then they plan to settle here in Nashville for the rest of their leave. That should give Harrison plenty of time to either find another nanny or marry Stephanie."

"Stephanie?"

"A woman from church he's started dating."

"You're hurting, aren't you?"

"Yes, but you did warn me."

"I know, but being warned doesn't make it hurt any less. I love you. Call me anytime you need to, and I'll be praying extra hard for you."

"Thanks, Daddy. I love you, too, and I can't wait to come home."

"I can't wait either, Bear. Good-bye for now."

The month that followed was as icy cold inside the house as it was outside in the January weather. Neither Korby nor Harrison seemed to have the energy to be angry anymore. There were no more slamming doors, irritated glares, or enraged words. There was absolutely nothing except frigid silence—heavy, pain-filled quiet.

Harrison rarely arrived home before bedtime, so Korby assumed he spent all his spare moments with Stephanie. He often looked weary, and Korby's heart ached for him, but something invisible kept her from showing concern. Whether it was fear of rejection, pride, or self-preservation she didn't know, but she never summoned the courage to express the fact that she cared.

Korby started working in the nursery to avoid seeing Harrison and Stephanie together in Sunday school. Korby chose to work the opposite service, so she wouldn't have to sit with him in church either.

He and the kids had family outings on Sundays without her. They probably took Stephanie along. She and Harrison were polite, quiet strangers, sharing the responsibility of his children. Sometimes it hurt so much that all she could do was cry.

CHAPTER TEN

A chilly, quiet January carried over into February. Korby remained distant and untouchable. Harrison longed to clear the air but had no idea how. She spoke only in monosyllables and only when absolutely necessary. He booked more and more long flights with long layovers to avoid her as much as possible.

He and the kids had spent one Sunday at Stephanie's. She'd invited them for dinner, but no matter how badly he wanted her to be the answer to his problems, she just wasn't. The two times he dated her, New Year's Eve and the family dinner, all he could do was count the numerous ways she fell short of being Korby. Even in the midst of all this pain, he loved Korby with all his heart.

Valentine's Day was tomorrow. He'd looked at many different cards, but none of them seemed right for a noncouple who no longer spoke to one another. Maybe it was just as well he'd be away from home.

"Korby?" he called from outside the guesthouse. She no longer bid him good-bye in the mornings or handed him a lunch sack on his way out. He rarely saw her before he left for work unless the kids unexpectedly rose early.

She opened her door without speaking. Her brows lifted in

question, and in her eyes he saw a deep sadness. His heart responded with an unending sadness of its own. His arms ached to pull her close and drive all this distance between them away. Instead he clenched his fists tightly shut and held them at his sides.

"I wanted to let you know that I'll be in L.A. until Monday. Your parents invited me to stay with them, in case you need to get ahold of me. Would you mind taking the kids to church with you? I know I should have asked earlier since Sunday is normally your day off. If you can't—"

"I don't mind." Her lips quivered, and her eyes teared up. "Have a good flight." She closed her door before he could respond. They both hurt, and neither seemed to know how to comfort the other or themselves.

Harrison's flight was uneventful. Thank goodness, since his mind was a million miles away. All he could think of was Korby and those tear-filled eyes. Somehow he had to make things right between them. Somehow he had to bury the pride that kept him from reaching her. And then somehow he must find the strength to send her home.

Karl met Harrison at the Van Nuys airport. Harrison actually had three days to laze around until his return flight on Monday. Had things been different at home, he would have probably returned there for the weekend. But as things stood, he needed a break from all the tension.

Karl dropped him off at the house and had to return to his office. Kettie was gone as well, but they'd both be home for dinner in a few hours. Harrison carried his bag to his room and unpacked his Bible. An envelope addressed to him fell to the floor. He tore it open, feeling dread rising from the pit of his stomach.

Harrison,

I am resigning from my nanny position. When you return on Monday, I'll be gone. I know this is the coward's way, but I feel it's the easiest way as well. Your parents will be here when you return, and your mother has agreed to watch the children for as long as you need her to. So technically, you have nearly a year to either find another nanny or marry Stephanie.

It is with deep sadness that I leave Abby and Benjy. My heart breaks as I consider the possibility of perhaps never seeing them again. But as I'm sure you'll agree, it is with a deep sense of relief that you and I part company.

If it's OK with you, I'd like to wean Abby and Benjy slowly. I do not wish to cause them more pain than they have already experienced in their young lives. Perhaps I'll call them daily for a couple of weeks, then every other day for the next couple of weeks. Well, you get the idea. Please let me know if this is acceptable to you.

I'm not sure I understand how or why, but somehow the feelings between us have became tangled and knotted and painful. I feel I owe you an apology for letting myself become caught up in a dream that could never happen. I'm sorry for any pain I caused you, any hurtful words I spoke, and any ill feelings between us. Please find it in your heart to forgive me and to remember me as the friend I once was.

In Christ,
Korby McCoy
PS I'm so glad you found your way back to Jesus.

Harrison wiped a tear from his cheek as he finished the letter. She was leaving. She'd be gone before he got back to Nashville. He'd lost his one true love before he'd ever even had her.

He reread the letter. His heart broke at the possibility of never seeing her again, and he felt no great sense of relief like she had predicated, only an overwhelming grief washing over him. He wept harder as he read her apology a second time. "Will you remember *me* as the friend I once was? Has your heart forgiven *me*, Korby McCoy?" he asked aloud.

Dear Lord, please enable us to forgive, to move on without all this pain, and to one day be friends again. Heal our broken hearts, and somehow use this pain to lead us into a closer walk with you.

Harrison spent a couple of hours on his knees before God. He kept remembering Korby's favorite verses, Matthew 11:28-30. It was as if he heard the Father say, *Come to me, Harrison. Come to my love. There you will find rest. There you will find answers.* When he rose, he had truly laid Korby and their future at the foot of the cross, and he walked away a free man—free from the pain, the hurt, and the worry.

Harrison found Kettie in the kitchen preparing dinner. "We have a three-day conference at church starting tomorrow. The speaker, Curtis Lee, will be joining us for dinner. I think you'll enjoy him. He has a wonderful testimony."

"Sounds good." Harrison really wanted time alone with Karl. "Can I help you with anything?"

"Do you mind setting the table?"

"Not at all."

Karl and Curtis showed up a few minutes later. After introductions, they all settled around the table for Kettie's homemade spaghetti and meatballs. "Your daughter inherited your cooking skills. She's quite talented in the kitchen."

"She's the only one who enjoyed being in the kitchen with me, and also the only one of the girls capable of making much more than toast."

"Are you married, Curtis?" Harrison asked, not wanting to discuss Korby even though he had brought her up.

"Yes. Deb is God's gift to me, and he gave us three beautiful children to boot."

"You sound like a lucky man." Harrison wished Korby

could be God's gift to him, but he no longer qualified for a godly wife.

"Luck didn't have much to do with it. I'm a man living out the grace of God in his life."

"What do you mean?" Harrison's curiosity was piqued.

"Do you know the meaning of *grace?*"

"Undeserved favor?"

"That's right. Deb is God's undeserved favor in my life. And I almost passed her by because I didn't think I deserved her, which, by the way, I don't. Thankfully God doesn't give any of us what we truly deserve but showers us with blessings instead."

"If you don't mind my asking, why did you think Deb wasn't right for you?"

"I have quite a past. My goal in life was to sleep with a woman from every state in the Union. I managed over one hundred 'conquests' before I recommitted my life to the Lord. Then I met Deb. . . ." His voice cracked with the emotion he felt for her. "I fell for her fast and hard. She was a godly woman who loved Jesus with all her heart. She had no past at all. How could I even consider her for a moment? She was pure and everything good, and the only thing I was, was forgiven."

Harrison's heart began to pound. "So what changed your mind? How did you know she was God's gift to you?"

"As I read that passage in James—'Whatever is good and perfect comes to us from God above'—I knew he had brought Deb into my life to be my wife. I can't explain it, but I knew. I'd never felt more humbled than at that moment—or more loved by God. The best part of the story is that Deb considers me to be God's good and perfect gift to her. *Me!* Can you believe that?"

Harrison grinned with Curtis and shared his excitement. He knew God had a message in that story for him, too. Kettie wiped a stray tear, and even Karl cleared his throat.

After dinner Harrison took a long, prayerful walk. He realized that he had sentenced himself to a life without hope because of his past mistakes. He'd never even prayed about God's will regarding Korby. He just assumed he knew. He'd been so certain God would never give him someone like Korby but only someone who'd made as many mistakes as he had. But his heart knew, as he listened to Curtis, that Korby was part of God's plan for him.

Later that evening Harrison knocked on the door to Karl's study. "Come in," Karl called from inside.

"Excuse me for interrupting." Harrison noticed Karl's Bible lying open and a pad full of notes next to it. "Do you have a few minutes to talk?"

"Of course. What's on your mind?"

Harrison took a seat in the straight-back chair facing Karl. "I'm in love with your daughter." Karl smiled and nodded. *That's a good sign,* Harrison thought. "Until tonight I considered myself unworthy of her. Well, I still consider myself unworthy, so I'm asking for your unmerited favor in allowing me to marry her, if she'll have me. I know I don't deserve her, and I feel like I have nothing to offer her but a life of poor choices and mistakes." His vision blurred slightly as his eyes teared up. "But if you will allow me the honor, I'll cherish her always. I promise never to forget that she is an expression of God's grace in my life."

"Harrison, you have my blessing. I can think of no finer man I could have for a son-in-law." They both rose and met halfway around the desk for a hug.

"I'm leaving in fifteen minutes. I have a seat on a red-eye.

I'm too tired to fly myself, and I need to see her as soon as I can. I need her to hear my heart."

"I'll give you a ride to the airport."

Korby lay in the dark playroom, dreading another Valentineless, roseless Valentine's Day. This was her least favorite holiday. An unhappy reminder that she had no love in her life, never had, and possibly never would.

As she had shopped for cards and small gifts for the kids earlier, she made the mistake of reading some of the verses printed in the "I love you" greeting cards. They only served to remind her how alone she truly was.

God, I'm sorry. Here I go focusing on my desires again, instead of just delighting in you. Forgive me for once again forgetting. Korby fell asleep reciting all the reasons she had to be thankful.

In the early morning a noise startled her awake. When Harrison was gone, she slept lightly. She heard the sound again, and fear rose up within her. Something was rattling the front door. Grabbing her pepper spray off the coffee table, she got there just as the door creaked open.

She reached around it, blindly aiming her spray, but a hand captured her wrist. She screamed as her weapon fell to the floor.

"Korby, it's me." Harrison came around the door, and she fell into his arms. Terror robbed her strength; she felt faint. Her entire body shook with the aftermath of her fear, and she held on to him for dear life.

He whispered close to her ear, but at first nothing registered. Slowly her mind translated his words. "It's all right. I'm here, and nothing can hurt you. Shh, baby. It's OK. I promise, it'll be OK." He kissed her temple and pushed her hair back out of her face.

"What are you doing home?" Her teeth chattered as she spoke. They still stood with the door wide open.

"A change in plans. I should have phoned you. I'm sorry. I never thought about frightening you." Then he lifted her into his arms, carrying her into the living room. He sat her in a chair close to the fireplace and lit a match to get the logs going. "This will warm you up in no time. I'll be right back."

Korby closed her eyes, trying to relax. He must have come home early to spend Valentine's Day with Stephanie. *But why is he being so nice to me? The letter* . . . She heard him close and lock the front door.

Returning, he sat on the hearth, placing her feet in his lap. "Your feet are freezing." He began to rub them. She wore sweats and a sweatshirt, but her feet were bare.

"Did you find the letter I tucked inside your Bible?"

"Yes."

"Is that why you're here?"

He shook his head and smiled.

"To spend Valentine's Day with Stephanie?"

Again he only grinned and shook his head. "Why is it you think I have a thing for Stephanie? We only went on that one date, and she invited the kids and me for Sunday dinner once. That does not constitute a relationship or grounds for a marriage proposal, as your letter implied."

"Is there someone else?" She dreaded his answer but had to know.

This time he nodded, and her heart constricted. He pushed her feet aside and was on his knees in front of her chair, taking her hands in his. "She's the most beautiful woman I've ever seen, inside and out. Her lips are completely inviting." To prove his point he placed a quick kiss there. "And her father gave me his blessing—and permission to ask her to be my wife."

Korby wondered if this was a dream. Suddenly, there was

nothing but tenderness between them. "And what did she say?"

"I don't know yet." His eyes sent messages of love, and her heart leaped in joy. His voice sounded husky. "Korby—"

"Yes! She said yes!" Korby laughed.

He drew her to him. "I love you, Korby. I have almost since the day you moved into the guesthouse." He gently pushed her hair behind her ear. "I felt unworthy of someone like you, someone pure, but I couldn't stop loving you. I think that's why everything got so tangled and knotted between us—because we tried to fight the inevitable."

She smiled as he quoted her words from the letter. "I love you, too." She laid her hand against his cheek.

He pulled a long white florist's box from behind the chair and laid it across her lap. Korby smiled at him through tear-filled eyes. "This is my first Valentine's gift."

"I promise it won't be your last."

She removed the lid and folded back the green tissue. Lying there were twelve perfect, long-stemmed red rosebuds. Their heavenly scent filled her. She removed the small card from its envelope.

> *Korby,*
> *I lay my heart and soul bare before you and offer myself to you. Will you come to my love and be my love? If you'll take me, mistakes and all, I promise before God to cherish you as a gift from his hand each day of my life.*
>
> *Forever and always yours,*
> *Harrison*

She smiled at him. Gentle tears rolled down her cheeks. "Becoming your wife is the greatest privilege I have ever been offered, besides becoming a child of God. I can't believe that you chose me."

Their tears mingled as they sealed their future with a kiss. A kiss that spoke of today and forever. A kiss that reminded her to delight in the Lord, today and always. And a kiss that stated that three was definitely a charm.

A NOTE FROM THE AUTHOR

As I wrote this book, it was only natural to me that Harrison would give Korby red roses. I never considered any other possibility. After all, a red rose means *I love you*.

Then, looking deeper, I realized that this year, as Dean and I celebrate our twenty-sixth Valentine's Day together as man and wife, it's inevitable that I'll receive a dozen red roses. No wonder they have such a deep and special meaning to me, for faithfully each year my husband delivers his gift of love on Valentine's Day.

And each year, I breathe in their sweet fragrance, enjoying them every time I pass by. I touch the velvet softness of their petals. I admire their vibrant color and am amazed at how a closed bud opens itself to the light and becomes a beautiful rose.

I hope as I open God's Word and allow his light to touch my life that I, too, will bloom into a more Christlike person. Like Harrison, I have made many mistakes, and sometimes they seem too big to overcome. Then I'm reminded that Jesus is the overcomer.

This story is especially dear to me because as I spent six years working in a high school youth group, someone I cared about very much made some bad choices much like those Harrison made. My heart grieved for this teen, and in my mind, I condemned this person to a hopeless future, believing my friend had forfeited the right to a godly spouse.

Thankfully, God is much more gracious and loving than I. While attending a writer's conference in Southern California, I heard a speaker share a testimony much like the fictional Curtis Lee's. God used it to remind me of how gentle, patient, and tender he really is and to restore my hope for this precious teen. He doesn't erase the consequences of bad choices, but he certainly fills lives with undeserved favor. So if you, like Harrison, have condemned yourself to a life of hopelessness and uselessness, my prayer is that you, too, may know God's incredible, forgiving love and accept his grace each day.

Jeri Odell

ABOUT THE AUTHOR

Jeri Odell discovered a love for writing in the sixth grade and is now living her dream. As a writer, her personal goals are to exalt Christ, edify the believer, and point the unsaved to Jesus. She hopes to reach beyond entertainment and challenge women to walk more closely with the Lord.

"Come to My Love" is her second Tyndale House novella. The first appears in the anthology *Reunited*. In addition, Jeri has written greeting cards, devotionals, short stories, and articles for *Focus on the Family* and *ParentLife*. She has been happily married to her high school sweetheart for more than twenty-five years. They live in Arizona and have three grown children.

Jeri welcomes letters written to her in care of Tyndale House Author Relations, P.O. Box 80, Wheaton, IL 60189-0080.

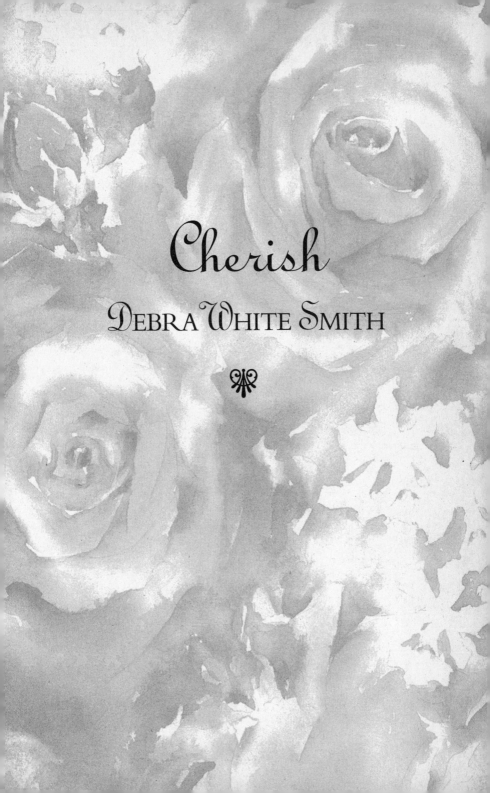

Cherish

Debra White Smith

TO MY HUSBAND, DANIEL,

who has put up with me for sixteen years.

Somebody give that man a medal!

CHAPTER ONE

Belle Anders gripped the pregnancy-test wand. Two pink stripes on the test's window meant she was pregnant. One pink stripe meant she wasn't. In one minute she would know whether her nausea was due to a virus or a baby.

Shoulders drooping, she slumped against the bathroom wall. The room's decor seemed to swirl together in streaks of mauve and gray and white.

Today she was going to leave her husband.

Joe didn't know she was leaving.

Not that he shouldn't know. Belle had tried to talk with him, share her unhappiness, but it never did any good. Eventually she built a wall between herself and her neglectful husband. Behind that wall, she still longed to be cherished. But Joe seemed more interested in his job, his sports, his own life than he was in Belle.

Now it was too late.

Belle felt as if her love had shriveled and died like a delicate rose without water.

She twisted the hem of her floppy T-shirt and wondered what she would do if the test was positive. Joe had never wanted children. Should she even tell him? Should she still leave?

Please, God, she prayed for the first time in weeks. *This is no time for a baby.*

Belle scrutinized the test wand. Two bright pink stripes marked it.

Pregnant!

As if the knowledge itself initiated another onslaught of nausea, she rushed toward the toilet and dropped to her knees. When the heaving subsided, Belle stumbled toward the kitchen.

Crackers. She had heard that crackers would ease the nausea. Belle fumbled through the cluttered white cabinets and found a box of saltines. She managed to down two of them, along with a few sips of water. The crackers covered the foul taste in her mouth, and the nausea subsided to a tolerable level.

Groaning, she rested her forehead in her hand. Belle often dreamed of a family. But not on the eve of a separation. This pregnancy must be the ultimate twist of irony.

At the very time in her life when she most needed to work, she would be out of a job. A flight attendant couldn't be sick for several months. She would surely be grounded. Belle had secretly saved some money, but it wasn't nearly enough to support herself for nine months.

Now what?

She thought of her older sister, Callie. Callie would know what to do. She had been helping Belle solve her problems since they were kids. Now Callie was a successful lawyer in Jacksonville, Texas, with a husband and two sons. Perhaps Callie would allow Belle to stay with her for a few weeks.

Jacksonville was a friendly little east-Texas town, where life unfolded with a comforting ebb and flow. Just the opposite of Dallas. Exactly the kind of solitude Belle needed. She reached for the cordless phone near the breakfast bar and punched in her sister's number.

Callie picked up on the second ring. "Hello."

Belle, biting her lips, brushed aside a warm tear. The very sound of her sister's voice made her want to burst into a fit of sobs.

"Hello . . . ," Callie repeated uncertainly.

"C-Callie?"

"Belle? Is that you?"

"Y-yes."

"Is everything OK? You don't sound like yourself."

"No. Everything isn't OK."

"Joe . . . is he sick? Has he—"

"Joe is fine." Belle glanced around the spacious living room, decorated in oriental tradition. For the first time, she wondered if she would miss the home she and Joe had built with laughter and love. But those days were over. They shared no laughs. No love. "I've got a problem, Callie. I—I—" A gulp. "I just found out I'm pregnant."

"Congratulations!" Callie exclaimed through gurgling laughter. "I didn't even know you and Joe were trying! How wonderful!"

"We weren't trying," Belle said flatly. "You know Joe has never really wanted a family."

"Oh, that doesn't matter. He'll come around. Rick did."

"But I'm leaving him today," she choked out as salty tears tickled the corners of her mouth.

"What?"

"Leaving. I'm leaving."

"But I thought you and Joe . . . You seemed so happy. . . . Even on Memorial Day when Rick and I were there—"

"It was all an act. I've been unhappy for two years and miserable for one."

"Does Joe know?"

"He should know. He's the one who's made me miserable."

"Why, Belle? What has he done? Has there been an—an affair?"

"Physically, no. Mentally, yes. He's more interested in himself and his own life than he is in me. I can't even remember the last time he told me he loved me. As a matter of fact, I don't really think he does love me." She perched on the corner of a bar stool.

"Well, does he know about the baby?"

"No. And I'm not going to tell him. Not right now, anyway."

Silence.

"I want to be gone when he comes home. I don't want to have a fight with him over this."

"But what about your job?"

"I'm so sick right now that the thought of flying makes me want to throw up again." Belle pictured herself, tall, lithe, and pale, vomiting all over first class. "I took a week off anyway to get settled into a new apartment, but if I don't work, I can't afford it. I'll just go in and see if I can arrange a leave of absence."

"And if they won't do that?"

"Then I'll quit," Belle snapped, feeling as if her sister were interrogating her on the witness stand. Why couldn't Callie leave her nit-picking questions in the courtroom?

"This isn't like you, Belle. You don't seem like yourself."

"Of course I don't. I'm pregnant, for pity's sake!" Her voice caught as a new wave of tears threatened.

"OK . . . OK . . . ," Callie soothed. "Just calm down. You can come here if you need to. The boys and Rick would love to have you."

"Good." Another sniffle. "I'm about to leave to go by the airline. After that, I'll head your way. I should be there sometime before dinner."

"I'll be waiting for you."

"And, Callie . . . don't tell Mom and Dad right now."

"Exactly how do you propose we keep it from them?" Callie said in a practical voice. "Have you forgotten how word spreads in a small town? And you sure can't hide in the closet the whole time you're here."

Rubbing her stinging eyes, Belle sighed. "I know. I just don't want to have to explain everything today. I hate to hurt them. And—" Belle hesitated. "And to tell you the truth, I don't want to have to listen to one of Mom's sermons."

"Belle!"

"I'm sorry. But that's the way I feel right now."

"All I can promise is that I won't tell them, but they'll find out—and soon."

"I know. But at least I'll have a little space."

"Well, be careful on your drive here," Callie said, her voice a troubled shadow of its former self.

"Thanks, I will."

They said their good-byes, and Belle bid farewell to her former life. She had already packed most of her clothing and personal items. The rest she would retrieve later. All that remained to be done was writing a note to Joe. Fingers trembling, Belle tore a piece of paper from the notepad hanging on the ebony refrigerator. And for the first time in a week, she felt adrift in an onslaught of doubt. Was this really what she wanted?

Perhaps if Joe would change . . . If he would only wake up and realize they had no relationship. She desperately needed affection. Someone to talk to. Honesty. To be cherished.

Joe, charmingly Latin, had gone out of his way to make her

feel special before they married. He had lovingly called her his "Southern Belle." Had he forgotten?

Perhaps Joe's problem was that he simply didn't understand Belle's needs. But she recalled three conversations in the last few months—if you could call them conversations—in which she had tried to share her unfulfilled heart. Joe either ignored her or pointedly asked her to hold the comments until after the basketball game on television. And he never even acknowledged that Valentine's Day was their anniversary. This year or last year.

She gripped the pen.

Her doubts vanished.

She knew Joe would never change.

Compressing her lips, Belle wrote her brief note. She then removed her simple gold wedding band and placed it atop the note. At once her insides twisted with a trio of conflicting emotions: relief, depression, courage. Belle had finally scraped together the strength to escape this trap Joe called a marriage, but deep inside a part of her sobbed. She had never imagined when she walked down the aisle that the man who made her feel so special would eventually come to ignore her. Belle never expected him to be Prince Charming, but she had expected him to at least invest some time and interest in their relationship.

Belle would stick to her decision to pursue a legal separation, no matter what Joe promised. He had already broken his promise to love, honor, and cherish her. Any new promises would be empty words.

CHAPTER TWO

As the unrelenting August sun stretched its blazing arms across the western horizon, Joe Anders walked from the Dallas fire station with one thought dogging him. *Flowers.* The dispatcher's husband had sent her a bouquet of red roses so large it bordered on ostentatious.

How long had it been since Joe had bought Belle flowers? He couldn't even remember.

Feeling restless, he slid into the seat of his dependable green truck. He loved its musty smell, its worn, comfortable interior. Belle used to fuss about the truck, and Joe would laughingly tell her real men didn't drive new vehicles. But Belle hadn't fussed at him about the truck, or anything else, in a long, long time.

He thoughtfully contemplated a lone male cardinal perched on the edge of the parking lot. The last couple of weeks, Joe had sensed an uneasiness in Belle. And she seemed withdrawn. Joe couldn't even remember the last time Belle had said she loved him.

Flowers. He would stop by the florist in the nearby mall and buy Belle a bouquet of yellow roses. Yellow had always been her favorite color. Perhaps a nice bouquet would solve Belle's problems.

Within an hour, Joe arrived at their north-Dallas home. As he pulled into the garage, the absence of Belle's Toyota surprised him. Today was supposed to be her day off. Maybe she had been called onto a flight. Perhaps that was part of Belle's problem. Her demanding job might be keeping her away from home more than she liked.

Using the utility-room doorway, Joe entered the kitchen. Immediately, a veil of uneasiness draped around him like a stifling pall. Something wasn't right. The house seemed more than quiet. It felt empty. Totally empty. Devoid of spirit.

At once Joe noticed Belle's wedding band lying on the white breakfast bar. He set the roses on the counter and slowly approached the ring, which was atop a note. Feeling as if he were in a slow-motion time warp, Joe picked up the ring, then the note. The words hit him like an unexpected punch in the gut.

Leaving . . .

It's over . . .

Nothing will reverse my decision. . . .

Joe's stomach clenched. His hands grew clammy. His upper lip beaded in sweat.

Trying to convince himself that he had misread the note, Joe rubbed his eyes and examined the words again. His first reading was correct.

Stunned. He was stunned.

How could Belle do this to him? Joe had supplied her with a comfortable home. He had never cheated on her. What was wrong with her?

As he stared downward, the blue kitchen tile blurred. A flood of memories washed over him. The first time Joe had seen Belle, he was flying back to Dallas after visiting his parents in Wyoming. Belle was his flight attendant. Willowy and blonde. Sunshine and joy. Joe planned to read a book on his journey, but instead of reading, he spent the whole flight making up excuses for Belle's services. Before the trip ended, every flight attendant was snickering. The next Valentine's Day, he and Belle got married.

Joe glanced toward the oversized painting hanging above the den's rock fireplace. Belle and Joe, a striking couple. Both smiling. Both aglow with love. Her fairness contrasted with Joe's traditional Latin coloring. His mother was half Hispanic. His father, Caucasian. Joe took after his mother.

The artist, in a stroke of genius, had captured the intensity of Joe and Belle's emotions. But that had been over four years ago.

In a frenzy, Joe clutched the vase of yellow roses and hurled them into the empty fireplace. "No!" he yelled as the vase shattered. "I won't let you do this to me! I have done nothing to deserve this!"

With an angry growl, he collapsed onto the garnet-colored sofa. What had gotten into that woman? This wasn't like Belle. She always seemed content in their marriage. Joe glared at the painting, at Belle's smiling face. Try as he might, he couldn't remember the last time she had smiled like that.

Perhaps she was in some kind of depression.

Joe stood and wondered if Belle would indeed stick to the separation. She had never been the assertive sort. More than likely, she would be back once she got over whatever was bugging her.

After a shower, Joe would call Belle's parents and see if she was there. He wouldn't beg her to come back by any means, but at least he would let her know he didn't appreciate her cowardly note.

After dinner, Callie dismissed everyone to the den, where she served Belle a ham sandwich. Belle had slept through dinner. Now she politely watched television with her nephews and brother-in-law while nibbling the sandwich and chips. Everyone remained conspicuously silent about Joe. Belle hoped the tense atmosphere would ease. And soon. As she rigidly sat on the sectional sofa, she felt nothing short of an intruder.

Not that Callie's home wasn't inviting. The den was a comfortable mix of plaids and beanbags and boy-worn tables. As Rick read the paper, the boys, Larry and Barry, lay on the scarlet oriental rug, which contrasted with their blue-jean cutoffs. Amidst a scattering of shoes and socks and books, they were engrossed in the Roadrunner and Wile E. Coyote.

The phone rang for the sixth time.

As she had done the other five times, Belle cringed. So far, every call had been for Callie's boys. But what about this one? Was this caller Joe?

She heard Callie's cheerful hello on the kitchen phone. Then a few muffled words. Finally, Callie, as blonde and tall as Belle, entered the den, a shadow in her gray eyes. "Telephone, Belle."

Belle swallowed hard against her churning stomach. Whoever had labeled "morning" sickness had been sorely mistaken. She had been nauseated for three days—morning, noon, and night. The more she ate, the worse the nausea. "Who—who is it?" she stammered, knowing it must be Joe. He would have read the note by now. He would be looking for her. He was most likely furious. And he probably would not accept her decision about a separation.

"It's Mom. If you like, you can take the call in Rick's office."

Rick, putting down his paper, nodded his agreement, a concerned glint in his dark eyes.

Belle relaxed against the sofa. So the confrontation with Joe was delayed. She absolutely hated confrontations. Perhaps that was part of the problem in their marriage. Belle had never been very assertive when confronting Joe with her needs. Even in recent months, her attempts at sharing her needs had been less than bold.

But now Belle faced a confrontation with her mother. She set the remaining sandwich on the coffee table, grabbed her Sprite, and walked toward the nearby office. "How did she know I was here?"

"She didn't. She just got off the phone with Joe. He thought you might have gone to Mom and Dad's. She called me to find out if you were here."

"I guess Joe told her about my leaving?"

Callie nodded.

"Great," Belle muttered.

"She's really worried." Callie placed a comforting hand on Belle's shoulder and followed her into the cluttered study. "And you would be, too."

A sigh. "I know. You didn't tell her about—"

"No. Nobody knows about the baby. Not even Rick," Callie whispered.

"I know I can't hide it forever. But I just need time to get my balance back. This has been very hard for me."

"I know." They embraced. "And I'm praying for you."

"Thanks."

Callie walked toward the heavy oak door. As she closed it behind her, Rick's concerned voice floated toward Belle. "She looks terribly pale."

Wondering how long she could hide her pregnancy, Belle nervously toyed with the hem of her University of Texas T-shirt and turned to Rick's imposing desk. She stiffly sat in the black chair, sipped her Sprite, and stared at the phone until the numbers blurred.

Callie's offer of prayer left Belle a bit uneasy. Many weeks had passed since Belle had sincerely prayed—or even gone to church, for that matter. Lately she let Joe go on Sunday mornings without her.

Her whole life she had attended church but never considered herself a strong Christian—not like Callie and Rick, who often read the Bible and prayed. Through the years, she had basically relied on her pastors to tell her what God's Word said.

Now Belle regretted that choice because she could use some comfort. If she knew where to turn in the Bible, perhaps she could find that comfort in the Word of God. Belle eyed the worn devotional Bible on the corner of Rick's disorganized desk. Maybe she would read it after talking with her mother.

Unable to put off the conversation any longer, Belle picked up the receiver. "Hello, Mom," she said with feigned cheerfulness.

"Belle?" Anna Runnel's voice was thick, as if she had been crying. A sniffle.

Her own eyes stinging, Belle struggled against a fresh rush of emotion. This was what she had dreaded the most. Hurting her parents. "I'm fine, Mom," Belle said, amazed at her voice's encouraging tones.

"I had no idea you and Joe were having problems."

"I've been miserable for a year."

"You've done a good job of hiding it."

"I know. That might be part of the problem."

"Joe just called. He seemed surprised."

"How could he be? He's the one who's made me miserable."

"Well, if you've hidden it, Belle—"

"I tried to tell him several times lately. He wouldn't listen." A pause. She toyed with the phone's cord and stared at the computer monitor. "And to top it off, he's forgotten my birthday and our anniversary for the past two years!" Belle, unable to hide the pain any longer, struggled against tears.

A high-pitched tone interrupted the call, and Belle thanked heaven that Callie had call waiting. "I think someone else is beeping in."

"OK. I'm not doing really well right now anyway. Maybe we can talk tomorrow."

Another beep.

And Belle felt as if she were being swept away in a hurricane of guilt. She hated being the cause of her mother's pain. Of anybody's pain, for that matter. Was there such a thing as a clean separation? Belle was beginning to think the whole thing might be uglier than she ever anticipated.

"I'll call you tomorrow," Belle soothed as the beep interrupted for the third time. "Maybe we can go out for lunch."

"Fine. That sounds fine," Anna said in a quivering voice.

After a quick good-bye, Belle pushed the phone's receiver button. "Hello," she said absently, her thoughts caught up in her mother's tears.

"Belle," Joe said, "we need to talk."

She had known he would eventually call. But Belle hadn't expected Joe's call on the heels of her mother's. She also hadn't expected the hint of vulnerability lacing his anger.

Speechless. Belle was speechless.

Chapter Three

Joe, clutching the cordless phone, sat rigidly at the kitchen table. As the deafening silence stretched into an ache, he waited for Belle's response. In the last few hours, his emotions had careened from fury to disgust to vulnerability. Could Belle really mean what she said in that note? Or would she be willing to talk about her feelings?

Still he waited. Waited in silence.

At last she spoke. "I tried to tell you about our problems several times in the last few months, and you wouldn't listen," she said, her voice strained and thick. "Now you want to talk?"

He methodically creased a royal blue place mat and tried to keep his cool. "When? I don't know what you're talking about."

"That's the whole point!" she snapped.

"Look, Belle—"

"Don't start with that tone."

"What tone?"

"The 'you've got a problem, and it has nothing to do with me' tone! I've listened to that for two years. When are you going to realize that you have some responsibilities in our marriage?"

"What are you talking about?" Joe's voice rose despite his efforts to keep it calm. "Up until a couple of weeks ago, I thought you were fine with our marriage."

She emitted an exasperated sound that seemed to be a cross between a growl and a yell. "Why are you so clueless?"

"Clueless?" He matched her decibel for decibel. "Why are you so selfish?"

"Selfish?"

"Yes! I don't appreciate the way you just walked out, leaving nothing behind but that cowardly note!"

Silence.

Joe hadn't intended for the conversation to grow so heated. He wanted to keep it calm. In retrospect he wondered at the feasibility of that. It seemed there was a load of explosive emotions under the surface of their seemingly placid relationship. Emotions Joe never knew existed. What had Belle tried to tell him? When had she tried to tell him?

As if those questions activated his otherwise defunct memory, Joe recalled a scene a few weeks ago. He had been relaxing in the recliner, engrossed in a sports documentary on television. . . .

"Joe, there's something important I think we need to discuss," Belle said, approaching from their bedroom.

Vaguely, Joe heard her words, but they didn't quite register.

"Joe? We need to talk," she said, more insistent than before.

He glanced at Belle, dressed in her oversized nightshirt, then back to the television. "Can it wait until after this show is over? I've been waiting to see this all week."

He felt her watching him. For several minutes she stood nearby as if she were trying to decide what to do. At last she turned, walked to their room, closed the door, and went to bed.

Joe followed her within the half hour, hoping she would be awake. He had a few needs that Belle seemed to be ignoring of late. Joe flipped on the bedside lamp to see that she was already asleep. His masculine urge for physical contact urged him to awaken her, but Joe didn't. He let her sleep.

Apparently, Joe hadn't realized that their marriage was going to sleep as well.

Belle's sniffles broke into his reflections. She was crying. The notion evoked both his sympathy and his fury. Even though Joe didn't understand everything, he truly ached for her. But at the same time, he resented her for pulling the crying act. Was it merely an attempt to soften him and therefore get her own way?

"You know, Belle," he said, measuring his words, "you aren't the only one in our marriage who isn't satisfied."

"What are you talking about?"

Joe wondered if Belle realized she had repeated his very words. "I mean that I have needs, too." He tried to remember how long it had been since they made love but couldn't recall the exact number of weeks.

"Well, there's much more to a marriage than sex, Joe," she sputtered. "As a matter of fact, that's about last on my list of needs."

"Well, since we're telling all," he said sarcastically, "it's about first on my list, and you've done precious little about it. And there's been more than one time lately that I've wanted to let you know it, too!" Restlessly, Joe began pacing the living room.

"Thank you for that report." Her sarcastic tone matched his. "Now I have a question for you."

"What?"

"Do you even know when our anniversary is?"

"Yes, I know. It's Valentine's Day."

"And what about my birthday?"

"June 13. What's the point in all this?"

"The point is—do you remember what you got me for our last two anniversaries and my last two birthdays?"

Joe frantically tried to recall the gifts.

"I'll tell you what you got me. Nothing! N-O-T-H-I-N-G! You ignored them both!"

His pacing stilled as he listened in impotent silence.

"And I've got news for you, mister. If you expect me to take care of your physical needs when you totally ignore my emotional needs, then you're crazy!"

"Is that what this is all about, Belle? That I forgot your birthday and our anniversary? Don't you think you could have told me with less drastic actions?"

She produced another of those half-growls, half-yells. This time, it held a condescending note. "You are beyond measure the most thickheaded man I've ever met! This is about way more than birthdays and anniversaries! I can't—I just can't— You are so— I cannot believe—" At last, she sputtered to a halt. Then the phone clicked in Joe's ear.

New fury surged through him. He turned off his cordless phone, turned it back on, and punched the redial button. Halfway through the succession of rapid beeps, he disconnected the call. His first instinct had been to call her back and explain to her in vivid detail why he didn't appreciate being hung up on.

But something stopped him.

What good would that do? It would only add to their explosive list of accusations.

Joe gripped the base of his neck and stared up at the painting of Belle and him that was hanging over the mantel. Their enraptured expressions seemed to taunt him, to challenge him, to mock what had become of their marriage. Without another thought, Joe dropped the phone on the sofa and grabbed the painting from its hook. Impulsively, he raised the painting, ready to dash it across the black, lacquered coffee table.

But he stopped in midswing.

His hands trembling, Joe took a series of deep breaths and allowed the painting to slip to the thick carpet. With a muffled thud, it landed faceup. He slumped into his favorite recliner and stared at the painted images of him and Belle. Had their whole marriage been a hoax? Nothing more than a painted image? A mirage that was fading—and fading fast?

Her accusations about the anniversaries and birthdays began to fully penetrate his thoughts. And Joe was stunned. How could he have slipped into the habit of forgetting Belle on those important days? Frankly, Joe never cared one way or the other if Belle remembered his birthday or anniversary. Had he assumed she felt the same?

She told him her leaving was about much more than his forgetfulness. Did Belle have needs that Joe never realized existed? Somehow he thought that if they had a healthy sex life and he provided for her, then she would be content.

But Belle said Joe was clueless. Was he? Did he even begin to understand his wife?

Shaking uncontrollably, Belle sat with her face in her hands and tried to silence the sobs coming from the bottom of her soul. Somewhere in the recesses of her mind, she knew she needed to get a grip on her emotions, but she couldn't quite fathom how to accomplish that feat.

Hearing Joe's scorn and anger only heightened her resolve

to maintain the separation. The chasm in their marriage was beyond mending—so wide that Belle didn't see how either could ever cross it.

Yet on a very deep level, Belle still yearned for Joe's affection. Even now, some empty spot within wished Joe would wrap his arms around her and soothe her taut emotions.

But that would never happen. That was the whole reason for this separation. Joe Anders was interested only in having his needs met. He cared precious little about Belle's needs.

Her breath catching on a hiccup, Belle searched the desk for a tissue. At last she discovered some in the bottom drawer. Grabbing several, she mopped at her swollen eyes, stood, and contemplated the best way to slip unnoticed into her room.

Her stomach twisted with nausea.

Her heart twisted with grief.

Her mind twisted with turmoil.

She had no desire to sit and make small talk. With anyone.

On the way to the door, Belle picked up Rick's devotional Bible. She opened the study door to see that Callie had joined her family in the den. Rick and she sat side by side on the sofa, casually holding hands. The sight left Belle even more distraught. Her sister's marriage seemed to be flourishing while hers was dying—or was already dead.

Rick and Callie both looked at Belle.

"I'm going to turn in for the night." She held up the Bible. "Mind if I borrow this?" she asked, her voice a watery reflection of its normal tones.

"No, not at all." A concerned, brotherly light stirred in Rick's kind eyes. Rick was such a considerate man that Belle often wondered if his gentleness was wasted in that computer store he owned. He should have been a family counselor or a pastor or a pediatrician.

On her way toward the hallway, Belle felt both Rick and

Callie watching her. She didn't doubt that they had heard her raise her voice on the phone. Obviously, they could see that she had been crying. Belle felt she owed them an explanation. But she simply didn't trust herself to talk. She would probably collapse into a fit of sobs with the first word.

Belle made short work of donning her nightshirt, brushing her teeth, and washing her face. It was barely eight o'clock when she settled into the spacious guest room. Even though she had napped all afternoon, Belle felt as if she hadn't slept in weeks. *The pregnancy must be making me tired,* she mused as she slipped between the cool sheets and propped her head on the stack of pillows. Gently she stroked her abdomen. For the first time, Belle marveled at the life within her. What would this child be like? Would it come into the world with parents who were at each other's throats?

As she gripped Rick's Bible, Belle compressed her lips in an attempt to stay the threatening tears. Trying to distract herself from her own heartache, she opened the Bible to Psalms. She hadn't read the Bible much since she had left home to go to college. But when Belle and Callie were small, their mother softly read the Psalms to them as they fell asleep. Perhaps those verses would calm and comfort her now.

Joe, tangled in the bedsheets, stared through the darkness, wishing to somehow annihilate the scent of Belle's perfume from his pillow. He had removed the pillowcase. But, heaven help him, he was still in the clutches of the light floral scent.

Onslaughts of emotion washed over him, each more potent than the previous. Like a lone boulder in the ocean, buffeted by one wave after another, his heart was the victim of his own mixed feelings.

Pride. Anger. Emptiness. Confusion. Desire. Loneliness. Desperation.

Sitting up, Joe rubbed his gritty eyes and stared at the digital clock. Two o'clock glared back at him. The longest night of his life.

Belle was gone.

Would she ever return?

Impatiently, he disentangled his legs from the sheets and stalked toward the kitchen. After pouring himself some milk, Joe leaned against the kitchen counter. As if his mind were bent on tormenting him, Joe involuntarily found himself remembering their first night in this house.

They had been married only a year. Surrounded by boxes, they made bologna sandwiches. Belle discovered a bag of chips and a candle. With the smug look of an arrogant waitress, she covered a box with a towel, placed the candle and sandwiches on it, and lit the candle. Joe found their cassette player and put their favorite saxophone music on. After eating their sandwiches, they twirled around the room in time to the music. Eventually, they tripped over a box in the living room and landed on the floor in a giggling heap. Their laughter gave way to heartfelt passion.

Try as he might, Joe couldn't remember if they had ever again behaved so spontaneously. In the following years, they gradually fell into the pattern that many "old married folks" fall into. The thought was disturbing.

Joe dashed the rest of his milk down his throat as if the act could erase the troubling thoughts. Unceremoniously, he dropped the plastic tumbler into the sink and moved to pick up Belle's wedding band from the breakfast bar. He slipped it onto the end of his pinky and once more wondered if he knew—really knew—his wife of five years.

At last he made a decision. The drive from Dallas to Jacksonville took just over two hours. If Joe left at seven, he would arrive at Callie and Rick's shortly after nine.

Life without Belle was no life at all. Joe would get her back. With a little reason and a little love, Belle would be home that very day.

CHAPTER FOUR

Belle groaned as the final heave subsided. She fumbled for a washcloth, dampened it, and bathed her face. The bathroom mirror told her she looked worse than she had ever looked in her life. At least she had showered and put on her jeans and shirt this time before the vomiting started. Maybe that was a good sign. Perhaps the nausea was beginning later in the day and would soon subside altogether.

When the doorbell rang, Belle's first thought was that Callie would answer it. Then she remembered. Callie had taken Larry and Barry shopping for their school supplies. On unsteady legs, Belle walked through the formal living room toward the door. She glanced out the large picture window to see if perhaps she could determine the identity of the caller. The sight of a worn Ford truck in the driveway sent her heart to her knees.

Joe.

Although Belle had anticipated his phoning again, she had never suspected he would come in person. She stopped and stood in silent dilemma. Had he heard her approaching the doorway? Perhaps if she kept still, he would assume no one was home and leave. But that went against everything Joe Anders was. Joe would sit on the front porch and wait until somebody came home, even if he had to wait all day.

Belle wasn't certain how she scraped up the bravado to open the front door, but she soon found herself staring into Joe's searching eyes.

"Mind if I come in?" he asked.

"No," she mumbled, wondering where she had found her voice. Belle's heart pounded out hard, even beats, and she prayed for the strength to survive this surprise encounter.

"You look pale," he said as she closed the door behind him.

"Yes."

"Have you been sick?"

"Yes."

After a pause, he once again exposed her to a searching gaze. Belle felt as if they were tossing a hand grenade back and forth and pretending it wouldn't explode.

"There's been a virus going around the fire station," Joe finally said.

"Oh, really." Belle hated to lie, but she didn't have the courage to alter his assumptions. Joe would find out about the baby soon enough. Right now there was no need to complicate an already volatile situation.

He offered her a slight smile, and a shadow of relief scurried across his features. Belle wondered if he thought that her resolve to maintain the separation was melting. His next words confirmed her assumption.

"Why don't you come back home, Belle?" Slowly, he reached for her hand.

Belle stepped away from him and walked behind the wing chair. "I told you last night—"

"About last night—we were both a little on edge."

"Maybe you can explain your part away as being on edge, but I wasn't," she snapped. "I meant every word I said."

He narrowed his weary eyes, and Belle wondered if he

might turn and leave. As if Joe were trying to compose himself, he walked toward the room's center. "If you would agree to come back, I can promise that I'll try to—"

"I've already heard that once."

"What?"

"Your promise. When we got married, you promised. Quite frankly, Joe, you've broken your first promise. How do I know you won't woo me long enough to get me back, then drop me again?" Quivering like a sapling in a tornado, Belle couldn't believe she actually had the courage to speak her true feelings.

"Drop you? I never dropped you."

"Yes, you did! Before we were married, you talked to me, you showed me affection, you gave me your attention, you cherished me, Joe. After our first couple of years of marriage, it seemed you somehow forgot about my feelings and my needs. Just as long as you got everything you wanted physically, then you seemed to think everything was hunky-dory."

"Who says I always got everything I wanted physically?" He paced the formal room, his brow furrowed in brooding accusation. "A few years into our marriage, you seemed to turn cold."

"That was because you turned cold emotionally. You stopped cherishing me. I can't just hop into bed and fulfill your every whim if you haven't shown me any affection. Women just don't work that way!" Her last words came out as a high shrill couched in a mound of frustration.

He stopped his pacing and looked at her as if she had just spoken in a foreign language.

She didn't flinch from his gaze.

"You were right last night," he finally said. "I've been clueless."

Belle hadn't expected him to actually admit it. At first she was stunned to silence. Then she experienced a new rush of anger. "You know, Joe Anders, I've been trying to get that through your thick head for months, and you wouldn't listen! Why did it take my leaving to get your attention? Why wouldn't you take the time to listen before now?"

"I don't know." He approached slowly, as if he was afraid a sudden move would send her flying from the room. Gradually, he took her hand in his.

She pressed her lips together and studied his lean, tanned hands. He wore her wedding band on the top half of one of his little fingers. She wondered if he had hoped she would put it back on.

His nearness almost destroyed every ounce of Belle's resolve. He hadn't shown her this much attention in years, and her affection-starved emotions clamored for more. Gradually, Joe slipped his arms around her and lowered his head to hers.

Feeling as if she were being hypnotized by the venomous gaze of a cobra, Belle leaned toward him. But her common sense crashed in upon her capitulation with a series of valid assertions: *You have solved nothing in your marriage. How do you know you can trust him to keep his word? He has ignored you for years. Do you honestly think he will change overnight?*

As if she had been punched in the gut, Belle stumbled backward. "No, don't," she said, her husky voice a clear indicator of the effect Joe Anders still had on her.

"Belle—"

"I guess you think all you have to do is kiss me a few times and everything will be fine," she accused.

"I never said that," he ground out, his nostrils flaring.

"No, but that's the way you act." She balled her fists so tightly that her fingernails ate into her palms. "There's something you need to understand, Joe. You have wounded me very deeply. You have almost destroyed every bit of love I ever had for you." She continued, more slowly, "And I don't trust you. I didn't leave on a whim or because I'm in some kind of emotional frenzy. I left because our marriage is dead. And I still don't think you have a clue. I think you think all you have to do is put a Band-Aid on the whole thing and that will fix it." She crossed her arms. "Well, this is a wound that's far too big for a Band-Aid. You have taken me for granted. You have been rude to me anytime I've tried to talk with you about our marriage. You have put zero energy into our marriage. Furthermore, if you want to know the absolute honest-to-goodness truth about something else—" She halted, amazed at her own honesty, amazed that in that honesty a new truth had just dawned upon her. "I have spent five years trying to do whatever it takes not to trigger that horrible temper of yours! And I'm tired of it."

She placed her hands on her hips. "I've already said it once, and I'll say it again. I do not trust you."

There. The whole thing was out in the open. Somehow, Belle felt that a load had been lifted from her. But nonetheless it had taken every ounce of courage she possessed.

Joe's brooding expression gradually grew into fury. His dark eyes flashed. His jaw clenched. His face reddened. He was going to blow up on her and prove everything she had just spoken. Somehow the knowledge brought her a twisted sense of satisfaction.

"You . . . you . . . you," he accused, directing his index finger at her nose. "While you're pointing the finger, you need to point it at yourself as well."

"What's that supposed to mean?"

"It's supposed to mean that I might be clueless in some areas, but it takes two to make a good marriage. Furthermore, you have done nothing—I repeat, *nothing*—to try to communicate with me—"

She threw her hands up. "Oh! I cannot believe—I told you that I've tried to talk with you for months, but you—"

As if another second in her presence would send him into orbit, Joe slammed out the front door.

Belle was shocked.

This wasn't like Joe. The few times in the past when she had tried to stand up to him, he had not left the room. He just yelled until his temper intimidated her into silence. Feeling as if she were playing a whole new game with Joe, Belle stood motionless and watched him through the front window as he got into his beloved truck, cranked it, and peeled off with far too much speed.

Suddenly the spacious living room seemed nothing but an empty cavity, and that emptiness fused itself to Belle's heart. It seemed they had gone from one extreme to the other, from no communication to screaming at each other.

As a lone tear rolled down her cheek, Belle hugged her midsection. She had told Joe that he had almost destroyed every bit of love she felt for him. Until today, she had wondered if he had destroyed *all* her love. But Belle now knew that in the deepest fathom of her soul, an ember of love still glowed fiercely for Joe.

He had said it takes two to make a good marriage. Could she be a part of their problems? Belle had been so busy focusing on Joe's failure that she hadn't contemplated the possibility that she, too, had some shortcomings.

Last night after reading Psalms, she had prayed vaguely for God's direction. But today, in the aftermath of their explosive encounter, Belle sensed that her prayers needed to be much more than vague. For the first time in her life, she went to her room, closed her door, and threw herself on the mercy of her heavenly Father.

North of Jacksonville, Joe sat at a picnic table at Love's Lookout Roadside Park. The park, atop Lookout Mountain, seemed more like a picture from a postcard than a state-maintained convenience stop. A warm summer breeze teased the massive trees, while birds frolicked in the surrounding piney woods.

Joe contemplated the expansive view across Lookout Valley and pondered the status of his marriage. Things were much more serious than he had ever imagined. He had no idea what to do next. Joe had heard all his life that every marriage has its ups and downs, much like the mountain and valley he now enjoyed. But he felt that the valley in his marriage was more the result of an earthquake than the natural descent from a mountain. It seemed there was a gaping canyon in their relationship. And when he and Belle tried to talk, they fell into never-ending echoes of accusation and anger.

Restlessly, Joe stood and walked along the short rock wall that prevented people from slipping down the side of the steep grade. Rather than driving straight back to Dallas, Joe had stopped ten minutes into his journey. Just to get his breath. Just to make sure he shouldn't turn around and approach Belle again. Just to be certain there was nothing more he could do.

"Oh, Lord," he breathed while gazing across the breathtaking splendor of God's creation. "I know I haven't spent a lot of time talking to you outside of church. I'm sorry for that. I know you're there. I know you understand all that's going on in my marriage. And quite frankly, I'm glad you do—because I don't. I really don't. I guess I've blown it in a big way. But, Lord, I'm not the only one to blame. I don't know if Belle sees it or not, but she's a part of our problem, too."

A stab of guilt pierced his soul as a new thought struck him, "OK. Maybe not as big a problem as I am, but still—part of it. And I really don't know what to do at this point. Do I go back to her now? Do I give her space? I don't want to push her farther away than she already is, but I don't want to lose her either."

Joe remembered that smoky something in the depths of her blue eyes when he had tried to kiss her. The same something that had been in her eyes early in their relationship. They had gone to Belle's family reunion. Joe was thrilled with the idea of meeting Belle's family. All day long, between the traditional barbecue spread and scoops of ice cream and hugs from dear old aunts, Joe sent Belle every positive signal he had ever learned and a few he made up. By the end of the day, his hand seemed permanently attached to hers. And there was no doubt in Joe's mind that he had met the answer to his prayers for a Christian wife. Joe glowed in the approval from her family. In short, he had been a hit. Everybody, including crotchety Great-aunt Agnes, gave hearty approval to Belle's new friend.

That night they had gone to the lake, taken off their shoes, and waded along the beach. Miraculously, they had the beach to themselves. The full moon spilled a honey-colored canopy across the lake, and the two halted to admire the moon's reflection across the rippling waters.

Joe, turning to Belle, had tucked a strand of hair behind her ear and gently brushed his thumb across her cheek. In the moonlight, that same smoky look he had seen at Callie's an hour ago had stirred in her eyes.

Belle certainly hadn't been immune to him then. And she wasn't now. Joe still affected her. The very thought gave him new hope. Perhaps things weren't as long gone as Belle heatedly claimed they were.

Another thought struck him. What would happen if he kept his distance but began sending her cards and flowers and all those things he had done before they were married? Would she gradually come around if Joe began to prove that he could cherish her? But Belle's earlier words attacked that idea in its infancy: *"How do I know you won't woo me long enough to get me back, then drop me again?"*

"Because I won't," he whispered. "I promise you I won't." Joe squared his shoulders, got into his worn truck, and drove back into Jacksonville. He had forgotten to do one thing before he left for Dallas. He needed to visit the florist. Belle was overdue for some yellow roses.

CHAPTER FIVE

Belle had never prayed facedown before. But she was so overwrought with the anguish of her marriage that she lay facedown on the mint green carpet with her forehead propped on her crossed arms.

"Oh, Father," she cried, "I don't know what to do. I don't think this is the way you intended things to turn out with Joe and me when we got married. But I just feel so . . . so betrayed by him. I'm not sure I understand everything that's going on inside me. But you've got to help me and—and show me what to do. I . . . I—" She thought about the baby. "I'm sorry I let Joe believe a lie about my being sick, but I just don't think I'm ready to argue with him over this baby. And I don't feel like I can trust him. You know all this. Please, please show me what to do."

Her prayer was interrupted by the doorbell. Belle stiffened. Was that Joe? She contemplated not answering the door. But if it was Joe, he knew she was home. He would probably keep ringing until she answered.

Mopping at her tearstained cheeks, Belle stumbled toward the door. Before opening it, she peeked out the front window to see a white van with a florist's logo painted on the side. Rick must have sent flowers to Callie. He was forever doing thoughtful things like that. Belle opened the door, and a huge bouquet of yellow roses greeted her. Behind the roses, a smiling woman extended the gift. Belle was crestfallen. Yellow roses were her favorite. She often dreamed of Joe's sending her yellow roses again, the way he had before they were married. Why had Rick chosen yellow? Any color but yellow.

"A delivery for Belle Anders," the lady said. "Are you Belle?" she continued gently as she noticed Belle's tears.

"Yes," Belle whispered. Her mouth dry, she took the roses and felt as if she were drowning in their heavenly scent. Why had Rick sent *her* flowers?

"Have a good day," the plump lady replied before turning back toward the van.

"Thanks," Belle called weakly. She wondered how many teary women the lady delivered flowers to in one day. Belle remembered once seeing a florist's billboard that said, "Just how mad is she?" Underneath the question were three bouquets that ranged from a bud vase to an arrangement resembling a flower garden. This arrangement was definitely the flower-garden variety.

Had Joe . . . ?

Belle closed the door and sat the bouquet on a nearby table. Hands unsteady, she removed the card from the explosion of yellow ribbon just below the blooms. She fumbled with the miniature envelope, which seemed to fight her every attempt at removing the signed card. In desperation, Belle tore the envelope away from the card. The message was brief.

To Belle,

All my love.
S. A.

It was Joe's handwriting. No mistaking that distinctive, oversized scrawl. But what did he mean by "S. A."?

New tears assaulted Belle. She was torn between two reactions: one, to angrily throw the roses out the front door; and the other, to embrace the roses and waltz around the room like a schoolgirl. Her response was a mixture of both. She cradled the roses to her as if they were a baby, took them into her room, lost her breath in their fragrance, then unceremoniously plopped them on the cherry dresser as if she were punishing them.

"Why are you so thickheaded, Joe Anders?" she demanded, as if he were still present. "Why did it take my leaving to get this kind of response from you?"

In that context, she wondered if the thought behind the roses was really sincere. After a few more teary sniffles, Belle decided she didn't know the answer to that one. How could she tell what was really going on in her husband's mind? He seemed to have his own complaints about their marriage. She had told him he was clueless. Perhaps she, too, had a touch of his clueless disease. Did she really know her husband? Had she even tried to know him?

As if her own mind were bent on fighting against her, Belle remembered a typical scene from early in their marriage. . . .

"Hey, Belle!" Joe called as he slammed through the kitchen doorway. "You'll never guess what I got today. Two tickets to the next Rangers game."

"Oh?" Belle looked at him blankly. "Who are you taking with you?" She thought she had endured enough of those meaningless baseball games before they were married to be obligated to attend them now.

A certain disappointment dampened the spark in Joe's eyes. "I thought you and I could go," he said uncertainly.

"Oh, Joe," Belle pleaded. "Would you be terribly disappointed if I didn't go?"

Joe shrugged and muttered something about taking one of the guys from work. Belle was relieved that he took her rejection so well.

But staring into that huge bouquet of roses, she now wondered if perhaps Joe had been more disappointed than she realized. How many times after that had he tried to get her to go places with him? A Dallas Cowboys game. His golf tournament. Fishing. Belle didn't remember how long he had persisted, but eventually he had stopped asking.

"If you had just been more affectionate, maybe I would have done more stuff like that with you," she whispered peevishly. Somehow, the words lacked the conviction she had felt previously. Joe had made it painstakingly clear that he wasn't the only problem in their marriage. However, Belle wasn't sure if she was quite ready to accept Joe's claim. Could his need for Belle's recreational companionship be as strong as her need for affection, communication, and honesty?

The question troubled her. Troubled her deeply.

She glanced at the clock, relieved to see the lunch hour quickly approaching. Callie and the boys were due back any minute. Belle would sling together a quick lunch for them. That chore would focus her attention elsewhere and end these disturbing thoughts.

CHAPTER SIX

Belle stretched and snuggled into the warm covers. Shortly, she would have to get up and begin breakfast for Callie's family. Belle was determined to earn her keep, so her day started early.

The wilted arrangement of yellow roses on her dresser caught her eye. Six weeks had passed since they had arrived, and they had long since turned an ugly shade of brown. However, Belle couldn't bring herself to throw them away. Something inside her wanted to cling to those flowers as if they could somehow infuse her marriage with life once again. Nonetheless, a doubtful voice deep within whispered hesitation about whether or not Belle should once again trust Joe with her true self.

Belle hadn't seen or talked with him since their last argument. But each week he had done something nice for her. Nothing elaborate, but nice. He sent her three cards, a teddy bear, and some of her favorite lotion. The cards were light and funny. Then the teddy bear came, "I love you" emblazoned on its tummy. The lotion arrived yesterday. The gold-embossed card accompanying it made Belle cry. All of his gifts or cards were signed "S. A." Belle and Callie had determined that the "S. A." stood for "Secret Admirer." Lately,

Belle wondered if perhaps it stood for "Silent Admirer." She had expected Joe to call and couldn't deny her disappointment in his continued silence.

The last several days when she had prayed, Belle had felt that she should contact Joe. Was this an answer to her heavenward request for guidance? Belle thought so. Today, as soon as she got a chance, she would call Joe and thank him. She hadn't really known what to say or how to say it . . . but this morning, staring across the room at Joe's gifts, Belle knew today was the day.

She gently stroked her rounding abdomen and pondered whether to tell him about the baby. Even though she didn't look pregnant at first glance, her weight gain was apparent. And from what the obstetrician said, she couldn't keep the secret from Joe much longer.

Thoughts of her pregnancy brought pangs of guilt. She knew deep in her heart that she should have told Joe about the baby before now. After all, he was the father. And the more she prayed, the more she read God's Word, the more she was convicted that Joe wasn't the only one who was responsible for the problems in their marriage.

"Oh, Lord," she whispered as she finally wrenched herself from the bed's claim, "please give me the strength to be totally honest with my husband."

Even though her family was silent on the subject, Belle knew that her parents and Callie thought Joe had a right to know about the baby. But after her mother's initial dismay over the separation, Belle's family had remained silently supportive. Belle was more thankful for them than she had ever been. They really were a good bunch.

Joe sat in the parking lot of the Jacksonville McDonald's and sipped the steaming black coffee. He had ordered the bitter liquid at the drive-through and now hoped it would give him the final edge he needed to face Belle. He was more nervous than he had been on their first date.

He had expected to hear from Belle long before this. Some note of thanks for the gifts. Perhaps a phone call. Anything. But his phone remained silent; his mailbox, empty.

For six weeks Joe had pondered her accusations. Even though his defenses had been high when Belle delivered her punch, Joe knew that every word she had said was true—especially the part about his temper. His mother had told him over and over, "One day that temper of yours is going to get you into trouble." Looked as if his mother was right.

And up until Belle confronted him about it, Joe had always excused himself by saying, "That's just the way I am." After hours of prayer and talking with his pastor, Joe finally came to the conclusion that he shouldn't make excuses for his sin. Rather, he should strive to be more like Christ. In short, something good was coming out of all this trouble with Belle. Joe had learned for the first time in his life that being a Christian meant focusing on Christ every day, not just attending church on Sundays. And once he started worshiping—really worshiping—God at home, Joe found that that worship spilled into his Sundays. In the past, he had expected his Sundays to spill into his week and take care of all the problems. But it just didn't work that way.

Draining the final sip of his coffee, Joe tossed the plastic cup onto his cluttered truck's seat. Accompanied by a series of prayers, he drove the short distance to Callie and Rick's Victorian home. Before he rang the doorbell, a last desperate prayer squeezed from his soul. *Please, God, help me not to lose my temper this time. No matter what she says or what happens, keep me from blowing up at her.*

Her throat dry, Belle sat behind Rick's cluttered desk and stared at the phone. With a mixture of dread and anticipation, Belle had spent the last hour preparing breakfast, seeing the family off, and cleaning up the mess. Now she knew she must call Joe. But what would she say? Belle wasn't certain she was ready to go back home—back to the way things were. Could she trust Joe to keep his promises this time? Or would he fall back into those well-learned patterns—the neglect, the coldness, the anger?

Perhaps if you begin changing your wrong patterns, he will too, a persistent voice whispered.

For the first time, Belle was seriously contemplating going back to Joe. She couldn't stay with Rick and Callie forever. The airline had granted her an extended leave of absence, but after the baby was born, Belle would be forced to go back to work if she were on her own. If she and Joe could solve their problems, Belle could quit her job and be a full-time mom. Wouldn't that be the best thing for the baby? The choices swirled through her mind, making her dizzy.

Just as she picked up the receiver, the doorbell rang. Belle dropped the receiver as if it were hot. As she rushed to the door, a flood of relief washed over her. The call had been postponed. Perhaps answering the door would give Belle enough time to come up with the right words for Joe.

Belle was so distracted that she forgot to glance through the front window to get a sneak preview of the person who stood outside. When she opened the door, she felt as if she had been punched in the gut.

CHAPTER SEVEN

Joe just stood there, silently appraising Belle, as if he didn't know whether she would run or ask him in. In his jeans and boots and starched white shirt, he looked more handsome than Belle ever remembered him looking. Was this her husband? The weeks away from him had somehow heightened her awareness of his attractiveness. No wonder she had married him in the first place.

Instantly she was aware of her own frumpy attire. A floppy T-shirt and sweatpants. That was about all she could fit into comfortably these days. This morning Belle had pledged to go to the maternity store for clothing. And soon.

"Do I get an invitation in, or do we just stand here and look at each other?" Joe asked, his smile a bit uncertain.

"Uh—" Belle gulped. "Come in." She opened the door wider. "You won't believe this, but I was about to call you."

"Oh, really?" Was that hope in his voice?

Belle shut the door behind him and collapsed onto the Chippendale sofa. Her knees refused to give her any support whatsoever. Joe settled across from her on a settee.

"So, why were you going to call me?" he prompted. Joe seemed much more at peace than ever before. The change in him left Belle's mind void of all thoughts. Could he have started seeking God as she had?

Suddenly the room's jade-and-burgundy tones seemed to blur together in a disconcerting way. Belle had yet to faint due to this pregnancy, but she often feared she might. "Uh . . . I was just going to . . . to thank you for the cards and the lotion and the little bear and . . . and the yellow roses," she finally rushed, and the room quit tilting.

"So my cover is blown," he said with a teasing smile. "You've discovered I'm your secret admirer?"

"It didn't exactly take Sherlock Holmes to figure that one out." Belle, her fingers shaking, gathered one of the jade-colored pillows onto her lap. Anything to hide the bulge of her abdomen. Nervously, she picked at the pillow's fringe.

She needed to tell Joe she was pregnant today.

She knew in her soul she needed to tell him today.

But she feared his reaction. She did not want him to explode.

"You seem high-strung," he said as if she were a shy gazelle he might spook. He leaned forward. "Is everything OK? Have you been ill? That virus . . . I assumed you got over it OK?"

The perfect chance to tell him. Instead, she simply stared at him in impotent silence. Her lips refused to move. Her tongue refused to disconnect from the roof of her mouth. As Joe's pondering gaze turned from concern to warmth, Belle's heart picked up its pace. She couldn't remember the last time he had looked at her so warmly.

She missed that look. She missed him, despite her better judgment. He wanted to take her in his arms. She felt his yearning, and her heart reached out to Joe as she hadn't reached out in a long time.

His warm gaze turned to hunger. An old, forgotten force

sprang between them, and she recalled the heat of their Hawaiian honeymoon. They had stayed in their room more than they had stayed on the beach. The incredible scenery was virtually wasted on them. They were so engrossed in the explosion of their love that the palm trees, ocean, and Pacific sunsets paled in comparison.

Her stomach twisted.

"Belle?" Joe whispered.

His husky tone jolted her common sense back into operation. If they became physical at this point, it would only complicate their problems. They needed to talk first. To do a lot of talking. And a lot of healing. And . . . and probably begin praying together like Callie and Rick did. Belle wasn't dead sure she was ready to move back today. And Joe would expect her to return to Dallas if they . . . if they . . .

She stood, more as a defense than anything else. "We should go get a Coke or something." Good. A nice public restaurant was the perfect solution.

"That's fine with me," he said simply, a shadow of disappointment twisting through his words.

"Uh—" She almost stumbled over her own feet as she tried to put some space between them. "I need to change. You're all dressed up, and I look like Raggedy Anne."

"No, you don't. You look beautiful," he said softly.

Belle, acting as if she didn't hear him, rushed to her room, shut the door, and collapsed on the edge of the bed. She never dreamed she would react to Joe Anders on that level again. Never dreamed she would feel that chemistry. How had she ever forgotten it? Closing her eyes, she took several cleansing breaths and tried to focus on what in creation she would wear. All Belle could come up with was one denim dress that might give her expanding midsection enough room.

As she donned the dress, she began praying. "OK, Lord. I've been asking for your help in this mess we've made of our marriage. But I've got to know, is this your idea of a joke? I never expected— You are simply going to have to give me the strength and wisdom to do what's right."

The telephone interrupted her prayer. But Belle was still wrestling with the zipper on the dress and didn't dare leave her bedroom in any state of undress. She pictured herself racing to answer the phone and Joe stepping behind her to zip her dress. The scene was far too intimate for Belle's peace of mind. They needed to do some talking first. Talking and healing.

Still, the phone kept ringing. Would the answering machine ever pick up? At last Belle heard Joe pick up the receiver and politely say, "Johnson residence." He must have decided the machine wasn't working.

Self-consciously, Belle examined her expanding figure in the princess-style denim dress. Thankfully, she looked more pudgy than pregnant. Belle ran a quick brush through her shoulder-length blonde hair and touched up her amber lipstick. Enough. She didn't want to be that obvious.

She stopped at the threshold of her bedroom door and forced herself to calm down. This was her husband, for pity's sake. She had lived with the man for five years. They should have known each other inside out by now.

But Belle had the feeling they barely knew each other. Did she really know Joe? He certainly didn't know her.

With a strength that surprised her, Belle opened the door and walked down the hallway. The house seemed strangely quiet. Ominously silent. And Belle had an unearthly dread of entering the living room. As if October's autumn chill were draping its arms around her shoulders, a certain coldness settled upon Belle. By the time she entered the living room, she couldn't so much as take another step past the threshold.

Joe stood, hands on hips, in the middle of the living room, glaring at her. Mute fury flashed from his eyes. His nostrils flared. He worked his jaw. His lips were thin, white lines.

In the deepest recess of her heart, Belle realized that he knew. Somehow he had discovered she was pregnant. Somehow he had learned that Belle had been less than honest.

But how? The telephone call. That was the only thing. But who . . . ?

Confirming her silent assumptions, Joe narrowed his eyes and said, "Rhonda at Dr. Brown's office called for you. When I told her I was your husband, she supplied the necessary details." He paused for added emphasis. "It seems you've missed your routine pregnancy appointment this morning."

Her appointment. She completely forgot.

Belle had never seen Joe so furious. He had every right to be angry with her, but not this angry. Her eyes stung. She felt compelled to scurry from the room, to avoid the inevitable scene. He spoke again before she had the chance to escape.

"Were you even going to tell me?" he demanded.

She couldn't speak.

"That virus—it wasn't a virus at all, was it? It was morning sickness! I noticed you had gained weight, but I thought—"

Still, she remained unable to utter a word.

"And you let me think—" He hit his forehead with his palm. "When did you find out?"

She stared in round-eyed scrutiny and stood her ground. She was proud of herself for that. She might have been in the wrong, but she didn't deserve this treatment.

"Tell me when!" Joe stomped his foot.

As if his physical action jostled her vocal cords, Belle finally spoke. "The day I left."

"The day you—" Throwing his hands into the air, he turned from her and stared out the front window. "And you still left," he said nastily, turning a disgusted gaze upon her. "Even though you knew there was a little one involved in all this? You still left!" He closed the space between them and lowered his face to only inches above hers.

"That is my child you're carrying." His hot breath fanned her cheek. "I deserved the respect of knowing about it. And I deserved to know from you. Not from some doctor's secretary."

Belle, her own fury rising, pressed her lips together and determined not to look away. She refused to cower to his anger.

"Don't you ever, *ever* whine to me about anything I have done wrong in our marriage! Because what you've done tops it all! You didn't even have the—the courage to tell me you were leaving. You just left that blasted note. And now this!" He motioned to her abdomen.

Grinding her teeth, Belle now knew there was no way they could ever recover what they had once shared. The chasm between them was too wide and quickly getting wider. Joe would never understand her confusion at the moment she discovered she was pregnant. He would never understand the pain he had dealt her, the pain he dealt her even now.

"I was going to tell you at the restaurant," she said through clamped teeth. "And if it's any consolation, I was also going to ask you to forgive me for not telling you sooner. But I guess none of that is good enough for you."

Silence.

"Why don't you just leave?" she finally ground out.

Joe's dark eyes, only centimeters from hers, seem to ignite in flames of new rage. "I believe that's the best suggestion you have ever made," he snarled.

Gripping his steering wheel as if he were punishing it, Joe sped along I-20. Bluish, turbulent clouds claimed the sky overhead—clouds that became a threatening, ebony mass along the western horizon. Joe felt as if those clouds were a symbol of his own fury. Just as he had been hurled headlong into that wretched argument, so he was hurling himself toward those clouds.

Joe had never felt so betrayed, not only by Belle, but also by her whole family. Especially by Rick. Why hadn't his brother-in-law called him? They had been buddies from the start.

"Maybe Rick doesn't even know about the baby," Joe mumbled as rain began to pelt the windshield.

Wearily, he rubbed his forehead and turned on the windshield wipers. Now what? He was at a total loss. In new territory.

His desire to control his anger had vanished when he discovered Belle's secret. Thoughts of her dishonesty now left him exasperated. At this point, Joe wasn't even ashamed of his anger. What man wouldn't have been angered? She said she planned to tell him about the baby at the restaurant. But could Joe believe that? After the way she had hidden it?

As the rain increased, he recalled his prayer before ringing Callie and Rick's doorbell—*Please, God, help me not to lose my temper this time. No matter what she says or what happens, keep me from blowing up at her.*

With a groan, Joe turned up the windshield wipers in order to accommodate the increasing rain. At last, feelings of guilt started assaulting his conscience. Once again Joe had blown it.

Totally.

In his mind, he played out an alternative scene. A scene

where he joyfully twirled Belle around the room. A scene where their mutual laughter blended together in a harmony of love.

Joe was going to be a father! He was thrilled at the prospect. For years he told Belle he really didn't care if they ever had children. But faced with the prospect of a baby—his baby—Joe was absolutely delighted.

As he continued to drive along the freeway, Joe imagined himself in a rocking chair, cuddling a warm bundle in the crook of his arm. Singing lullabies. Changing diapers. Getting up in the night. Feeling precious, tiny fingers wrapped around his finger. The whole notion of fatherhood left his eyes a bit misty.

A threatening streak of lightning reached its jagged fingers toward a nearby scattering of trees. The following boom seemed to inject Joe with more feelings of betrayal, which tainted his momentary delight. Belle had been less than honest with him. Was Joe that hard to live with—such an ogre that his wife felt compelled to withhold life's most precious moments from him? What other moments had he missed with Belle?

Sighing, Joe turned the windshield wipers to their highest speed and instinctively slowed the truck. Visibility was decreasing. And fast. The black, churning clouds obliterated almost every ray of sun, but the increasing flashes of lightning provided ample light. At once there was more light than Joe even desired. He suddenly wanted to hide his eyes from what he at long last realized he had driven into.

When had the storm become so violent? Joe's mind flashed through the gradual progression from what seemed a normal rain to . . . to this. He had been so distracted that he hadn't paid enough attention to his surroundings.

In panic, he slowed his truck to a crawl and strained to see the roadside through the wall of roaring rain. He glimpsed several towering pine trees whose tops were being forced closer and closer to the earth.

Even though this part of Texas was notorious for spring and autumn tornadoes, Joe never altered his plans in concession to an approaching storm. In fact, he always scoffed a bit at Belle's fear of severe weather. But these turbulent clouds left him wondering if he had been dreadfully unwise in his scoffing.

Hands trembling, Joe followed the example of the vehicles in front of him. He steered to the roadside, stopped, and switched on the easy-listening radio station he and Belle enjoyed. The shrill tone that in the past had annoyed Joe filled the truck and sent chills down his spine. A meteorologist's urgent, strained voice soon followed:

"This is an alert of the emergency broadcast system. This is a tornado warning. A tornado has been spotted along I-20, just northwest of Tyler. I repeat, a tornado has been spotted. If you are in this vicinity, take immediate cover, and stay tuned to—"

The meteorologist's warning was drowned out by a train-like roaring that obliterated every other noise in its wake. Joe's limited visibility was reduced to nothing. Nothing but swirling rain and debris that assaulted the windshield as if it were being blasted from the bowels of an infuriated monster.

A tree limb careened against the windshield. The glass shattered, and Joe instinctively covered his face and dove onto the floorboard. The truck tilted and shivered as if a mean-spirited giant were indecisive about whether to turn the vehicle over or leave it upright.

Joe's stomach clenched in horror. "Oh, Lord," he prayed, "save me!" No other prayer came to his mind. Only the panicked plea of a desperate man.

As that awful roaring continued, Joe lambasted himself for not paying more attention to the weather and not using more caution. If nothing else, he should have been listening to the radio. But his mind had been consumed with his own anger. His own emotions. And nothing else. Perhaps he did the same thing with Belle. Focused too much on himself and not enough on her. He hadn't seen the storm brewing in their marriage until it had unleashed its fury—and then, perhaps, it was too late.

While the truck continued its sickening tilting, Joe wondered if his baby would arrive into the world without a father. Only a miracle could save Joe's life. Facing his own mortality, he made one vow. *If I survive this, I will do everything in my power to make my marriage work. Whatever it takes.*

"I mean that, Lord," he whispered just before the truck crashed to its side and everything went black.

CHAPTER EIGHT

The telephone's shrill ring interrupted Belle's dinner preparations. She wondered if Callie was calling again. She had phoned an hour ago to alert Belle to the approaching thunderstorm, which now pummeled the windows with rain and produced ominous rolls of thunder.

Belle once again thought of Joe. He had been so angry when he left—she wondered if he was paying any heed whatsoever to the weather. Joe had never been the least bit afraid of storms. Time after time, he daringly defied them and won. Sighing, Belle tried to squelch the tendril of worry that wouldn't be ignored. Even though her anger had yet to die, Joe was still her husband. And Belle did care for his safety.

She reached for the cordless phone sitting on the breakfast bar. "Hello." Fully expecting Callie's cheerful voice, Belle walked back to the roast she had been preparing.

"This is the Smith County Sheriff's Department," a sanitized masculine voice said.

Belle's heart dropped to her stomach. This was about Joe. She knew it was about Joe. Suddenly, Belle wanted to hang up, as if that act would delete the whole call. "Yes?" she whispered.

"We found this number in the billfold of a Joe Anders.

We're searching for his nearest relative. Is there anyone there by chance related to him?"

Her stomach knotted, and Belle swallowed against a clump of nausea pressing the back of her throat. "This is his wife." She choked back a sob. "Is he—has he been—"

"No—oh no," the officer rushed. "He isn't dead—"

"Thank God!" Belle exploded and sagged against the kitchen counter. The tears drenching her cheeks seemed akin to the heavy rain pounding the roof.

"But he is in the hospital. He was caught out in a tornado. His truck was overturned, and he is currently unconscious."

"Is he—how badly is he hurt?" Belle automatically washed her hands, dried them, and ran for her bedroom.

"That I don't know. But he's in a hospital here in Tyler."

Once she learned which hospital he was in, Belle grabbed her car keys and raced outside, oblivious to the rain. Once in her car, she remembered the pot roast left sitting on the counter. Callie would worry. Belle turned on her cell phone and called her sister.

After relating the news, she broke into a fit of tears. "Oh, Callie," she wailed while steering through the diminishing rain. "The last thing I said to him was, 'Why don't you just leave?' Now he's in a hospital. Unconscious. And only God knows what all is wrong with him. He might—what if he—" Belle slowed the car to a stop at a red light.

"Now, listen," Callie said in a firm, kind voice. "You need to calm down. Going into hysterics won't do anybody any good."

Those wise words worked to slow Belle's tears.

"Whatever the two of you said to one another can be apologized for."

"If he ever wakes up."

"He's going to wake up," Callie said as if she could see into

the future. "He's got to. That's all there is to it." Her last as-
sertion wasn't quite as certain as the first one. "I'm going to
be praying like crazy."

"OK. Do that. And . . . and can you call his parents,
please?" Belle recited the number from memory, then disconnected the call.

Joe awoke off and on all evening to the blurred impression of
antiseptic smells, a white room, and starched uniforms. At last
he gained consciousness with clarity of mind. The first thing
he felt was the pressure of a hand in his and the pleasing smell
of soft, floral perfume. The same perfume that graced his bed
pillows at home. He opened his eyes to stare into Belle's
anxious face.

"Hi," she said with a tremulous smile.

"Hi," he croaked. "Where am I?"

"You're in the hospital."

"Hospital?"

"Yes."

"How long have I been here?"

"Several hours. They say you have a concussion, and they
want to watch you overnight."

"What happened?"

"You had a near miss with a tornado."

Then Joe remembered. He remembered the rain. The
roaring. The truck turning over. He also remembered the argument he and Belle had had before he drove into the storm.
And he remembered the vow he made before he lost consciousness. The vow to restore his marriage.

Slowly, Joe placed his hand on the side of her rounded abdomen.

Belle covered his hand with hers.

"I'm sorry," he said against his dry tongue.

"Me too," she replied, her eyes teary.

His head aching, Joe struggled to sit up. Belle plumped some pillows behind him. An awkward silence settled around them as Belle poured him a cup of ice water. Trying to clear his head, Joe wondered where they went from here.

"Looks like you're going to need somebody to take care of you for a few days," Belle said as she handed him the small water cup. An uncertain light flickered in the depths of her light blue eyes.

Joe hesitated. "Are you suggesting you should move back in?"

"I—" Belle shrugged.

He downed the cold water. "Are you offering to come home only because you thought I'd been killed and now you feel terrible about everything?" He produced a tired, teasing smile and tried to ignore his pounding head.

As if she wanted to avoid answering him, Belle took his cup and refilled it. She seemed more unsure of him—and herself, for that matter—than Joe ever remembered her being. He didn't know whether her uncertainty was a good sign or a bad sign. He didn't even know if he wanted her back home on the terms she was obviously offering. Whether he had a concussion or a broken arm or was half dead, that did nothing to sweep away their problems.

The problems still existed.

The only difference was that Joe was now ready to work through them. Before the tornado, he had been more inclined to stuff them in a closet somewhere and get on with life. Now he saw that that was no answer at all. Belle had told him that he wanted to just put a Band-Aid on things. Perhaps she was right. The problems they had were too big for Band-Aids—or greeting cards or even yellow roses, for that matter. Joe saw with clarity that until they were willing do some serious talking, their problems would only get larger.

Today's argument proved that.

Belle stood at the window, thoughtfully watching the diminishing clouds.

He wondered if she was thinking what he was thinking.

"Why didn't you tell me about the baby?" he asked gently. As hard as he tried to hide it, a forlorn thread laced his question. He was too tired and too beaten up to successfully play his hand at masquerade.

She hugged herself and rubbed her upper arms. "I guess I was running like crazy from our marriage," she said, directing a painful smile his way. "Inside, I was even running from the pregnancy." Her chuckle lacked humor. "I know that sounds wild, but it's true. And the irony of the whole thing is that I've wanted children so much—" Her voice broke, and she silently fought the tears.

Joe wanted to kick himself. How many times had Belle mentioned having children and he put her off? Who had he been in this marriage for anyway? The answer left him disgusted. He had been in the marriage for himself. Just as he had been so focused on himself that he had driven smack into a tornado. And as long as everything went the way Joe wanted, he thought Belle would be happy, too. He couldn't have been any more immature if he tried.

He suppressed a frustrated moan and realized that, even in his praying, he continued to point his finger at Belle. Sure, God heard his prayers—even answered them—but those prayers now seemed an infantile attempt at "straightening out" his wife. Joe had admitted to God that he had problems, too, but half his focus had been on Belle's problems. Joe now saw that he needed to allow God to deal with Belle. There was too much wrong with Joe for him to worry about what was wrong with his wife.

After Belle got her emotions under control, she continued, "Anyway, once I found out I was pregnant, I didn't want to tell you because I knew you would use it to try to get me to stay."

"I would have. I would have used anything."

She nodded silently and looked back out the window.

"So . . . are you still running from our marriage?" he asked softly.

"I don't think so." She turned and sat on the metal air-conditioning vent protruding from the wall.

"Are you running toward it?"

"I drove up here like a maniac, didn't I?"

Her teary smile instigated a song of hope in Joe's heart. Nonetheless, Joe had one more question to ask—the toughest of all. "Was there any chance of your running toward our marriage when I left earlier today?"

Belle's eyes widened, and a sea of resentment seemed to pour from them. "No way," she said honestly.

"So nothing has really changed, then, has it? That tornado didn't blow all our problems away."

With a weary sigh, Belle walked to his bedside and took his hand. "I guess not. We've got a lot to work through, don't we?"

"Yes."

He pulled her onto the bed beside him and wrapped his arm around her. Belle slowly placed her head on his shoulder. Only the Lord knew how much he had missed her closeness. Joe's world seemed so empty without Belle.

"In all honesty, Belle, what do you want to do? Would you rather go back to Callie's or come home?"

"I would feel awful not coming home with you. I feel like I ought to."

Her words weren't the ones Joe hoped for, and he tried to stay the tide of disappointment washing over him. These were words of duty. Words of *should* and *ought* and *had better*. Something inside Joe whispered that Belle needed more time. And for once in his marriage, Joe was willing to wait. To wait and give her the time she needed to heal.

Some things in life couldn't be rushed.

At last Joe spoke the hardest words he had ever spoken in his life. "Why don't you go on back to Callie's. And when you get ready, Belle—*really ready*—then come home. Not because of a tornado, but because you can't imagine another day without me. Those are the terms I want you back on, and those are the terms I'm willing to wait for."

She sat upright and stared into his eyes. A combination of shock and disbelief danced across her features. "You really mean that, don't you?"

"Yes—" Joe swallowed hard—"I mean it."

"But how will you—"

"I'll manage fine. I'm a big boy. I'm barely injured." He touched a small bandage at his hairline. "I'll call my bossy sister to come down and take me home tomorrow. She owes me, anyway."

"Well, if you're sure . . ."

"I'm sure. And let's just leave everything like this—the ball's in your court now. When you feel like talking, call me. I'm ready when you are."

"OK," she said, a mystified note in her voice.

Joe dared to stroke her cheek. When she didn't pull away, he tugged her toward him. With a restraint he was far from feeling, Joe gently brushed his lips against hers. She responded as if she expected more. Joe forced himself to stop. He didn't want to rush her. Closing his eyes, he pulled her back into the crook of his arm.

For once in his marriage, Joe knew he had done the right thing.

CHAPTER NINE

Belle didn't leave the hospital until almost midnight. When she walked through Callie's front door, her sister was waiting for her. Belle felt as if she were in high school and Callie was playing the role of protector.

"Hey," Belle said softly.

"How is he?" Callie asked. "Rick and I debated about whether or not to come up there."

"He's fine. They're just keeping him overnight for observation."

"So how are things between the two of you?"

"I don't really know." Belle shrugged. She had never been so bewildered by Joe's behavior. "I offered to go back home with him, and he told me he didn't want me back until I came back because I couldn't imagine another day without him, not because of a tornado."

"Wow! Now that sounds like a man with a head on his shoulders," Callie said as she followed Belle into her room.

Belle collapsed on the bed. The evening had been exhausting, emotionally and physically.

"Are you going to be OK?" Callie closed the door behind them.

"Yes. I'm just tired."

"You aren't going to throw up or anything, are you? You look horribly pale."

"No, like I said, I'm just tired." Belle propped herself up, and Callie settled on the end of the bed. "It's been a draining day. First, Joe and I had that whopper of a fight, and then the tornado . . ."

Callie's kind gray eyes remained calm, impartial, just as they had been from the start of this mess.

"You don't think I was right in leaving the note and not telling Joe that I'm pregnant, do you?" Belle challenged. For some reason, she felt she needed to get these issues out in the open with Callie. Her sister had remained ominously silent about them.

"Do you?"

"No." Belle sighed and crossed her legs. At last she told Callie what she hadn't told Joe at the hospital. "But, Callie, I've been so tired of his neglecting me, and I'm tired of worrying if I'm going to set off his temper," she said desperately. "I didn't trust him before, but after he blew up today, I really don't. It doesn't matter much how he acted at the hospital. How do I know that the next time I see him he won't go into a tailspin again? Joe said a mouthful when he said that tornado didn't blow our problems away."

"Are you thinking of divorcing him?" Each of Callie's words seemed to be wrapped snugly with concern.

Divorce.

The word sounded like a death knell. Belle knew deep in her heart that she didn't want a divorce. She didn't want to be yet another American statistic. Furthermore, the more she read the Bible, the more she prayed, Belle didn't much think God would condone her divorcing Joe. Perhaps if Joe were an unrepentant adulterer . . . but despite his faults, Belle knew beyond a doubt that he had been faithful to her. Joe Anders was not a womanizer.

"Well?" Callie said as if she was really worried.

"No. No divorce. A few weeks ago I might have entertained the thought, but not now. I—" Belle swallowed. "The more I pray, the more I see that . . . that—" That what? That perhaps Joe was right? That perhaps they were both to blame for their marital problems? "Oh, Callie—" Belle sniffled. "Joe seemed so much different at the hospital than earlier today. I don't know if that tornado traumatized him or what. But I'm so confused, I feel like I'm the one who's been in the tornado. I thought he would be delighted at my offer to go home with him, and then he said what he did about waiting. I have never been so shocked in my life. Joe has never—absolutely *never*—had that kind of patience. What in the world has come over him? I wonder if he even knew what he was saying."

"Oh, it sounds to me like he knew exactly what he was saying. I think that maybe it just took a tornado to help him get his priorities right, that's all."

"So what do you think I should do?"

"I thought you'd never ask," Callie said ruefully.

Belle socked her with a pillow.

"Hey! Let's not get violent here!" Callie teased, tossing the pillow back.

"I know you and Mom both have been just dying to tell me what you think!"

"But we haven't said a word." Callie shook her finger.

"Yes, I know. Thanks for staying out of it. I think I've needed this time to think and sort some things through on my own."

"But now . . ."

"Now I think I'm ready to listen. Or perhaps I need to listen. But quite frankly, I don't know how you think you're going to help with Joe and me," Belle said in sisterly candor. "After all, you married 'wonder husband.' Your marriage seems heavenly."

"Yeah, after eighteen years of hard labor!"

"What's that supposed to mean?"

"It's supposed to mean that more than once in our marriage I contemplated throwing Rick, his bowling ball, his computer, and his various assortments of dirty socks out onto the lawn."

Belle's mouth dropped. "No! Really? Are you talking about the same Rick Johnson I know?"

"Yes, indeed. The tall, thin guy. The one we ate breakfast with this morning."

"What on earth is wrong with you? The man is perfect!"

"I beg your pardon," Callie said in a mock offended tone. *"I'm* the one in our marriage who's perfect."

"Yeah, right. I grew up with you, remember?" Belle reflected over the various times Callie's exacting tendencies had driven her nuts. But those same tendencies had also turned her into a dynamite lawyer.

Callie chuckled. "I know you'll find this hard to believe—" she raised her thin brows—"but five years ago Rick told me that he was convinced I would never die of natural causes."

"Why?"

"He said one day I would exasperate somebody so much that they would just kill me."

"You?" Belle feigned a gasp. "Miss Perfection?"

"Yes, yes, I know, I know. It's hard to believe, but Rick actually spoke those very words to me."

A companionable silence settled between them.

"So what are you saying?" Belle asked, already sure of Callie's general intent.

"I'm saying that marriage is hard work. The challenge isn't falling in love and creating a romance with your husband before you're married. Most anybody can do that. The challenge is keeping the romance alive after you know everything there is to know about him."

Callie paused and thoughtfully chewed her thumbnail. "Quite frankly, I've come to a few other conclusions as well. I think that every couple who has been together any length of time has done one of two things: They've either swept a lot of issues with all the pain under the rug, or they've been open and honest with each other and have a healthy marriage."

She looked Belle in the eyes. "You know, just because a couple has stayed married thirty or forty years doesn't mean they have a healthy marriage. A lot of people seem to mistake a long marriage for a good relationship. But I've decided something, Belle."

As always, Belle was impressed with Callie's wisdom.

"Lots of people sweep so many issues under the rug that it's like there's this mound of stuff between them. And after you do that for twenty years or so, I'm afraid the pile gets stuck somehow. And it's so huge that neither the husband or wife are willing to dig into it. It's like this mountain of hidden problems is between them. And the mountain's so high, they can't even see each other."

Belle nervously picked at the pillow. "I've only been married five years, but I've been there. Or rather, I *am* there."

"Well, since we're being completely truthful, here, I've been there, too. And one day, when my boys were in preschool, I decided that if I wanted them to have healthy marriages, then I was going to have to do some heavy-duty living of one in front of them."

"Mom and Dad don't really have a healthy marriage, do they?" Belle was stunned by that sudden realization.

"No, they don't. They've got a mountain of accumulated issues between them. And guess what—you and I—" Callie pointed to Belle, then herself—"have just followed in their footsteps. We've approached marriage the same way they did: Just stay silent and let the resentment build. Let's don't discuss our problems or our real feelings. Let's just show up at church and pretend everything is OK. Quite frankly, I don't ever remember Mom or Dad telling me any of that. But they lived it. They still live it, and that's much stronger than any words."

Belle chewed her bottom lip. "But I tried for months to talk with Joe, and he just wouldn't listen."

"Sounds like he's ready to listen now. And sometimes—" Callie laid her hand on Belle's shoulder—"you just gotta keep trying until he's ready. And as much as I hate to admit it, there have been times when Rick has had to just keep trying until I was ready."

"So you think that now that Joe's ready to listen, I should call him, beg his forgiveness, and move back in?"

Callie chuckled. "How big is that mound under the rug?"

"It feels like Mount Everest."

"It's going to take a lot of guts, but maybe you should just start pulling those issues out from under the rug one at a time and talking—calmly talking—them over until you feel at peace about moving to another issue. Then—" she shrugged—"you'll be calling Joe and telling him you can't imagine another day without him."

"Do you really think so?"

"I know so. I've been there. Just wait. You're going to be pleasantly surprised."

After several silent moments, Callie stood and walked toward the door. "That chocolate pie you made is calling me," she said with a smile over her shoulder. Then her eyes widened with something close to horror. "I just realized that if you and Joe get everything worked out, I'll be without a cook. You've spoiled me so thoroughly, I might have to actually hire somebody to replace you!"

"Don't rush things," Belle replied. "We're still a long way from where you and Rick are."

That night Belle began her first letter to Joe. He responded. She wrote back. So did he. Again and again. For the next two months, through phone calls and letters, they gradually extracted one issue after another from under that proverbial rug, hacked the life out of it, sought forgiveness from God and each other, and went on to another issue. Belle slowly began to awaken to feelings deep within her that she was shocked to encounter.

She needed Joe.

And her daily prayer time—which had started as a desperate attempt to understand God's will in the mess of her marriage—turned into a time of praise and worship. Soon Belle began to intercede for her husband in a new and empowering way. At that point, her feelings for Joe underwent a radical transformation.

CHAPTER TEN

With Christmas only a week away, Belle sat in the obstetrician's office. Having grown uncomfortably large, she shifted from one position to another. The baby wasn't due until March, but Belle already looked eight months pregnant. Naturally her doctor suspected twins, but up until her most recent visit, the doctor had detected only one heartbeat, and the original sonogram showed only one baby. But Dr. Brown had thought she detected two heartbeats on the last visit. She surmised that perhaps one twin had been behind the other. Today Belle would receive her second sonogram. But in her soul, she already knew what the doctor would find.

Two babies.

Belle was going to have twins!

The thought both thrilled and dismayed her. How would she ever care for two babies?

Once again Belle shifted in her seat and contemplated the Christmas tree gracing the waiting room's corner. The tree blended with the hunter green wallpaper behind it. All Belle could think about was her family—Joe and these two precious lives within her. Joe was going to be an excellent father. Belle was certain of it. If only the two of them could learn how to create a good marriage. It seemed they had worked their way through most of the issues under that rug. Now they should be able to move forward and create new memories. Belle, still a bit unsure, frantically hoped they didn't fall back into their old habits.

Joe had visited Belle twice recently. Their last visit ended on a strained note. Joe had pointed out some difficulties in Belle that she would have preferred to leave hidden under that rug. But this extracting of the pile of issues between them involved both of their shortcomings.

Belle's musings were halted when a couple entered the waiting room. There was nothing particularly arresting about them. Jeans and T-shirts. Canvas shoes. Average build. They looked about like any couple you might see on the street. But they were holding hands and exchanging lovers' glances. The wife, obviously pregnant, seemed aglow with happiness. And her doting husband went out of his way to make sure she was comfortable.

Although Belle had long since left morning sickness behind, she felt as if she were having another onslaught of it. Her stomach twisted in a combination of anxiety and longing. Her eyes stung. There was a time before they married when Joe showed Belle that kind of affection. Would he ever relearn that behavior and understand how much Belle needed it?

She continued gazing at the young couple and wondered what it would be like to have Joe with her during her doctor visits. So far, Belle had gone it alone. The presence of a supportive husband would be so nice.

Someone took the seat beside her, and Belle automatically moved her oversized purse to give the person more foot room. "Excuse me," she muttered. Glancing up, she encountered Joe's humorous gaze.

"Hi," he said, his dark eyes dancing with mirth.

Belle blinked in confusion. Had her imagination conjured him up, or was Joe really sitting beside her?

"You look like you've seen a ghost," he teased.

"How did you know I was here?"

"I went by the house. You weren't there. I went by the law office and asked Callie if she knew where you were. She sent me here. Looks like I caught you before the sonogram." He leaned forward. "When I got your letter yesterday about the possibility of twins, I couldn't stand it. I had to come." He hesitated, and his mouth turned up in an unsure way. "Is that OK?"

"Uh . . . yes. It's fine. Just fine." Belle forced herself not to gape. Was this her husband? He seemed like a version of the doting man Belle had just been observing. Except there was nothing nondescript about Joe. There never had been. He wasn't perfectly handsome, but his height, dark hair, and dark eyes never left him without feminine admiration. Many women would call Joe a good catch.

"Mrs. Anders," the nurse said from the doorway.

Belle stood, Joe at her side.

The young nurse greeted them with an overly charming smile, which she never used with Belle. And Belle suspected the reason for the smile was Joe. Her tall, dark husband. She had the overwhelming urge to wipe that sugary smile right off the cute nurse's face. Years had passed since Belle had felt the possessiveness she now experienced.

Soon Belle stretched herself on the examination table, and that same cute nurse prepared her for the sonogram.

"So, how long have the two of you lived in Jacksonville?" she asked cheerfully.

"Uh . . ." Belle searched for the right words and finally looked to Joe in desperation.

361

"Belle is just here for a . . . hmm, hmm . . . visit. Our home, that is, I live in Dallas."

"Oh," the nurse said, her glossy lips forming an embarrassed pucker.

As the nurse applied the warm contact jelly to Belle's midsection, an awkward silence settled around them. Belle examined the nurse's name tag in an attempt to remember her name. C. Crank. She remembered Dr. Brown referring to her as Charlie. At the time Belle had considered Charlie an appropriate name for the attractive young woman.

What must Charlie think of her and Joe? Belle still didn't wear her wedding band. Did the nurse assume they weren't even married? Then she remembered her calling her Mrs. Anders, so she must know they were married. Belle glanced toward Joe's hands. Her wedding band still claimed a spot on his little finger. Seeing Joe's wedding band in its rightful place thrilled her beyond expression.

Charlie moved to fetch an implement near Joe. "Excuse me," she said with another of those sugary smiles.

Joe returned the smile. Then he glanced toward Belle, who comically rolled her eyes. His grin increased. He was enjoying every minute of this.

The jerk!

Why did he have to look so good?

Within seconds, the nurse began moving the device across Belle's stomach. Joe hovered nearby, straining to see the picture on the computer monitor.

"Aha!" Charlie turned to Joe. "Looks like there are two babies! Congratulations!"

Joe gripped Belle's hand, his dark eyes filling with love and adoration. Warmth rushed into Belle's heart. She had told Joe the doctor was speculating about twins, so the confirming news didn't surprise her in the least. She was more warmed by her renewed attraction to her own husband and his reaction to the news.

"Are they boys or girls? Can you tell?" Joe questioned, leaning closer to the monitor.

"Let's see. . . ."

Out of the corner of her eye, Belle watched the computer monitor. Various shades of gray moved across the screen. At first, the shapes meant nothing to Belle. But when she looked closely, Belle began to see tiny fingers, toes, and two little faces. All at once, she ached to hold the babies in her arms. And Belle knew in the core of her being that she could never go back to work when two helpless infants desperately needed her. If for no other reason than her children, Belle would move back to Dallas.

But the return to Dallas would be for other reasons besides the babies. She loved Joe. At that moment, as he waited impatiently to hear about the babies, Belle loved him more than she had ever loved him in her life.

"OK, I can tell that one of them is a boy. See." Pointing to the definitive parts, Charlie glanced over her shoulder toward Joe. "This one on the right."

Forgetting the nurse, Belle strained to see her son.

"He's beautiful," Joe whispered, holding one of Belle's hands in both of his.

"The other baby is turning just right," Charlie continued. "Hold steady, darlin'. Nice pose. Let me see. Now, are you a girl or a boy?"

Belle held her breath. Not because she preferred one or the other. But her suspense was like an unrelenting tidal wave.

"This one's a girl." As with the boy, she pointed to the screen.

"One of each." Joe pulled Belle's fingers to his lips.

A tremulous smile tilting her mouth, Belle held Joe's ardent gaze.

"You did a good job, darlin'," he whispered.

"*We* did," she insisted.

"Yes, we did."

Ironically, their marriage's darkest days had conceived the source of their greatest joy.

"Would you like a picture?" Charlie asked professionally, and Belle wondered if she had imagined the young woman's attraction to Joe.

"Yes," they answered together.

"OK." Charlie exposed Joe to another smile. "I guess I can do two, so you'll each have one." She left the implied meaning unsaid. Since they obviously weren't living together, they would each need a separate copy.

Immediately Belle knew she had not imagined Charlie's attraction to Joe. The young woman had done nothing unprofessional, but Belle still picked up on a heavy undercurrent of "Wow! This guy's adorable." All the nurse's body language supported the undercurrent. Belle recognized it so much because it was the same body language she had used shortly into her relationship with Joe. . . .

Their second date. They went to Six Flags over Texas with his church group. The whole day was filled with opportunities to get to know each other. And with every hour that passed, every time they got off yet another roller coaster or enjoyed their cotton candy or watched the live entertainment, Belle was thinking, *Wow! This guy's adorable.*

Everything about Joe pleased Belle—his infectious grin, the way he inclined his ear to catch each word she said, his obvious respect for her as a woman. Belle even liked the tiny white scar below his left eye. "A childhood injury," he explained in mock solemnity before they embarked on the log ride. "I tripped myself with a stick I was carrying. Almost put my own eye out."

She needed every ounce of her willpower to keep from placing a light kiss on the scar and saying, "I like it."

Joe's eyes widened, as if she had indeed kissed him. Belle's thoughts must have been more obvious than she knew. Halfway through the log ride, Joe slipped his arm around her waist. Belle smiled, glad he had taken the hint.

Where had that magic gone in their relationship? How had they let it slip away?

The expectancy.

The sparkle.

The anticipation.

The two of them really hadn't changed that much. Perhaps they could rekindle what they had initially shared. Perhaps they were already rekindling it. At once, Belle was more excited about her marriage than she had been in years. And she realized that, beyond any human doubt, God had answered her prayers. The romance was back in their marriage. Somehow, in the middle of all their human bumbling, God had directed their journey back to one another.

Well, Lord, she thought, spontaneously squeezing Joe's hand, still entwined with hers. *You're just great. That's all there is to it! Thanks a million!* What a blessing to know that God had created romance, then extended the great gift of marriage through which to freely express that romance.

"Here are your pictures," the cheerful nurse said, thoroughly disrupting Belle's musings.

"Oh, thanks," Belle said blankly. She took the picture and stroked the image of two tiny faces, side by side.

"They look like they're talking to each other," Joe mused.

"Maybe that's a good sign," Belle said.

"Oh, twins are like that, Mr. Anders," Charlie said. "They arrive into the world bonded."

In a matter of minutes, the nurse cleared the clutter and invited Belle to sit back up. Joe briefly excused himself for a trip to the rest room.

Belle was still lost in admiration for her babies when Charlie patted her shoulder in feminine conspiracy. "Don't let him get away, now." She pointed toward the door Joe had just exited. "He's a good catch." She winked.

Belle wondered momentarily if Joe had paid this nurse to conspire on his behalf. Upon dismissing the crazy thought, she was immediately flooded with new appreciation for her husband. "I agree," Belle said. "He is a good catch."

Joe at her side, Belle settled her account with the matronly secretary and automatically made an appointment for her next visit. Then another thought struck her. "What would be involved in my changing doctors at this point?"

The dismayed secretary gave Belle a look that said, "What have we done wrong?"

"Oh no," Belle assured her before she could verbalize any concern. "I'm perfectly pleased with Dr. Brown and—and all the staff. It's just that I really live in Dallas. I've been temporarily staying with my sister, and it looks as though I'll be going back to Dallas . . . soon . . . uh, maybe today."

Belle couldn't miss Joe's surprised intake of air. He slowly wrapped his arm around her waist, and Belle felt as if she were drowning in the waters of a tingling sea. It was like their second date—like the log ride—all over again. Once more, Belle was glad Joe had taken the hint and put his arm around her.

"Would Dr. Brown mind moving my records to my usual doctor in Dallas?"

"Oh no, not at all," the secretary said cheerfully. "I didn't realize . . . that um . . ." She shuffled some paperwork in an attempt to cover the awkward moment. "All you need to do is have your doctor call Dr. Brown, and she'll authorize the transfer of your records."

"OK. Well, if I don't see you again—" *and I know I won't,* Belle added to herself—"thanks for everything. You all have been a delight."

"Yes and—and thank you." The secretary beamed. "And I hope everything continues to go well for you."

An electrified silence engulfing them, Joe and Belle walked toward her red Toyota. Joe kept his arm around her until they stopped near the car, and Belle was as thrilled by his presence as if they were newlyweds. She turned to face him and reveled in a new surge of freedom to express her feelings for Joe. For the first time in their marriage, she gave in to the urge to act in a completely uninhibited fashion. At last she succumbed to the impulse she had squelched years ago at Six Flags. She grabbed the front of his starched white shirt, stood on her tiptoes, and passionately pressed her lips to his.

After an astonished gasp, Joe lost no time taking advantage of the moment. He wrapped his arms around Belle and pulled her closer. The kiss deepened, lengthened.

Belle felt as if she were engulfed in an ocean of pleasure. Oh, she had missed this. How long had it been since they had shared such an explosion of passion?

A car's distant honk reminded them that they stood in full view of the public, and they simultaneously broke the embrace.

"Wow!" Joe said, his breathing as uneven as Belle's. "You haven't kissed me like that in . . . in— You've *never* kissed me like that!"

"Well," she said huskily, "you've never been as open with me as you have in the last two months."

"In that case, just consider me 'Mr. Open' from now on."

Backing out of his embrace, she reached for his hand and removed her wedding band from his little finger. "And just consider me Mrs. Joe Anders." She forced the ring onto her swollen ring finger. "And don't ever forget it!"

Joe's eyes widened as if he understood all too well. "I think you must be a wee bit jealous," he said with glee.

"And you loved every minute of it. Didn't you?"

"Well . . ."

"What did you do—pay her to act that way?" she said, fluttering her eyelashes in an exaggerated way.

"As a matter of fact—"

"Do you know what she said when you left?"

"What? Tell me. I'm dying to know." His face beamed with an incredulous joy Belle felt herself.

"She said, 'Don't let him get away, now. He's a good catch.'"

Joe roared with laughter. "That's the best advice I've ever heard."

Belle rolled her eyes. "Men!" she said in mock disgust.

"And do you believe what she said, Belle?" Suddenly very serious, Joe stroked her cheek.

"I do," Belle said, the simple words reverberating with the vows she and Joe had made almost six years before.

EPILOGUE

Joe paced the waiting room, engulfed in the smell of stale coffee. He had attempted to sit by Callie and her parents but managed to stay still only a few seconds before the need to move had prevailed. Callie sat, biting her lip, her face dark with worry. Her gray-haired parents' expression mirrored Callie's.

Poor Belle. With every scrap of energy, she had tried to give birth. An hour ago, when her blood pressure escalated to dangerous levels, the doctor had ordered an emergency C-section. Highly concerned, the doctor wasted no time in demanding the administration of anesthesia and suggesting that Joe might be better off in the waiting area. Unsure whether or not to insist on staying with his unconscious wife, Joe decided he could pray more fervently in the waiting room.

Dear Lord, Joe silently prayed, *be with Belle. Give the babies a safe delivery. Please, God, bring all three through this.*

"Mr. Anders," the doctor said from the doorway. "Congratulations! You have a healthy boy and girl."

Joe stopped pacing. His heart raced. His mind whirled. "And Belle? How is my wife?"

"She's fine. Just fine. Everything went great. She's in recovery now, but she'll soon be in her room. You can wait here or in her room—or you might want to go to the nurs-ery—"

Joe didn't wait for the doctor to finish. Forgetting Callie and her parents, he whizzed past the doctor like a man half-crazed. His babies were here! Joe had to see them or he would explode.

He rushed to the nursery window and pressed his forehead against the cool glass, straining to read the various name tags. In the back of the nursery, two nurses busily bathed and dressed two dark-haired babies.

The twins. Brett and Brooke. Joe knew beyond any doubt those were his babies. His stomach did a flip-flop. And he un-derstood the true meaning of love at first sight.

One of the nurses noticed him and waved happily. She turned to speak to a nearby nurse's aide who came to the nursery door.

"Are you Mr. Anders?" she asked.

"Yes."

"Would you like to hold your son and daughter?"

"May I?" he replied, unable to believe they would actually allow him to hold the babies so soon.

"Sure. Step right in here." She opened the door wider to admit Joe into a small, brightly decorated room with a rock-ing chair and changing table. "This room is just right for your first introduction."

"Thanks," Joe whispered.

Within seconds he settled into the rocking chair, and the two smiling nurses nestled those whimpering bundles into Joe's arms. All that showed was their wrinkled red faces. They wore warm, knit hats and seemed oblivious to the upheaval they had caused.

"You are quite a pair," Joe whispered. His eyes stinging, he kissed them both on the forehead and relished their newborn smell. "I'm your dad, in case you didn't know. And one day when you get a little bigger, I'm going to take you for ice-cream cones, and we'll go swimming in the summer, and if it ever snows, we'll make a snowman in the winter. But it doesn't snow much in Texas. I know, I know, that's quite a disappointment, but maybe your mom and I can make up for the loss. . . ."

While the babies dozed, Joe continued the soft words. He was awestruck—truly awestruck—at God's miraculous timing. What could be better than to have their babies on Valentine's Day? For the rest of their lives, Belle and Joe would celebrate three special events every February 14—their anniversary, Valentine's Day, and the birth of their beautiful children.

Joe didn't know how long he marveled over the miracle of birth, but he did know he had tasted a wee bit of heaven. He glanced up to see Callie, along with Belle's parents, standing in the doorway. Joe had forgotten all about them. They must have held back to give him a few moments alone with his new son and daughter. With a smile, he beckoned them into the room and began showing off his pride and joy.

Fatherhood was going to be great!

Belle awoke to the sound of someone shuffling about. She gazed around the dimly lit room, groggily trying to place where she was. Then she remembered.

"The babies," she rasped against a tongue that felt like thick, dried leather.

Immediately, Joe was at her side. "You're awake," he said, gently pushing her hair from her forehead.

"The babies. Where are they?" She gripped his hand, her anxiety high.

"They're in the nursery. Everything's OK. The three of you did great. I'm so proud of you." As he assisted her with a few sips of water, his dark eyes shone with new depths of love.

She relaxed against the pillows. "Labor was awful."

"I know. No, I guess I don't know. But I'd have done it for you if I could."

She smiled and knew Joe meant it.

He turned to grab a huge arrangement of yellow roses from near the dark window. "I was just adding water to the roses when you woke up. Want to take a smell?"

"Sure." Belle snuggled her nose into the softness of what seemed to be a thousand blooms. "You're spoiling me rotten," she said groggily. "If you don't bring me flowers every day from now on, I think I'll sob uncontrollably."

"Happy anniversary. Happy Valentine's Day," Joe responded over a chuckle.

"Today is our anniversary, isn't it? I forgot."

"You forgot!" Joe's brows rose. "But there's no excuse for that!"

"Oh, you—" She lazily slapped at him.

He gently kissed her forehead.

"I want to see the babies."

"I know. The nurse came by a few minutes ago and said they were bringing them in soon. But until then, we have something to say to each other. We were going to restate our wedding vows, remember?" Joe replaced the roses and sat on the edge of her bed.

Belle nodded, her foggy mind calling up the memory of their agreeing to restate their vows. During the last two weeks, Belle had been banished to bed. Joe took part of his vacation and was at her side during the whole wretched ordeal. As Valentine's Day and their sixth anniversary approached, the two prayed together, shared, and bonded as never before. Last week they decided to restate their wedding vows today.

"But do you feel like it?" he asked with concern.

"What?" Belle asked blankly.

"The wedding vows. Do you feel up to restating them now?"

She hesitated. Belle's main thoughts were with her babies. She wanted to see them. And soon. She wasn't sure she could concentrate enough to say her own name, let alone wedding vows.

"It's just that before we meet the babies together, I want our commitment to be fresh and renewed," Joe continued. "We were a couple before Brett and Brooke, and we will be after they leave home. As important as these twins are, our marriage is just as important."

She recalled Callie's saying that if Larry and Barry were going to have good marriages, she and Rick must model a good marriage for them. Belle decided it was never too early to start.

"OK," she said, her heart warming with Joe's earnestness.

Silently he pulled a piece of paper from the pocket of his starched white shirt. "I wrote my own special vows last week."

"But I didn't," Belle said guiltily. She had assumed they would simply repeat what they'd said at their wedding.

"It's OK. You've been busy. I'll let you off the hook . . . this time." He produced an exaggerated wink, then reclaimed her hand and read the most beautiful words Belle had ever heard.

"My dearest Belle, I love you. I realize now that I've done a lousy job showing you that love in recent years. But I want you to know that life without you is no life at all." His voice cracked.

And Belle allowed a tear to flow freely down the side of her face.

"I know I'm not perfect, and I know I'll mess up a lot in the future, but I want to pledge to you today that I'm going to try harder than ever to make our marriage work. I may not be a knight in shining armor. I'm probably not anybody's dream man, either, for that matter. But I am a man who loves you with every fiber of his being. And I promise before God that I will cherish you, openly and in my heart. I will never break that vow again. I also promise to talk with you and listen to you, and most of all, Belle—" Joe stopped to stroke her face— "I promise to pray *with* you and *for* you every day of our lives." He gently kissed her cheek. "Let's keep the magic alive."

"I will," Belle replied, straining to think of a special vow for Joe. At last she came up with something. "And I promise to go to the next Dallas Cowboys game with you," she finished groggily.

"You're so romantic," Joe said with mirth, the flush of happiness on his face.

"Thanks—I'm trying."

Belle felt Joe's happiness in her own heart, and she didn't think it could increase—until the nurse arrived with their two bundles of joy.

A NOTE FROM THE AUTHOR

D ear Reader,
When the editors at Tyndale House asked me to choose a flower to use in this novella, I chose the rose as a symbol of the care marriages require. If you've ever grown roses, you know they require a great amount of care. Without special attention, rosebushes develop diseases, accumulate aphids, and shrivel away to an ugly shadow of their former selves.

Marriage is the same way. If romance is to stay alive in marriage, both husband and wife must give special care to the relationship. Creating a romantic relationship *before* marriage requires little work; we're usually caught up in the newness of each other and excited about what lies ahead. But once a couple marries, the work must begin.

In writing "Cherish," I relied heavily on the concepts found in the book *His Needs, Her Needs* by Willard F. Harley Jr. (Fleming H. Revell, 1986). If the romance has vanished from your marriage, I strongly recommend that you read Harley's book or visit his Web site at www.mariage-builders.com. Intercede on behalf of your mate, roll up your sleeves, and begin the work. You'll never be sorry.

Blessings!
Debra White Smith

ABOUT THE AUTHOR

Debra White Smith lives in east Texas with her husband and two small children. She is a full-time writer who has published numerous novels, is working on several nonfiction books, and speaks at conferences and retreats. In 1997 Debra was voted one of the top-ten favorite Heartsong Presents authors, and in the same year readers ranked her novel *The Neighbor* as one of their top-ten favorite Heartsong Presents novels. Debra's Tyndale House novellas appear in *A Victorian Christmas Quilt* and *A Bouquet of Love*.

You can write to Debra at P.O. Box 1482, Jacksonville, TX 75766, or visit her Web site at www.getset.com/DebraWhite Smith. She would love to hear from you about her writing or about potential speaking engagements.

Current HeartQuest Releases

- *A Bouquet of Love*, Ginny Aiken, Ranee McCollum, Jeri Odell, and Debra White Smith
- *Faith*, Lori Copeland
- *June*, Lori Copeland
- *Prairie Rose*, Catherine Palmer
- *Prairie Fire*, Catherine Palmer
- *Prairie Storm*, Catherine Palmer
- *Reunited*, Judy Baer, Jeri Odell, Jan Duffy, and Peggy Stoks
- *The Treasure of Timbuktu*, Catherine Palmer
- *The Treasure of Zanzibar*, Catherine Palmer
- *A Victorian Christmas Quilt*, Catherine Palmer, Peggy Stoks, Debra White Smith, and Ginny Aiken
- *A Victorian Christmas Tea*, Catherine Palmer, Dianna Crawford, Peggy Stoks, and Katherine Chute
- *With This Ring*, Lori Copeland, Dianna Crawford, Ginny Aiken, and Catherine Palmer
- *Finders Keepers*, Catherine Palmer—coming soon (Fall 1999)
- *Hope*, Lori Copeland—coming soon (Fall 1999)

Other Great Tyndale House Fiction

- *The Captive Voice*, B. J. Hoff
- *Dark River Legacy*, B. J. Hoff
- *Embers of Hope*, Sally Laity and Dianna Crawford
- *The Fires of Freedom*, Sally Laity and Dianna Crawford
- *The Gathering Dawn*, Sally Laity and Dianna Crawford
- *Jewels for a Crown*, Lawana Blackwell
- *The Kindled Flame*, Sally Laity and Dianna Crawford
- *Like a River Glorious*, Lawana Blackwell
- *Measures of Grace*, Lawana Blackwell
- *Song of a Soul*, Lawana Blackwell
- *Storm at Daybreak*, B. J. Hoff
- *The Tangled Web*, B. J. Hoff
- *The Tempering Blaze*, Sally Laity and Dianna Crawford
- *The Torch of Triumph*, Sally Laity and Dianna Crawford
- *Vow of Silence*, B. J. Hoff

Heartwarming Anthologies from HeartQuest

A Victorian Christmas Tea—Four novellas about life and love at Christmas-time. Stories by Catherine Palmer, Dianna Crawford, Peggy Stoks, and Katherine Chute.

A Victorian Christmas Quilt—A patchwork of four novellas about love and joy at Christmastime. Stories by Catherine Palmer, Peggy Stoks, Debra White Smith, and Ginny Aiken.

Reunited—Four stories about reuniting friends, old memories, and new romance. Includes favorite recipes from the authors. Stories by Judy Baer, Jeri Odell, Jan Duffy, and Peggy Stoks.

A Bouquet of Love—An arrangement of four beautiful novellas about friendship and love. Stories by Ginny Aiken, Ranee McCollum, Jeri Odell, and Debra White Smith.

With This Ring—A quartet of charming stories about four very special weddings. Stories by Lori Copeland, Dianna Crawford, Ginny Aiken, and Catherine Palmer.